'Oh my God . . . ! No!' She looked desperately about her at the sight of the camp on fire, thick black smoke rising up into the clear blue sky, the heat everywhere.

'Here . . . ! Mrs Mills? Here . . . !' The major had secured a ladder against the wall. 'We have to get up on to the roof . . . we . . .' He looked behind him as the first of the rabble came into view, soaked in blood and screaming . . . He raised his arm, aimed his pistol and fired. The man went down.

'Come on!' he yelled at Alicia, who stood almost para-lysed with fear. 'For God's sake! Come on!' . . . But it was already too late. As she stumbled towards the ladder, her legs gave way and she lost control of her bladder. Helpless, she sank to her knees weeping as a group of seepoys galloped into the grounds of the bungalow, slashing violently at the two officers holding the entrance and mutilating their bodies in a matter of seconds.

Major Reece never managed his second shot.

Much, much later, when the bloody chaos the mutineers had wrought was discovered, there was very little recognis-able left of either him or Alicia Mills.

DISHONOURED

Maria Barrett

WARNER BOOKS

A *Warner* Book

First published in Great Britain in 1995
by Little, Brown and Company
This edition published 1996 by Warner Books

A CIP catalogue record for this book
is available from the British Library.

ISBN 0 7515 0536 6

Typeset by Palimpsest Book Production Limited,
Polmont, Stirlingshire
Printed and bound in Great Britain by
Clays Ltd, St Ives plc

Warner Books
A Division of
Little, Brown and Company (UK)
Brettenham House
Lancaster Place
London WC2E 7EN

For my mother, Maureen.
With love and thanks for a lifetime of inspiration.

Acknowledgements

This book was probably the most difficult I have written, not alas, because of intellectual content but because of the arrival of one small member of our family who somehow managed to turn life upside down. No problem I thought, imagining the baby to come, I can sit it quietly in the corner of my study and it'll play with some educational toy while I trot out a couple of thousand words. Easy. No sweat. Ha! Big shock. Our son, a wonderful mix of unbelievable energy, mischief and joy, has never, not once, sat quietly since the day he arrived. Result, nine months of frantic, confused, muddled work in the bin and *Dishonoured* rewritten, from scratch, five months late and completed (Lord knows how) in record time.

Because of this, I owe a great deal of thanks to the people who looked after William with such love and care. I found it was only possible for me to write properly when I knew he was happy and content, so a huge thank you to Toi Hill, Mum, June and Pat and our 'wonder nanny' and friend Vanessa Buckland. Also thanks to Alison Baron whose help was brief but never the less important.

I owe enormous thanks to June Barrett for her help

with my research, answering even the most seemingly stupid questions about life in India in the sixties and for organising lunches with Indian contacts, importantly, Revati Kapoor and Chandra Vati Rajwade who corrected many of my cultural mistakes. Thank you to Dr Alan Taylor for his memories of his work in a leprosy colony in Pakistan, to Alison L. de L. in Newcastle for use of the university library for research and to Professor Pugh for his help and reading list. Finally, my thanks to Barbara Boote, for her patience with my late manuscript and her confidence, to Helen Anderson, who edits so well, my agent Mic Cheetham, who somehow always managed to call at the right moment with the right amount of encouragement and to Jules for his equanimity, love and support.

MB

PART 1

Chapter One

India, Moraphur
Saturday, 9th May, 1857

Colonel Reginald Mills strode through the garden, brushing aside the drooping branch of a jacaranda tree, and up the steps on to the verandah of his bungalow. He shouted out to his servant, squatting in the shade by the door. A stout, middle-aged man, he was sweating in the midday heat and his temper was up.

'Bearer! Where the devil are you? Bearer!' The servant scurried into view and bowed very low. 'Ah there you are! 'Bout time!' The colonel took off his hat, handed it across without looking at the Indian and began unbuckling his belt. 'Is the Memsahib resting?'

'Yes, Colonel Sahib.'

He turned towards the house. 'Bring me a whisky soda.' Handing over his jacket, he walked into the cool of the bungalow, the head bearer following two paces behind. 'And tell *khansama* we'll be in late for dinner tonight!'

He swore under his breath. 'Fraternising with the natives, it's too damn much!' And blotting his damp moustache on a clean, starched white handkerchief, he made his way across to his wife's bedroom.

'Oh, hello, Reggie.' Alicia Mills shushed away the attentions of the ayah with a brusque hand movement and turned her head towards the figure of her husband in the doorway. She was sitting at the dressing table in her chemise and loosened corset, her thick blonde hair only half unfastened, a few strands of it heavy on her shoulders. She turned back to her reflection. The colonel looked at her for a moment, the flushed youth of her skin in the hot afternoon, and felt the sudden need of her.

'You can go,' he said over his shoulder to the ayah as he walked towards his wife. Alicia caught his eye and a small smile crossed her lips.

'Damn wretched party tonight,' he said as he stood behind her and finished unpinning her hair. He rested his hands on her shoulders, again caught by the fresh dewy quality of her skin, and looked at her face in the mirror.

'The commanding officer's duty, darling,' she reminded him. She moved her hand up to his and eased it down to the swell of her bosom under the chemise. Alicia Mills had married well, she was proud of her wealth and position and Reggie was really quite sweet, so long as she kept him that way. 'It won't be all that bad . . .' she murmured as he bent to kiss her neck. 'It does well to keep in with these people . . .' She tilted her chin up so that he could nuzzle the hollow of it. 'I think it's rather exciting . . . he's the maharajah's jeweller you said . . . ?'

The colonel stopped what he was doing. 'He's a bally

darkie, Alicia! Remember that!' His nostrils flared and the muscle in his left cheek twitched momentarily. Stiffening, he moved away. Colonel Reginald Mills had been in India too long; as far as he was concerned, it was them and us.

Alicia swivelled round on her stool. 'Oh Reggie, don't be so short . . .' She unfastened the tiny mother-of-pearl buttons on her chemise, letting it fall open over the very pale skin of her breast. 'Come back here . . .' she said quietly. She saw his face relax slightly and she smiled. 'You'll feel better after a lie down.' Standing, in just her petticoats and corset, she closed on him and put her hand up to his face, trailing her finger along the line of his luxurious whiskers. 'Much, much better,' she finished, and, walking across to the bed, she parted the mosquito nets and lay down ready for him.

'Colonel Sahib! Colonel Sahib!' The knocking on the door increased in its intensity. 'Colonel Sahib! Quick! Please quick, Colonel Sahib!'

The colonel gritted his teeth, panting hard. 'Go away!' he snarled. Alicia moaned.

'Colonel Sahib! Please come, Colonel Sahib!' The knocking had stopped and the bearer had his ear to the door, listening for sounds of the Sahib.

'Go . . . away . . .' The colonel gripped the sheet by Alicia's shoulder. His breathing quickened.

'Colonel Sahib!' The door handle rattled. 'Colonel Sahib!'

'Ah, damn it!' Reginald flicked his eyes open. 'What the hell . . . ?'

'Reggie darling!' Alicia dragged her gaze away from the

wall at the sound of her husband's swearing and focused on his damp red face above her. She brought her mind back to the present. 'What is . . . ?'

The colonel sat up. 'Damn people! Can't get a minute's peace!' He glanced down at Alicia, half naked on the bed. 'I'm sorry,' he muttered, yanking his breeches up from around his thighs.

She waved her hand to dismiss his apology and reached for the sheet. She was peckish anyway, she could do with tea.

'I'll have to go and see what's . . .' The colonel had tucked his shirt in and was pulling on his braces. 'I'm coming, bearer!' he shouted as the knocking on the door started again. He strode towards the door and moments later had left the room. Alicia rang for tea.

'What the devil is all this about . . . ?' The bearer cowered, his head bent and his palms folded together in the Hindu way. 'Please, Colonel Sahib . . .' he hissed, 'the secretary sahib for His Majesty the Maharajah is here . . . please, Colonel Sahib, he is outside, please . . .'

Colonel Mills swiped his right hand across the bent head of his servant. 'I never see anyone in the afternoon! You know that!'

The bearer looked up, pleading. 'But Colonel Sahib . . . the secretary sahib to the maharajah! Please, you must come!'

Colonel Mills closed his eyes for a second. The heat of the afternoon had begun to close in and his head ached. He wanted to be lying down inside in the cool, not sweating outside with a bloody native! He held tightly on to his temper, his face reddening and snarled at the bearer, 'Where is he?'

'Outside, Colonel Sahib,' the servant bent even lower. 'On the verandah. He is waiting to be invited inside, Colonel Sahib.'

'Get my jacket and boots.' Colonel Mills had no intention of inviting an Indian into his bungalow. He would see the chap on the verandah and nowhere else. 'And hurry up!'

The bearer scurried off and returned almost immediately. The colonel pulled on his coat and sat ready to be assisted with his boots. Minutes later he stood again, smoothed his fingers over the tips of his moustache and walked out towards the verandah.

'Colonel Mills.' An elderly Indian dressed in dark grey silk *sherwani* and *churidar* pyjamas folded his palms and bowed his head. 'Good afternoon to you, sir. His Royal Highness the Maharajah sends you his good wishes.'

The colonel nodded in reply. He refused to acknowledge Indian royalty; they were all natives to him. Insolently leaning back against the wall of the bungalow, the searing heat enveloped him and he shut his eyes for a moment. 'What is it?' he demanded, not even looking at Nanda. 'You have a message from the maharajah?'

'Yes, colonel sir.' Ever courteous, the Indian's English was smooth and polished. He raised his head and looked directly at the officer, red and damp in the heat. He concealed the slightest of smiles. 'We have had rumours today from the north, colonel, from Meerut. There is news of terrible unrest. This problem of the pig and beef fat to grease the new cartridges has caused much upset, colonel sir, with the Hindus and the Mohammedans. It is an awful prob—'

'I am well aware of the situation, Mr Nanda!' the colonel interrupted. 'You have no need to remind me.' He stood away from the wall to assert himself. 'Was this the only thing that you—'

'Oh no, colonel sir!' Nanda was not in the least intimidated. 'We have heard this morning that the soldiers who would not touch these things have been humiliated, colonel sir, all eighty-five of these men have been stripped of their uniforms, their ankles shackled. It is most upsetting, I really do not think . . .'

'Mr Nanda!' Moving forward a pace, Colonel Mills towered above the slight, elegant Indian. 'I really don't see what it could possibly have to do with my command here in Moraphur! These men directly disobeyed the order to use the cartridges and their officers have punished them.' The colonel gave no hint of the alarm that Nanda's words had caused him. 'It really is nothing to do with me,' he went on, all the time wondering what the hell that fool Hewitt was doing in command up at Meerut, 'and as far as I am concerned, that is the end of the matter!'

'Perhaps so, colonel sir, but I fear that this incident has caused much anger in the lines. From Meerut, just now, we have heard of terrible rumours . . .'

'Rumours? Pah! I am not in the business of listening to rumours! I command this division of the regiment on fact, that accounts for my judgement, not blasted rumours!' Colonel Mills felt a small rivulet of sweat trickle down the side of his face and, thoroughly irritated by the heat, Nanda's sly superiority and the bloody fiasco up at Meerut, he turned towards the door.

'But forgive me, colonel,' – Nanda had dropped the pretence of 'sir' – 'the news was of feelings of great anger and offence,' he lowered his voice, 'even of mutiny!' He stepped forward a pace to keep himself level with the officer. 'I really do think that you should . . .'

Colonel Mills swung round. 'I should go inside now and get out of this blasted heat, that's what I should do, Mr Nanda!' To be spoken to in that manner by a native incensed him; his temper finally snapped. 'And I'll thank you to refrain from idle gossip and rumour! You chaps are all the same, far too taken up with loose talk and meddling! When you have some facts, then perhaps I will see you. But, until then, please, Mr Nanda, stop wasting my time!' And without the courtesy of an adieu, the colonel stamped off inside.

The darkened interior of the bungalow, although not much cooler than outside, was at least a relief from the glare of the sun. The colonel slumped into an armchair and shouted for the bearer, wiping his face on his handkerchief. Nanda had infuriated him, he was getting above himself. It would do to remind the maharajah exactly who ran this state, he thought angrily.

Still, the situation in Meerut was alarming, Nanda was right. His own officers had talked of unease in the lines, the men were restless, upset and trouble amongst the ranks spread like wild fire. He couldn't afford to let any strife at Meerut eat its way into his own troops, he would have to take a ride up there in the morning to gauge the seriousness of Nanda's rumours.

'Bearer!' he shouted a second time, the thought of a day-break start and a ride in the stifling heat up to

Meerut fuelling his already foul temper. 'Bearer!' he hollered. 'Where the hell are you?'

He slumped back in the chair as the servant finally hurried into view. 'Blasted party!' he muttered under his breath. The last thing he needed was a late night. 'Get these ruddy boots off me!' he snarled. 'And be quick about it! You damn natives are so damned slow!'

The colonel and Mrs Mills sat silent in their carriage at seven o'clock precisely that evening, as it swung into the impressive grounds of Indrajit Rai's house, royal jeweller to the Maharajah of Jupthana. Alicia felt the colonel stiffen beside her at the sight of such native opulence and placed a pale cool hand on his arm reassuringly. Looking out at the torch-lined driveway, she leant a little closer to the open window and breathed in the warm, jasmine-scented air as they drove through the flame trees hung with lanterns and approached the house, ablaze with light.

The carriage drew to a halt in front of the ornate and sprawling bungalow and a young house boy stepped forward to help the guests down; he was instantly dismissed. Colonel Mills turned and offered his hand to his wife; the thought of strange dark fingers on her skin incensed him.

'Alicia?'

'Thank you, Reggie.' Alicia held the hem of her evening dress in one hand and tilted her head back in a manner she assumed fitting; they mounted the steps up the verandah towards their host.

Indrajit Rai stood, with his son on his right, waiting humbly to receive his honoured British guests. It was a great coup for him that the colonel and Mrs Mills had accepted his invitation and it was essential that they be given the very best hospitality. As they approached him, he bowed his head and pressed his hands together, smiling all the time but keeping his eyes averted so as not to offend.

'Colonel Mills Sahib! And Mrs Mills Memsahib. How good of you to come, you do a great honour to me and my family.' Indrajit Rai's English, like Nanda's, was precise and carefully modulated. He had studied it fastidiously and practised his accent tirelessly. 'Please, you are most welcome.'

Colonel Mills nodded in reply and glanced over the Indian's head into the house to see who had already arrived.

'May I please introduce you to my son, Colonel Mills?' Indrajit Rai motioned frantically with his left hand behind his back for his son to step forward and bow his head. 'This is my son, colonel, Jagat. It is a great honour for him to meet you.'

From behind the host, a tall lean young man of seventeen stepped forward and held out his hand to the colonel. He looked directly ahead and smiled. 'How nice to meet you, Colonel Mills.' He kept his right hand extended even though it was ignored. 'And Mrs Mills.' He turned and smiled at Alicia. 'It is a pleasure indeed.'

Colonel Mills felt a hot rush of blood to his face and his nostrils flared. Who the hell did this young devil think he was? Didn't he know the form? He opened his mouth to protest at such damned ruddy impudence when Alicia touched him gently on the arm. He started, noticed the sudden staring silence around them and held his tongue.

Alicia was right, it wouldn't do to cause a scene, not in his position.

'Please, Colonel Sahib, please go into my house and the bearer will bring you a drink!' Indrajit stepped in front of his son, his eyes lowered and edged the colonel towards the interior of the bungalow. He had begun to sweat anxiously. 'This way, Colonel Sahib and Mrs Mills Memsahib, please to have a nice cool drink inside.' He blocked the view of his son in an attempt to dismiss his rudeness. 'It is such an honour,' he rushed on, 'to have you as guests in my house, such a great honour for me and my family! Please, please to go inside . . .'

At last the colonel smiled.

'A drink for the colonel and Mrs Mills, bearer!' The host shouted above the chatter of the party, 'Quickly!' He clapped his hands loudly. 'Quickly, a drink!' The bearer came into sight, carrying a large silver tray, and Indrajit Rai fussed extravagantly over the refreshments. Alicia smiled at several of their acquaintances, nodding to the left and the right and the colonel relaxed slightly. He took a long gulp of his whisky soda and glanced around him. The difficult moment was over, at least for the interim and the party continued, much to the relief of the agitated host.

'But what I do not understand is why so many of our countrymen do not question the supremacy of the British. Pah! It would seem to me that we are all too afraid of putting the situation right.' Jagat Rai had his back to the rest of the party as he spoke to a small group of young men in the corner of his father's large open drawing room. He knew nothing of the true situation in Meerut

12

or of the tension in the military community and spoke simply off the top of his head; he enjoyed the thrill of indulging in dangerous talk. 'It would seem to me—' he broke off as one of his friends jabbed him in the ribs. The colonel was within earshot and had glanced several times in their direction; his ear was constantly tuned to any talk of unrest. Jagat was undeterred. 'It would seem to me,' he went on, but louder this time, his voice rising above the swell of small talk, 'that where the British are concerned, we are frightened of speaking our minds, it would seem to me—' Jagat received a sharp prod with a bony elbow and turned towards his friend to protest. He saw then, quite clearly, that the colonel had stopped talking and was staring hard at him, a prominent vein in his temple distended and throbbing. The chatter around the room died away but he matched the colonel's stare.

'It would seem to you what exactly?' Colonel Mills demanded. He had no intention of restraining himself this time; the boy needed to be embarrassed, put in his place. He was aware of the room's attention focused on their exchange and he waited for the boy to back down.

'It would seem to me,' Jagat answered, 'that the British superiority in India is a figment of their imagination.' He spoke with cool assurance, his face set and his gaze steady on Colonel Mills. A shocked murmur ran through the room. Jagat Rai, an intelligent, educated and angry young man, was not going to back down. 'The British are no better than any other ruler in this country and perhaps they are even worse.' He saw the colonel's face flush deep red but he went on. 'Whatever they are, colonel, the people of India are not happy with them. The situation is not a comfortable one and I think that it is going to have to change.'

'Well I . . . I . . .' For the first time in his life, Colonel Mills was lost for words and the whole party looked on with horror and dismay as he floundered. He had never, in all his military career, been spoken to with such insolence by an inferior, and never, never by a native! His face took on a peculiar bilious look as the blood pounded beneath the surface of the skin and such a sudden, overwhelming urge for violence overtook him that he had to grip the leather gloves he held in one hand to stop himself from lunging forward and taking the blighter by the throat.

Jagat Rai simply smiled, nodded his head and then turned away, back to his friends, as if nothing untoward had happened. The only thing that perturbed him was the fact that he might have offended his father.

'Alicia!' Colonel Mills finally announced to the still hushed room. 'We are leaving. I will not stay here to be insulted!' He glared across the room and shouted for the bearer.

'Oh my goodness! Colonel Mills Sahib!' Indrajit Rai rushed in from the verandah where he had been talking to more guests and bowed humbly low. He had heard the colonel's remark and his mind was in turmoil. 'Please, colonel, you must not be leaving so soon! My cook has prepared some European canapés, please, you must stay to taste of them!' He glanced up and smiled hopefully.

'Alicia, are you ready?' Colonel Mills did not even acknowledge the man. He waited a few moments for the boy to bring Alicia's wrap and then he held his arm for her and turned towards the door. 'We are leaving,' he announced to the room, and, as Indrajit Rai stared desolately after them, the colonel and Mrs Mills swept arrogantly out of the party.

'Damned impudent darkie!' the colonel exploded as soon as the carriage moved off. 'I've never heard such bloody rudeness in my entire life!' He took out his handkerchief and wiped his forehead. 'Stuff and bloody nonsense too! If you ask me that blasted boy . . .'

'Reggie!' Alicia protested at the bad language and Colonel Mills grudgingly apologised. They sat in silence for several minutes. 'I don't know where the hell these fellahs think they'd be without the British!' He went on, too angry to let it drop. 'I mean, really! They have no idea of the skill and organisation it takes to—' He stopped short. Alicia had placed her hand at the top of his thigh, her long elegant fingers applying a little pressure before edging higher. There was only one way to calm her husband down and Alicia moved her hand expertly, her touch light and exciting. Besides, she thought, hearing his breathing slow and regulate, he always lasted much, much longer after a temper.

Colonel Mills swallowed hard, finally losing his train of thought and relaxed back against the padded velvet of the seat. It was a long drive home and he was glad of that. Damn and blast the events of the day, he thought, not quite letting himself go, and damn and blast tomorrow as well, with that wretched bally ride up to Meerut; it was the last thing he needed! He eased his shoulders back as Alicia deftly stroked and let out a sigh. Had to be done though, he thought, before his mind drifted into pleasure, no doubt about that, not after tonight there wasn't. He closed his eyes and the face of Jagat Rai flashed into view. 'Ruddy Indians,' he murmured as a cool hand wrapped around his flesh. He blinked them open to check the blinds were down, then settled back once more. Couldn't trust them an inch, he mused, only moments before his whole body shivered and Alicia's hands worked their magic.

Chapter Two

Sunday, 11th May, 1857

Colonel Mills took the crop proffered to him by his Syce and tapped it against his thigh impatiently. It was still dark and only a faint glimmer of day could be spotted on the horizon. Already the heat had begun. He was in a foul temper; they should have left some time ago, if they'd been able to find the servants.

'You ready?' he shouted across at Captain Boyd.

The captain nodded. He jarred his mount forward, regardless of the young horse boy under foot, and adjusted himself in the saddle. The massive dark stallion was jittery, it wanted to be off and the small boy cowered against the stable wall as the horse shifted fretfully about.

'Right! We'll head up to the Lohagarh Fort and then out across the open plain towards Meerut. We can stop in a couple of hours for a break on the Sariska Pass, find one of the caves for shade.'

'Fine.' Captain Boyd dug his heels in and the horse

moved off. He glanced over his shoulder at the colonel, slowing to let him take the lead, and minutes later they had left the camp boundaries and were heading out into open countryside.

However, at the same time that they set out, eighty miles to the north, the Meerut that Colonel Mills and Captain Boyd rode towards lay in chaos and devastation. Nanda's rumours had become reality: the native troops had mutinied.

Dense smoke from burning buildings rose up into the dark sky above the town, obscuring the very last of the moon, and as the new day broke, the terrible remains of frenzied and savage attacks on the Europeans could be seen as only dark, gruesome shapes in the faint dawn light. They had slaughtered everything in their path and while the command dithered, shocked and confused, the bloodthirsty band of rebel seepoys had ridden on over the Abu Nullah bridge and out on to the Delhi road. They were headed south, to march on Delhi and to murder the Europeans, screaming with violent anger and hatred.

'Whoa! Steady, boy! Whoa!' Colonel Mills pulled hard on the reins and dug his thighs tight against his mount's flank, gripping to keep his balance. 'Whoa!' He kept his seat but only just, somehow managing to calm the horse. He was an expert equestrian but he struggled for several minutes to bring the animal back under his control. 'Christ! Boyd!' He glanced back over his shoulder at the captain as the horse steadied. 'Boyd? You all right?'

His companion's horse had also reared up in panic at the sudden terrifying screams that came out of nowhere but Captain Boyd, less experienced, had taken a fall and lay on the hard, dry ground, moaning in agony. His mount had bolted and, as Colonel Mills dismounted, hurrying his own horse over to Boyd, the same blood-curdling yells sounded again.

'Good God! What the hell . . . !' Colonel Mills bent down, glancing behind him as he did so. He could see a cloud of dust on the horizon and he knew they didn't have much time. 'Boyd? Boyd, can you move? We have to get out of sight, can you get up?'

Boyd managed to nod.

'Here man, take my arm.' The colonel slipped his arm behind the captain and wrenched him to his feet. He groaned, his legs buckling, but the colonel held him up. Still clenching the reins, he dragged Captain Boyd over to the cover of some rocks where he slumped down, the rock supporting him, his face white with pain. 'It's my shoulder,' he moaned, 'I think I've broken my shoulder.'

'All right. Just stay there, man.' Colonel Mills secured the reins of his mount and then ran out on to the track to collect up Boyd's cap. He swept his foot over their tracks and darted back to the cover of the rock. Standing close to his horse, he held her nose and waited. For the first time in his life he felt frightened. Not for himself and Boyd, he didn't give a damn about his own life, but Nanda's words came back to him and an image of the angry young man at the party swam before his eyes. It was for Alicia he was afraid. It was for Alicia that his heart pounded in his chest as the thunder of galloping hooves neared and hysterical Indian voices were carried screaming on the wind.

It was over in seconds.

The rabble of men, whose uniforms, torn and blood-stained, told him everything, had passed out of sight, a stray bullet clipping the edge of the rock where Boyd crouched and the colonel's mount screeching in fear for a few terrifying moments. They had galloped by and the captain and Colonel Mills remained undiscovered.

'What in God's name . . . ?'

'Meerut!' Colonel Mills answered, standing and wiping the sweat out of his eyes. 'They've come from Meerut.' Without wasting another moment, he led his horse out on to the track and stared into the distance. 'I've got to get up there,' he said, 'find out what's happened!' He put his foot in the stirrup, ready to mount, then glanced back at Boyd. 'Will you be all right?'

Captain Boyd nodded.

'I'll send someone back for you as soon as I reach there.' They were about ten miles south of Meerut. He mounted and pulled the reins in.

'D'you think they'll come back?'

'No, I don't think they will.' In truth he had no idea what they would do. In his experience the Indian was wholly unpredictable, save for one thing: vengeance. And the thought of that chilled him to the core.

'Ayah!' Alicia Mills sat forward and put her breakfast tray down on the bed beside her. 'Ayah! Where are you?' She called out again to her servant, this time more impatiently for fear of having to get up herself. 'Ayah! Where are you?' Her voice rose. 'Please come here!' she shouted. 'The baby is crying!'

Moments later, she sighed, exasperated, and swung her

legs over the side of the bed, reluctant to get up. Just then the ayah came running into the room.

'Where have you been?' Alicia demanded. 'Did you not hear the baby crying?'

'No, Memsahib!' The ayah's voice trembled as she spoke. 'I have been outside!' A small sob suddenly escaped her and she rushed to the crib. Alicia jumped off the bed and ran across to her. She gripped the ayah's arm. 'What is it? What's happened?' For some reason she felt an instant panic. Things had been so odd that morning, no servants, a deathly quiet in the house. She shook the ayah who had bent to pick up the baby. 'What? What is it? Tell me!'

The ayah yanked her arm free and cradled the infant to her breast, trying to soothe him. She wiped her cheeks on the skin of her wrist, unable to stop her frightened crying. 'We must go, Memsahib,' she stammered. 'Please, we must go now, please to hurry . . . !' She was shaking and her anxiety made the baby scream even louder. Alicia grabbed the ayah's shoulders, fear making her long fingers dig painfully into the flesh. 'What has happened?' she cried. 'Tell me . . . ?'

'Mrs Mills! Mrs Mills!' They were interrupted by an urgent banging on the door. 'Mrs Mills! Are you in there? It's Major Reece!'

'Yes . . . ! Oh my God!' Alicia ran to the door, flinging it open. 'What is it?' The panic was making her dizzy, she could hardly breathe. 'What's happened?' She looked frantically past the major into the sitting-room of the house. 'Bearer!' she shouted. 'Bearer? Where are . . .'

'The bearer has gone, m'am!' Major Reece cut her short. 'So have most of the servants. There's trouble here . . .'

He was armed with his sword and a pistol. 'We have to leave now!'

Alicia glanced back at the ayah. She tried to take some deep breaths, to calm herself down.

'Can you dress quickly? We don't have much time . . .' In the distance they heard a scream, a wild, animal sound and Alicia began to shake. 'Yes, yes I can . . . Oh God . . .' She ran back into the room and began to pull open the drawers in her chest, grabbing at her clothes, throwing them into a heap on the floor. She couldn't think, she was too frightened. Suddenly the sound of the rabble hit them; a terrifying murderous yell and the ayah let out a sob. It brought Alicia to her senses.

Opening the top drawer, she grabbed the baby's layette, flinging the tiny garments at the ayah. She ripped the silk shawl from around her shoulders and ran forward, throwing it across the baby to hide it. 'Go,' she cried urgently, 'take the baby and hide under the verandah . . . right down into the corner where the wine is kept!' She pushed the ayah towards the back door of her bedroom. 'Go on! Go . . . !' Alicia had started to cry as the ayah clung weeping to her hand. She wrenched it free, not able to look at the baby. 'Go, I tell you!' she shouted. 'Go on . . .! Go! . . . Go now!' She turned away as Major Reece ran into the room. 'Mrs Mills! Hurry! Please hurry!' He was white and sweating, his pistol in one hand. 'There's no time! Please, come with me!' Alicia wiped her face on the sleeve of her silk night-dress, unable to stop her crying now and, barefoot, she ran after the major out on to the verandah.

'Oh my God . . . ! No . . . !' She looked desperately about her at the sight of the camp on fire, thick black smoke rising up into the clear blue sky, the heat every-where.

'Here . . . ! Mrs Mills? Here . . . !' The major had secured a ladder against the wall. 'We have to get up on to the roof . . . we . . .' He looked behind him as the first of the rabble came into view, soaked in blood and screaming, the steel of his blade flashing menacingly as it caught the light. He raised his arm, aimed his pistol and fired. The man went down.

'Come on!' he yelled at Alicia, who stood almost paralysed with fear. 'For God's sake . . . ! Come on!' He would not go up the ladder without her. 'Come on . . . !' But it was already too late. As she stumbled towards the ladder, her legs gave way and she lost control of her bladder. Helpless, she sank to her knees weeping as a group of seepoys galloped into the grounds of the bungalow, slashing violently at the two officers holding the entrance and mutilating their bodies in a matter of seconds.

Major Reece never managed his second shot.

Much, much later, when the bloody chaos the muti-neers had wrought was discovered, there was very little recognisable left of either him or Alicia Mills.

Chapter Three

It was dark by the time Colonel Mills set out again for Moraphur. He had ten men and three officers of the Sixth Dragoon Guards with him; that was all the command at Meerut could spare. They rode long and hard, the colonel sick to the pit of his stomach at the sight of the devastation he had witnessed in Meerut, terrified for the peril of his own camp. He had been shocked and ashamed at the disorganised and futile response of the senior officers at Meerut. It seemed the command, despite the repeated warnings, was totally unprepared for what had just happened; it had no idea what to do.

As each mile passed on the road to Moraphur, the colonel felt the raging ache of despair as images of the carnage flashed in and out of his mind. The hot, dusty landscape bore witness to the chaos, littered every now and then with the charred remains of a burnt-out carriage or the carcass of a slaughtered donkey, already foul smelling and fly infested in the stifling heat.

Finally they reached Moraphur. Passing through a silent, closed town, as the boundary of the camp neared, the party slowed to a walk and continued on in grim, shocked silence. Moraphur had not escaped.

The colonel dismounted, several of the men did the same. He gripped the reins of his horse and swallowed down the bile that rose in his throat. As he bent to pick up a small bloodstained lady's slipper, he saw the foot, severed at the ankle, was still in it. Behind him the wretched noise of one of the soldiers vomiting echoed in the silence and he closed his eyes.

'Dear God,' he murmured. 'Oh dear God . . .' Walking on, he kept his eyes ahead and passed the carnage all around him in a daze. He followed the main road of the camp up to the grounds of his own bungalow and for a moment his body froze. The bungalow stood, almost untouched, it appeared. He dropped the reins of the horse and ran ahead. 'Bearer!' he shouted. 'Alicia! Alicia!' But as he ran, he caught his foot on something and stumbled, nearly losing his balance. He glanced down at the ground, back at his path and it was then that he saw it. He dropped to his knees and buried his face in his hands. He made no sound. He recognised Alicia's hand; it still wore the ring he had given her for her birthday.

Sometime later, although Colonel Mills was never exactly sure when, as the ghastly task of collecting together what was left of the butchered bodies and digging graves for them was under way, a massive earth tremor ripped through the ground and the whole sky was momentarily lit up, a vivid white, then orange light. The magazine, an immense store of ammunition in Delhi, had been blown up by the British forces to stop it falling into enemy hands and the effect of that explosion was felt for miles around.

The small rabble of servants that had remained in camp ran screaming from what they were doing and cowered together, wailing and praying. Several of the soldiers dropped their tools, one lost his balance and stumbled.

'What the damned hell was that?' Colonel Mills was perspiring heavily, large dark stains of sweat ran into the patches of black blood on his uniform. 'Get up, man!' he shouted at a dhobiwallah, swinging his leg out and kicking him hard in the back. 'Get up, I said!'

'It came from the direction of Delhi!' one of the young officers called out. His uniform was also drenched in blood. He wiped his arm across his brow as he looked up and left a trail of dirt, sweat and blood on his skin. The colonel couldn't bear to look at it; he turned away. 'God only knows what's happening there,' the young officer went on, 'it could be any . . .' Suddenly his voice trailed away as he looked past the colonel's shoulder. He saw a figure, a woman with a European shawl over her head. 'What the devil . . . !' Dropping his spade, he broke into a run.

Colonel Mills swung round. 'My God! Alicia!' He recognised the silk and his whole body froze in shocked disbelief for a moment. Then he was running, down after the young man, sprinting across the patch of open ground and on the road towards his bungalow.

*   *   *

The ayah had crawled out from under the eaves of the bungalow, terrified by the earth's gross shudder and she stumbled forward into the last of the daylight, momentarily blinded after her hours of darkness. She still wore the memsahib's shawl over her head and she clutched the baby to her breast, desperately trying to shush him quiet, his pathetic wails smothered by her grip. She made only a small anguished sound, a stifled sob, but her eyes were wild with panic, darting frantically over the ground as she moved out of the cover of the house; searching for any terror.

The young officer reached her first. He gripped her shoulder with one hand to hold her steady and yanked the shawl from her head. Already he could see that she wasn't what he had thought and the disappointment flared his anger. 'What the hell is this . . . ?' He clenched the edge of the shawl in his fingers, a French patterned silk and crushed it. 'Jesus! You impudent . . .' He raised his arm to hit her.

'Leave her!' Colonel Mills stopped several feet away, panting hard. The realisation of who the figure was sent a pain of such intensity through him that he had to bend double for a moment and hold his chest to ease it. He glanced up at the young officer. 'It's the ayah,' he said slowly, 'Mrs Mills' ayah.' He straightened, making an almighty effort to regain his composure and took several deep breaths. Finally, he walked across to them. 'You can leave us, major,' he said. Without looking at the servant, he reached out for the baby and took his son into his arms.

'I said leave us!' he ordered and the baby whimpered at the force of his voice. The young officer turned away.

Holding his son, Colonel Mills started for the bungalow, oblivious to the sobs of the ayah behind him. He carried the baby badly, inexperienced and disabled in his sorrow and the child began to howl, a thin weak cry against the blanket of deathly silence that covered them all.

It was dark when Colonel Mills finally came out of the bungalow. The ayah had gone in after a while and taken the baby from him to feed it and change it, but he had barely realised. He had sat, for a long time, in the eerie darkness amidst the horrible chaos the mob had left behind, and stared blankly out at what was left of the garden, Alicia's precious garden. He did not try to make any sense of it all, he had seen too much of men and war for that, but he did try to find someone to blame. In his ordered military mind he believed there was someone or something responsible for everything. Nothing ever just happened, events were made. And in the time that he sat, his anger and grief focused on that one fact, Colonel Mills found the someone responsible he needed. In the distorted logic of pain and misery, he blamed Indrajit Rai.

The trouble in Moraphur had been growing for some time, he realised that now. Hadn't Rai's son said so? What was it he'd said? That the situation was not a comfortable one? He must have known, Colonel Mills reasoned, he must have had some idea! And if he had known, then his father would have known! Indrajit Rai would most definitely have known, could probably have even been behind the whole thing! Smiling, gracious Indians, with their parties and European canapés; it was all a ruse, a trap to lull the British into a false sense of security. But that upstart of a son couldn't keep quiet! He couldn't keep his filthy native mouth shut, could he? Colonel Mills stood, for the first time in hours, his legs weak and stiff from sitting, he paced the floor. It all began to slot into place, the visit from Nanda, the party, the whole scene was so damn clear he wondered why the hell he hadn't seen it before! As he paced, he worked it through. Nanda must have got wind of the mutiny, he worked for the maharajah, Rai was the maharajah's jeweller. What if Rai had been planning something like this for years and then found the chance in the unrest amongst the ranks. He could have stirred it, raked the hornets' nest, he could have incited anything in the atmosphere there was.

The colonel stood on the steps of his ransacked home and looked at the torchlight dotted around the camp, torches to light the way for burying the dead. He gripped the balustrade as his head swam and he swayed precariously, dizzy with anger and fatigue. 'Jesus Christ, that man will pay!' he muttered through clenched lips. 'God damn it he will pay for his part in all . . .' He stopped as the wail of an infant pierced the silence and made him shiver with pain. It was his own son crying. Henry Reginald Mills was crying for his mother.

'Captain!' Colonel Mills called out to the officer in charge of digging a grave at the back of the mess. The young man stood straight and wiped the sweat out of his eyes but his vision didn't clear. They had been working all day in the choking heat and the scene had begun to blur into one mass of sweat, dirt and blood.

'Yes, colonel?' He averted his gaze, not wanting to look his superior in the eye. He had buried the remains of the man's wife; how could he face the poor devil after that?

'Captain, I want you to go into Moraphur. There are people to hold accountable for the trouble today and I want them brought in for questioning.'

The captain swallowed, the hard lump of his Adam's apple moving uncomfortably in his throat. 'Sir, I think that we should try to finish up here tonight if we possibly can. I—'

'I have given you an order, captain!' the colonel interrupted. 'I am not interested in what you think!' He jutted his chin out and squared his shoulders. 'There is justice to be done and we must see to it. The men I want brought in are both in the same family: Rai. There are business premises in the town and a bungalow out towards Deeg. I want them here tonight.'

'Yes, sir.' The captain drove the spade hard into the ground and left it there. He walked across to the small party of soldiers still digging and shouted out his orders. What the colonel was doing God only knew but he wasn't in any position to question him. He hoped there wasn't going to be any trouble; the poor bastard was obviously out of his mind with grief and with him in command, the last thing they needed now was trouble.

'It is the British Army, master! Come quickly! Please . . . there are soldiers outside!'

Indrajit Rai hurried down the corridor from the bedroom he shared with his wife, straightening the cotton *kurta* he had pulled on in the past few minutes. The main room of the bungalow was dark and the bearer stood with a lamp by the door. He could hear movement from Jagat's bedroom and he called out to his son.

'Jagat! It is all right, please, go back to bed, I am sure

it is nothing.' Taking the lamp from the bearer, he paused a moment to compose himself and then swung open the front door.

'Indrajit Rai?'

'Yes. I am Rai. What is it you want?' Indrajit blinked rapidly in the glare of the torchlight but could only make out several indistinct figures behind the officer in command.

'Indrajit Rai, I am here to place you and your son under arrest. You will come with me to the British Army headquarters for questioning.' The young captain kept his voice even and stared at a spot directly above the other man's head. He was damned nervous but didn't dare show it. If you let that sort of thing slip then the crafty buggers really took advantage. He had never trusted the natives and he had no intention of starting now. 'Is your son inside? Ask the bearer to tell him we are waiting.'

Indrajit Rai took a pace back and held on to the wall for support. 'But please . . . I don't understand. Please, there must be some mistake.' A sweat had broken out on his upper lip as he looked at the officer. 'What could you want with—'

'I am placing you both under arrest as of this moment,' the captain interrupted and continued to look over his prisoner's head. 'You may inform your household.'

'But I . . .'

Two of the soldiers moved forward behind the captain and Indrajit Rai backed into the house. He could not believe this was happening, it was impossible! There must be some mistake. His legs buckled under him.

'Papa? Papaji!' Jagat hurried across to the door and took the weight of his father just in time. He helped him across to a chair. 'What is it, Papa? What has happened?' He glanced up at the army out on the verandah. The small group of grimy and bloody-uniformed men were menacing in the light of the torches.

He swallowed hard and looked back at his father. 'What do these men want, Papa? What?'

Indrajit Rai clutched his chest and took a deep breath to ease the pain there before he spoke. 'It is the British Army, Jagat, they have come to arrest us both.'

'No!' Jagat stood. 'No! It cannot be! Why? What have we done?' He looked from his father to the men outside and then back to his father. 'They cannot do this!' he hissed urgently. 'Papa, they cannot just arrest us! Call the servants! They cannot just take us away!' Jagat's voice had risen with panic and the young captain outside shifted uncomfortably. He couldn't hear the conversation but he could catch the tone and it was beginning to make him damned nervous.

'Hurry up in there!' he called out. 'I don't want to have to send my men in after you!'

Jagat swung round angrily. 'You just try! Dammit!' He shouted across to the bearer in Hindi to fetch the rest of the servants. 'Go! Now! And quickly, tell them to come with sticks!'

'Jagat, no!' Indrajit contradicted his son and the bearer stopped short. 'It is a misunderstanding, Jagat, that is all!' He rose to his feet and straightened his clothes. 'We will see the colonel about all this, it is simply a mistake, Jagat. You will see. Come!' Indrajit faced the door. The events of the past day in Meerut and in Moraphur had left Indrajit Rai shocked and exhausted; he had never seen such violence and hatred in his countrymen. He had been helpless, frightened for the safety of his own family and he had watched, in shame and anger, the annihilation of innocents. The world was in chaos, this was simply another part. 'Come, Jagat!' he ordered. The young man looked at him, totally uncertain of his words or actions. 'Tell Mrs Rai that we will be back as soon as this mistake is found out.' Indrajit laid his hand on the bearer's arm. 'Look after her,' he said quietly in Hindi. 'Jagat?'

Jagat took one last long look at his father. Unlike the man he loved and respected, he had no regard for the British sense of justice. He glanced back at the light in the corridor and saw the figure of his mother watching them. 'Yes, Papa,' he answered finally and together they walked out of the house.

Chapter Four

Colonel Mills sat alone in the officers' mess with his head in his hands. The heat was choking and he was in full dress uniform, the sweat running almost continuously down the side of his face but he was oblivious to it. In these small private moments, he was oblivious to everything; his mind was completely blank.

In the past two weeks Colonel Mills had brought Moraphur back under British command. With the small battalion of men from Meerut he had wielded extraordinary power over the small community. He had rounded up anyone he had reason to suspect, he executed at his will and he kept large numbers of wealthy and powerful Indians under armed guard. He neither knew nor cared whether what he was doing was right or wrong, he was driven by grief and anger; he had a crusade.

Glancing at his pocket-watch on the table in front of him, he realised it was almost time for the enquiry board to assemble and he sat upright, straightening his jacket. Despite the chaos, Colonel Mills always looked immaculate; it had become an obsession with him, after the dirt and blood of clearing up the massacre. He wiped his face on his handkerchief, newly laundered, the second that morning, and set his papers in a neat pile ready. Moments later, he called out in answer to a knock and the three other officers who made up the enquiry board filed in.

'Good morning, gentlemen.' He didn't smile, he never did.

The officers sat, each for his own reasons highly uncomfortable with the situation, and the colonel addressed the matter in hand. 'Rai,' he said, without looking up. 'I want to pass a motion that they be executed the day after tomorrow and that all business, property and land belonging to the said party be requisitioned by Her Majesty's Government in India.'

One of the officers coughed nervously and the colonel glared across at him. There was an awkward silence while the young captain in question struggled to find the nerve to disagree but it was short-lived. He knew what was happening wasn't right but he just didn't have the courage to speak out. Reinforcements were arriving in a couple of days and with them very probably a new command, thank God. He would have to leave it until then. He kept quiet as the colonel addressed the other two and said, 'Those in favour say Aye.' Assent was mumbled and the motion passed. The young captain looked at his colleagues with a weary, exasperated expression and the colonel went on to the next matter. This meeting was as ridiculous as it had been each day so far; the enquiry board was a mere formality, Colonel Mills was in command, he gave the orders and regardless of how bad those orders were, for the moment at least, they had to be carried out.

'Papaji. Papaji!' Jagat Rai touched his father on the shoulder and shook him gently. The older man opened his eyes and attempted to smile, the effort of which seemed to exhaust him and he closed them again.

'What is it, Jagat?' he murmured.

'Papa, there is something to eat. Here, you must try to take a little.' Jagat held out a rusting tin plate. 'Please, Papaji, just try a little.'

But Indrajit held his hand up and gestured for Jagat to take the plate away. The food had not been prepared by his own cook, by someone of the right caste, and as a fastidiously religious man, it would defile him to eat it. He had gone a fortnight now without food and he was frail, dehydrated by the lack of water or nourishment in the intense heat and ill, infected by the dirt and excrement in the cell. Jagat sighed bitterly, wondering whether to try again and then stood, knowing it was useless. He walked to the far wall of the cell and placed the plate in the corner on the floor. He gave the disgusting mess they had been served to the cockroaches.

'Jagat?'

Turning back to his father, Jagat saw that he wanted to say something. He hurried to his side. 'Papa? What is it?' He took the strip of cotton he had ripped from his shirt and dipped it in the cup of water they shared. He gently smoothed it across his father's brow to soak up the sweat. 'Papaji?'

'Jagat, you are sure that your mother is all right?' Indrajit opened his eyes now and stared at his son. 'You have had word that she is all right?'

Jagat looked away. 'Yes, Papa,' he answered quietly, 'I have had word.' He clenched his fists by his side and willed his father to avert his gaze. Jagat had never been able to lie, especially not to the man he loved and respected. There had been no word of his mother, there had been no word of anyone but he was too afraid of what the worry would do to his father to tell him that. So he had lied, two days ago he had lied, and now Indrajit, in his fevered, exhausted state woke every few hours and asked the same question. It was agony to Jagat to have to answer him and to have to repeat his lie over and over again.

'Jagat, I am afraid that they have forgotten us,' Indrajit Rai breathed. His throat was so dry that he had lost his voice and could barely whisper. 'I want you to ask for a meeting with the colonel, with Colonel Mills . . .' Indrajit broke off and rested for a few moments. 'The colonel is a fair man, Jagat . . .' Again he had to rest, the effort seemed to drain the life from him and he was on the edge of unconsciousness. 'I want you to insist to see him . . .' he murmured before his eye-lids fluttered and closed. 'He will help us, I know he will.'

Colonel Mills stood with his back to the room and stared out at the remains of the camp. The officers' mess had miraculously survived but most of the other buildings were burnt out, thankfully in places, leaving only the ashes of some of the slaughter. He put his hand up to shield his eyes from the glare of the sun and remained

standing there as a knock sounded on the door and he
called out for the person to enter.

'Excuse me, colonel, but may I have a word?'

The same officer who had gone to arrest Indrajit Rai
stood by the door in the officers' mess dining-room and
waited for the colonel to acknowledge him.

'Go ahead, captain.' Colonel Mills kept his back to
the officer.

'Em . . . We have a bit of a problem with Rai, sir,
he is making a fuss in his cell, he says his father is ill,
unconscious and that he, em . . .' The captain cleared
his throat. 'He demands to see you, sir, he demands an
interview with—'

'He demands! He demands an interview!' Colonel Mills
swung round, his face white with rage. 'He demands an
interview . . . !' He stopped, breathing with difficulty and
in the glare of the bright sunlight the captain was shocked
by how much events in the past two weeks had aged him.
The once plump, ruddy features had become pallid, the
flesh hanging in loose folds around his neck and jowls.
'That boy should have been taught a lesson years ago!' he
shouted. 'Bloody upstart! He demands . . . !'

The captain took a step backwards. 'Sir, I don't think . . .'

'I want that man's property confiscated! I want his
family removed from their home . . . I want . . .' He
stamped across the room and yanked open the door,
hollering into the anteroom. 'Sergeant! Sergeant!'

The captain pressed himself against the wall, the force
of Colonel Mills' anger almost physical; it knocked him
back. The thought that he should take the colonel's orders
momentarily crossed his mind. The sergeant was a thug
and his party of men were little more than hooligans. But

he dismissed the idea. The brutality of the past weeks had turned his stomach; he didn't believe in an eye for an eye. He wanted no part in it.

'Bloody sergeant! Bloody anus of a man! Where the hell is he?' Colonel Mills strode back to the table and took up his stick, cracking it violently down on the edge before tucking it under his arm. He didn't realise the captain was still in the room and was talking to himself. 'I'll have those fucking darkies if it's the last thing I do . . .' he muttered vehemently and, turning to leave, he walked straight out of the room without even seeing the other man.

'Open up! Open up!' The sergeant thumped continuously on the door with the end of his truncheon, making a hell of a noise. He smiled as the wood started to give way and cracked under the force of the blows. 'Open up I said! It's the British Army!' His truncheon went through, the top panel of the door splitting down the centre. 'Open up in there!' He saw the door rattling as someone on the other side attempted to unlock it and he couldn't resist giving it another smack, just to let them know he meant business.

Indrajit Rai's bearer fumbled anxiously with the bolts inside as his mistress stood behind him. They had kept the house locked up, despite the heat, ever since the master had been arrested, afraid every waking moment of the soldiers' return. But now that it had happened, Mrs Rai was oddly calm. She had suspected that this was inevitable and she would face her fate with dignity.

Like her son, Mrs Rai had no faith in British justice, she had seen in the past two weeks that they were as bad as any other nation when it came to greed and power. They had arrested her husband and her son, killed them for all she knew, and now they had come for their property. She had hidden what she could, taken the valuables she could find but she had no clear idea of what her husband owned, she could not hide everything.

'Hurry up in there!' The sergeant kicked the door, impatient with the bearer's slow-handedness. 'Get a bloody move on!' he shouted, kicking again. He was a bully, with a deep hatred of Indians and he relished the job in hand: he could hardly wait for the door to open. ''Bout time!' he snarled as the last bolt gave way, and, aiming his foot at the centre of the door, he smacked it open with the full force of his boot. The party of soldiers was inside in a matter of seconds.

Knocking the bearer down with a violent crack of his truncheon, the sergeant grabbed Mrs Rai, tearing her arm up behind her back and shoving her through the house towards the bedroom. She made no sound, though her face had crumpled in pain. There he pushed her on to the bed, held her down with his knees pinned to her chest and ripped at her sari, yanking it away from her hips and thighs. When he had exposed her, her flesh red and scratched from the struggle, he stood back and sneered at her shock and humiliation. 'I wouldn't touch you,' he spat, 'you filthy native!' And, as she began to sob with relief, he slapped her hard across the face and left her slumped on the bed.

The rest of the house was being ransacked. As the sergeant came out of the bedroom he put his foot up the bare arse of one of the soldiers raping the ayah and laughed. The young woman was sobbing silently, her eyes wide open and blank with fear and pain. He joined another of the men in the study and started emptying the contents of a bureau, hurling books, papers, anything he found of no value across the room. The things he wanted, he chucked into a sack they had brought for that purpose, any money he pocketed.

It took less than an hour to work through the house and leave a trail of total devastation. The sergeant took the sack and loaded it on to the wagon outside, leaving the men to take the last of what they wanted from the bungalow. When he had done that he gave the order to leave. If he'd had his way, he'd have torched the place but for some reason the colonel wanted it left. He glanced back at their handiwork and smiled. If he'd had his way there'd be no fucking Indians left in this God-forsaken place.

Colonel Mills dismounted and tied the reins of his horse to a tree. He walked up the rest of the drive towards the bungalow, hardly remembering it from the night of the party, and climbed the steps up on to the verandah. It seemed an age ago that he had been here with his wife. He stood, looking into the broken remains of Indrajit Rai's home and, for the first time in seven days, he smiled, a bitter sardonic smile. This was what he wanted, this was justice.

He took the small gold and jewelled bird his men had looted from the house out of his pocket and held it in the palm of his hand. He looked down at the uncut stones, the smooth polished rubies and diamonds, gleaming in the evening sun. Alicia would have liked this, he thought, it was a perfect example of Rai's workmanship. He closed his fingers around it, clutching it so tightly that it dug painfully into his flesh. Alicia was dead and buried, what was left of her, along with the rest of them. Alicia would never see it.

Turning, Colonel Mills stepped down off the verandah and walked away from the house. The deathly silence of it pleased him. He untied the reins of his horse and glanced back before mounting. He would execute the Rais the day after tomorrow, before the new command arrived, he would not let them deny him that. That was really what he wanted, he thought finally, that was justice.

Chapter Five

The camp was deserted in the midday sun, just as Nanda knew it would be. As he approached its boundaries with his carriage the driver drew to a halt and he stood, as if he had spotted an eagle up in the sky, and pointed it out to the driver. He gave his men exactly enough time to crawl out from under the coach and into the grounds of the camp. Then, a couple of minutes later, the first part of the plan complete, the carriage pulled off and continued on to the guard at the entrance, where Nanda made a request to see the colonel at his pleasure.

Within the quarter hour, permission was granted for this visit and Nanda rode along the main thoroughfare towards the officers' mess, his eyes averted from the sight of the small wooden crosses marking the graves that were littered throughout the camp. He was ashamed of the mutiny but he understood it and he knew that Colonel Mills had gone too far in his reprisals for the massacre.

The driver set him down at the officers' mess and Nanda gave him instructions to wait. He knew that he wouldn't have much time with the colonel so they'd have to move quickly. Straightening the sleeves of his *sherwani*, Nanda nodded to the sergeant on the door at the mess and, hoping he could stall the colonel long enough, went inside to await his interview.

The prison block was a building directly across from the officers' mess, a lucky coincidence for Nanda. As he went inside, his driver jumped down from the carriage and leant back against it, his eyes on the soldier Nanda had indicated.

'Psst . . . Psst, soldier,' he hissed. 'I have something to show you.' He smiled and brought out a bundle from the folds of his trousers. He held it up, a packet of postcards, and saw he had the sergeant's attention. 'Over here . . .' he whispered, nodding to the back of the carriage. 'I have nice photos . . .' again he smiled, winking, 'nice photos of girls, white girls . . .'

The sergeant stood, a flicker of excitement licking the pit of his stomach, and, leaving his desk, he went out into the sun and followed the driver to the back of the carriage.

'Show me,' he said, reaching for the packet of postcards. He wasn't going to pay unless they were really good. But the driver held on to them as he'd been told to do and untied the bundle himself. Squatting on the ground, his back to the prison block, he laid the first of the pornographic pictures that Nanda had given him on the ground so that the sergeant had to squat beside him to see it. He watched the man's face very closely and, seeing he had his full attention, he gave the signal behind his back, and began to display the rest of the packet, very slowly, one by one.

In a matter of seconds, Nanda's men were inside the prison block. The guard was taken out with a sharp blow to the back of the neck, his keys removed and the Rais' cell located. He would be unconscious for only a few minutes, they had to be swift.

'Indrajit Rai?' The first man unlocked the door while the second kept watch. 'Indrajit Rai . . .' His voice was barely audible for fear of the other prisoners overhearing. He cracked open the door, covering his nose and mouth against the stench in the cell. Jagat looked up. He had been kneeling by his father's side, cooling his brow with the last of their water and as he saw the man, he struggled to his feet, his legs weak.

'Malika Shuker! Praise the Gods . . .' His voice broke. 'My father . . . he is too ill . . . he—' The man gripped his arm to stop him, putting his hand over his mouth.

'We will come back tonight for you,' he whispered urgently, 'not now, Nanda is in the camp, he would be suspected now, arrested . . .' The man pulled a knife from his belt. 'Here! You must call the guard in tonight, when you hear the eagle cry . . . you must use this . . .' He glanced nervously behind him. 'Be ready, after dark, we will not be able to get in again but we will be waiting. The ground at the back will be clear to the boundary, run across there, keep low, we will have you covered. Listen for the eagle . . .' He let Jagat go and moved back to the door. 'That is the signal . . . when you hear that it is clear . . .' There was a groan from the guard as he began to come round, the man started. 'The eagle,' he hissed. Seconds later, without another word, he was gone.

Jagat ran to the door but it had been relocked. He fell against it, groaning and slumped to the floor. With the other man there might have been a chance, with his help he might have done it. But he would never get out of there alive carrying his father, he would never make it to the boundary in time. He put his hands up to his face and closed his eyes. How could he leave his father here? He dug his fists into his eyes, trying to stop the tears of anger and frustration. How could he do that?

'Rai?'

He started and swallowed painfully.

'Rai? Answer me!'

The small panel in the door was slid back and the guard looked into the cell, checking the prisoners. 'Rai?'

Jagat glanced up and called out hoarsely. The guard moved on. He never usually did his round until dusk but he had dropped off to sleep, gone out like a light in the afternoon heat, waking with his head slumped on the desk. It was something he had never done before and it made him nervous. Satisfied that everything was in order, the guard went back to his post and Jagat listened to his heavy footsteps recede. He stood, rubbing to try and relieve the ache in his legs, and walked across to his father.

I can't leave him, he thought, kneeling and dipping the rag into the water, I know I can't. A pain of sheer desperation shot through him. But, as he put his hand on Indrajit's brow, he realised that he would have to.

His father was dead.

'Mr Nanda, I really don't see what this petty ruling of the maharajah's has to do with me!' Colonel Mills sat at the head of the long dining table in the mess and glared down the length of it at the Indian. If he'd had his way he'd have thrown Nanda into prison along with the rest of them but the man was too highly connected, not just in Jupthana but across the country; the colonel didn't dare. 'I would appreciate it if you would stop wasting my time!' he growled.

Nanda bowed, one eye trained on the window. 'But colonel sir, the maharajah wishes your approval. He would not like to be seen to be doing—' Nanda broke off. He caught sight of the sun glinting off a piece of polished silver in the distance and breathed a sigh of relief. 'He would like to be doing right at all times, colonel sir.' The signal had been given, the first half of the plan was complete. 'Perhaps I can assure him that is so?' He had managed to talk for some length about practically nothing and was now eager to be away.

'Yes, yes, man! If that's what this is all about, then yes! For God's sake be done with it and leave me to get on with some work!'

'Oh, thanking you most kindly, colonel sir!' Nanda bowed, backing towards the door. 'Thanking you for your time.' He glanced up and saw that the colonel had already dismissed him. He took no offence. He'd got what he came for, fifteen minutes of the colonel's time wasted and smiling to himself, he turned and left the room.

It was black. A low, thick cloud covered the sky, obscuring the moon and stars, cutting out the light and it was silent, the heat and air trapped close to the ground making it humid and still.

Jagat Rai sat, his father's hand in his, the flesh white and cold as he looked through the bars on the small window at the ink blue sky outside. He waited. He had no idea of the time, or how long he had held his father like that, he was conscious of nothing but the silence. The silence enveloped him. He was listening so hard for the eagle that his whole body strained and the silence seemed as if it would go on for ever.

Then he started.

The cry came twice. The first time it was muffled, smothered by the cloud, the second time it was high and clear almost as if the bird circled overhead. It was the signal, they had come for him. Jagat looked down at his father. He leant forward, kissed the icy brow and stroked it with his fingertips. Then he stood, took the knife from his belt and went to the door. He banged, thumping his fists hard against it and shouted for the guard. He called out that his father was dead, knowing this was the only way the door would be opened and positioning himself, he held the knife ready. As the man came into the cell, Jagat gripped him from behind, and swiftly and silently cut his throat.

Nanda waited. He sat by the roadside with his bearer in the cover of the trees and glanced every few minutes at the horizon. They were forty miles west of Moraphur where the border of Jupthana met the next state. From there it went on to Balisthan and out of British jurisdiction. They had everything ready.

The next time he looked out he saw the dust. Spurring his horse forward, he made off in that direction, leaving the bearer with the spare mounts, and, nearing the riders, he slowed to a trot, realising there were only two.

'Jagat?' He drew alongside his friend's son. 'What's happened? Your father?'

Jagat shook his head. He couldn't look at Nanda.

'Dead?' Nanda reached out to touch the boy. 'What . . . ?' He saw the pain in Jagat's eyes and broke off. 'Come,' he said, 'you need to rest a while . . .' Turning the horse, he led the way back to the bearer.

The bearer had set a pot of water over a fire and Jagat sat near it, the firelight illuminating his face, a face much older than its seventeen years. He drank his tea in silence, conscious of the relief to be able to drink without guilt. Unlike his father, Jagat had eaten to keep alive, every mouthful tasting foul in the knowledge that it was deeply against his religion.

Nanda watched him as he drank, his own sadness at the loss of his friend mixed with a deep pity for the boy. He had secured him a future, with the help of the maharajah, but it was nothing compared to what he had lost. The British government would requisition his inheritance and he would never be able to set foot in the state again. He had escaped execution but Nanda was still not sure if that was preferable to a life of shame.

'Jagat?' The boy looked up. 'It is time for you to go. You must be out of the state before they find you have gone.'

Jagat stayed where he was. 'But my mother, where is she?'

'She is safe, Jagat,' Nanda answered. 'She is in hiding with one of the maharajah's relatives. She will wait for you to send for her.' He stood. 'Please, Jagat, you must leave!'

Finally Jagat nodded and slowly got to his feet. Nanda walked with him to the horses while the bearer stamped out the fire and began covering traces of it. The two men faced each other, then Nanda embraced his friend's son.

'Jagat, you must avenge the gods for this murder,' he said quietly. 'You will find a way.'

Jagat held on to Nanda and the years fell away; he felt like a child again. 'I know . . .' his voice broke. Moments later, he turned away.

'Here.' Nanda handed him a small leather pouch. 'Your papers, letters from the maharajah, money . . .' He waited while Jagat checked through the information, then he held out a small cloth-covered bundle. 'Jagat, after the soldiers had gone, your mother, when she went back to the house . . .' He saw the boy flinch at his words, hit by the sudden realisation that his home had been ransacked. He stopped and gave him a little time. 'This,' he went on, a few moments later, 'she found this, she wanted you to have it.' He removed the cloth and held a small jewelled bird in the palm of his hand, one of a pair and probably the most beautiful thing Indrajit Rai had ever made. Jagat took it. 'The other one had gone, but this was . . .'

'This was all that they left me!' Jagat suddenly spat. 'This!' He closed his hand over the bird and clenched his fist. 'This . . .' He looked up at Nanda. 'This is the British justice that my father believed in,' he said quietly. Nanda heard the icy anger in his voice and his heart leapt. The boy would need that anger.

'Yes,' he whispered urgently, 'this is the British justice that he died for!' He gripped Jagat's arm. 'Remember that,' he urged, 'every time you look at the bird remember that!' Nanda released him. 'Now go! Hurry, before any more time is lost!' He helped Jagat mount, looking up at his figure as he pulled the headdress around his mouth and covered his face. He slapped the horse's flank and Jagat moved off.

'Ride like the wind!' he called out and the boy looked back at him, a look so like his father's that Nanda's heart ached. 'Go on! Go!' he shouted. 'Go!' And, straining his eyes in the darkness, he watched the horse and rider until they were just a tiny dot on the horizon and the sound of them had blurred into the muffled noises of the night.

PART 2

PART 3

Chapter Six

London, March, 1965

Mitchell Harvey's long black Bentley pulled up at the entrance to the departures terminal at Heathrow airport and parked on a double yellow line. The driver climbed out, beckoned to a porter and went around the back to open up the boot. The two pieces of luggage were loaded on to the trolley, the porter directed to the check-in desk and the driver climbed back in. He glanced in the rear-view mirror, saw that the glass screen was up, and, staring straight ahead, waited for further instructions.

In the back of the car, Mitchell Harvey sat with his wife. He took her left hand, briefly glanced down at the three-carat diamond on her fourth finger and held her hand loosely in his own.

'Suzanna?'

She turned to him, her face cold and impassive.

'I will be arriving at the villa in five days' time,' he said,

'Margaret has my flight details and my itinerary, she will be in touch.'

Suzy nodded.

'I expect you'll want to do a bit of shopping,' he remarked. 'With the season fast approaching.' Again she nodded without speaking. Mitchell reached into the breast pocket of his suit and took out a thick roll of fifty-pound notes; he laid them carefully in Suzanna's lap.

'Suzanna?'

She looked down at the money and then turned away from him, her nostrils flaring with distaste. Mitchell squeezed her fingers, knowing the diamond cut into her flesh.

'Thank you, Mitchell,' she said after a few moments.

He nodded, keeping up the pressure, then he said quietly, 'You will remember what we discussed, won't you, Suzy?'

He waited for her to answer, slowly crushing her fingers as she took her time to reply. She winced at the pain but remained silent.

'I asked you a question, Suzanna!' he suddenly snapped, wrenching her hand towards him and making her cry out with the pain. He held his fist up, her long, thin fingers white and bloodless in his hand. 'I won't have it,' he snarled. 'Not now, not any more!' With his other hand he pulled her face round, pressing his nails into her cheeks. 'I have been very patient, but people are talking, they are talking about a kept man, a gigolo and they are laughing at me, Suzanna! I don't like to be laughed at!' He let go of her face and she dropped her head, forcing back the tears. 'Do you understand me?'

Swallowing down the urge to scream at the pain in

her hand she managed to nod. Then Mitchell suddenly released her fingers and a sharp pain shot up her wrist as the blood flowed back.

'I will not tolerate the situation any more,' Mitchell said calmly, smoothing his suit jacket as if nothing had happened. 'And don't try to lie to me, Suzy; I know exactly what you are doing.' He reached forward and pressed the buzzer. 'Always.' Seconds later the door was opened by his driver and he climbed out while Suzanna waited for her own door. Wearily, she stepped on to the pavement, shivered in the cool early-morning air and took Mitchell's arm, escorting him to the check-in desk. She waited, smiled at the young blond man behind the counter and wondered vaguely whether he was Mitchell's type. Then Mitchell turned to her, kissed her cheek and taking his briefcase from the driver, he turned heel without another word and strode towards passport control.

'Goodbye, Mitchell,' she murmured under her breath and, thoroughly miserable, walked slowly back to the car.

Later that morning, Suzanna Harvey walked out of Biba, laden with carrier bags. She had spent Mitchell's money; all of it. It was the only thing about her husband that gave her any pleasure – the money. It was the only reason she had married him. She held the door open for the young man behind her and he followed her out on to the pavement, carrying another four huge black and gold bags and watching the slim curved shape of her bottom in front, clearly visible in her tight, bright red miniskirt. The taxi that had transported her here was still waiting, the meter ticking away and the driver jumped out at the sight of her, opening the back door and letting his eyes travel over the expanse of thigh she showed as she climbed into the cab. Crossing her legs, she bent and smoothed the soft black suede on her knee-length boots and then looked up at the driver who hadn't taken his eyes off her legs.

'The bags?'

'Oh, yes, sorry . . .' He coughed, embarrassed and turned to the young man, taking the bags and placing them neatly alongside the front seat in the cab. Suzanna leant out of the window, handed the young sales assistant a ten-shilling note and glanced nervously behind her. Satisfied that there was no one following her, she relaxed back and opened a copy of *Harpers and Queen*.

'Where to, Mrs Harvey?' The driver strained to look at her over his shoulder; it was a while since he'd seen a pair of pins like that.

She glanced up. 'Home of course,' she answered archly. Despite the shopping, her mood hadn't lightened.

'Of course,' he muttered under his breath as he indicated and pulled out into the traffic. 'I'm a bleedin' mind reader, ain't I?'

Major Phillip Mills let himself into the flat in Grosvenor Square, dropped the keys of Suzy's Mercedes in an ashtray on the hall table and put his suitcase down by the front door, calling out to Suzy. He smoothed his hair back off his temples and checked his appearance in the mirror. The tan suited him, his clean-cut angular face was more pronounced by the deep brown and his hair had lightened to almost blond. He smiled, pleased with himself and called out again.

'Suzy? Darling?' He could hardly wait to see her.

He strode through to the huge sitting-room, then the bedroom and realised she was out. Disappointed, he dropped on to the sofa, put his feet up and reached for the top copy off a pile of *Vogue*s. He lit himself a cigarette. This was Suzanna Harvey's *pied-à-terre*, a base she used when she came up to London and didn't want the bother of opening up the Regent's Park house. It was a present from her husband, a sweetener they called it privately, and Phillip Mills had helped her decorate it, had bought the furniture with her, chosen the bed. Naturally, he treated it as he would his own home.

Settling back and placing a cushion behind his head, he opened the magazine, drew on the cigarette and took the ashtray from the side table, balancing it on the arm of the sofa. He glanced at the glossy ads, flicked through the features, then ground out the fag, closed his eyes and promptly fell asleep. It was eleven o'clock in the morning and he had just flown in from Delhi.

'Phillip! Darling!' Suzanna stood poised in the doorway, one small Biba carrier bag in her hand and a stocky, red-faced taxi driver behind her, laden with the other seven. 'I wasn't expecting you until this afternoon!' She glanced behind her at the driver. 'You can go,' she said curtly. 'Leave the bags there.'

Digging in her purse, she followed the cab driver out into the hallway and pulled out a tenner. She handed it across. 'Thank you,' she said and Phillip kicked off his shoes, hearing the slam of the front door. He sat forward and peered out into the hall.

'Suzy?' The only reply he got was the soft rustle of

what he thought were her clothes, then the sharp click of her boots on the parquet floor. He waited.

'Have you missed me?' she asked from the doorway.

He turned to look at her. She stood in her black panties and boots, the bare skin on her round, firm breasts the same nut brown as her long, smooth thighs. She flicked a strand of chestnut-coloured hair back off her shoulder and smiled.

'My God . . . Have I . . . ?' He held out his arms. 'Come here . . .'

Moving across to him, she stood in front of him while he kissed her chest, trailing his mouth down across her breast to the erect tip of her nipple. She was so filled with longing that it took her breath away. She needed him, it was like a drug, the sex between them.

'Well show me, then,' she murmured, taking his hand from her hip and pressing it gently against the lace-covered mound between her thighs. Then she knelt, one knee either side of him on the sofa and unbuckled his belt. 'Show me how much . . .'

Some time later, wandering naked from the bedroom to the kitchen to make some tea, Phillip heard the phone ring and went to answer it.

'No!' Suzy had jumped out of bed and was at the door of the sitting-room. His hand froze above the receiver. 'I'll get it, darling,' she said casually in an attempt to cover her tension. 'Oh, and put something on, will you?' she smiled. 'You never know who can see into this flat.'

Phillip narrowed his eyes and looked at her as she answered the call but she ignored him. He walked towards the kitchen.

'Oh, hello, Poppy! Yes, yes fine, darling!' She perched on the edge of the table and looked down, pretending to inspect her nails. Phillip watched her for a few moments, then went on into the kitchen to make tea. He kept one ear tuned into the conversation. 'No, no I didn't know,' Suzy went on. 'Oh, really? Well, if he does I'll let you know. Of course, but things change, Poppy, you never know what . . .' Suzy broke off as Phillip came back into the sitting-room and placed a tray on the sofa table. 'All right, I'll let you know. Yes, yes thanks, Poppy. See you!' She hung up.

Still naked, Phillip poured the tea. 'What things change?' he asked, handing her a cup. 'And who's the mysterious "he"?' Sitting, Phillip saw Suzy blush but she quickly turned away to hide it and fiddled, tying the belt of her silk wrap.

'"He" is no one important,' she answered. 'And lots of things change.' She smiled nervously and disappeared into the bedroom. A few moments later she stood in the doorway and chucked a towel at him. He caught it and held it up.

'What's this for?'

'Don't be churlish, Phillip,' she answered, 'put it on and make yourself decent.'

He reached for his cigarettes, still ignoring the request and lit two, handing one across to her. 'Why?' he asked, leaning back. 'You've never complained before.' He glanced down, then up at her, making his point. 'And why not answer the telephone? It's never bothered you in the past.'

Suzy shrugged, avoiding his eye, and, bending forward, she flicked her ash. Phillip caught her arm and held her wrist. He felt a moment of panic. 'What is it, Suzanna? You're not tired of me?'

She jerked her arm free. 'No! Of course I'm not tired of you! For God's sake, Phillip, you should know that at least!' She looked away. They had been together for over three years and Phillip Mills was her life. 'It's not you, it's . . .' she broke off and stood up, crossing to the window. She didn't want this confrontation now, not on his first day home. 'It's nothing,' she said. She turned her back on him and looked out of the window at the street six floors below. She felt suddenly very desperate.

Phillip waited. He stared at her back, at the tense line of her body as she hugged her arms around her and hunched her shoulders. He could feel an intense fear rising in his chest.

'Have you met someone else?'

Suzy spun round. 'Oh God, no!' She laughed; the question was so ridiculous. It was a sharp painful sound and it seemed to break her. Suddenly she put her hands up to her face. 'Oh God!' She started to cry.

'Christ, Suzy! What is it?' Phillip sprung forward and pulled her close to him. He had never seen her cry before, in three years, he had never seen a tear. 'Suzy?' He kissed her hair as she pressed her head against his chest. 'Suzy, please, it can't be that bad.' He tilted her face up. 'Hey! Come on.' He kissed the corner of her mouth as she wiped her tears on the back of her hand, sniffing loudly. 'Come on.' He led her over to the sofa and sat, pulling her down beside him and reaching for the towel to cover himself. He was suddenly embarrassed by his nakedness.

'You OK now?'

She nodded, fumbling in her pocket for a handkerchief.

'Are you going to tell me what's the matter?' Suzy looked away. 'What is all this stupid "don't answer the phone, don't walk around without any clothes on" about?' He stared at her profile, a perfect face framed with soft dark hair and he loved her so completely that it frightened him. 'Am I the "he"?'

She started. 'And you don't know I'm in England, you haven't seen me?' His voice took on an angry edge. 'You don't even want Poppy to know, your best friend?'

She kept her face turned away from him and gripped the handkerchief, twisting and wringing the silk around her fingers.

'Why, Suzy?' Phillip asked it almost lazily, as if he couldn't care less but the blood was pounding in his ears. 'Why all this drama?'

'Because . . .' She broke off helplessly and reached forward for her cigarettes.

He caught her wrist. 'Because what? What, Suzy?'

'Because of bloody Mitchell!' she cried, wrenching her arm free and jumping up. 'Bloody, bloody Mitchell!' A sob caught in the back of her throat. 'Mitchell is watching me, his spies, they're everywhere, they know all about me, about you!' Her voice was high and tight, the pain strangling her. 'He wants a knighthood, he wants you out, gone! Out of my life! He made threats, he hurt me! He said . . .' She was shouting, her face crumpled with grief. 'He said people are saying you're a gigolo, a kept man, he said people are laughing at him, that I'm causing a scandal!' She covered her face with her hands and began to weep.

All Phillip could do was sit motionless and stare at her. He was so shocked he didn't know what to say, how to comfort her. Mitchell Harvey had never been part of the equation, he had been a blank face in the background, a ruthless homosexual who had married Suzanna as a cover for his sexuality. He didn't care what they did so long as they were discreet within their own circles. He didn't care about anything, least of all Suzanna.

Phillip looked helplessly down at his hands. 'Suzy, please,' he said quietly. 'Please don't cry like this.'

'Like what?' she suddenly screamed. 'Like I'm going to lose the only thing that I've ever wanted, ever loved! Don't you care? Don't you . . .' She lashed out at him but he caught her arm.

'For God's sake, Suzy!' He yanked her towards him and held her, pinned her body tight to his own, his arms locked across her back. 'For God's sake, stop it,' he cried hoarsely, as she struggled against him. 'Jesus, Suzy . . .'

But her violence stopped as abruptly as it had started and she slumped against him, her face buried in his chest. Phillip stroked her hair, wrapping his fingers in it. He looked above her head at the picture on the wall, a picture they had bought together in Bond Street, a Chagall, and he remembered handing the money over in cash, Mitchell's cash, he remembered the thrill of it, the sexual excitement that the power of money could bring. He remembered fucking Suzy all night, the picture propped up against the wall in the bedroom and her face turned towards it every time she climaxed. Gently he tugged on her hair and tilted her head back.

'You OK?'

She nodded and tried to hide her face again.

'It's all right,' he said, 'I love you, remember? You won't put me off with baggy eyes and a red nose.' He did love her, it was the truth. He loved everything about her, her beauty, the lifestyle they shared, her money.

Suzy smiled, a sad, half-smile then she moved away from him, across the room and picked up the packet of cigarettes, lighting two, as was their habit. She held Phillip's out to him and he came over.

'Thanks.'

'I have to go to Spain,' she said flatly. 'At the end of the week. Mitchell is entertaining at the villa.' She smoked as she spoke, almost continually, holding the cigarette close to her face. When she finished one, she immediately lit up another. 'And he wants to do the season, all of it, poncing around with him, dressed up, lying to people, pretending!' She stood up and walked away. 'I won't be able to see you, he'll make sure of that. I won't . . .' She broke off, unable to go on. Swallowing hard, she managed to calm herself. 'He means it,' she said quietly, coldly. 'He wants the House of Lords, he has some deal, some bloody deal to finance and he needs respectability, he needs me! Ha! What a fucking joke! Mitchell, the East End thug in the House of Lords! Lord Harvey, duffing up his wife!' The bitterness in her voice shocked Phillip. She hardly ever talked about Mitchell, he knew very little about the other side of her life. 'I've missed you so much,' she said, looking away. Her voice had changed again, it was small, like a child's. 'All the time you've been in India I've thought about you, about this.' She glanced around the flat, their flat. 'Being together.' She dropped her head and put her hands up to her face. 'I don't think I can live without you any more,' she whispered, 'I really don't.'

'You won't have to live without me,' Phillip answered. He reached out to her and took her hands. 'Suzy? Look at me, Suzy.' She lifted her head. 'Listen, I promise you that we'll find a way out of this.'

She shook her head helplessly.

'Yes! I promise!' Pulling her towards him, he held her hands up and kissed her palms, her wrists. 'I don't know how, I can't pretend that I do, but there will be a way.' He eased her in closer so that she stood before him and dropped her hands, slipping his fingers inside the silk, touching her warm flesh. 'Have I ever let you down?'

'No.'

He edged the robe down, exposing her bare shoulder and her breast. He put his mouth to her nipple and ran his tongue over the tip, making her shiver. 'I would do anything for you, Suzanna,' he murmured. 'Anything.' He parted the rest of the silk and looked at her body, a body he cherished. 'I won't let you go,' he said, and, closing her eyes, Suzanna almost believed it was true.

Chapter Seven

Phillip jumped off the bus at the corner of the Ritz and Green Park, ignored the shouts from the conductor and dug his hands in his pockets. He was in a black mood. Suzy was off to Malaga in the morning, he'd had to find himself somewhere to stay at bloody short notice and he no longer had the car. Being without the Mercedes really got to him. Striding off in the direction of St James's Palace, he took a left turn and walked along St James's Street, glancing miserably in the window of Lock & Co. at a panama he could not afford and hurrying past Berry Bros and Rudd. Without Suzy to finance his living expenses, wine on account and expensive head gear were out of the question. He carried on down the street, keeping his eyes ahead and turned the corner into Marlborough Road.

'Good evening, sir.'

He took his hands out of his pockets and nodded at the policeman on duty. 'Major Phillip Mills,' he said.

'Mills . . . Mills . . .' The policeman ran his finger along the list he had on his clipboard. 'Ah, here it is.' He looked up and smiled. 'Thank you, major. Go on through.'

Phillip walked past the barrier towards the palace and took the third door on the right. He was meeting Bertram in the mess to collect the key to his flat and finalise a few details. He hoped to God the man didn't have any cats to feed.

'Evening, sir.'

'Hello, corporal.' Phillip handed his raincoat over. 'I'll have a gin and tonic.' The corporal nodded. 'Is Captain Bertram in the mess yet, d'you know?'

'No, sir, he's been called away, he left a message for you, sir.'

'Called away?' Phillip held down his irritation. If Bertram had skipped off without making arrangements for him he would be well and truly beggared.

'It's Major Mills, isn't it?'

'Yes!' Phillip snapped. He was in no mood to be civil.

'Erm, Major Latham is in the mess, sir, he's expecting you.'

'Who the devil is Major Latham?' Phillip sighed irritably and straightened his jacket. He turned and walked into the mess, wondering what the hell he was going to do; the last thing he wanted was to go home to his mother in Weybridge.

'Phillip?'

Phillip looked across the room. 'My God! Teddy Latham!' His face broke into a broad grin as he hurried across to his old chum. 'Of course, Major Latham! What the hell are you doing here?' The two men shook hands warmly.

'I haven't seen you for bloody years, you old dog!' Phillip beamed. 'The last time was . . . ?'

'Old boys cricket,' Teddy filled in for him. 'Fifteen years ago this summer! You got drunk as a skunk on Sussex ale and passed out on Smythe's parents' Chinese rug just before dinner!'

Phillip burst out laughing. 'And everyone apparently just stepped over me to get to the dining-room!'

'Sir?'

Phillip turned and took his gin and tonic from the tray. 'Can I get you a drink, Teddy?'

'No, no thanks, Pip, I'll have to make tracks in a few minutes.'

'Oh, go on! It's not every day that you meet up with an old school chum.' Phillip took a large gulp of his gin. 'To tell the truth I could do with some cheering up.'

'All right then!' Teddy laughed, in exactly the same way that Phillip remembered from school, a loud noisy chuckle coming from the back of his throat. 'I'll have a pint of ale please, corporal.'

'Yes, sir.'

They walked across to the seating and Teddy stood by the fireplace while Phillip made himself comfortable in an old leather armchair. He took out his cigarettes and offered one to Teddy.

'So what are you doing here?' he asked, lighting up.

'Ceremonial duties, a sixth-month stint by the Welsh Dragoon Guards.'

'Good Lord! I'd completely forgotten you'd gone into the Welsh Guards. Couldn't for the life of me think who Major Latham was when the corporal mentioned you.' Teddy laughed again just as his drink arrived. Phillip motioned for the corporal to bring him an ashtray. 'So where're you living during this stint?'

'Clare's family have a flat in Kensington. We're . . .' Teddy broke off and grinned at Phillip's face. 'I've been married for almost a year now, Pip! Didn't you know?'

'No! Congratulations!' Of course he didn't know, since meeting Suzy, Phillip had lost touch with nearly all the old set, he hardly bothered to keep up his Christmas cards. Covering his dismay he said, 'Who's the lucky girl, then?'

'Clare Bennet, now Mrs Clare Latham. She's the younger daughter of Brigadier Sir John Bennet?'

'Well, well, well.' Phillip smiled. 'I'm pleased for you, Teddy! Not a bad career move!'

Teddy grinned. 'She's a fabulous girl, Pip! Twenty-one, gorgeous looking and all mine! You'd love her!' He swallowed down the last of his beer. 'Hey, listen! I've just had an idea. Clare's got her sister coming up from Sussex tonight, for the weekend. Why don't we make up a four and go out for a meal?' He stopped, suddenly remembering an old piece of gossip about Phillip and some married woman. 'Erm, if you don't have any other plans that is?'

Phillip aimed his cigarette at the fireplace and lobbed the butt perfectly into the grate. 'I don't know, Teddy, I've got quite a lot to organise, I'm moving into Bertram's flat while he's away and I've got to get hold of the keys . . .'

'God! Bertram!' Teddy suddenly fumbled in his pocket and pulled out a set of keys. '*Voilà*! He asked me to give these to you and said he's sorry but he had to leave early to fix something to do with his boat. It apparently came adrift from its mooring.' Teddy chucked the keys and Phillip caught them in one hand. 'Why anyone would want to sail round the British Isles for his holiday, I don't know. I'd be off in the Med or somewhere else hot and sunny, if it was me.'

Phillip looked at the bunch, then up at Teddy. 'Any other message? No cats to feed?'

Teddy grinned. 'Don't think so.'

Phillip made a snap decision. 'OK then, you're on for tonight!' The thought of a Friday night alone in Bertram's flat was a miserable one. 'A couple of drinks at the Ritz, then dinner at a small Italian place I know! How's that?'

'Sounds good to me! Clare'll be delighted.'

Phillip drained his glass and left it on the floor. He glanced at his watch. 'D'you want to have a few more here or . . . ?'

'No, let's get going.' Teddy patted the pocket of his blazer to check his keys were there and Phillip stood, smoothed the crease in his trousers and looked across at his old school friend.

'Ready?'

'Yup, sure! D'you have a car here?' Teddy asked.

Phillip turned away abruptly. He was so used to driving the Mercedes, impressing people with it, that he felt bereft without it. 'No,' he said over his shoulder, keeping his face averted. God, he'd have loved the car now, Teddy would have been wowed by it.

'Right, we'll go in mine then.' Teddy rang for the corporal and asked for Phillip's raincoat. It arrived seconds later and he led the way down the stairs, stopping in the hallway to make a telephone call to Clare at her office. Phillip waited for him outside in the cold.

'I'm parked round the back,' Teddy said as he came out. 'Shall I bring the car round?'

'Yes, all right.' Phillip watched Teddy go, watched his jaunty stride and heard him whistle as he went. For a moment he envied Teddy. What have I got, he thought, his mind drifting back to the awful scene with Suzanna, what exactly? But Teddy came round the corner just then, peeped the horn of his Austin and Phillip put all of that from his mind. He climbed into the passenger seat, the policeman lifted the barrier and together they set off for Kensington.

Clare Latham yanked the navy wool dress she had been wearing for work over her head as soon as she slammed the front door of the flat shut behind her and kicked off her shoes. She ran barefoot into the bedroom, threw the dress on the bed and turned on the transistor radio, singing along loudly to the Beatles, 'Love love me do!' Pulling out a black miniskirt and red tunic top, she dived into a drawer for a matching scarf and finally untangled her boots from a heap of shoes. She carried the clothes into the bathroom, ran the bath, splashing a liberal amount of perfume into the water and began removing her make-up. Jane was arriving at six-thirty, Teddy and Phillip Mills were on their way home right now and tonight was an opportunity that Clare was definitely going to make the most of.

Jane climbed out of the taxi, reached into her bag for her purse and mentally calculated the right tip, exactly. She handed over the money, smiled politely and picked up her bags. Glancing up at the building, she saw that the lights were on in the flat and was relieved that Clare was home. She was early, it was just after six and she was dying for a cup of tea.

Climbing the front steps, she rang on the buzzer and waited for the door release. Inside the entrance hall, she called the lift, taking off her jacket as she watched the floor numbers light up and tutting because someone had obviously just gone up. She unfastened the top two buttons on her blouse, took off her shoes and moaned when she saw the swelling on her ankles. The weather had turned suddenly warm for spring and she couldn't wait to peel off her woollen stockings and soak her feet in cold water.

The lift finally arrived, she travelled up to the fifth floor and rang the front door bell, leaning against the wall, unclipping her suspenders and rolling down the stocking on her right leg with great relief. She looked up as the door was opened and said, 'I don't know why, Clare, but that suspender belt I bought when I was up last time really digs into my legs!' She lifted her skirt and rubbed a red mark at the top of her thigh. 'Ouch, see what I mean?'

'Gosh, yes. That looks quite nasty.'

Jane started and looked up aghast. She dropped her skirt, pressed herself back against the wall and flushed.

'Who's that? Phillip?'

Clare's face suddenly appeared over Phillip's shoulder. 'Jane! Oh no! Oh . . .' Clare darted round Phillip in the doorway and leapt in front of her sister. 'Jane! How lovely to see you!' She glanced behind her. 'Go on in, Phillip,

Teddy'll get you a drink.' She laughed nervously, her voice high with excitement. 'We'll be in right away!' She covered Jane from view and shooed him away with her hand. In a loud whisper, she hissed, 'My God, Jane! What on earth . . .' She gripped Jane's elbow and ushered her inside, her bags, shoes and jacket left in a heap in the hall, one stocking baggy and wrinkled around her ankle. She propelled her older sister along the corridor to the bedroom and flung the door open, pushing her inside.

'Phew! That was close!' Clare locked her bedroom door and leant against it, her make-up shiny with sweat. 'D'you think he was shocked?'

Jane turned and stared at her. 'Shocked?'

'Yes! Phillip! D'you think it put him off?' Clare started to pace the floor, her fingers pinched across the bridge of her nose. 'If we hurry and find you something to wear and do your make—'

'Clare!' Jane held her hands up. 'Stop! Stop right there!' She sank down on to the bed and removed both stockings then she rubbed her ankles, shuffled back on the bed so that her feet were up and said, 'Firstly, who is Phillip and secondly, we are not finding me anything to wear or doing my make-up! Understood?' Clare nodded sheepishly. 'And thirdly, what is going on?'

Clare sat down opposite her sister on a wicker bath chair and leant forward. 'Phillip is Major Phillip Mills,' she said urgently, 'equerry to the Duke of Cumberland. He's thirty-five, in the Scots Guards, went to the same school as Teddy and he's single!' She said the last word with triumph and Jane shuddered. 'Oh, Jane,' she exclaimed, 'he's perfect for you! I can hardly believe it!

We're supposed to be going out to dinner, the four of us, tonight! We're having a few drinks at the—'

'Clare . . .' Jane shook her head.

'It's just that he told Teddy he needed cheering up and he's at a loose end while he's on leave, he works in India at the moment, some sort of job for the maharajah and he said . . .'

'Clare—'

'He's jolly good-looking, don't you think, Jane? And much nearer your age than any of the other people we've introduced you to—'

'Clare! That's enough!' Jane stood up. She knew that Clare had the best intentions but she really didn't think this was a good idea. She was tired, she had the beginnings of a headache and she'd been on enough of Clare's blind dates to last her a lifetime. 'Look,' she said, as kindly as she could, 'why don't you go out with this Phillip chap and leave me behind. I'm sure you'd be able to rustle up one of your glamorous girlfriends to make up a four.' Jane smiled, one of her no-nonsense, older sister smiles, and straightened her skirt. 'How about Abby?' she suggested but looking across at her sister, she saw Clare's face drop. 'Perhaps not Abby,' she said lamely.

Clare stood and walked across to the door. 'I'd better tell them you're not coming,' she said miserably.

Jane caught the hint of a tear in her voice and heard a faint sniff. She hated herself.

'Oh all right,' she said a few moments later, just as Clare pulled the door open. 'If it means that much to you I'll come!'

Clare spun round. 'Really? You will?'

'Yes.' Jane smiled despite her irritation and longed for

a stronger will power. 'Give me a few minutes to smarten myself up,' she said. 'But I'm warning you, I'm not putting on anything fancy!'

'No, no of course not!' Clare beamed, thoroughly pleased with herself. She was convinced this was it, she had at last found the right man for Jane. In her book, twenty-six and unmarried was practically a sin. 'See you in a few minutes then?'

'Yes, a few minutes.' Clare shut the door behind her and Jane sighed heavily. 'Not that I've got anything fancy,' she muttered, looking in the mirror and smoothing her hair. 'And even if I did,' she said aloud to her reflection, 'it wouldn't make the slightest bit of difference.'

The cocktail bar at the Ritz was full and as Phillip sat across the table from Jane in silence the noise and hub of conversation around them served only to make him feel more miserable. It was a mistake, this evening, he was in a bad mood, depressed even, and he should never have agreed to come out.

He looked across the room at Teddy and Clare who had by chance met up with a friend of Teddy's and who stood at the bar talking animatedly and laughing, Clare furtively glancing over every now and then to check how her sister was getting on. She was a good-looking girl, he thought, watching as she slipped on to a bar stool and showed an expanse of long slim thigh, and she was giving it her best shot, leaving them alone to chat, giving them plenty of time to get to know each other. He turned his attention back to Jane and attempted a smile. It was a shame, he was really too down to enjoy himself.

'Would you like to smoke?' he said, to make conversation.

'Yes, please.' Phillip held out his cigarette case and Jane took one. She waited for him to offer her a light, then said, 'It's pretty ghastly this, isn't it?'

'What?' Phillip sat back.

'This evening. Clare glancing over every five seconds to see if we're having a good time, leaving us alone expectantly.' She smiled, genuinely amused at Phillip's shock. 'Oh it's all right,' she said, 'I'm quite used to it! Clare and her matchmaking, she's always miles out!'

He smiled back. 'You don't mind?'

'Not really. Every time she does it I say never again, but then,' Jane shrugged, 'I try not to take it too seriously.'

'You're very tolerant.'

'Yes, yes I think I must be.' They both smiled. 'Look,' she said, leaning forward and noticing Clare out of the corner of her eye, craning her neck to see what they were doing. 'I don't think I can stand much more of this agony. I have to be up early in the morning to do some painting and I could really do with an early night. Would you be agreeable to me having a headache and you offering to take me home?' She smiled. 'That way Clare isn't disappointed.'

The relief on Phillip's face was obvious. Jane bent and picked her bag up off the floor. 'Good,' she said, 'that's decided then.'

Phillip finished his drink. 'Thanks, Jane, I appreciate . . .'

She shrugged and cut him short. 'Shall we go? We can nip over and tell them on the way out.'

'Right.' He stood, offered her his arm and she took it. Jane, pressing her hand to her brow and Phillip looking concerned made their way over to tell Clare and Teddy that they were leaving.

Outside the hotel Phillip stood with Jane while the doorman hailed a cab. He glanced at her neat navy suit, low-heeled shoes and matching bag and thought briefly how nice she looked; sensible and smart. The cab arrived and the doorman helped her inside.

'I hope you feel better,' Phillip said.

Jane smiled. 'Thanks. Nice to meet you, Phillip.'

'And you.' He slammed the door shut and waved at Jane through the window. 'Thank you!' he called as the cab pulled off, but Jane didn't hear him. She had already turned away and was looking straight ahead. The likes of Major Phillip Mills, good-looking, charming and sophisticated, were not for her. She had known that for years – never had been and never would be. 'Plain Jane,' she murmured, without bitterness or regret and she settled back to enjoy the ride home.

Chapter Eight

Phillip reached over and switched on the bedside lamp. The light outside was just breaking.

'Are you awake?' He sat up.

'No.' Suzanna rolled onto her side and put her arm up over her eyes. 'Not yet.'

Phillip smiled. 'It's six-thirty,' he said. 'This is your early-morning alarm call.' He bent and kissed the side of her face as she moved her arm and opened her eyes. 'Oh God, is it really?'

'Yes.' Phillip dropped his legs over the side of the bed and stood, reaching for his cigarettes. 'I'll put the kettle on,' he said, moving towards the kitchen. Suzanna sat up and, rubbing her eyes, she watched him walk naked from the bedroom. She knew she had to get up, make tracks but she couldn't face it. She shouldn't even have been at the flat, it was dangerous, too risky. She felt tense and miserable.

'I shouldn't have come,' she said as Phillip came back into the bedroom and took his trousers from the chair. 'I should have stayed at the house, Mitchell will find out, I know he will. It was a mistake!'

Phillip pulled the flannels up over his hips and fastened the fly. He walked across to the bed. 'Suzanna, stop it! You're being paranoid, it wasn't a mistake.' He leant towards her and kissed the hollow of her neck. 'I needed you last night, I couldn't have stayed in Bertram's flat on my own, I needed to say goodbye to you properly.'

He moved his mouth down to her breast and she caught her breath. 'Phillip, don't,' she murmured. 'Please, I have to get dressed, I have to go.'

He pulled back. 'OK.' Turning away abruptly, he finished dressing, pulling his half-buttoned shirt over his head and rolling up his tie, stuffing it in the pocket of his jacket. 'What time is the driver coming to the house?' He fiddled with his cufflinks, not looking at her. He didn't really want to know, he didn't want to know anything about the other side of her life but he felt he had to ask. He was making conversation, small talk to ease the misery they both felt.

Suzy climbed out of bed, reaching for her wrap. 'Seven-thirty,' she answered. 'But Margaret's coming to the house at seven. She has some papers she wants me to take out for Mitchell.'

'I see.' Phillip picked up his loose change from the dressing-table and caught sight of Suzy's reflection in the mirror as he did so. He swung round and caught her up in his arms. 'God, Suzanna!' He held her close, breathing in the smell of her, the smell of their sex, her perfume, all of it making him dizzy with longing. 'I love you, Suzy,' he whispered, 'I can't bear the thought of being without you.' She clung to him. Her fingers gripped the flesh on his shoulders and her body, pressed tight against him, seemed at once so frail and so strong, his inspiration. He didn't know how he would ever live without her.

'What are we going to do?' she murmured.

He pulled back and looked at her face. 'I don't know,' he said, 'but I'll think of something, I promise you . . .' She nodded and dropped away from him. She didn't believe him, he knew that. Walking to the bed, she straightened the covers, not properly, just wasting time, fiddling.

'I'd better go.' Phillip moved towards the door. He had his jacket over his shoulder. Suzy looked at him. 'You don't have to.'

'Yes, I do. I don't want to be here when you've gone, I want to remember the flat with you in it.' He saw Suzy's face collapse and closed his eyes for a moment. When he opened them she had composed herself and, ashen-faced, she stared at him. 'Will you ring me when you get back? Let me know you're all right?' She nodded. 'I've left the number of Bertram's flat on the pad.' He turned.

'Phillip?'

'Yes?'

She didn't know what to say, she just wanted to look at him, to keep the image of his face in her mind, to seal it in her memory.

'Take care.'

He smiled. 'You too.' And without another word, he walked away from her and out of the flat. She heard the front door slam then nothing, and slumping down on the bed, she gave in to her grief.

Stepping out into the cold early morning air, Phillip

turned up the collar of his jacket and wondered what the hell he was going to do. It was too early to embark on anything constructive and too late to go back to bed. He was miserable and the thought of his loneliness, of being without Suzy, filled him with desolation. He decided to walk. Heading in the direction of Park Lane, he made his way towards Hyde Park Corner and an early morning trek through the park, the heels of his shoes clicking smartly on the pavement as he went.

Jane left the flat in Queen's Gate just after seven. She carried her painting stool, a small collapsible easel and her water-colour case along with a huge handbag slung over her shoulder that contained a thermos of coffee and some sandwiches that she'd made the night before: egg and bacon, her favourite. Heading up to the Serpentine, she had already decided on the view she would tackle first and was looking forward to it. She walked quickly, the cool mist of the morning chilling her and making her wish that she'd worn her scarf as well as her hat. She swung her arms and stamped her feet as she walked to keep warm as well as humming 'Don't put your daughter on the stage, Mrs Worthington', loudly and badly out of tune.

Phillip sat down on a bench and looked at the ducks on the water. He pulled his jacket in tight around him, suddenly cold, and rested his head in his hands, closing his eyes. He felt thoroughly wretched. As he listened to the empty silence all around him, punctuated only by the odd quack and splash of the birds, he thought of Suzy, of the warmth of her body next to him in bed, and realised that he had never felt so dismal or alone.

He slumped forward and hung his head and it was like this that Jane first spotted him.

Walking past the Albert Memorial and cutting briskly across the park to the Serpentine, Jane headed straight for the view she had decided on and the bench she wanted to use. She came through a clump of trees, her feet wet from the dew on the grass and stopped at the edge of the water. Her bench was taken. Digging in her bag for her glasses, she hurriedly put them on and peered across the twenty-yard gap at the obstruction. She couldn't see his face properly but from the slump of his figure he looked pretty miserable. She tutted irritably and scanned the lake for another view, one eye on the bench to see if the man had any intention of moving. At this point Phillip looked up.

For a few moments both Jane and Phillip just stared, each trying to place the other, then Jane realised who it was and smiled. 'Hello, erm . . . Jane Bennet!' she called. 'We met last night?' She pulled off her hat and shook her head so that her hair fell into place.

'Yes, I remember.' Phillip straightened as she came up to the bench. 'How's the headache?'

'It miraculously disappeared in the cab on the way home. Isn't that extraordinary?'

He smiled. 'Yes, quite extraordinary.' Sitting back, he rubbed his hands wearily over his face, then looked at Jane. 'So, what are you doing, Jane Bennet, in Hyde Park at seven in the morning?' He glanced down at the pile of stuff she had been carrying.

'Painting,' she answered. 'Water-colour, for the West Sommerton Water-colour Society, study of land and sky.'

'How interesting.'

'Not really.' Jane shrugged. 'Pretty dull in fact. I lecture, one night a week to a group with an average age of seventy and if anyone is awake at the end of the evening it's been a good night!'

Phillip smiled again and stood. 'Well, I think I'll leave you to it, then,' he said. He dug his hands in his pockets and glanced across the park.

Jane watched his face, pale under the suntan, miserable despite the smile and said, 'Would you like a cup of coffee? I've brought a thermos.'

He glanced back at her.

'You look as if you could do with one.'

She was frowning, a crease between her eyes that made her look fiercely concerned and Phillip liked that; he warmed to it. 'Yes,' he replied, 'I could do with one, thanks.' He sat down again on the bench and Jane dug in her bag, pulling out a huge black flask and a packet of sandwiches. 'Here,' she said, handing the tin foil packet to him. 'Bacon and egg. If they don't cheer you up then nothing will.'

He took the packet, not at all hungry and opened it, peering in at the sandwiches. 'D'you want one?'

'No, not yet, I'll save mine for later. Go on though, tuck in!' Jane poured the coffee and handed that across as well.

Phillip took a bite of bacon and egg. 'Hmmmmm.'

'They do that,' Jane commented as Phillip moved on to a second sandwich. 'You think you're not hungry and then, wham, one bite and you've got to finish the pack.'

He looked at her, his mouth full, and then down at the packet. 'Are you always right?' he mumbled, still eating.

'God no! But when I'm wrong I don't tell anyone.' She sat back on her heels and looked at him. Then suddenly she said, 'Is it anything you want to talk about?'

Phillip stopped eating. 'No,' he answered abruptly and looked down at his lap. He hardly knew her, who the devil did she think she was?

When he glanced up again Jane was still watching him. 'It's just that you look so miserable . . .' she shrugged as she got to her feet. 'And sometimes it helps to talk.' She bent and picked up the top of her thermos. 'Finished?'

'Yes.' Phillip started to rewrap the left-over sandwiches, then suddenly changed his mind and looked up at her. 'I mean no. Is there enough for another cup?'

He smiled as Jane's face relaxed. 'I think so,' she answered. He moved on the bench to make room for her and she sat down next to him, pouring a second cup of coffee into the little plastic top of the thermos.

'Jane?' She stopped what she was doing and turned her face towards him. 'What would you do if you thought you might lose the only thing that really mattered to you?' He averted his eyes as he asked her, not wanting her to see the pain there.

Jane was silent for a while. 'I don't know,' she answered honestly, then a few moments later said, 'I think, if it really meant that much to me that I'd probably do anything to keep it.'

Phillip looked at her. 'Anything?'

'Yes, I believe I would do anything.' She smiled, a rather sad smile Phillip thought. 'Although I've never been in that position,' she said quietly, 'I mean, having something or someone that mattered more than anything else.'

Phillip reached over and took her hand. It was an

extraordinarily candid statement and he respected her courage. 'Thank you, Jane,' he said.

'Good Lord!' She laughed, a short embarrassed snort. 'What on earth for?' And easing her hand away, she stood, picked up her bag and plonked it down on the bench between them. 'I'd better get started,' she said, pulling out her paints, 'before this place is flooded with American tourists!'

Phillip stood as well and, chucking the dregs of the coffee away, he screwed the cap back on the thermos and handed Jane what was left of her sandwiches. He dug his hands in his pockets.

'We should get together sometime for a drink or something,' he said, more out of courtesy than anything else and Jane nodded, knowing as much. 'Thanks for the coffee, Jane.'

She turned to him and smiled. 'My pleasure, Phillip.'

'And thanks for . . .' But Jane had pulled on her hat and bent to set up her stool so he didn't bother to finish his sentence. 'Goodbye, Miss Jane Bennet.'

She glanced up at him. He was probably the best-looking man she had ever seen, she thought briefly. 'Goodbye, Major Phillip Mills,' she said. And watching him stride away she sighed, both with regret and relief, and went about her water-colour.

Later that same morning, as Jane finished her first painting, Phillip let himself into Bertram's flat in Chelsea, having walked the whole way from Hyde Park. He switched on the heating, drawing the curtains in the sitting-room and opened the top window to air the place. Then he walked through to the small galley kitchen to make himself a cup of coffee. He peered hopefully in the fridge but found nothing except half a lemon and a bottle of brown ale. If he hadn't had a lunch appointment at Kensington Palace he would have been tempted to forget the coffee and open the beer.

Filling the kettle, he turned on the gas and put it on to boil while he rifled the cupboards for the coffee and sugar. He wasn't used to worrying about this sort of thing; at the flat in Grosvenor Square, Suzy's housekeeper took care of everything domestic, she even bought his own brand of toothpaste. Finally locating a tin, he scraped the bottom of it for half a teaspoon of stale instant and made himself a cup of coffee. He took it through to the bedroom, sat down on the small double bed with only one blanket and looked miserably at his luggage. He had six cases and four boxes, an enormous amount of stuff that had piled up at Suzanna's place and that needed to be sorted if he was going to make it through his leave in Bertram's tiny flat. It was a depressing thought.

First things first though, he decided, spotting his wash bag, he had to bath and change for lunch, then find his briefcase. It was his first meeting with the duke since arriving back in the UK and he was due to brief Edward and his staff on the details of the job in Baijur. He stood, left the disgusting coffee on the bedside table and looked through his things, finding his suit bag, the case with his shirts in and his ties; they were all in the luggage he had brought from India. Then he went into the bathroom to unpack his toiletries.

Twenty minutes later, lying up to his chin in hot water with the radio blaring and Jane's words fresh in his mind, Phillip began to feel better than he had done in days. Bertram's flat wasn't Grosvenor Square admittedly but it was comfortable and it would do for the time being. It was talking to Jane though that had finally made Phillip feel better; it had somehow clarified the matter. It wasn't that Jane had said anything particularly wise or revelatory, she had simply stated what he had known to be true, said the words he had been thinking, and hearing them from her made them seem all the more realistic, all the more possible. He didn't have any answers yet, he couldn't see a way out but he knew for certain now that he could find one.

Turning on the tap with his toe, Phillip let the bath fill another couple of inches with piping water, submerged himself completely, then stood up, reached for one of Bertram's grey, stiff towels and dried himself briskly. He pulled on his towelling robe, glanced out of the window up at the sky and blew a kiss to Suzy, somewhere up there on her BOAC flight to Malaga. He walked through to the bedroom to dress. It was eleven-thirty and he was due for lunch in an hour.

Phillip's taxi drew up outside Kensington Palace and he jumped out, handing the driver a pound note and telling him to keep the change. He crossed to the policeman on duty, cleared security and made his way to the duke's office, straightening his tie as he went.

'Hello, Phillip.' Sir David Pulling, the duke's attaché, was waiting for him as he arrived and the two men shook hands. 'How are you? How's Baijur?'

'Fine, thanks, David. How're you?'

'Very well, very well indeed.'

'And Laura?'

'She's fine. Up to her eyes in it with committees, schools, the children.' He laughed. 'All the chaos of family life!'

'I can imagine!' Phillip laughed too, politely.

'Phillip, we're having lunch in Edward's apartment this afternoon,' Sir David said, leading the way down the corridor and opening the doors at the end. 'It's this way.' He stood back and Phillip walked ahead of him, waiting for Sir David to close the door behind them.

'It's just us,' Sir David continued as they made their way along to the private apartments.

'I see.' Phillip tried to cover his surprise. He hadn't expected this.

'Lunch *à trois*!' Sir David laughed. 'Go on through, Phillip, Edward is waiting for us.'

'Right, fine.' Phillip cleared his throat as he stepped into the duke's apartment and fixed a smile on his face.

'Phillip!' Edward came through from the sitting-room as he heard the door open. 'Good to see you! How are you? You look well!' He crossed and shook Phillip's hand.

'Hello, sir. I am well, thank you, very well indeed.'

'Good! Nice tan!' He laughed, a deep, hearty chuckle, and Phillip relaxed slightly. 'I hope you're doing some work over there, not lying by Viki's pool and playing polo all day!'

Phillip smiled. 'I have had the odd game of polo with the maharajah, sir.'

'Ah! I told you as much, David!' He laughed again. 'Come on in, Phillip, and we'll get you a drink.' He glanced at his watch. 'In Indian circles, if I remember correctly, Phillip, at a quarter to one you'd be on your second burrapeg whisky soda by now!' He led the way into the sitting-room and motioned for Phillip to sit. 'Gin? Whisky?'

'A gin and tonic please, sir.'

'Right. David?'

'The same please.' The duke ordered the drinks and came across to the sofa opposite Phillip. The room was decorated in cream and gold brocade and, as he sat down, Phillip noticed that it had been designed to suit the duke's own colouring; he looked perfectly in place here.

'Phillip, I've asked you here today because I've a number of things I wanted to discuss with you, your progress with the maharajah's security arrangements for his wedding included of course.' Phillip nodded and the duke broke off while the drinks were served. 'But that isn't the main reason, and it isn't why I've interrupted your weekend.' He lifted his glass. 'And David's.' Taking a gulp of his drink, after the duke had done so, Phillip felt his initial tension return.

'Phillip, I thought, if you'll forgive me for being blunt, that we would get on to the main business of this luncheon straight away. I don't want to waste time on peripherals at this point.'

Phillip agreed, holding his drink tightly in his hand.

'Good.' The duke glanced briefly at Sir David and then began. 'Phillip, I was informed earlier this week of the resignation of a senior member of my staff, a very important member of my household and I am naturally very disappointed and upset.'

Phillip nodded.

'It was a surprise for everyone, I think I'm right in saying that, am I, David?'

'Yes, it was very unexpected.'

'Yes, unexpected, definitely that.' The duke finished his drink and motioned for another. 'It is my personal secretary, Phillip, Lord Balfont, who has resigned.' He swirled the ice around his second glass of whisky. 'With this terrible illness his wife has suffered he's found it impossible to divide his loyalties. His place is, quite rightly I think, by his wife's side.'

'Yes, yes absolutely.' Phillip felt his chest tighten.

'So, I am in the position of having to find a replacement, not immediately of course but within a reasonable time span and it has been suggested to me that I should consider someone younger this time, someone with a little more . . .' he smiled, 'verve! A little more life!'

Phillip didn't trust himself to speak. He gripped his glass and nodded, watching Sir David Pulling out of the corner of his eye.

'Buckingham Palace is becoming more and more concerned with public opinion, Phillip,' Sir David said, 'the public are becoming more and more interested in the royal family and we have to look after their image. Someone younger, with a wife and young family, would be ideal for Edward's household. It would help to take the pressure off.'

Both men nodded and Phillip sipped his drink. A single man would not be suitable, that much he realised, it would only add to the already speculative rumours about the duke's private life. 'Of course there are only a very limited number of people who would be at all suited to this position,' Sir David went on, 'and obviously for the right person to be already married is more than we could have hoped for.' Sir David leant forward. 'Although at some future point it would of course be necessary.'

He placed his drink on the sofa table and glanced over at the duke.

'Phillip, I have been very pleased with your work as my equerry over the past two years,' the duke said, 'very pleased with your reputation within our circles.' He smiled. 'I have discussed the matter with a number of my advisors over the past few days and, Phillip, if you are agreeable, I would like to offer you the position of personal secretary when Lord Balfont retires at the end of the year.' He watched Phillip's face and saw the open shock there. 'Of course there are a great many things that you'll want to ask and that we'll need to discuss. I expect this has come as a bit of a surprise?'

'Yes, yes it has, sir. I, erm . . .' Phillip coughed. 'I don't really know what to say.'

'Well don't say anything yet, Phillip,' Sir David interrupted, 'let's go on into lunch and discuss the matter at length. I'm sure you must have an awful lot of questions.'

Phillip placed his drink on the table and glanced down at his hands, folding them quickly in his lap to stop them trembling. Of course a senior position in the royal household was what he had always aspired to, it was his lifetime ambition. But for it to come now, at his age, the opportunity of his whole career, it left him almost speechless! He cleared his throat. 'You said Lord Balfont was leaving at the end of the year?'

'Yes, that's right. I would naturally expect you to finish the job in India, Phillip, and then of course to sort out your personal arrangements . . .' The duke broke off and glanced across at Sir David.

'A family apartment here at Kensington Palace would

be decorated for you ready for, say, January the first?' Sir David said.

Phillip nodded and took a deep breath.

'Right, well I think lunch is ready for us now.' The duke stood. 'Why don't we continue this discussion at the table?'

'Quite.' Sir David waited for Phillip to follow the duke and pulled up the rear. The three men went into the dining-room, the doors were closed behind them and the details of the royal appointment discussed in complete privacy.

Phillip stood on the pavement outside Harrods and looked at his reflection in the plate-glass window. It was four o'clock in the afternoon. He had left the palace at three and had wandered round for an hour, through Kensington Gardens, on into Hyde Park and the Serpentine to see if Jane was still there painting and had ended up in Knightsbridge, feeling flat, looking at himself in the glass and wishing he could see Suzy, that he had someone, anyone to share this incredible news with.

He straightened his tie, his regimental tie and slicked back his hair. He did have a nice tan, he decided, Edward was right. 'Edward,' he mouthed silently. He was on first name terms with the duke and would very probably be on first name terms with other members of the royal family when he took up his appointment. When he took up his appointment! The job was already his, Phillip could think no other way. The details escaped him, marriage, a wife and family, they were unimportant, lost in the excitement of the moment. Suddenly Phillip let out a whoop and an elderly lady next to him tutted irritably. He shrugged and went into the shop. He wanted to buy something, something to celebrate today and made his way through the crowds of people to the gentleman's outfitters. He would buy a new suit, or maybe a sports jacket and some flannels, even a raincoat from Burberrys. Stopping by a row of navy wool blazers, he ran his fingers over the cloth and saw the sales assistant make his way over.

'Jane!' he suddenly said out loud.

'Sorry, sir?' The assistant shifted the jackets very slightly on the rack and smiled at Phillip. 'May I help at all?'

'No, erm, no thank you.' Phillip instantly made up his mind. He wanted to celebrate but not with a jacket, he had too many clothes already. He wanted an excellent dinner, an extremely expensive bottle of wine and a bloody good night out. I'll ring Jane, he thought, hurrying towards the telephones, Jane was the perfect choice. Who else could he ring on a Saturday afternoon and expect to be free for the evening?

Jane climbed out of the lift and pulled off her hat and coat before she went back for her things. The afternoon had warmed up considerably and she was sweating with all her gear on. Dropping them on the floor by the front door of the flat, she rang the bell and went back to the lift to fetch her bag, stool and easel. She was tired after painting all day and they seemed heavier now than when she had left this morning. She struggled, quite out of breath, and glanced up wearily as Clare darted out of the flat and ran across to her, yanking her bag from her hands.

'Jane! There's someone on the phone!' Her arm dropped visibly with the weight of the bag. 'Hurry up, Janey! Quick!'

Jane placed her easel and fold-up stool down by her feet and straightened. 'For me?'

'Yeeeess! Of course it's for you! Go on!'

'Oh!' She left the things there and walked towards the flat, stopping by the door. 'Are you all right, Clare?' she called over her shoulder. Clare seemed very agitated.

'Yeeesss!' Clare made frantic shooing motions. 'Go on, Jane!' she cried, quite desperately and Jane shrugged, disappearing inside to take her call.

'Hello?' The telephone was in the sitting-room and she slumped down into an armchair as she spoke, holding the receiver in the crook of her shoulder. 'Ah!' she said, glancing up at Clare who had hurried in after her, and scowling at her. 'Hello, Phillip.' The earlier desperation made perfect sense now. 'Fine thanks. Yes, yes I did, thank you. Yes, I'm sure the West Sommerton Water-colour Society will be delighted, if they stay awake long enough to see all three!'

Clare heard Phillip's laughter down the line while she busied herself with rearranging the photograph frames on the bureau. She smiled reassuringly at Jane.

'No, I hadn't planned to do anything . . .' Jane rubbed her legs as she spoke and saw Clare inching closer to the phone. She swapped the receiver to the other ear. 'Oh, I see. Well congratulations!' Her knees were aching from sitting on that ruddy stool for so long and she couldn't wait to get in the bath. She stopped rubbing. 'Well, that's very kind of you, Phillip, but I honestly don't think that I can tonight.' Jane turned away from Clare's face, aghast with shock and horror. 'Yes I am free but . . .' Clare had darted round to where Jane could see her and was hopping up and down nodding her head, and wringing her hands. 'At your club? Yes, yes I do know it . . .' Jane suddenly broke off. 'Could you hold for one minute please, Phillip?' She put her hand over the receiver and said, 'For God's sake, Clare, bugger off! If I want to go out with Phillip Mills I am sure I can make up my mind without your help!'

'But, Jane! You can't turn him down, you can't . . .'

Jane stood and one hand in the middle of her sister's back, she propelled Clare out of the room with a sharp shove. 'I can do whatever I like,' she snapped and slammed the door shut.

'Sorry about that, Phillip,' she said, as calmly as she could manage.

Phillip laughed on the other end of the line. 'Clare's right you know,' he said, 'you can't turn me down.'

Jane blushed, cringing with embarrassment. 'Oh God! I . . .'

'Look, why don't you let her back into the room and tell her that I'll pick you up in a cab at seven. If we arrange to meet at the club you might not turn up!'

Jane was flummoxed. She still had time to back out but she'd lost her nerve. 'All right,' she said. 'Thank you, I'll be ready by seven.'

'Good, I'll see you then.'

'Yes, see you then. Goodbye, Phillip.' Jane glanced over at Clare who had sneaked back into the room. 'He'll pick me up at seven in a cab,' she said, banging the receiver down. 'He's been offered some sort of promotion and wanted someone to celebrate with.'

'And he rang you!' Clare clasped her hand to her breast. 'He wanted to celebrate with you, Jane! Oh, I can hardly believe it . . .'

'Well don't then!' Jane snapped. She stomped off

towards the door and turned, scowling over her shoulder at Clare. 'He wanted to celebrate, Clare, that's all! And I would imagine, that at four o'clock on a Saturday afternoon, he couldn't find anyone else mug enough to be free!'

It was still only very early spring and the night air was chilly. As Jane and Phillip left the Savoy Hotel to wait for a taxi, Jane pulled her coat in a little tighter around the dress that Clare had lent her and shivered.

'Are you all right, Jane? Would you like to sit inside and I'll call you when the taxi arrives?'

Jane smiled. 'No, thanks, Phillip, but I'm fine.' He placed his hand on her elbow as they moved forward down the steps of the hotel towards the doorman.

'Taxi, sir?'

'Yes please.'

They stood for a few moments in silence.

'You two off as well!'

Both Jane and Phillip turned as an old friend of Jane's father's came down the steps towards them, his arm around his wife. They had met Colonel and Mrs Graves in the Savoy Grill.

'Yes, yes we are, Monty!' Jane said.

'Good meal?'

'Superb.'

'Excellent, excellent!' He laughed heartily and his wife rolled her eyes at Jane. 'Come on, dear,' she said, tutting. 'We've interrupted quite enough of Jane and Major Mills' evening already.'

'Nonsense, nonsense!'

Jane laughed as Monty's wife cuffed him on the arm then leant forward and kissed her cheek. 'Good to see you looking so well, Jane dear. We're off! Come on, Monty!' she called over to her husband who had struck up another conversation with Phillip. 'We're walking back, hopefully the air will sober you up a bit!'

Monty laughed again and shook hands with Phillip. 'Love, honour and obey!' he said jovially. 'We seem to have got it the wrong way round!' He kissed Jane. 'Goodnight, Jane dear. Send our good wishes to your parents!'

'I will, Monty, thanks! Goodnight, Sybil!' Jane called. The colonel's wife waved as Monty joined her and they linked arms, walking off down towards the Strand.

'What a nice couple!' Phillip faced Jane and turned the collar of her overcoat up. 'Old friends of the family?'

'Yes.' Jane blushed as he continued to hold the lapels of her coat. 'I enjoyed meeting them,' he said.

'Good.'

He meant it but Jane didn't really believe him. For Phillip, eating at the high-profile Savoy Grill, a restaurant that was way out of bounds when he was with Suzanna, and being able to meet people without worrying about who would say what, was a refreshing change. 'I enjoyed tonight,' he said. 'Thank you.'

Jane looked up at him. 'So did I,' she answered, surprised even now that she had. Phillip was good company and if she had been second, or even third choice for tonight, she hadn't felt it.

'Can I see you again?'

Jane looked away. Phillip was very attractive but she

was getting past wasting time on flings or friendships that didn't lead anywhere.

'We could go to the British Museum,' Phillip added. 'I could show you some of the pieces my family have donated.'

'Give you the chance to show off you mean!'

Phillip laughed. 'Yes, all right. Please come out with me and let me brag to you all afternoon about how important my family were in India!'

'Oh, go on then!' Jane laughed as well. 'As it's half-term this week and I've nothing else to do!' Besides, she thought, what was another friendship to add to her long list? At least she wouldn't be under any illusions with Phillip; a friendship was all it would ever be, a man like him would never see anything in her. 'Thank you, I'd love to come,' she said more seriously.

'Tuesday?'

'Yes, Tuesday. I can come up for the day.' A black cab pulled up at that moment and the doorman opened the door for Jane. 'Kensington, Queen's Gate and then Chelsea,' Phillip said to the driver.

Jane turned round. 'Oh, don't bother to come all the way over to Kensington, Phillip! Please, I can see myself home, honestly!' She smiled. 'Get another cab and go straight home.'

He hesitated, not knowing what to do. 'Are you sure?' It was very sensible but few women would have suggested it.

'Of course I'm sure!' Jane pulled the door shut and pressed the window down. 'Goodnight, Phillip,' she said. 'Thank you for a lovely evening.'

He stepped back, making no attempt to kiss her and

smiled. 'Goodnight, Jane. It was a pleasure.' And tapping the roof of the cab with his fist, he watched as it pulled off and Jane settled down into the seat, waving briefly as she disappeared from view.

Chapter Nine

The second floor of Selfridges was packed, it was a Saturday afternoon and the ladies fashion department was doing brisk business. As Jane followed Clare up the staircase towards the throng of shoppers she felt a pang of misgiving and wondered for the umpteenth time that day why on earth she had let Clare talk her into this. It was her birthday and the last thing she wanted to do was fight her way through a department store looking for a dress that Clare considered suitable for her date. She sighed heavily as Clare turned to her and said irritably, 'Come on, Janey! Anyone would think that you weren't in the slightest bit interested in doing this!'

But she knew Clare had her best interests at heart, it was her and Teddy's present to her, so she smiled and replied, 'Sorry, but I'm not as young as I used to be!'

'Ha ha!' Clare shook her head. 'You shouldn't keep

mentioning your age, Jane! And certainly don't mention it to Phillip tonight!'

Jane burst out laughing.

'What's so funny?' Clare demanded, hands on her hips.

'Oh, Clare, you are!' Jane stopped laughing and curbed her smile; Clare's face was like thunder. 'You surely don't think that Phillip doesn't know how old I am?!'

'Well, I, erm . . . I just thought it might, erm . . .'

Jane smiled. 'Might put him off, eh? If he knows I'm an old spinster just dying to get married!'

'Don't make fun of me, Jane.'

Jane climbed the three steps between them and kissed Clare on the cheek. 'I'm not,' she said. Clare could be remarkably immature for twenty-one but Jane still adored her. 'Come on, let's go and buy that dress you promised me for my birthday.'

'All right.' Clare linked her arm through Jane's as they climbed up to the second floor. 'Where shall we start?' she asked, scanning the scene.

'You choose.'

'OK. How about over there?' She pointed to a part of the shop that had been done out like a boutique, at a mannequin in a black minidress. Jane swallowed back her automatic response; it was far from her idea of a nice dress but she let herself be led over.

Clare began her search.

'So Phillip knows you're twenty-seven today, does he?' she asked, rifling through a rack of minidresses like the one on display. She pulled one out in purple and held it up for inspection.

'Yes, he knows my age,' Jane answered, silently praying

that Clare put the dress back. The last thing she wanted was to come to blows over the first choice.

'Oh.' Clare did put the dress back. She moved on to the next rack. 'I suppose if you're really good friends it doesn't matter.' Clare glanced up. 'Does it?'

'No, no it doesn't.' Jane moved away and fiddled with a rail of skirts and matching tunics.

'Is that what it is then?'

Jane took a completely unsuitable miniskirt off the rail and held it up, avoiding the question. 'Hmmmm?'

Clare walked over to her and shook her head. She swapped the skirt for a dress she had chosen and hung it in front of Jane's body. She looked at her sister. 'Is it just a friendship between you and Phillip?'

Jane sighed, removed the dress from Clare's hands and stuffed it back on the rail.

'It's just that you've seen an awful lot of each other in the past couple of weeks and I was wondering . . .'

'Clare!' Jane snapped, a little more abruptly than she'd meant to and moved off towards another section.

'If it was more than that, if . . .' Clare hurried after Jane. 'If it might be . . .'

'To be perfectly honest with you,' Jane said, swinging round to face her sister, 'I really don't know what it is!' And she headed straight for the designer section, leaving Clare speechless behind her.

Jane walked through the rails of cashmere and silk, the beautifully cut suits and dresses and ran her fingers every now and then along the sleeve of a blouse or jacket, luxuriating in the fine quality of the fabric. She stopped, glanced at herself in a full-length mirror and sighed heavily. What she'd just said to Clare was true, although she'd been avoiding thinking about it for as long as she could. In all honesty she had no idea about her relationship with Phillip Mills. She had no idea at all.

If she was frank with herself, she thought, picking up a coat and holding it in front of her, she didn't really know what she felt about Phillip, let alone what he felt about her. She had seen a lot of him, Clare was right, he was difficult to refuse. But was it only a month since they'd met? It felt so much longer, it felt as if she'd known him for ever.

Phillip was a type, Jane had decided, after only the second time they went out. He was typical public school and army, traditional, rather set in his ways but he was fun, he was intelligent, witty and attentive and he was also extremely good-looking. Jane put the coat back and swopped it for a jacket, but that didn't suit her either. She stood and stared at her reflection, squinting her eyes and peering at her face. He was definitely good-looking, she thought, a small flame of excitement flaring in the pit of her stomach. If she was honest with herself he was the dishiest man she had ever been out with, he had everything, he was as close to the mark as a man could get.

Jane put the jacket down and, still staring at her face, she unclipped her hair and let it fall down. Well, God knows what he sees in me, she mused, tucking the long strands of brown behind her ear and making her already rather long angular features look even longer and more angular. She shifted from one foot to the other. She was tall and slim, she had nice legs and a good neat figure but no one could call her beautiful, or even pretty. She could possibly pass for attractive, she reckoned, in candlelight with full make-up on but she would never turn heads, not the way Phillip did whenever they were out together.

'It must be my personality,' she said to her face but even as she said it she doubted it. She amused Phillip, she knew that, they had friends in common and she did her best to entertain but she always felt there was a part of him missing, like he wasn't really with her and it puzzled her, because he was always the one to ask her out, he was the one so keen to continue their friendship.

Jane finally moved away from the mirror. Was it a friendship? If it was it was pretty close. They hadn't been to bed yet but Jane had the feeling it was inevitable, that things were working their way towards it, as they so often did. Only this time she really wanted it. She wasn't 'in love' with Phillip, or at least she didn't think so, she wasn't sure she knew what love was, but she recognised her feelings, she knew she wanted him, was sure he would be a good lover. She could sense that, in his glance, in the slightest touch of his hand, and she felt the familiar ache of excitement at the very thought of it.

'Janey! There you are!' Clare suddenly appeared behind an enormous rail of dresses and Jane blushed, feeling guilty about her thoughts. 'Look! Tadah!' She held up a black silk jersey dress with a high neck and a long flowing shape. Jane was impressed. 'I had to go through practically every rail in the shop,' she said, handing it across, 'but there it was in the end, all alone, just waiting for you!'

Jane laughed. 'You are so melodramatic, Clare Latham!' She looked at the dress and checked the size. 'It's very nice. Shall I try it on?'

'Yes, go on.' Clare glanced around the shop. 'Over there!' she said, pointing to the fitting rooms. 'I'll come with you.'

Jane smiled. 'It's all right, I think I can manage. You wait here.'

'But you'll want me to hold your hair up and advise on jewellery and . . . ' She broke off and shrugged. 'I'll wait here,' she finished.

'Right. See you in a minute then.'

Clare watched her sister go, holding the dress up and weaving her way through the other shoppers. Clare didn't really understand Jane, she wasn't like any of her girlfriends, or even their mother for that matter but Clare did like her sister, she liked her very much indeed. In fact, she thought, as Jane came out of the fitting room wearing the dress and looking really quite nice, she didn't know anyone who didn't like Jane, it was really impossible not to.

Across the other side of town, Phillip Mills, having just put down the phone after a long call to an old friend from the regiment, thought exactly the same thing and smiled as he went through to the sitting-room. He dropped down on to the sofa and put his feet up on the coffee table. Reaching for his cigarettes, he lit one up. So Wendy Peterson was at school with Jane, he thought, and Jerry just phoned to invite him and Jane to lunch next Sunday, having heard that they had struck up a close friendship. Jane was a 'thoroughly nice girl' to quote Jerry and they were delighted that Phillip thought so too. Phillip grinned as he flicked his ash into a saucer. After three years out on a limb with Suzy, he had miraculously re-entered polite society again and the invitations were starting to flood in.

'Jane is a thoroughly nice girl,' he said aloud. 'She's clever, talented, kind, funny and sensible. Sir!' He saluted to the empty room and stubbed out his cigarette, feeling suddenly flat. Jane wasn't Suzanna. He stood and walked across to the window, looking down at the traffic on the road. His body ached with longing for her. But he knew he had to put Suzy from his mind, at least for the time being, he couldn't let her get in the way, not at the moment, not until things were clear, settled. He walked back to the sofa and lit another cigarette. He had to focus on one thing. If he didn't, if he let anything else get in the way he knew he'd never be able to go through with it. He had to keep it clear in his mind, he had to know what he wanted. I'd do anything to keep it, Jane had said that first time they met. She was right, it was worth anything and all he needed was a little more time.

Glancing at his watch, Phillip realised he was running late and went through to the bedroom to lay out his clothes for the evening ahead. He took his dinner jacket out of the wardrobe, lay it neatly on the bed, checked the trousers and found his dress shirt, studs, cufflinks, socks and polished black patent shoes. He had bought tickets for the first night at Covent Garden of *Madame Butterfly*, it had cost a fortune but he was really looking forward to surprising Jane. It was her birthday and she loved the opera, it was also a month since they'd first met and Phillip had decided it was about time he moved things forward.

Taking some fresh underwear from the drawer, Phillip carried it through to the bathroom with him, left it on the chair and bent to run his bath. He sprinkled a liberal amount of Penhaligon's oil into the water for good measure, then on the spur of the moment carried the bottle into the bedroom, pulled back the bed cover, and pouring some into the palm of his hand, sprinkled it over the pillows and sheets. Satisfied that he was prepared, he went back to his bath.

Suzanna and Mitchell Harvey arrived at Covent Garden with plenty of time before the performance; it was just after seven o'clock. Mitchell had ordered champagne in the circle bar for his guests, a couple of board members of a merchant bank with their wives and he wanted to make sure they were there to greet them. The Bentley pulled up outside the entrance of the Royal Opera House and the driver hopped out, walking round to open the door for Suzanna. She took his hand and he helped her out of the car as she held the hem of her Givenchy evening gown up off the ground and stepped carefully on to the pavement. She stood and waited for Mitchell. Suzanna hated the opera, she hated it as much as she hated all the things she did with Mitchell: Ascot, Wimbledon, first nights, Glyndebourne and countless, countless dinners. She stifled a yawn and turned as Mitchell joined her.

'Ready?' She nodded and Mitchell took her arm. 'At least try and look the part,' Mitchell hissed as they walked past the small crowd formed to catch a glimpse of the princess when she arrived.

Suzanna smiled at a flashlight and Mitchell's grip relaxed slightly. 'That's better,' he said. 'Now keep that up all evening and I'll be happy.' And, smiling, together they walked on inside.

*   *   *

Phillip and Jane ran all the way up the Strand. They were late, the traffic had been terrible and they'd jumped out of the taxi cab at Charing Cross and decided to go the rest of the way on foot. Phillip held Jane's hand and pulling her onward, her hair and coat flying behind her, he led the way up past Covent Garden market and on to the Royal Opera House. Jane pulled back as they approached the building, its white columned façade lit up against the black night sky.

'The opera!'

Phillip stopped. 'Very observant.' He turned and looked at her face. 'Is that all right?'

'Yes! Yes it's wonderful, I . . .'

He took her hand again. 'Come on, Janey! They'll close the doors if we arrive much later!' He started to run, pulling Jane behind him and, laughing, they sprinted the rest of the way and arrived, out of breath but just in time.

'Phew!' Jane dropped Phillip's hand as they entered the theatre and glanced round the foyer looking for the hat check. 'I'll do the coats and you get the chocs!' she said, locating the cloakroom. He peeled off his overcoat, handed it to her and she hurried over. Phillip checked his tickets with the young man on the door of the stalls, quickly chose a box of Bendicks and joined Jane, took their coat tags and put them in his pocket.

'Ready?'

'Yes, I can't wait!'

He looked at her face, all of a sudden crimson from the rush of blood to her cheeks and leaning forward, he planted a cool kiss on her forehead. 'Happy birthday, Janey,' he said.

Jane shivered, a tiny, imperceptible response to his touch. 'Thank you, Phillip.'

He took her hand, she laid her head on his shoulder for a moment and they walked down to their seats at the front of the stalls as the orchestra warmed up and the lights began to dim.

Suzanna was surveying the scene with her opera glasses, a pair decorated with mother-of-pearl and a gift from Mitchell for Christmas. They had a box, opposite the royal box and Suzy was waiting for a first glimpse of the princess as she took her seat. She ignored the business chatter behind her and the talk of children and schools from the women and stared around the opera house, trying to spot the couturier dresses and any jewellery worth more than her own. She saw a couple come in late, the last to arrive and catching sight of what looked like a very attractive man with a rather plain woman, she focused her lenses on them, out of idle curiosity.

For a moment the whole opera house went silent. Suzanna dropped her glasses.

'Are you all right, Suzanna dear?' One of the wives leant forward and picked them up, handing them over and glimpsing Suzy's face, ashen with shock.

'Yes, I'm fine . . . I . . .' Suzanna put the glasses up to her eyes again as the blood rushed in her ears. She saw Phillip help Jane into her seat and take her hand again. She saw his face as he leant in close and whispered something in her ear. Jane laughed and Phillip held her hand up to his lips, gently kissing it. Suzanna's chest constricted and she felt as if she might suffocate. 'My God, I . . .'

The glasses fell a second time to the floor and Mitchell looked over.

'Suzanna!'

Suzy turned. She stared at him wild-eyed, her breath coming in short gasps and suddenly she stood, knocking back her chair and staggering forward. 'I have to get some air . . . I'm sorry . . .' She pushed her way to the back of the box and struggled for a moment with the door. 'I don't feel well, I . . .'

One of the men stood and opened it for her but Mitchell glared. Suzy stumbled out into the passage and gripped the wall for support.

'Please excuse me,' Mitchell said as he stood and nodded to his guests. 'I must see if she's all right.' He followed Suzy out of the box and found her in the passage, slumped down on the floor, her head back against the wall. He clicked the door shut behind him knowing the boxes were sound-proofed.

'What the hell are you playing at?' he snarled, yanking her up by her arm. 'Get back inside that box!' He pulled her again and she cried out. She was lifeless, useless. 'What the hell . . . !' He held his hand up to smack her across the face but she cowered and he stopped himself. He moved away and swallowed down his anger.

'Suzanna, you know how important this evening is to me,' he said coldly. 'I have an awful lot resting on my reputation here.' He dug his hands in his pockets, his fists clenched and looked down at her but she couldn't even face him. Suddenly he swore and kicked the wall. 'Jesus! This had better not be one of your silly little tantrums!' he threatened. 'If it is . . .' he broke off as the muffled sound of applause came through from the auditorium. 'OK, have it your way this time, then,' he said, calmly moving back towards the box. Then he turned, suddenly vicious. 'But if you ever do this again!' He jabbed his finger at her, his face ugly with rage. 'Embarrass me! Then I'll make sure you pay for it! D'you understand?' He leant down and pinched her cheeks between his thumb and finger, snapping her head round to face him. 'D'you understand?' She nodded, the fear bright in her eyes.

'Good.' He stood straight, smoothed his dinner jacket and glanced down at her a last time. 'God, you're pathetic,' he said and, turning, he went back to join his guests.

Suzy heard the door of the box open, the whisper of hushed voices and then silence. She could just make out the National Anthem and she looked up. Slowly getting to her feet, she spread her hands over the jade silk of her evening gown and smoothed the creases, straightening the skirt. She glanced down at her bag, unclipped it and counted the cash inside. She had enough for a taxi home.

Taking a deep breath, she shrugged back her shoulders and held her head up. She felt sick, sick and dizzy, but if she could just make it back to the flat, if she could just speak to him, just hear his voice then she'd be all right. Suzanna knew she would be able to tell, she knew that just from the sound of his voice she would be able to judge whether or not Phillip had deceived her, if he still loved her. She turned and walked along the passage, following the exit signs to the stairs at the end, then down and out into the cool night air. As soon as he said her name, she thought, I'll know, I'll know whether to live or die.

*   *   *

It was after eleven when the crowd spilt out on to the pavement in front of the opera house. Cars, voices and a hubbub of excited noise filled the air, black overcoats, brilliant white dress shirts and an array of brightly coloured silk evening gowns ablaze under the lights.

Jane held tightly on to Phillip's arm as he led her through the throng and out of the way of the queue for taxi cabs. She was a little drunk from the champagne Phillip had ordered in the interval and high on the music and singing. The whole evening had been a success, her dress, the hairstyle Clare had fixed up for her and Phillip, unusually attentive, unusually attractive in his black and bright white. They stopped, twenty yards away from the crowd, in the shadow of the market and Phillip turned to her, placing his hands on her shoulders. Jane looked up at him. 'Jane.' He stopped and cleared his throat. 'Jane, I was wondering if . . .' Again he hesitated. This was harder than he had thought it would be; it wasn't natural, it felt odd. 'If you wanted to have dinner somewhere now or if . . .' He brushed a piece of dust from her shoulder.

Jane put her hand softly over his, she loved to touch him. She stopped his fiddling and said, 'Or if I might like to come back and have a coffee with you?' She smiled. She had been waiting for this and was ready.

'Yes.' He shrugged and smiled back. 'Would you?'

Jane reached up to touch his face. She traced the shape of his mouth with her fingertip. She wanted to be loved by him, she wanted the warmth and comfort of his body next to hers. 'Yes,' she said, 'I would.'

He bent his head and kissed her. 'Good.' Then he looked at her, at her face soft and relaxed and he knew it was right; it had to be right. 'Let's go then,' he said and he led her down to the corner of the Strand and found them both a taxi.

Suzanna sat, a small glass of vodka balanced precariously on the arm of the sofa, the telephone in her lap. She stared at the painting on the wall opposite, not really seeing it but just blankly focused on something, anything to take away the fear, a fear that ground down in the pit of her stomach. She looked at her watch.

Phillip would be leaving the Royal Opera House now, he would be taking his friend home, or maybe out for a bite to eat; whatever he was doing, he wouldn't be back at Bertram's flat for another hour, maybe two. She looked at her watch again, as she had done almost every ten minutes since she'd left the opera. There was no point in ringing yet, she knew that but she still dialled his number, just to be sure. The phone rang. It rang and rang and rang, a terrible empty sound that filled her with horror. She slammed the receiver down. I'll try again in twenty minutes, she thought as she drank down the remainder of her vodka. Then she stood to refill her glass.

Phillip ran up the last three stairs and fumbled with the key, desperate to get it in the lock. 'Sorry,' he called over his shoulder to Jane. She shrugged and continued up slowly as he dashed inside the flat and lunged for the phone. The line was dead. Replacing the receiver, he walked back to the stairs and put his hand out for Jane. 'The person hung up,' he said. She took his hand as she climbed the last step and he pulled her in towards him, holding her close. 'Thank goodness.' He stroked her hair and breathed in the fresh smell of her shampoo. 'Come on, let's go in.'

She nodded and with his arm around her shoulder, he led her into the flat. 'D'you want coffee?'

She smiled and shook her head.

'No. Me neither.' Dropping his arm, he faced Jane and, leaning down, he kissed her, gently moving his hands to her coat and slipping it off her shoulders. It fell to the floor. Silently, he took her hand and guided her towards the bedroom. He opened the door, went to reach for the lamp on the chest but Jane stopped him. 'Leave it off,' she whispered. 'Please.' He smiled at her in the half-light and nodded. 'To bed then,' he said gently, 'in the dark.'

'Yes,' Jane answered and she relaxed against him as he pushed the door shut with his foot.

'Damn!' Phillip moved away from Jane and sat up. He stretched for the bedside lamp. 'D'you mind, Janey? I don't think this person's going to bloody give up!'

Jane ran her fingers along his back and then rolled over, snuggling down under the sheets. 'OK. It's safe now,' she said and Phillip switched on the light. They smiled at each other.

'I'm really sorry, Jane.'

She shrugged. 'Go on, it might be important.'

Phillip pulled back the sheets and stood, taking a towel off the chair and tying it round his waist. 'I won't be long.' He glanced back at her.

'Go on!' She shooed him off and pulled the sheet up to her chin. 'Hurry up!' Phillip left the bedroom and Jane clicked the light off as he shut the door behind him.

He strode through to the hall and grabbed the receiver,

really annoyed at being called at this time of night. 'Hello?' It was cold in the hall and he shivered as he stood there in just a towel. 'Hello?' He began to lose his patience and went to hang up.

'Phillip?'

Suddenly he gripped the phone, slumping back against the wall. 'Christ! Suzy?' His mouth went dry. 'Suzy? Is that you?' His voice dropped to a whisper and he strained to hear her on the other end. 'Suzy? What is it? Suzanna?' He could hear her breathing, a congested sound and his stomach flipped over with fear. 'Are you all right? What is it, Suzy?' The line went quiet for a few moments then he heard a sob; he realised she was crying. 'Oh God, Suzy. Please, please don't cry. What is it?'

'I saw you,' she said, 'I saw you tonight, with someone, with . . .' She broke off and the few seconds Phillip waited seemed to last for ever. 'I saw you with another woman, Phillip!' she cried suddenly. 'My God, I couldn't believe it, I saw you kiss her, I saw . . .'

'Stop it, Suzy!' he hissed. 'Stop it!' He could sense the hysterics in her voice; he knew the signs. 'Calm down! Please.' He kept his voice steady, his breathing controlled. He didn't want her to catch his fear. 'Suzy, listen to me, listen, just for a moment.' He looked down the hall at the bedroom, still dark and willed Jane to stay in bed. He took a deep breath. 'Suzanna, I made a promise to you, only a few weeks back, I promised you something, didn't I?' He waited, holding his breath.

'Yes, but . . .'

'I said that I wouldn't let you down, that I'd find a way for us. Did I say that, Suzy?'

'Yes.'

'Suzy, you have to trust me. I know what I'm doing and I won't disappoint you, I promise. Please, you have to trust me!' She was crying still, he heard her sniff but she was calmer, he could feel it. 'You will trust me, won't you? You know that I want what's best for both of us?' His voice had changed, he was cajoling, persuasive. 'Please? Hmmm?'

Suzanna laid her head back against the sofa as she held the receiver and closed her eyes. She trusted him, she always had and she knew, she knew from the sound of his voice that he loved her, she didn't need any more words, any more talk, she could tell. She had always been able to tell.

'I trust you,' she said quietly. She felt the room spin for a moment and opened her eyes quickly. 'You won't let me down, will you?'

Phillip heard her words slur. 'No, I won't let you down.' He shivered again, more from relief than cold. 'Go to bed, Suzy,' he said. 'You're tired; go and tuck yourself in bed and try and get some sleep.'

'Yes, yes I'll do that. You always look after me, don't you, Phillip?' She closed her eyes once more and felt the spinning, only she was too tired to open them again. She swallowed down the faint taste of nausea and let her head flop to the side. 'Goodnight, darling,' she murmured. 'I love you, I . . .' She dropped the receiver back into its cradle and curled on to her side. 'I love you so much,' she whispered, but Phillip didn't hear her; she had cut him off.

Phillip held the phone for a few moments longer, then quickly replaced the receiver. He rubbed his hands wearily over his face and turned towards the bedroom. He felt sick, sick and cold and miserable but he knew he had to go through with it. He walked down the hall and softly clicked the door open.

'Jane?' He heard the rustle of the sheets and moved towards the bed. 'I'm sorry about that, Jane,' he whispered. 'It was business.' And he sank gratefully into bed beside her and curled towards the warmth and comfort of her body.

Chapter Ten

The weather had stayed warm through March and into the beginning of April but the middle two weeks it began to rain. It rained almost continuously for seven days and as Jane sat at the table in the dining-room, the soft light of the candles flickering on the polished wood and the hum of conversation around her, she watched the water run down the long panes of glass in the sash windows and make complicated vertical patterns that merged into each other and disappeared as quickly as they formed. They fascinated her but as she glanced up around the table, she saw that her father was watching her and quickly tuned back into the conversation, smiling briefly at him for catching her out. She turned her head towards Phillip on her right, holding court, with Clare, her mother and Teddy all focused on him, absorbed in his story and felt a glow of satisfaction. She took a sip of wine and listened.

'So what happened next?' Clare demanded, a mixture of horror and curiosity on her face.

'Well, the bird Colonel Mills had found was apparently one of a pair and the Indian had the other one. When he fled the state, he swore vengeance on the British and on Colonel Mills and his family for splitting the pair, killing his father and ruining his life.' Phillip stopped to take a sip of wine before he finished his tale. 'And, as far as we know, this oath still exists to this day.'

'Ooh!' Clare shivered. 'How incredible! Weren't you terrified going to India, Phillip? I would have been.'

Phillip smiled. 'I should think it's all forgotten by now, Clare. I'm the first Mills to go there since the whole episode "supposedly" happened and I'm not sure there's any real truth in it.' He shrugged. 'I should think it's pretty safe and, of course, I'm terribly brave!'

Clare laughed and turned to Jane. 'Isn't that the most amazing story, Janey?'

Jane smiled. 'Of course, but then Phillip has great skill at story telling.'

Phillip placed his hand over hers and squeezed it. 'Do I detect a hint of sarcasm in your voice, Jane Bennet?' He smiled.

'No, me?' The whole table laughed.

'And you've seen the bird, have you, Jane, in the British Museum?' her father asked.

'Yes, it's very beautiful. Stunning in fact.'

Clare shook her head. 'I'm surprised that you ever went to India, Phillip! I wouldn't step foot anywhere near danger like that.'

'That's why you're not in the army,' Teddy said, smiling.

'Did your family's connection with India have much influence with your present job, Phillip?' Brigadier Bennet asked.

'No, I don't think so, sir. Of course it was useful that I had been to India when this appointment came up and that I'd some experience of the customs and culture but I don't think I was appointed as equerry for those reasons.' He shrugged and finished his glass of wine. 'Jane, that was a superb dinner,' he said, patting his mouth with his napkin. 'And an excellent Burgundy, sir. Thank you.'

'Jane is a very good cook,' Mrs Bennet said. 'She always cooks for us when we entertain, doesn't she, John?'

'Yes, yes she does.' He smiled at his daughter. 'And Clare washes up usually. Clare is an excellent washer-upper, isn't she, Teddy?'

Teddy laughed. 'Excellent.'

'Now, would you like a brandy, Phillip, or a glass of port?' Brigadier Bennet stood and went to the sideboard. 'Teddy? You'll join me in a port, won't you?'

'Please.'

Phillip went to stand as Jane got up to help her mother with the plates. 'Don't get up,' she said quietly, her hand on his shoulder. 'We'll leave you to it,' she called across to her father.

'Don't you want a brandy, Janey?'

Jane shook her head.

'What about your mother? Caroline? Like a glass of something?'

'No thanks, John. I think we'll do the dishes and put the coffee on.' Mrs Bennet had started removing the plates and handing them to Clare. 'Make sure the fire's stoked in the sitting-room will you?' she said as she held the door open for the girls. 'We'll join you in there in half an hour.' And she followed her daughters out across the hallway and along the passage to the kitchen.

'Isn't he divine?' Clare whispered to her mother as Jane stood across the kitchen from them covering leftovers in tin foil and packing them in the fridge. 'He's besotted with Jane as well!'

'Hardly besotted,' Jane called over to them. 'We get on well, that's all there is to it!'

Caroline Bennet shook her head and continued stacking dishes by the sink. She didn't want to get involved; it was Jane's business and it should stay that way. She put the last plate on the pile and turned the taps on full blast to fill the sink, squirting a measure of Fairy Liquid under the running water. She hoped it wasn't serious with Jane and Phillip. He seemed a nice enough man, she thought, as she watched the sink fill up, but Jane hardly knew him and before long he'd be off again to India and Jane would mope around the place making everyone's life a misery. She wrenched the taps off and reached for her rubber gloves. What on earth was Jane doing inviting him down on Mrs Jones's day off, it really was too much. Dinner parties were all very well but only when the help was in, any other time simply shouldn't be considered.

'Pass me the plates, will you, Clare?' Caroline said, turning to her daughter 'And, Jane? You can dry.'

Jane started and looked round. She had been staring out at the rain again, at the remains of it drying on the window. 'Yup, sure!' She bent in towards the fridge, placed the last wrapped packet in and then closed the door. 'Just coming,' she said as she straightened and she walked over to join her mother and Clare.

'So I start feeding them in about May, as soon as the weather turns really, but I'm always careful. I measure each feed and catalogue it so I never lose track.' John Bennet broke off and took a puff on his cigar. Phillip had asked him about his roses so he'd told him, pity the young man didn't have the courtesy to listen to the answer. He waited, finished his port and turned towards Teddy. 'Pass the port please, Teddy.'

'Certainly.' Teddy reached for the decanter and passed it to his left. Phillip glanced up.

'I think the rain's stopped,' he said as the brigadier poured himself another small glass of Taylor's. 'I wonder if you'd mind me asking Jane to show me your roses, sir? See what all this careful feeding has produced.'

John Bennet smiled. He had been listening, just looked as if he hadn't. 'It's John,' he said. 'Please, Phillip, call me John. And not at all, I think Jane would love to show you the roses, she's almost as good with them as I am.'

'Thank you, John.' Phillip stood. 'If you two gentlemen will excuse me?'

'Certainly.'

Phillip moved towards the door. This was a lovely room, the French cherrywood table was so finely polished that the wood glowed in the candle light and reflected the image of the rose bowl, heavy with David Austin's Old English roses. He glanced at the seventeenth-century Dutch paintings on the walls, only knowing as much because Jane had told him so, and then at the long sash window where the garden trailed on seemingly for ever outside. This was a lovely house, it was the perfect background for him and it added to his determination.

'We'll be in for coffee,' he said and John nodded. Quickly, before he lost his brandy-fuelled nerve, he left the dining-room, crossed the stone flagged hallway and found his way along to the kitchen. He knocked and then walked straight in.

The garden did go on for ever, Phillip thought, as he followed Jane on past the rose beds and through an arch in the box hedge to another level of lawn, edged either side by an English country garden border, the scent of lavender and sweet peas, hollyhocks and honeysuckle strong in the damp, rain-filled air. He reached for her hand and she turned to glance at him over her shoulder.

'The kissing seat is down here,' she said. 'Right at the very end of the garden.'

'Is it especially for kissing?'

Jane smiled. 'No, not especially.' They continued on, Phillip's shoes getting increasingly wet from the grass and his socks beginning to feel clammy, until they reached the white wrought-iron bench against a hedge of wild roses that grew over a bramble bush. Jane took the tea towel she had brought in her pocket and wiped the seat down.

'Here you are.'

'D'you mind if I stand?' Phillip dug his hands in his pocket and moved away from Jane. He glanced down at the longer, thicker grass and felt the hem of his trousers saturate. Not quite what I'd pictured, he thought. 'Erm, Jane?'

Jane had sat and was looking behind her at the bramble

bush to see how much fruit it would bear that September. She turned to look at him.

'Jane, I wanted to speak to you about something,' he said. 'Something important.'

Jane put her hands in the pockets of her Barbour and crossed her legs, the top of her welly hitting the bench as she did so. 'I thought as much,' she said quietly. 'It's very unlike you to ring at the last minute and invite yourself down.' She shrugged and smiled to cover her disappointment. 'What is it?' She had been waiting all evening for this, it was probably the old elbow but at least he had the decency to tell her to her face.

'Well, I feel a bit embarrassed to be honest,' Phillip said. 'I'm not really sure where to start.'

'Just say it,' Jane answered. 'Get it out in the open.'

Phillip raised an eyebrow. 'OK.' He cleared his throat and Jane thought, oh boy, how to make a right dog's dinner of it. She switched off.

'Jane, will you marry me?'

'That's OK, I was expecting it anyway.'

'Sorry? Jane, did you hear what I said?'

Jane raised her head; she was sick of humouring people. 'No, what did you say, Phillip?' she asked with weary sarcasm; he obviously wanted to make things absolutely clear.

'I said, will you marry me?'

Jane narrowed her eyes and looked at him. 'You said what?'

Phillip held down an irritated sigh and wondered briefly if she was making fun of him. 'I asked you to marry me, Jane.'

Jane stared at him. 'I see,' she said.

Phillip stood where he was, his socks now sodden and felt a spot of rain on his face. 'Is that all?'

'Well, no, it isn't.' Jane bit her lip. 'Why?' she asked.

Phillip came over to the bench and sat down next to her. 'Why do I want to marry you?'

'Yes. Why?'

This was the part he had rehearsed: perfectly. 'Because we make a good couple. Because we get on very well, we have a lot in common.' He took her hand. 'You're intelligent, witty, attractive, kind and I think you'd make a very good wife for me, Jane.' He kissed the palm of her hand. 'We're compatible in bed as well, that's very important.'

Jane took a breath and held it, then she let it out very slowly, in one long exhalation. She felt momentarily shocked by what he'd just said; she felt dizzy, she tried hard to think straight. Phillip hadn't mentioned love, but then why should he? They couldn't possibly fall in love in a matter of weeks, love took years, it took marriage and children. What he had said made sense, they did get on well, they did have friends in common and they were certainly compatible in bed, that was something she had never expected! Love would come, surely? Love would grow. That's how one would view it rationally. Was it possible to view it rationally, she thought, putting her hand up to her flushed cheek. She looked at him.

'What about India?' she asked

'You would come with me. We could get married before the end of my leave.' Phillip sensed her hesitation, it wasn't what he had anticipated. 'India is an incredible opportunity, Janey, you've always wanted to go there, haven't you?'

'Yes, but . . .'

'But what? Your job? Teaching a bunch of sixth-formers how to draw straight lines, the Sommerton Water-colour Society, average-age group – geriatric! Think of the painting you could do in India, Jane, thousands of years of culture for you to discover! You would love it, I know!'

'You seem to have thought it all through,' she said, easing her hand away from him and standing up. She walked over to a gap in the hedge and stared out at the field beyond. Phillip watched her for a few minutes, then he walked over and stood behind her, encircling her with his arms. 'I've had to,' he said quietly, 'I'm thirty-five, I know what I want and I also have just two weeks of my six-week leave left.'

'I see.'

Phillip gently turned her round to face him. 'You said that before.'

'I know.'

He tilted her chin up. 'Face me, Janey, look at me.' He pushed a strand of hair back and tucked it behind her ear. She immediately responded to his touch. 'Will you marry me, Jane Bennet?' he asked softly.

Jane looked at his eyes, cool and grey, she studied his face for a few moments, easily the most beautiful face she had ever seen on a man and then she reached up and touched his cheek with affection. 'Kiss me,' she answered. 'Kiss me first.'

'And then?'

'And then we'll see,' she said.

Brigadier John Bennet carefully closed the bedroom door

behind him so as not to wake Caroline and glanced down at his watch, the dial luminous in the dark; it was one a.m. He tied the belt of his dressing-gown and bent to put on his slippers. Then he crept down the stairs, missing the two at the bottom that creaked, and walked across the hall to the sitting-room. He opened the door and peered inside.

'Janey?'

Jane was sitting on the floor by the fire. She turned and smiled at her father. 'Come in, Daddy.'

'You all right?'

'Yes, yes I'm fine.'

He entered the room and came over to her, sitting down in the armchair. 'I heard Phillip go but you didn't come up.' He bent and picked up the poker, stirring the last of the burning coals. 'I wondered if you were all right.'

Jane smiled. 'Thank you.' They were silent for a while.

'Did Phillip enjoy his evening, d'you think?'

'Yes, I think so.'

'Was it a last-minute thing or did you just forget to tell your mother?'

Jane pulled her knees up and hugged them in close. She rested her chin on them. 'It was a last-minute thing,' she said. 'Phillip wanted to speak to me.'

'Oh?'

Jane suddenly reached out and touched her father's leg, laughing gently at him. 'Oh, Daddy, you're so predictable!'

'Am I?'

'Yes!' Her laughter slowly died. 'Phillip has asked me to marry him,' she said after a while. 'I would've told you first anyway.'

'I see.' John Bennet stirred the fire again, for something to do. 'Are you in love with him, Janey?'

Jane shrugged, not knowing what to answer.

'Well, then I should think very carefully about it if I were you.'

Jane lifted her head. 'Did you think I wouldn't?'

'No, no of course not, but I do think that it's very easy to be caught up in the romance of the moment, though.'

Jane was silent. She laid her head back on her knees and watched the dying fire. 'I'm twenty-seven, Daddy,' she said quietly, 'it's an opportunity that won't come along again. He's a wonderful man, he'd be a good husband. We're good friends, Daddy, we make a good partnership.' She suddenly looked up. 'It's an opportunity to travel, to do something with my life, to get out of teaching and experience something! I don't want to stay in Sussex all my life. Phillip is right, there's so much I can do in India and it's not just India, Daddy, it's a whole lifetime of things ahead of me, if I marry Phillip!'

John held his tongue. He wanted to explain so much to her but he didn't know how. 'What about love?' he asked.

'I don't know about love, how can I say if I love him or not, I've no experience of love, of anything like that but I think love can grow.'

'You don't need experience, Janey,' John said. 'You'd know if you loved him.' He leant forward and held out his hands. Jane took them and he squeezed her fingers. 'I don't want you to spend your life wondering what it might be like to truly love someone, with your heart and soul and I don't want you to find that someone when it's too late.' He dropped her hands and looked away at the fire. Jane saw the colour drain out of his face and realised with a jolt how old he was and how sad. She wondered what he had missed in his life.

'Daddy, I know what I'm doing. Please believe me, I'm old enough to know what I want.'

'Do you, Janey, really know what you want?'

She looked straight at him. 'Yes,' she said, 'I do.'

Finally he stood up. 'Well, I'll leave you to make your decision then,' he said. 'Goodnight, Jane darling.' He bent and Jane reached up to kiss his cheek. 'Think about it carefully.'

Jane nodded but when he reached the door she called him back. 'I have thought about it, Daddy,' she said.

He turned. 'And?'

'And I said yes,' she answered.

Without another word John Bennet opened the door and silently left the room. He understood but her decision filled him with disappointment. No wealth of travel or opportunity could ever replace an all-consuming love and he hoped with his whole heart that would be a truth she would never have to face.

Chapter Eleven

It was another Saturday afternoon, just one week on and Jane found herself in Selfridges again, this time with Phillip but still with the same lack of enthusiasm and commitment to shopping. She sat opposite him in the restaurant, sipping her glass of wine, looking idly past his shoulder at the other diners in the restaurant and wondering what on earth she was doing all of this for. She was getting married in a week's time, cream silk suit and small marquee in the garden but as she listened to Phillip's voice, running through the final version of their wedding list she felt very little excitement, she felt very little of anything, leaving most of that up to Clare, who had enough zeal for all of them.

It wasn't that she didn't want to get married, she longed to be Mrs Mills, to be on her way to India. It was more that the occasion meant little to her, that she felt no emotion for it. She wanted it over and done with. She wanted to start her new life.

'Are you happy with that, Janey?' Phillip had his pen poised over the list.

'Yes.' Jane dragged her eyes away from a rather odd-looking couple in the corner and looked at Phillip.

'And you think the Royal Doulton is better than the Spode, a bit more fashionable?'

She hadn't a clue what he was talking about. 'Yes.'

'Good! That's settled then.' Phillip made a note on the list, crossed something out that Jane tried surreptitiously to read and then glanced at his watch. 'What time is Clare meeting you?'

'Oh, erm, one-thirty I think. I'm not sure.'

He corrected the sleeve of his jacket to exactly half an inch over his shirt cuff and smoothed his hair back. Jane watched his movements with fascination. She had only just begun to notice how often he attended to himself, smoothing creases, adjusting ties, jackets, trouser pleats. It made her feel self-conscious now when she had always been the type of woman not to notice a ladder in her stocking until it had climbed the entire length of her leg and formed a gaping hole at the top. She patted her own hair, gently forcing a loose strand back into the bun at the back. There were a number of things she had begun to notice about Phillip but she pushed them from her mind. The creases will smooth out, she told herself, love will grow stronger with time.

Phillip reached for her hand. 'Jane darling, would you mind terribly if I left on time, even if she's not here?'

Jane shrugged. She didn't mind at all, in fact she had

a rather good novel in her bag and would be glad of the time to herself.

'You are good to me,' he said and kissed her left hand, holding it up to the light so that her diamond engagement ring glittered. A young woman on the next table noticed the gesture and smiled wistfully, whispering, 'How romantic!' loudly to her mother.

Jane eased her hand away and bent for her bag. 'What time's your meeting?' she asked, taking the paperback out and laying it on her lap under the table.

'Two-thirty.'

'Perhaps you should leave now,' she suggested. 'You don't want to be late.'

'Are you sure you don't mind?'

'No of course not. Clare will be here shortly and I'll just order another drink until she arrives.'

Phillip smiled, one of his most charming smiles. 'All right then, I'll get off.' He stood, came round to her side of the table and bent to kiss her cheek. 'See you tonight, then. What time do the Lythes want us?'

They were dining with some old friends of Jane's parents in Cadogan Square. 'Eight o'clock,' Jane said.

'Right, I'll pick you up from Teddy and Clare's at seven forty-five.'

It was just like him to be precise. Fifteen minutes for travelling across London, five minutes to park, five minutes to find the house and at ten-past eight ring the door bell; perfect timing. Jane smiled to cover the tiniest flicker of irritation she felt.

'See you later then,' she said, as he straightened, checked his jacket was in line and moved away from the table.

'Bye, darling.' He strode across the restaurant, stopped at the door to wave and disappeared from view. Jane took her book out from under the table, opened it at the page she had marked and without another thought of Phillip, she bent her head and started to read.

Suzanna lit a cigarette from the packet on her dressing-table. She inhaled deeply, blew the smoke out of the side of her mouth and leant forward to study her face in the mirror. I look good, she thought, I look really good and I'm ready for him. She took another drag of her cigarette, reached for her bottle of Chanel and sprayed it generously over her throat and chest, opening her robe to perfume her breasts and rubbing her hands over the flesh warming it to give off the scent. She was excited, she felt better than she had done in weeks and tracing the tip of her nipple with her finger, she felt the warm glow of sex spread through her whole body. God she'd missed him, she had missed him so much it hurt.

Suzy stood up. She slipped the robe off her shoulders and left it on the floor, walking naked to the bed and sitting on the edge to pull on her sheer black stockings and lace suspender belt. She reached for her dress. It was a simple red shift dress that fitted close to her body, cut to her shape exactly and she wore nothing except her stockings under it. She slid her feet into her shoes, black suede stilettos and walked through to the sitting-room.

Checking the fridge in the kitchen, she ran her eye over the champagne, the plate of smoked salmon and the small tin of beluga caviar. She had bought in Phillip's favourites, wanting to impress him, to spoil him in these few precious hours together. She shut the fridge door and stretched up to the cupboard for a teacup. Just a small gulp of vodka, she thought, to calm my nerves and she unscrewed the top of the bottle, sloshing the colourless spirit into her cup. She drank it down in one. She was nervous, excited, it was only natural that she would be. But it was Phillip who had made the first move, he had rung her, asked to see her and that in itself should give her confidence. Suzy took another cigarette from a packet on the sideboard. She had taken to doing that, leaving packets everywhere so that she always had one ready, it reassured her to have them handy all the time. She lit up and taking a saucer to use as an ashtray, she walked back to the sitting-room and sat down to wait. He should be here soon, she thought, glancing at her watch, but if he isn't here by twenty-past two I'll have another quick drink to keep me calm.

Phillip paid the driver, looked up at the building and ran up the steps to the main doors. He buzzed Suzy, waited and then let himself in as the door release went. He took the stairs to the sixth floor, a knot of tension in the pit of his stomach making him unable to relax in the lift, and arrived at the flat only a little out of breath. Suzanna had left the door open as she always did and he walked in, calling to her.

'I'm in here!' she answered from the sitting-room. He walked through.

'Hello, Suzy.' Phillip stood in the door and looked at her. She was the most beautiful woman he had ever known, long-limbed and thin, her face and features, everything about her delicate almost to the point of frailty, but not quite. She stood, brushed her hair off her face, her wonderful thick dark hair, and smiled at him.

'I've missed you,' she said.

Within seconds he had crossed the room and swept her into his arms. It wasn't what he'd planned, he knew he had to stay calm, aloof, but he couldn't stop himself.

'Jesus, Suzy, I've missed you too!' He hugged her in tight, his eyes closed, the smell of her, the feel of her overpowered him. 'You feel so good . . . You . . .' He kissed her hair. 'You smell incredible.'

She pulled back and laughed. 'Do I? Do I really?'

Phillip saw the doubt on her face despite the laughter. 'Yes, you do.' He pulled her in to his body again and found her mouth. He hadn't wanted to touch her, he'd thought that he could do it without getting close, without complicating things. As she kissed him, as their bodies melted together he thought what a fool he'd been, things were complicated, they always had been.

Suzy ran her hands up under his jacket along the taut muscle of his back and opened her mouth to him, darting her tongue across his lips, gently biting him. He moaned and held the hem of her dress, pulling it up over her hips. 'My God . . . Suzy . . .' The feel of her naked body pressed against his clothes incited him. Holding her buttocks, he lifted her and she clenched her legs around his hips, all the time their mouths locked together. He manoeuvred her over to the sofa and leant her back so that she was perched half on, half off the edge. He eased himself away just far enough to unfasten his trousers, his fingers fumbling with the belt, his heart pounding and with his other hand he ripped the neck of her dress, the sharp tearing sound, the sudden violence of it making her jump. He shunted his body into place and bent his head, tearing his mouth away from hers, down to her breasts and she moaned, murmuring his name over and over again. He felt as if the moment would go on for ever. Then, gripping her hips, he pulled back, he looked at her face, at her eyes half closed, her mouth parted, the lips swollen, and he said, 'I love you, Suzy, I love you so much.' But it was the faintest whisper. He had lost the words, lost all thought, all reason, everything except her. He took her then, thinking that nothing else mattered, unable to stop himself, caught up in a physical power he neither wanted nor understood.

Later, lying next to him, both of them naked, Suzy trailed her finger along the entire length of Phillip's torso, from the hollow of his neck to the ridge of muscle between his hips. She felt him shiver and watched his face. His eyelids fluttered but he didn't open his eyes. She was chilly, she could do with a drink, she thought, just a quick sip of vodka to warm her up, provided he was asleep. So, carefully moving her head, she eased her body away from his and sat up, slowly standing so as not to disturb him. She padded naked through to the kitchen, found the bottle and took her cup from the sink, filling it. She swallowed down the contents, half filled it again and quickly drank that. Then she put the bottle away and went back to Phillip. He was awake as she sank down again next to him.

'We'd better get dressed,' he said, reaching out and stroking the smooth skin on her shoulder. 'I can't stay too long.'

'You can't?' Her voice was instantly panicky and he regretted his carelessness.

'You have to get back to Mitchell,' he said. 'You don't want him to know where you've been, do you?'

She shook her head. 'No, but . . .'

Phillip smiled and knelt up. 'But what?' He leant forward and nuzzled her neck. It was always the same, once he'd touched her he found he couldn't leave her body alone, she excited him so much that he had to keep on, stroking her, caressing her, making contact.

'I got a bottle of champagne,' Suzy said, 'and some smoked salmon, some beluga.'

Phillip sat back. He looked at her face, turned away from him, her lip trembling slightly, and cursed himself. Christ he'd been an idiot, he should've seen this coming! He should have left her alone, come in, said what he had to and gone. He should never have touched her. God, why did he always have to touch her. He took a breath and tried to think it through.

'I've been so miserable,' she said hoarsely, 'I've missed you so much, I thought maybe we could spend some time together, I thought you wanted to see me.' She bit her finger nail hard, making him wince.

'Suzy, I did want to see you, I do want to see you, all the time.'

She glanced up. 'Really?'

'Yes, really.' He stood and took up his trousers and underwear, quickly pulling them on. He had almost forgotten why he'd come, for a few moments back there he had imagined that it was all going to be perfectly all right. He swallowed down the tension that had started again in his stomach and said, 'Why not open the champagne. We can have a glass or two, can't we?'

She nodded, her face brightening. She got to her feet

and reached down for her dress. There was a time when she wouldn't have bothered, when they both spent the whole time naked, making love whenever they wanted to, wherever they wanted to. She pulled it over her head, pulling at the ripped neck, reaching for a safety pin from the drawer to pin it up and cover her chest. 'D'you want something to eat?' she called as she went into the kitchen. 'Shall I open the caviar?'

'Yes, do!' Phillip answered as he fastened his cufflinks. He didn't feel at all like eating, he felt sick.

Suzy came back with a tray and left the bottle for Phillip to open while she arranged the dry toast and caviar. He popped the cork, filled two flutes and handed one across to her. She was sitting back on her heels, watching him as he passed her the glass.

'This is nice,' she said, holding her glass up. 'Like old times.'

Phillip nodded and raised his glass.

'To us.' Suzy toasted.

'Yes.' Phillip gulped down a mouthful of champagne. He could feel his stomach churning as the wine hit the nervous acid in there. 'Suzy?'

'Hmmm.' She had taken two cigarettes from the packet on the sofa table and put them in her mouth. She leant forward for her lighter.

'Suzy, I need to tell you something,' he said. She handed him a lit cigarette and he took it, not really wanting to smoke.

'Yes?' She smiled at him, vaguely content, for the first time since he had walked out of the flat six weeks ago.

'Suzy, I have found a way for us to be together, long-term I mean, for ever . . .' He broke off to swallow, his mouth suddenly dry and saw that Suzy was staring at him, her face registering disbelief. She sat perfectly still, hardly daring to breathe and he could see the brightness in her eyes, the excitement, the beginning of tears. He gripped the stem of the glass.

'It's weird, it's an odd way out but it's perfect, Suzy, it'll mean we're safe.' He had started to speak more quickly, needing to convince her, to convince himself almost. 'No one would ever bother us, we'd have the perfect alibi and, besides, I'd have the cover of the palace, the safety of my reputation.' He stopped, the tightness in his chest making him slightly breathless. Suzanna was still staring but her face had changed, her colour had drained and her eyes were hard, hard and frightened.

'The palace?' Her voice cracked and she had to cough to clear her throat. She swallowed down most of her glass of champagne and reached for the bottle.

'I've been appointed personal secretary to the duke,' Phillip said quietly. 'The announcement will be made next week.'

She started and her hand jerked, sloshing the champagne over the table. She continued to fill her glass, letting the wine spill over the top. 'Congratulations,' she said. She sat back on her heels and took a swig of champagne. Her hand was trembling. 'How nice for you.' She hadn't meant it to sound so harsh and dry but she couldn't help herself. The fact that he hadn't told her was like a physical blow. She willed herself to stay together.

'I'm sorry, I should have told you.' Phillip couldn't bear to see the pain on her face and he hung his head. 'Suzy, look, I don't know how to tell you this but I want you to try and understand it for what it is.' He raised his head slightly and saw that she was staring at him, her face seemed almost paralysed in its expression. 'It's something that sounds awful but it isn't, it's our way out, our chance.' He stopped a third time, the dryness in his throat now painful. 'Suzy, I'm getting married,' he said quickly. 'I need a wife for my appointment to the duke and I've found someone who's prepared to take me and the job on.' He paused momentarily, then rushed on, frightened to stop talking. 'I know it sounds bizarre, I know it sounds as if I'm deserting you, as if it's over between us, but it isn't! It's just the beginning, Suzy! You must understand that, it's the freedom we need, Suzy, the perfect alibi: me, married, a family man! Who'd ever expect . . .' He broke off, waiting for her response, bracing himself for the torrent of emotion. He looked up and saw that she was still, completely motionless. Then silently she stood up, gripping the edge of the sofa to steady herself and walked into the kitchen. She grabbed the bottle of vodka, almost letting it drop, her hands felt so numb, and she unscrewed the top, slugging a great mouthful down from the bottle. She wiped her mouth on her sleeve and held onto the sideboard for support.

'Suzanna?' Phillip stood in the doorway. He moved towards her. 'Suzy, please?'

'Don't you come near me!' she screamed, suddenly swinging round and lashing out, the bottle in her hand. Phillip leapt back. 'Don't you dare come near me!' Her face crumpled and she started to sob.

'Suzy, please don't cry, please don't . . .'

'Don't cry?' She wiped her face on the back of her hand. 'Don't cry? Don't say a word because I've got it all so neatly worked out and I don't want you to make a fuss!' She snorted derisively then dropped her head into her hands. 'Oh God, Phillip, how could you?' The pain in her voice cut him like a razor and he moved towards her again. He went to put his arms around her but she shoved him angrily away, knocking him back.

'Do you really expect me to believe all this crap? Do you?' She shook her finger at him, jabbing the space between them. 'Because I don't! I don't believe a fucking word of it, Phillip! A way out, a chance? For us? Bullshit! A way out for you! Yeah, sure!' She spat the words at him, making him wince at the force of her anger. 'And you know what really hurts?' She picked up the bottle of vodka from the side and stabbed the air with it. 'It's the fact that you couldn't come in here and tell me straight, you had to have your fuck, didn't you, Phillip? You had to have your last fill of me.' She pushed past him, smacking her side on the door frame. 'God, you make me sick!' she screamed from the sitting-room. 'You make me sick! D'you hear me? Sick!' She smacked the bottle of vodka down against the edge of the sofa table and suddenly it smashed, the glass shattering everywhere.

'Ahh! My God!' Her hands flew up to her face and Phillip realised in an instant that she'd been hit. Blood spurted out through her fingers and splattered over the white carpet.

'Suzanna!' He ran forward and grabbed her hands, tearing them away from her face. It was covered in blood and his heart flipped. 'Come here! Jesus, Suzy!' She was hysterical, he had to calm her down. 'Look, it's all right, Suzanna, it's all right. Come here, darling, come on!' He led her screaming into the kitchen and wrenched the cold tap on, all the time the fear pounding so hard in his body that his hands were shaking.

'Breathe, Suzy, breathe!' She was hyper-ventilating and the blood was pouring from her face. His shirt was covered in it. 'Breathe deeply, come on!' He drenched a towel in cold water and pressed it up to her cheek. 'Come on, Suzy, it's all right, it's all right.' He kept saying this over and over as he rinsed the towel time after time and reapplied it. 'It's all right, my darling, I'm here, I won't leave you, I promise . . .'

The flow of blood started to ease. Suzanna was calmer, the hiccupping of her sobs quieter, less frequent. She held one of his hands so tight that it was white but she kept her face still as Phillip looked at it and examined the cut. She would need stitches, it was a cut to the right of her eye but the bleeding had been deceptive; it wasn't as bad as he had originally thought. Pressing the towel to her face for the last time, Phillip led her out of the kitchen and into the sitting-room. He sat, helping her down beside him.

'You OK?'

She managed to nod. He still held her hand and he put it up to his mouth, kissing the bloodless knuckles. 'Christ, you scared me,' he said quietly. 'I couldn't bear it if anything happened to . . .' He stopped as a warm drop of water fell on to his hand. 'Oh Suzy, please, please don't cry.'

'But you love me,' she whispered, 'I know you do.'

'Yes, yes I love you,' he said, 'I always have, from the first time I met you, remember? At Cowdray Park? You were with Mitchell, newly married and you looked so unhappy, so beautiful and unhappy and it made my heart ache just looking at you.'

Suzy sniffed and Phillip took his handkerchief from his pocket, carefully drying her eyes. 'I will always love you, Suzy. You need me, I won't ever leave you.'

'But you have . . . You . . .'

'No, I haven't left you!' He turned her face gently towards him. 'I promised you weeks ago that I would find a way out for us and I have. I'm not marrying someone I love, how could I do that? I love you! I am marrying Jane Bennet, a nice girl, twenty-seven, sensible and a friend. She isn't and never will be you. Please, Suzy, please understand that.' He took a breath, his own heart beginning to slow at last. 'My appointment to the duke's permanent staff is a huge achievement, Suzy, it's what I've always wanted. I'll be based in London, Jane will be in the country, and we can be together. What can Mitchell say? What can anyone say?' Phillip leant towards her and kissed her. 'Oh God, Suzy, trust me, please, just trust me.'

Suzanna hung her head. How could she doubt him? How could she even begin to live without him? Her life was a mess, she was married to a violent homosexual, a bitter mistake, done for the money and the only happiness she had ever known was with Phillip. She had to trust him, she had nothing else left.

'My eye,' she said. 'Do I need stitches?'

'Yes, I'll have to ring someone, you'll have to get to the hospital.'

'No! Phillip, please don't leave me! Take me to the hospital, you have to, I can't go on my own!' She started to cry again and Phillip rubbed his hands wearily over his face. He was running out of time and he was tired, exhausted from the emotional strain. 'Can I phone Poppy?'

Suzy was silent.

'I can't take you to casualty, Suzy. What about Mitchell? It might even make the papers. Be sensible please.'

'Like Jane?'

Phillip bit back an angry retort. 'Let me call Poppy. Hmmm?' He said patiently, 'She'll take you, she can handle the press if there's anyone there.' Phillip stood. 'Poppy will look after you.'

'Yes, all right, Phillip.' Suzy sat back, resting her head against the sofa. She was drained of energy and she needed a drink. 'Phone Poppy then, her number's in my book.'

Phillip went to Suzy's bag and took out her book, then he crossed to the phone, glancing quickly at his watch as he did so; it was six-thirty. If Poppy could get here in half an hour and he could ring Jane from the box on the corner of Oxford Street then he might just be all right. If not, then God knows what he was going to say. He dialled Suzy's best friend and waited for the line to connect. It wasn't even as if he could go straight there, he thought, looking briefly down at his shirt, with this amount of blood he would have to bath and change first. He heard Poppy's voice and concentrated on the present, not the future. 'Hello, Poppy? It's Phillip Mills. I'm round at Suzy's flat, we've had a bit of an accident. Can you come over and help?' He listened to her reply and tried to keep the relief from his voice. 'Oh great, thanks, thanks a lot, Poppy. Yes, I'll wait for you.' He put his thumb up to Suzy but she hardly registered the gesture. 'Yes, see you in half an hour then.' He smiled as he hung up.

'Poppy's coming round,' he said, walking back to Suzy. 'She'll be here in a while.' But Suzanna didn't hear what he said. She had passed out.

*   *   *

Jane was in the bedroom when Clare called her from the sitting-room; she was finishing dressing. She went straight to the phone, a small frown of worry on her face, and said: 'Hello, are you all right, Phillip?' Then she smiled.

'No, of course not, I'm sure they won't mind!' She wrapped the telephone wire around her fingers. 'I'll ring them now and explain.' She paused. 'Honestly, it's fine! Now don't worry at all, Phillip, just get here when you can . . . and don't kill yourself in the rush! Yes, all right, see you then. Bye.' She hung up. 'Phillip's been held up,' she said, looking around for her bag. 'Poor dear, something at the palace. I'll just ring the Lythes and tell them we'll be late.' And, totally unfussed, she found it, took out her book and dialled her parents' friends.

Chapter Twelve

It was a glorious spring day, warm, with the lightest south-westerly breeze that came in off the Sussex coast and cooled the edges. The ancient wisteria that framed the back of the house rustled with the wind, its heavy lavender blooms drooping and scattering their tiny petals over the grass. The marquee stood in the centre of the second lawn, behind the box hedge, its high tented roof only visible over the top, a trail of white ribbons on sticks, white balloons and rich green ivy led down to it.

Jane sat in her room, her things packed for the trip to India, a mass of cases and bags, her suit hanging neatly on a padded hanger in front of the wardrobe and half her hair in curlers. She listened to the hairdresser's prattle as she unclipped and unravelled without taking any of it in and watched Clare put the final touches to her own silk-suited appearance. She wasn't nervous or excited even, she was simply longing for it all to be over, for a deep hot bath at the hotel tonight, and a tumbler full of single malt.

'Gosh!' Clare turned away from her own reflection in the dressing-table mirror and stared at Jane. 'That does look, erm . . .' She stopped and coughed. 'It looks really something, Janey.'

Jane narrowed her eyes. She couldn't see herself but she'd had her doubts when the curlers began to come out. 'What does something mean?'

Clare shrugged and glanced away. Jane immediately stood up and marched across to the mirror. 'Oh no!' She pulled at a tightly curled strand of hair and it bounced right back into position. 'Oh dear Lord!' The whole effect was frightful. 'I'm terribly sorry,' she said, turning towards the hairdresser, 'but I'm afraid I'll have to wash this out.'

'Oh, Janey, no!' Clare darted around her, patting bits of her hair into place. 'There isn't time! You have to be ready in twenty minutes.'

'Don't worry, I will be!' Jane started for the door. 'I should never have listened to you and Mummy,' she said, taking the towel off her shoulders and chucking it on to the bed. 'I'll be back in a minute.' And she left the room with Clare and the hairdresser speechless behind her.

John Bennet slammed the door of the car and smiled at Caroline and Clare inside. He tapped the roof and the driver swung the old Jaguar round, its wheels crunching on the gravel drive. He tipped his cap and the car drove off. What a different affair this was from Clare and Teddy's wedding, he thought, nodding to one of the caterers carrying a case of champagne round to the marquee, an altogether much quieter and understated nuptial.

He walked into the house, dark after the bright sunshine outside, and wandered through to the sitting-room, decked with May blossom and early huge white old-fashioned roses, their scents mixed with the smell of beeswax polish and pot-pourri. He sat on the edge of the sofa and looked at the photograph of Jane on the piano, Jane as a young girl, always his favourite and so like him that he could honestly say it never bothered him not having a son. He wondered if he should give her a shout, she was late and probably up there reading, or doing a quick sketch of the marquee from her bedroom window. He smiled to himself and slowly got to his feet.

'Jane!' As he turned he saw her and he stood looking at her for a few moments, one hand resting against the doorframe, her tall slim figure neat in the pale cream silk suit and matching shoes, her hair tied back off her face in its usual loose pony tail and the only adornment her bouquet, a bunch she had tied herself from the garden.

'You look beautiful, Janey,' he said.

She smiled. 'Thank you.' She came across to him and took his arm. 'I look nice, Daddy, better than usual,' she said, her eyes laughing up at him, 'but never beautiful.'

He bent and kissed her cheek. 'You always have been and always will be beautiful to me, Jane,' he said quietly, 'because I love you.' He saw her look away quickly and he touched her hand on his arm. 'Are you ready?'

'Yes.' She put her finger up to her eye and wiped away the beginning of a tear. 'Yes, I'm ready.'

'Good.' But John stood where he was for a moment

as if deciding on something. Then taking Jane's hand, he held it and faced her. 'Janey, are you absolutely sure about this?'

Jane looked at him, at the concern in his eyes. 'Yes,' she answered, 'I am sure.'

He nodded but still didn't move. After a few moments he said, 'Jane, I want you to understand that if ever anything goes wrong, if ever you need me, I will be here for you.'

She lowered her eyes.

'You will remember that, won't you?'

Finally she faced him. 'Yes, I will always remember that,' she said. 'Thank you.'

He took the hand he was holding and placed it back on his arm. 'Let's go then.' He smiled, proud of her, and they walked towards the door. As they stepped outside into the bright summer sunshine the caterers, marquee people and flower arrangers all broke into a round of applause.

'Thank you, thank you so much!' John held the door of the car open for her and Jane waved, smiling and laughing at the fuss, as she climbed inside. She wound down the window and waved again while her father climbed in beside her and patted her knee.

'To the church then,' he said.

'Yes.' Jane held her bouquet up to her nose and breathed in the scent of the flowers. 'To the church.' The car pulled off and Jane went to her wedding, followed by cheers and cries of good luck.

Suzanna Harvey sat in the Bentley with Mitchell by her side. It was early on Saturday morning and they had just left their country house in Wiltshire for a lunch party in Wimbledon. It was warm, there was a high over the whole country and most of the last week had been in the high sixties. Suzy wore her Hardy Amies sleeveless dress and bolero jacket, the dress was cut low and the jacket had three-quarter sleeves. It wasn't one of her favourite outfits but Mitchell had asked her specifically to wear it, though God knows why, she thought as she glanced down at it, the colour didn't really suit her and he'd never taken any interest in her clothes before. She looked from the dress to the window and stared out at the view. It was so early that the mist still clung to the hills and valleys and the sky was leaden with the expectation of morning. Suzy stifled a yawn and shifted away from Mitchell as he opened the morning's newspaper and folded it on to the page that he wanted.

'Suzanna?'

She continued to stare out of the window. 'Yes?'

'Suzy, I have a small gift for you,' Mitchell said as he bent and took a box out of his briefcase by his feet. Suzy watched him out of the corner of her eye but didn't turn her head away from the window.

'Here.'

She held out her hand, only slightly turning to look at him. 'Thank you,' she said.

'Aren't you going to open it?' His voice had a steely edge to it and she felt her insides recoil.

'Yes, yes of course.' Taking the small dark leather box, she lifted the top and saw the Asprey's name and crest in gold on the padded silk. She looked down. 'It's lovely, Mitchell,' she said flatly, taking the pearl choker out and holding it up. It was three ropes of large uncultured pearls, almost pink in colour with a ruby and diamond clasp.

'There's something else.' Mitchell bent across and lifted the top tier of the box. Underneath were the same three ropes of pearls and clasp but cut to fit her wrist. He motioned for her arm. 'Here, let me help you with it.'

She held out her wrist and watched Mitchell's long wrinkled fingers, his gnarled knuckles fiddle with the pearls. He fastened the bracelet and said, 'Lean forward, dear, let me do the choker as well.' She did as he asked and let him finger her neck, admiring his taste. So this was why he'd chosen the outfit; to show off his gifts. She shuddered.

'You've been a good girl, Suzanna,' he said, smiling. 'I'm pleased with you.' He took the paper up and handed it across to her, a small high giggle escaping him as he did so. 'I expect you've already seen this?'

Suzy took *The Times* and glanced down at the page Mitchell had marked. She started, holding the paper tightly between her fingers. She held her breath, the nails of her other hand digging hard into the leather of the seat. 'Yes,' she said, 'I have.' The pain was so intense that she wondered if she was going to faint. She let her breath go and refilled her lungs. She would be all right, she had to be all right.

'It's a lovely shot, isn't it?' Mitchell leant towards her and looked at the photograph of Jane and Phillip running through a shower of rose petals outside the Church of St Michael in West Sommerton, West Sussex, as the duke and several other members of the House of Lords looked on. 'So natural, so happy . . .'

Suzy swallowed back the nausea that rose in her throat. 'Yes,' she managed to say, 'it is.'

Mitchell smiled again and touched the pearls at her neck. 'Good girl,' he said, 'I knew you'd agree with me.' And as he let his fingers drop away from her throat and turned towards the window Suzanna thought for a moment his present would choke her. But that was exactly the way he had meant her to feel.

Chapter Thirteen

Shiva Rai stood at the long carved teak wood desk in his study and waited for the operator to connect his line to Bombay. He was motionless, staring out at the profusion of green, the vivid purple of the jacaranda and the burning red and orange of the flame trees, ablaze in the early morning sun. He waited. He was close now, closer than he had ever dared believe he would be and the bitterness, the acrid taste of revenge was heavy on his tongue. So much time, too much had passed; it had taken a lifetime, too long. He sighed. If things had been different, if his son had lived, had not been cut down in his youth struggling for Independence, if . . . Shiva turned away from the garden. No more if, no more waiting. The gods had smiled on him and at last he had been given his chance. His lifetime's chance.

The line rang and Shiva picked the receiver up. He listened for a few moments and then said, 'Good, I will be ready for them.' He smiled, the briefest and most chilling of smiles and hung up. He rang for his secretary.

'Shekhai, you can tell my grandson to come in now.'

He remained standing at the desk, one hand resting on the edge, the other folded inside the opening of his *kurta*, between the third and fifth pearl buttons. He was a tall man, tall and heavy, his jet black hair smoothed back off his face and oiled with a hair oil he had specially prepared for him in Bombay; it smelled of jasmine and sandalwood. On the last finger of his left hand he wore a ring, gold, worked to resemble the head of a serpent and set with rubies and diamonds. It was a beautiful piece, intricately set with the finest stones from Agra and it signified power, the power of the man.

Ramesh Rai had been sitting outside his grandfather's study in silence. The corridor was dark, the polished, cool, grey marble floor like glass, the walls of white silk as flat and smooth as the floor. He sat and stared at the collection of paintings, the same works he had sat and looked at as a boy, ten in all, small elaborate images, worked on silk and telling the stories of the men in his family, his own father's life and heroic death, the history of his inheritance. He followed the fortunes of his family in the paintings, a family ruined once, only to go on to recover its fortunes, a brave, independent family, a family of honour and as he sat there he felt like a child again, waiting to be called by Shiva, waiting for the few moments with his grandfather. He started as Shekhai came out and stood, fastening the buttons on his jacket, straightening his tie. He had lived his life in awe of his grandfather and now, at twenty-five, it was still no different.

'Please, Shivaji is ready for you, Ramesh.' Shekhai bowed and indicated for Rami to go in. Rami bowed as well and, standing erect, he walked into his grandfather's study.

'*Namaste*, Ramesh.' Shiva stepped forward but did not remove the hand from his *kurta* or make any attempt to embrace his grandson. Rami pressed his hands together and bowed his head.

'Grandfather.' He walked across the room and bent to touch Shiva's feet, the customary sign of respect. Then he stood and smiled.

'I have missed you and I have missed India, Dadaji.'

Shiva nodded, patting his grandson on the back and placing an arm around his shoulder. 'Please, let us sit.' They moved towards the low silk-covered divan. 'You look well, Rami, we are glad to have you home.' At last Shiva smiled. 'It is a very good suit you are wearing.' Shiva fingered the cloth of Rami's jacket and Rami smiled proudly. 'But,' Shiva said, dropping his hand away, 'it is not Indian. We must get you some Indian clothes, Ramesh. I will telephone the tailor.'

Rami nodded, disappointed already at the way the meeting was going. He had wanted praise and affection, he had always wanted those things but he had never got them, not from Shiva. 'So,' Shiva sat on the divan and crossed his ankles, pulling his legs up under him. 'You have done well, Ramesh, your mother and sisters are very proud of you. You liked London? It is a lively city, yes?'

'Yes, yes it is.' Rami hesitated. He found, having spoken English for so long now, that he was having trouble with his Hindi. He flushed as Shiva frowned and said coldly, 'Have you forgotten your native tongue, Ramesh?'

'No! No of course not, Dadaji, it's just that I . . .' He broke off as Shiva turned his attention to some papers on the table at his side. Shiva never listened to excuses. Rami folded his hands in his lap and waited for his grandfather to finish. It was hardly unimaginable that he should be a little out of practice speaking Hindustani, he thought, he had been in England for six years now, with only a short break each summer at home. Oxford, then Lancaster Gate, the job at Whitfield, Stacy, Chance; it was Shiva's idea in the first place, to train him up for the business. Rami turned to look out of the window at the gardens. He had never understood his grandfather, never felt anything but frustration and remorse at not being able to please him, but he had hoped, in his long absence, that things might in some way have changed. He was wrong.

'Ramesh, I wanted to speak to you this morning,' Shiva said, placing the last paper in the file, 'because I have something that I want you to do.' He looked up at his grandson. 'Your excellent English will be most beneficial.' The sarcasm in his voice was humourless and Rami turned away for as long as he dared to cover his exasperation. His spirits sank.

'The maharajah has some guests arriving at the palace bungalow this afternoon, Ramesh, an English couple, Major and Mrs Mills.' Rami turned back. 'The maharajah decided earlier this year that he needed some professional advice on the security arrangements for his wedding. He contacted the Duke of Cumberland who sent out Major Mills, his personal equerry.'

'That's right! Viki said something about it the other day, he—' Rami stopped as Shiva raised an eyebrow. The royal family were always addressed by their titles not their first names; Shiva disapproved strongly of over-familiarisation.

'The maharajah said that Major Mills is bringing back his new wife. Is that right?'

'Yes, that is quite correct.' Shiva smiled. 'And that is where I would like your assistance, Ramesh.'

'I'm sorry?' Rami watched Shiva's face; it was cold and impassive. He had no idea of what was going on in his grandfather's mind.

'I would like you to offer your friendship and hospitality to Mrs Mills for a few weeks, look after her, Ramesh. She will be at odds in a new country and will probably feel homesick. You can show her the city, entertain her, relieve her boredom to some degree.' Shiva faced his grandson. 'Is there something the matter with this?'

Rami was silent. He averted his gaze but kept his face respectfully towards his grandfather. There was a great deal the matter with this. He had been expecting to be given a real job, to be included in the business not asked to be nursemaid to an Englishwoman. Rami could feel his grandfather's impatience, the force of Shiva's irritation made him reticent to say anything, but his disappointment fuelled him. He had been independent for a long time now, it was difficult to suddenly take on the mantle of his grandfather's wishes.

'Is this not a thing that my sister could do, Dadaji?'

Shiva uncrossed his legs and stood, walking away to the window to show his dissatisfaction. 'I am sorry. Do you have a problem with this, Ramesh? It is not suitable for your sister to do, it is what I want you to do, therefore I have asked you.'

'Yes I know, but I had thought . . .' Rami stopped. He

was talking to Shiva's back and suddenly felt deflated. He may have lived in England, be qualified in English law but he was still an Indian son; it was a question of respect. 'I will visit these people tomorrow,' Rami said quietly.

Shiva turned and smiled for only the second time at his grandson. 'Good, it is settled then.' He came back to the divan. 'I think that is all for now, Ramesh,' he said. Rami stood; he had been dismissed.

'Will you be in for dinner, Grandfather?'

Shiva walked across to the desk and glanced down at his diary, open at the day's page and marked with a slither of silk. 'No, not tonight, Ramesh, I have an appointment. But tomorrow.' He looked up. 'I will be here tomorrow night and you must invite the Mills for drinks at the club, as our guests.'

'Yes, fine.' There was never any time for the family, always meetings, appointments, drinks with guests. Rami folded his palms before turning towards the door. '*Namaste*, Dadaji,' he bowed his head and walked across the room.

'Ramesh?'

Rami glanced back.

'Your father would have been proud of you,' Shiva said.

'Thank you.' Once more he bowed and then silently he left the room. My father would have been proud, Rami thought, but never you, and, removing his tie along with his jacket, he went in search of his mother and the easy, idle chatter of his sisters.

Phillip had hold of Jane's arm as he steered her aggressively through the crowd. He was hot, confused and very irritated. He gripped her elbow, his fingers pinching her bare skin and she clutched her handbag tightly to her chest as he'd told her to do, looking from right to left, mesmerised by the noise, the animation and colour of India. She wasn't watching where she was going.

'Mind your step, Jane!' Phillip tripped badly behind her and swore at a small group of men squatting on the ground, still pinching her elbow. 'Bloody place! Jesus!' Again, he stumbled and yanked on Jane's arm as he did so. 'Christ! These bloody people! It's a bloody mad house! Where the hell is that man from the palace? The maharajah . . .'

'Major Mills! Major Mills!'

Phillip stopped and put his hand up to his eyes. He was sweating profusely and the underarm of his shirt was saturated. He had begun to smell. 'Did you hear that Jane? Where . . . ?'

'Please! Major Mills! Over here!'

It was the final leg of their journey and they were changing platforms for the last train that day to Baijur. Phillip darted his eyes over the station, heaving with bodies, bicycles, baggage, live chickens and hens in baskets, produce, great sacks of grain and boxes of vegetables and saw, much to his amazement, an elderly Indian gentleman dressed in a baggy cream linen suit standing three feet above all of this on a pile of boxes stacked up on top of each other and about to topple. He waved his arms about frantically and as soon as Phillip spotted him, he threw his own arms up in the air and shouted, 'We're over here!' He shut his eyes and waited for the crash but nothing came. 'This way, Janey!' he said with relief and wiped his face with his handkerchief.

'Not before time.' He took her arm again. 'You'll have to get used to this.' He steered her once more through the throng of people as she smiled back at the mass of Indian faces grinning at her. 'This is India,' he finished crossly although she couldn't really see what all his fuss was about. 'Nothing ever goes right.'

'Oh my God! Major Mills Sahib! Oh thank God for that! And Mrs Mills! Oh what relief! I have been looking for the last hour and was thinking that I had lost you both!' The small Indian reached them, smiling and wringing his hands and had said all this before he actually stopped. He took off a battered old panama with the Ghurka colours on the band. 'This is a great pleasure, Mrs Mills, Major Sahib. Dr Bodi Yadav, at your great service.' Then he folded his palms together and bowed his head.

Jane smiled, her widest and most spontaneous smile and held out her hand. 'How lovely to meet you, Dr Yadav.'

'Oh, madam, a pleasure to meet you as well!'

Phillip looked on, keeping his own hand by his side; he never shook with the natives if he could help it.

'I have a porter, Major Sahib, over here. Please, this way. Your baggage? It is with the station master?'

'No, it's with a porter on the platform that we came in on. I was trying to locate someone before we moved it. You can go back for it when we get to the train.'

Jane winced. She saw Dr Yadav flare his nostrils but he kept his face indifferent. She had never seen Phillip behave like this. It must be the heat, she thought, removing his hand from her elbow, and the travel, he was tired, exhausted probably.

They followed the Indian across the station, up a flight of steps and on to a rickety ironwork bridge that swung as they crossed it. They walked over to the other platform, Jane noticing that few Indians did the same, most preferring to take the easy route across the rails and up on to the train. They walked the length of the locomotive to the end, to the last carriage where already a small crowd had formed expecting to see someone important.

'We have taken the whole carriage,' Doctor Yadav said, as the door was opened for them, 'so that you will not be bothered.'

Phillip nodded and made way for Jane to climb on board, but she hung back for a few moments. 'You go on, Phillip,' she said, glancing up at the pristine first class carriage, 'I'll follow in a few moments.' Phillip raised an eyebrow and Jane saw a distinct flash of irritation cross his face but she ignored it. She wanted to look back at the train already laden with people and what looked like the entire contents of their lives, she wanted a couple of minutes to enjoy the wonderful chaos of the station, the noise, the colours, the smells. She noticed Dr Yadav on her right and said, 'It seems like the whole of India is travelling from this station.'

He smiled. 'Wherever you go in this country it feels like that. You always have the whole of India with you.' Then he laughed, a short, round chuckle and Jane knew that she liked him. 'Most Europeans are hating it,' he said. 'What do you think, Mrs Mills?'

'Me?' Jane turned away from the noise, from the people crowding into carriages, squeezing in baskets with chickens squawking and passing up shouting, wriggling children. 'I think it's wonderful,' she answered, 'But for God's sake don't ask me why.' They both smiled.

'Shall we?' He motioned for her to climb into the carriage.

'The luggage?'

'It is taken care of.'

'But?' Jane hadn't even seen him look away for a moment, how on earth had he organised the luggage? She turned to him, puzzled, but he simply smiled and tipped his hat.

'After you, Mrs Mills, please.'

Jane climbed up the three steps and went on into the carriage where Phillip had already seated himself and was reading a three-day-old copy of *The Times*. 'Ah, Jane!' He glanced at her over the top of his paper. 'All right?'

'Yes, thank you, Phillip.' She sat down, placing her bag on the floor and looked behind her at Dr Yadav. 'What time does the train pull out?'

The doctor felt in his top pocket and pulled on his gold watch chain, lifting a large round watch from his waistcoat. 'Ten minutes ago,' he said, perfectly seriously.

Jane laughed. She leant her head forward to the window, straining to see out then said, 'Does this open?'

'Yes, please, allow me, Mrs Mills.'

'Oh, thank you.' Jane moved back while Dr Yadav yanked the window down, letting in a rush of warm air and the noise and smell of the station. Phillip tutted and lowered *The Times*. 'Janey, really!'

'Sorry, Phillip.' Jane went to lift the window again but couldn't. 'Oh dear, it appears to be stuck.'

'Typical! Dr Yadav? Would you be so kind as to help my wife.'

Jane flushed but Dr Yadav ignored Phillip's tone and stepped forward a second time. 'Please move to the side,

Mrs Mills.' He placed both hands on the window lever ready to tug. 'Goodness me! It is a very stubborn thing, oh dear . . .' He lost his balance momentarily as the train jerked into life, then all of a sudden fell backwards into Jane. 'Oh goodness! Mrs Mills, please, oh my God! Are you all right, dear lady?'

Jane managed to right them both, holding the profoundly apologetic Dr Yadav from the back in a sort of bear hug. She started to laugh. 'Yes I'm fine. Hey, the train's moving, isn't it?'

'Yes, here, please to have a look!' The doctor moved away and Jane hurried forward, sticking her head out of the window. She stared behind her at the rest of the train, packed with bodies, hanging on to the doors, sitting on the roof, leaning out of windows and all waving, smiling and shouting as the train left the station. 'My God! It's . . .' Jane darted her head back in again, her face already dotted with grit. 'Phillip! Come and look at this! I've never seen anything like it!'

But Phillip really was too tired. He lifted his paper and ignored his wife's behaviour. Jane sighed and went back to the sight, waving, herself, at the people behind her. She hung out of the window for several kilometres down the track, waving both arms and smiling and finally came back into the carriage some way away from the station. Her face was streaked and smeared with dirt and grime.

'Oh Lord, Janey!' Phillip let out an exasperated sigh, then attempted to cover his irritation with a smile. 'Here!' He handed her his handkerchief and she took it, spitting on it and then wiping her face. She saw Dr Yadav suppress a smile.

'Dr Yadav, is there a bathroom that I could use?'

'Yes, certainly. Please, Mrs Mills, please to be calling me Bodi, that is my first name.'

'Thank you, Bodi!' Jane flicked a look at Phillip and saw that he'd gone back to his paper. For the first time since she had met him, Jane experienced the slightest feeling of exasperation at Phillip. She decided to put it behind her. 'And you must call me Jane,' she replied to Bodi and saw the irritated rustle of *The Times* to note Phillip's disapproval.

It was a glorious morning, hot and fragrant with a cool breeze rustling the leaves on the flame trees every now and then and the sun dancing on the sprays of water from the fountains, sending up a rainbow of colours into the air. Jasmine scented the wind and rose petals were scattered over the grass. It was a rich, perfumed and gold-spun Indian day.

Jane woke early. She lifted the gauze of the mosquito net and climbed out of bed, walking barefoot to the carved sandalwood shutters that were closed over the French doors. She folded them back and stood in the brilliant sunlight, looking out over the white marbled terrace to the palace gardens beyond, to the sprays of the fountains just visible in the distance, sending jets of water high up into the azure blue sky. She rubbed her eyes, pulled on her robe and opened the doors, then she stepped out into the morning and smiled; she had never seen anything so beautiful.

'Good morning, Jane.'

She started and looked to the right. Phillip was lounging on a cane sofa in riding breeches and a shirt, drinking tea. He stood and came across to her, lightly kissing her cheek. 'Did you sleep well?'

168

'Yes, thank you, I did.' Phillip had decided on separate bedrooms. Jane had been disappointed but he had managed to convince her. He would be working long hours, he said, and with the unbearable heat, his difficulty sleeping and his snoring, he thought it was better all round to sleep separately, just sleep, of course. In the end he had convinced her; she was still disillusioned though.

Moving out on to the terrace, Jane glanced at his attire. 'Have you been riding?'

'No, not yet. I'm off in a few minutes with the maharajah. He wants me to try out one or two of his new ponies.' Phillip looked at his watch. 'Would you like tea? I can ring for some before I go.'

'No, I think I'll dress first. You get off.' Jane put her hand on his shoulder and smoothed the crisp cotton of his shirt. 'Are you back for lunch?'

'Yes, hopefully. Around one?'

'Good, I'll see you then.'

Phillip went across to the small cane table and finished the last of his tea. He took a handful of sugar lumps from the bowl and wrapped them in a napkin. 'Not for me,' he said.

Jane laughed. 'I hope not.' She watched him straighten and smooth his hair back. '*Au revoir*,' he called, heading down the steps of the verandah and out into the sunshine. The sheen of his boots was so high that they gleamed in the sunlight.

'Have a good morning!' Jane noticed how well the jodhpurs suited him, the tight muscular shape of his buttocks clearly visible as he strode off. He disappeared from view and she turned back towards her room. It was good to see him back on form, she was relieved that this was the Phillip she knew and had married.

Ramesh Rai had been drinking coffee with the maharajah on the terrace of the palace, discussing the two new polo ponies he had just bought from Argentina, when he saw the figure of Major Mills in the distance, walking through the palace gardens and up towards the terrace. He stood and called out to Vikrem who had gone in to change.

'The major is here, Viki!'

The maharajah came out, fastening the top button on his polo shirt and carrying his hat. 'Thank you, Rami. Are you sure you won't join us?'

'No, thanks, but I have something I must do for my grandfather.' Rami held down an irritated sigh; he would have loved a ride.

'Phillip!' The young maharajah walked towards the steps of the terrace as Phillip came up. They shook hands and Viki turned to Ramesh. 'Phillip, this is an old friend of mine, Ramesh Rai. His family have been associated with mine for many, many years. Major Phillip Mills, Ramesh Rai.'

Phillip nodded, but as Rami stepped forward he was obliged to shake hands. 'Pleased to meet you,' he said without warmth.

'And you, major.'

Viki smiled, his usual broad grin. 'Rami and I were at the same college at Oxford, Phillip.'

Phillip nodded. He wasn't the slightest bit interested in Ramesh Rai. 'Really?' He looked over Rami's head.

'Of course Rami gained a much better degree than me but then I was only there for the women and the alcohol!'

Viki laughed and patted Rami on the back. 'Come, Phillip, shall we make tracks?'

'Yes, of course.'

Rami held out his hand again but as the maharajah had turned away Phillip ignored it, pretending he didn't see it. There was something about educated upper class Indians that really got up his nose.

'See you later, Rami, eh?'

'Yes. Have a good ride!'

The maharajah led the way across the terrace and Rami watched them go, the heels of two pairs of long riding boots clicking smartly on the marble. He went to dig his hands in the pockets of his jacket and realised he was wearing a *kurta*, the long Indian tunic worn over *churidar*, loose trousers. He smiled and shook his head. Once an Indian, always an Indian, he thought, despite too long in England. And he walked down the steps towards the gardens and the palace bungalow, in search of Mrs Mills.

Unpacking took far less time than Jane had thought it would. Unused to help, she trailed the ayah around the room for an hour or so trying to do her bit and then realised she was only in the way. She gave directions as to where things should be put with hand actions and much pointing and decided to leave the girl alone. Putting on her straw sunhat and a pair of dark glasses, she slipped her phrase book into the pocket of her skirt and set off for a tour of the garden. She didn't know what else to do with her time.

An hour later, Jane took off her hat and scratched her head. She had got rather hot under the straw and her scalp had begun to itch. Dropping it on to the ground, she turned back to her phrase book and held one of the drooping rose heads in her hand. A sweat had broken out on her upper lip with the effort of it all.

'Greenfly,' she said to the head *mali* and the two other gardeners that stood with him. 'It's riddled with bugs.' She pointed to the brown patches on the leaves and the tiny almost invisible fly, then she thumbed the pages of her book frantically searching for the right word. 'Bad!' she announced, shaking her head and wagging her finger. 'Very bad!' The head *mali* nodded and smiled. 'Oh dear Lord,' Jane muttered. She found the word for fly, aviation and tried that. '*Ud na.*' The gardeners tittered.

'You . . . need . . . to . . . treat . . . it . . .' she said slowly and carefully but all three faces stared blankly at her. She felt near to tears with the sheer frustration of it, she'd been here for nearly an hour, trying to explain in the heat of the midday sun and she wished she'd never opened her mouth in the first place. She searched the book a last time and wiped her damp face on the corner of her skirt, lifting it up and showing her knees. She flushed, realising what she'd done and saw the hasty glances of all three men. 'Oh God,' she murmured, 'three randy gardeners is all I need.'

'Hello.' She instantly looked up from the book.

'Er, Mrs Mills? Hello? Over here!'

She turned, overwhelmed to hear an English voice. 'Oh! Yes, I, erm . . .'

'Are you having a spot of bother?'

Jane stared at the man coming towards her. He was in Indian dress, dark grey silk *kurta* and white cotton trousers and he was smiling.

'You're Indian!'

'Yes, well the last time I looked, I believe I was.' He was laughing at her and she blushed. Her face, already pink from the sun, turned an angry red. 'I'm sorry, I meant that you didn't sound, erm . . .' She held out her hand. 'Jane Mills,' she said and smiled. 'I didn't mean any offence.'

'No offence taken, Mrs Mills.'

Jane stared for a few moments at the man's face. It was an extraordinary face, she thought briefly, cool and classic as if someone had chiselled the features from dark brown sandstone and then, he smiled; it came alive when he smiled. 'Jane,' she said quickly, 'please call me Jane.'

'Thank you, I will.. Ramesh Rai.' He still held her hand. 'Please, call me Mr Rai.' Suddenly Jane burst out laughing and Rami decided almost immediately that he liked her. 'Rami,' he said, 'my friends call me Rami.'

Jane's laughter died away but she stood smiling at him. 'Nice to meet you, Rami.'

'The pleasure is all mine, Jane.' He glanced down and realised he was still holding her hand, a long, elegant, strong hand. He let the fingers go slowly, reluctantly and she dropped her arm by her side. 'You were having a bit of trouble?'

'Oh! Yes, I . . .' Jane glanced to her right and saw all three gardeners absorbed in the scene in front of them. She blushed a second time. 'I was trying to tell them that the roses have greenfly.' She turned and took one of the flowers in her hand. 'Look, it's awful! And they need feeding, I have some wonderful stuff at home that my father uses, we developed it together, it's organic fertiliser, I could ask him to send some over and . . .' she stopped.

'And I do go on, I know. Roses are my specialist subject.' She smiled. 'Sorry.'

'Not at all, Jane.' Rami took the phrase book Jane was clutching and looked at it. He shook his head, smiling at it. 'Would you like me to explain all of this?'

'I don't know if it's worth it really.'

'Do you know how to treat greenfly?'

'Of course!'

'Then it's worth it. Roses are the maharanhi's passion, that's the maharajah's mother. Look, you explain, I'll translate.' He dropped the phrase book on the ground. 'Fire away.'

Jane hesitated, not quite sure if he was serious.

'Go on!' Rami spoke in Hindi to the head *mali* and he nodded, turning towards Jane. 'He's all yours!'

Jane smiled. 'OK then,' she said. 'Now the first thing about roses and greenfly,' she began, and Rami translated it. Together they went through Jane's lecture stage by stage, with the head *mali* nodding and smiling and the two under-gardeners hanging on every word.

'You know that really was very interesting,' Rami said, sitting on the verandah of the bungalow an hour later and sipping a *nimbupani*. 'I didn't realise there was so much to know about roses.' He smirked as he said it.

Jane turned to him. She had been watching the gardener in the far distance already carrying out some of her instructions regarding the greenfly. 'There's no need to be sarcastic, Mr Rai.' She smiled. 'Some people are very interested in roses.'

'But presumably they are all over sixty.'

'No!' Jane laughed as she protested and thought about

the advice given to her at the West Sommerton Water-colour Society on the subject of her roses. 'Well, yes, all right then, perhaps it is mainly the older generation but . . .' She stopped. 'What's so funny?'

'You are!'

'I am?' Jane had started to laugh as well now, not for any reason but because Rami's chuckle was infectious. 'Why am I?'

'Why are you what?'

Suddenly Jane sat up and turned. 'Oh, Phillip!' For a moment she felt intensely guilty and then she thought: what on earth for? She stood, smiling again and said, 'Phillip, this is Ramesh Rai.' She moved towards her husband. 'Rami, my hus—'

'Jane,' Phillip said coldly, 'we've already met.'

'Oh? Have you?' She glanced up at Phillip and saw that he had turned his face away from her and was clicking his fingers for the bearer. She waited for an explanation but none came.

'Phillip, Rami came to ask us to join him and his grandfather for drinks tonight at the club,' she said, attempting to cover Phillip's rudeness. 'I more or less accepted but I said I'd better check with you that we're not busy.' She smiled at Rami as Phillip sat down. He reached for his wife's hand. 'Well, I'm afraid we are.' He looked across at Ramesh and without warmth or courtesy said, 'Sorry, but no can do.'

Jane pulled away. She was shocked at such a lack of manners. 'Ah bearer, could we have some more drinks please,' she said, keeping her voice calm. 'Rami? Would you like another *nimbupani*?'

'A what?' Phillip interrupted.

'A lime and soda,' Jane answered.

'I see.' Phillip picked up the paper. 'Say it in English then.' He glanced at the bearer. 'I'll have a cold beer please, bearer.'

Jane clenched her jaw and forced a smile. 'Rami?'

Rami stood. 'No, thank you, Jane, but I must be getting off.'

'Must you?'

'Yes. Thank you for the drink.'

'Thank you for the help.'

Phillip kept his head in the paper.

'Goodbye, major.'

He glanced up momentarily and nodded.

'I'll see you out, Rami.' Jane was fit to burst. She had never seen Phillip so surly.

'Thank you.'

'My pleasure,' she said and only just resisting the urge to kick Phillip, she led the way across the terrace and into the bungalow.

Five minutes later she was back.

'Phillip! What the hell has got into you?' she demanded angrily. She stood in front of him and put her hand in the middle of his paper, crushing it. 'I'm sorry, but that was unforgivably rude!'

'For God's sake, Jane!' Phillip folded the paper and stood up, walking away from her. 'It's no big deal. Forget it, all right?'

She followed him. 'No I won't forget it! What are we doing tonight that we can't go for drinks? Hmmm? And why didn't you tell me before?'

'Because we aren't doing anything,' he answered,

turning and leaning back against the balustrade. 'I am not going for drinks tonight and that is my last word.'

'But why?' Jane was exasperated; she simply didn't understand him. 'Why on earth not?'

Phillip looked out at the garden for a moment then he said, 'Because I don't socialise with Indians, that's why.'

'You what?' Jane's eyes flashed.

'You heard,' Phillip snapped. He walked past her towards the bungalow. 'It's them and us, Jane,' he said. 'And the sooner you realise that the better.' He walked inside without another word and left Jane speechless with anger behind him.

Chapter Fourteen

Jane sat on the edge of her bed in the white, high-ceilinged bedroom of the bungalow with the sun streaming in through the windows and dropped her feet down on to the cool marble floor. The coldness of it against the warmth of her skin was delicious. It was still early morning, seven a.m. but even so it was hot and, looking out at the terrace at the intense blue sky beyond it, Jane knew that this was just the beginning, that by mid-morning it would be stifling.

Walking naked to the bathroom, Jane turned on the cold tap and splashed her face and neck with water, taking a sharp breath as it hit her skin. Then she ran the shower, adjusting the temperature to exactly the right degree, tepid, just above cold, tied her hair up and stepped under the jet. It was the only way she could face the day.

Twenty minutes later, she joined Phillip in the shade

of the terrace for breakfast. She walked out of the cool sitting-room, wondering why on earth he insisted on taking breakfast out in the heat and the warm air suddenly rushed at her, rendering her momentarily breathless. She waited for the feeling to pass, ran her fingers across her brow already slightly damp with sweat, then walked on to where he was sitting.

'Good morning, Jane,' he said, without lowering his paper.

'Morning.' Jane smiled at the bearer as he helped her into her chair and shook out the napkin for her. 'Thank you, DhaniRam, and how are you this morning?'

'Very well, memsahib. And you?'

'Fine thank you.' Jane glanced across at Phillip's plate, pushed to the side with its half eaten full English breakfast already congealing and wondered how the hell he could eat that in this heat. 'I'd like some tea please,' she said, 'with lemon and some papaya, melon and orange.'

'Yes, memsahib, certainly.'

'Oh and some yoghurt, please, DhaniRam.'

Jane smiled again. 'Thank you.' She waited for the bearer to move out of earshot then said, 'And how are you, Jane? Fine thank you, Phillip. Did you sleep well? Yes, very well, despite the heat. It shows, my dear, you look most refreshed this morning. Why, thank you.'

Phillip lowered the paper. 'Have you finished?'

'Yes, I think so.' Jane drummed her fingertips on the table and stared out at the gardens in brilliant sunshine.

'So, what are you up to today, Janey?' Phillip folded away *The Times* and poured himself a second coffee. He didn't want another day to get off to a bad start.

Jane turned. 'I thought I might cycle up to the Khali

Temple, on the road out to Chittawar; Dr Yadav recommended it. He said it's terribly cool there, all leafy and shady. I thought I'd do some sketching.'

'Are you going alone?' This was a thinly veiled reference to Ramesh Rai. He had called in several times over the past ten days but Jane seemed to keep missing him. His persistence annoyed Phillip; he didn't want his wife friendly with Indians.

'Yes. I've asked DhaniRam to pack me some lunch, I thought I'd make a day of it, get some good work done.'

Phillip nodded but said nothing. He didn't understand Jane's need to be busy, he thought she should be at the club, playing bridge, having lunch, getting to know the other wives. That's what upper-class English women did, for God's sake.

The bearer arrived with Jane's breakfast and Phillip clicked his fingers and motioned for his place to be cleared. Jane bent her head and concentrated on her fruit, embarrassed by the way he handled the servants. Phillip lit a cigarette.

'I'll be in late tonight,' he said, blowing smoke away from the table.

'Oh?'

'Yes, I've got a meeting that'll probably go on late. Go ahead and eat without me if you like.'

Jane tucked her hair behind her ear. She hated eating alone but was getting pretty used to it. 'How late's late?'

Phillip shrugged and stubbed out his cigarette. 'I'll ring you,' he said, standing, 'from the office, let you know.' He drank the last of his coffee and reached for his jacket on the back of the chair. He wore one of his several linen suits, as always immaculately kept, perfectly wrinkled in the right places, tortoiseshell buttons and a knife-edge crease along the trousers. He arranged his panama exactly on his head, tipping it forward slightly and tightened the knot on his tie. Jane saw this every morning but she still couldn't get used to it, the constant attention to his every personal detail. He came around the table and kissed her.

'Bye, darling. Have a good day.'

'Yes, bye, Phillip.'

He picked up his briefcase. 'You know you ought to pop down to the gymkhana club one of these days, have a swim, get to know one or two of the other girls out here.'

Jane nodded.

'Right, good. I'll get one of the chaps' wives to ring you then, Marjorie maybe or Phyllis.' He turned and waving without looking at her, he walked into the house, whistling as he went.

Jane rolled her eyes and plopped an ice-cold piece of melon into her mouth. The club, she thought, how awful. She listened to the noises of her husband's departure and breathed a sigh of relief when he finally left the house and the peaceful silence was resumed. Recently, she realised, looking out at the garden, she had begun to tire of Phillip and his typically English mannerisms. Only slightly of course, she told herself firmly as she sipped her tea and everyone tired of their spouse on occasions, didn't they? It couldn't be a honeymoon for ever after all, could it? And she turned away from the dazzling sunshine, went on with her breakfast, enjoying every mouthful, and thinking about the day ahead – hardly aware of the fact that Phillip had completely gone from her mind.

It took Jane quite some time to cycle out to the Khali temple, far longer than she had expected. It turned out to be a fair distance from the city, something she hadn't realised from the map and in the heat and sun it had taken a great deal of effort. She followed the directions that Dr Yadav had given her, coming off the main road at the crossroads after the small village of Dwalior and heading for the forest area in the distance. The landscape was flat and bordered by patches of scrub that every now and then led into clumps of forest. The dark air looked so cool and inviting there that Jane was tempted to abandon her goal and lie down for a while in the tent of cool green. But she cycled on.

Jane had been drawing most days since she arrived in Baijur. She was unused to doing nothing and the first few days had seemed to stretch for ever in front of her, leaving her feeling rather hopeless, at a loss with herself. On the third day in the bungalow on her own, she fetched her bag, took out her water-colours and set off into the city. She spent hours drawing, totally absorbed in the colour and movement of Baijur, fascinated by a city that seemed perpetually in motion. And from that day on there was no going back – Jane had found herself something to do.

Finally approaching the huge area of forest, Jane jumped off her bicycle and wheeled it to a lump of stone, propping it up and leaving it there. She took her things from the basket, slung her bags over her shoulder and dug in the pocket of her trousers for Bodi's map. The temple was half a mile into the undergrowth, it was marked by boulders of pale yellow carved sandstone and he had told her that she would find it perfectly easily if she followed these. That was exactly what she intended to do. Taking off her sunglasses, she walked forward, pushed back the branches of a jacaranda tree and started for the temple.

Fifteen minutes later, Jane found the last boulder. She had walked slowly, unnerved by the dark airlessness of the forest, frightened by its silence, punctuated every now and then by a scuttling or rustle, the sharp cry of a bird. She jumped at every sound, her heart thumping in her chest and found herself sweating, far more than she did in the heat of the sun. The trail she had followed was thin, roughly cut through the undergrowth and she had stumbled several times. Finally, when it opened out into a definite path, wide enough to walk easily, she breathed a sigh of relief. 'Thank God for that,' she murmured under her breath and, brushing back a thick, heavy palm, she stepped into a clearing. Suddenly, behind her a branch cracked underfoot. 'My God!' She gripped the branch she was holding and stood frozen to the spot. She heard footsteps.

'Jane? Jane Mills?'

She swung round. 'Oh my God! Rami! Thank goodness!' Jane put her hand up to her chest, her heart was pounding so hard that she could feel it though the thin cotton of her shirt. 'Jesus! You scared me half to death!' She laughed nervously.

'Come,' Rami held his hand out and Jane took it. He led her into the clearing and the brilliant white sunlight. Jane covered her eyes for a moment, blinded by the light.

'Are you all right, Jane?'

'Yes! Yes of course.' She removed her hand and felt in

her bag for her sunglasses, slipping them on. 'Sorry, it's just that I got a bit spooked, walking up here.'

'Spooked?'

'Yes! Nervous. It was so dark and creepy.'

'You shouldn't really be here on your own, you know.'

'Oh?'

'It's not dangerous or anything but it's . . .' Rami shrugged.

'It's what?'

'It's very isolated, too far away.'

Jane smiled; he looked so concerned. 'I didn't realise when I cycled here. I thought it was much nearer.' She dropped her bags down on the ground. 'What are you doing here, anyway?'

Rami turned away and walked across to where he had spread a rug and some of his things. He knelt and began packing them into a bag.

'I'm sorry, I didn't mean to be nosy.'

He glanced up at her and smiled. 'No, really. I, erm . . .' He held up a cloth-covered book. 'I come here sometimes, for the solitude. I write my verse here.'

'Verse? You write poetry?'

Rami laughed. 'Don't look so shocked, Jane Mills!' He came across to her. 'It's nothing special, just a bit of relaxation.'

'I see.'

'What about you? Are you sightseeing? This is one of Bodi's favourite places, I expect he told you to come here.'

'Yes! Yes, he did! Do you know Dr Yadav?'

'I know Dr Yadav very well, all my life in fact. He has been . . .' Rami stopped. Jane looked up at him. 'He has been the half of my grandfather that Shiva is not,' he finished and Jane frowned.

'I don't understand.'

'No.' Rami tucked his book into the pocket of his *churidar*. 'Nor do I.' He sighed. 'My grandfather finds it very hard to treat me as a grandson, Jane. Bodi has loved me unconditionally since the day I was born.' He didn't feel any need to explain, but he wanted to. 'He's my mother's uncle and he's been like a father to me.'

The small frown across Jane's forehead disappeared and she smiled. 'You're very lucky.'

'Yes, I think I am.' Rami could not resist her smile. It was a clear, honest smile, not coy or calculating; it showed her happiness, as simple as that. He smiled back. He had never said anything so intimate about his family before but he didn't regret it. 'So why are you here? You didn't answer me.'

'I came to sketch.'

He glanced down at the bags. 'Hence the luggage.'

'Yes, hence the luggage.'

'Well . . .' Rami shrugged and walked back to his spot. 'I shall leave you alone, then.' He began rolling the rug.

'Rami, please.' Jane took off her sunglasses. 'Please don't let me drive you away.' She walked over to him. 'Can you work with me here?'

He stared up at her. She was so tall, almost his height and the shape of her long slim thighs was visible through the cotton of her skirt with the sun behind her. Rami looked away, suddenly surprised at his response to her. 'I don't think . . .'

'Oh please!' she interrupted. 'I shall feel awful if you leave because of me.'

He let go of the rug and it unravelled itself. 'All right. I will stay.'

Jane grinned. 'And I will sit miles away from you and not say a word.' She went to her bags and began to unpack her paints. Within minutes she had set up her easel and small stool and, adjusting her hat, she sat down to start.

'Not a word,' Rami called. 'You promised!'

She dipped her brush into her water and flicked it across the space at him. 'Not a word,' she replied and they both laughed.

Towards the end of the morning, Jane sat back and looked at what she had done. She always painted very close to the paper and found she could only properly judge if she stood and took several paces back. She got to her feet, her legs aching, and stepped back. She had taken a corner of the temple, set against the backdrop of the forest and painted the carvings in exquisite detail. The colours were pinks and greens and azure blue, the sandstone, the trees and the sky.

'Have you finished?'

Jane started. True to her word, she had not said a thing for nearly three hours. She had been so absorbed in the work that she had forgotten Rami was there. She glanced over her shoulder at him.

'May I see?'

'Yes, of course.' Jane turned away and busied herself washing her brushes and tidying her paints as Rami came across to the painting.

He stood and stared for quite some time. Then he said, 'Jane, it's beautiful.'

She looked up and smiled. For some peculiar reason

his opinion was tremendously important to her. 'Thank you.' She straightened and wiped her hands on her apron. 'I have some lunch,' she said. 'Would you like to share it?'

'I would love to share it but I am afraid that I have lunch with my grandfather, Jane.' He remained standing in front of the picture. 'Jane?' He turned. 'I hope you don't mind me asking but would you be interested in selling this painting?'

Jane came to stand next to him. 'I don't mind you asking but I'm sorry, I don't sell my paintings.'

He smiled. 'No, I didn't think you would.' He walked back to the rug. 'Ah well.' He shrugged. 'I must go,' he said and bending, he packed everything away. 'Perhaps you might like to come sightseeing with me one afternoon, Jane,' he said as he strapped his things together, ready to attach to his bicycle. 'I did call a few times but I seem to have . . .'

'I know,' Jane interrupted. 'I've been out a lot, drawing.' She imagined Phillip's tutting disapproval. 'I'm very busy,' she said.

'Yes, of course.'

Rami walked back to her and held out his hand. 'It was nice to see you, Jane.'

Jane took his hand, the long, smooth brown fingers cool to touch. Phillip wasn't the only reason for her excuse, she knew that. 'It was nice to see you too, Rami,' she answered. 'Cycle carefully.'

He smiled and hitched his things up on to his shoulder. 'Goodbye!' he called as he strode off. He glanced over his shoulder at her and waved, then he disappeared off into the undergrowth.

*   *   *

An hour later, Shiva and Ramesh Rai stood on the intricate and delicate mosaic floor of the ante-room in the Lake Palace and waited for Vikram Singh, the Maharajah of Baijur. A cool breeze blew across the water and in through the open fretwork of the windows, in the lily pools it gently rocked the flowers and sent tiny ripples across the still, calm ponds. Ramesh thought about Jane, about how much she would love the beauty of this palace; he wondered what she was sketching now at the Khali temple and what she was having for her lunch. He heard his grandfather cough and glanced up

'You are some place else, I think, Ramesh,' Shiva said.

'I am sorry.' Rami looked away from his grandfather's harsh, penetrating stare.

'No matter, here is the maharajah!' Rami turned back in time to see his grandfather's face change, the smile, the warmth that suddenly appeared and he resented it.

'Shivaji! And Rami!' The maharajah, smartly dressed and relaxed, broke off talking with one of the royal officials and walked towards them. He was smiling broadly.

'You are well, Shivaji?' Shiva folded his palms and bowed his head. Viki turned to Rami who did the same.

'You missed a good ride last week, eh, Rami?' The advisor leant in towards the maharajah and whispered something, Viki nodded and then dismissed the man. 'No matter,' he said, continuing where he had left off, 'we must arrange for you to try out these ponies soon! In the next week, eh? I want your opinion, Ramesh!' He turned towards the garden. 'Come, we are lunching on the terrace today, there is a good breeze to cool us!' He led the way out through the water garden and on to the far terrace.

'Shiva, how is business?'

'Very good thank you, sir. We are about to open an office and show rooms in New York.'

Surprised, Rami turned to his grandfather. He had heard nothing of this before.

'Excellent, excellent!' They had crossed the terrace and the maharajah nodded to the bearer as they approached the table. 'Please, Shiva, Rami, be seated.'

Two uniformed servants stepped forward and both men took their places.

'So,' Viki said, 'we shall have a drink and then we must talk.' He clicked his fingers and a servant stepped forward to pour the *nimbupani*. 'We have important things to discuss.'

Rami took a sip and glanced sidelong at his grandfather while Shiva drank and chatted to Viki. He felt that Shiva knew what this lunch was for but hadn't told him and it made him uneasy.

'Well, Rami,' Viki crossed his long legs and the silk tie of his brocade cummerbund fell to the side. He waved his hand casually in the air and dismissed the servants with one sweep. Then he leant forward and Rami saw that the buttons on his *kurta* were set with tiny rubies in an intricate pattern; he recognised Shiva's work. He felt the atmosphere change.

'Rami, I have asked you here today because I have something important that I would like to talk with you about.' Viki glanced over his shoulder and saw one of the servants lingering by the drinks table. He clapped his hands and motioned for the boy to leave them. He waited several minutes, then, sure they were alone, he said, 'Your grandfather and I have been discussing the problems with Pakistan, Rami, and the implications for Baijur, being so close to the border.' He reached for a gold cigarette case and flipped it open, offering a cigarette to Rami. 'It is a difficult subject,' he said, 'a delicate one.' He lit up and smoked for a few moments. 'We are vulnerable here, Rami, the state is stable in so much as the house of Singh stays in power. And power is wealth.' He sat back and looked at the young man in front of him as if weighing him up. 'I have a job for you,' he said, 'an obscure job but one that I am positive is vital to the security of my position here.' He glanced over his shoulder again before he leant in close to the table. 'Your grandfather has told you that there have been threats to my life?'

'No!' Rami stopped and lowered his voice. 'I don't believe it!' he hissed. 'Who? And why?'

'This business with Pakistan, the Muslims everywhere are unhappy, here in Baijur even.' He shrugged. 'I don't know who, I can only guess that it is political, religious.' Viki was silent for a few moments, then he said, 'I need to protect myself, Rami, take precautions. If something should happen to me I need to be sure that Aeysha, the new maharani, would be safe.' He stubbed out his cigarette and Rami noticed that his face changed when he spoke of his wife to be. 'This is where you can help,' he said. 'You have a part to play. I have discussed it at great length with your grandfather and we were decided many months ago on the course of action.' Viki paused. 'Shiva and RJ International started work for me at the beginning of the year. They have been making copies of every item of jewellery that we own, part of it is already finished. They are making a counterfeit of the entire wealth of the Singh house.'

'My God!' Rami shook his head; it was almost unbelievable. The work involved was incredible, the collection of the old maharani alone was said to be worth millions.

'The work has been carried out overseas, Rami,' Shiva said. 'In my workshops in Paris and London. It is a matter of utmost secrecy.'

'But I don't understand, I—'

Viki held up his hands to interrupt Rami. 'I have done it for safety, Rami,' he said. 'I intend to hide the originals, at least until I know it is safe in Baijur.' He sat back and again looked at Rami as if weighing him up. He was silent for some time, then he said: 'I have chosen you to carry out this task.'

'Me?'

'Yes. I would like you to take care of it, to, how can I put it, to plan a route for the originals. It is not a simple case of hiding, there is too much at stake to take the risk of that. What I had envisaged is a serious and complicated procedure, Ramesh, something that you will have designed, using your skills, your knowledge of the land here, your verse perhaps, your intellect, something that only you know the answer to.'

Viki stopped talking and Rami sat motionless for a moment. He was dumbfounded. 'I'm not sure if I really understand you,' he said. 'You mean that you want me to set up some sort of maze, a puzzle of some kind, to where I decide to hide the wealth?'

The maharajah nodded.

Rami sat back. It was ludicrous, he couldn't possibly do it. He shook his head. 'It is far too great a responsibility,

Viki, I can't . . .' He broke off and looked at his grand-father.

'You are trusted, Ramesh, with the life of the maharajah and you think of refusing?' His dark eyes were like granite, cold and hard, impenetrable.

'No, it's not that, it's . . .' Again he stopped. 'How could you possibly trust me with all of this? What if something went wrong? What if someone found out what I was doing?'

Viki lit another cigarette and looked at Rami over the trail of smoke. 'You would have to ensure that these things didn't happen, Rami.'

'I don't know, I don't know if I can do it!' He shook his head again helplessly and sat silent for a while. Then, looking up, he said, 'How long would I have, if I were to do it?'

'I want it settled by the date of my wedding,' Viki answered. 'It is a big event, dangerous to some degree.'

Rami nodded. 'And if only I know the answer?'

'You will have prepared a text for me.'

'What? Like some kind of trail?'

'Perhaps. Perhaps a book of verse and illustrations. I don't know, that is up to you, Ramesh. But it must be ingenious, that is why I have asked you.'

Rami bowed his head and smiled tensely, acknowledg-ing the compliment. 'Can I use someone to help me? If I were to make a book of some sort?'

Viki's face darkened. 'You must think carefully, Rami, it has to be someone you would trust your life with.' He stubbed out his cigarette. 'That is what you would be doing.'

Rami nodded and fell silent again. The burden of what

he had been asked to do was enormous. He looked at Shiva. It was a burden but it was also a challenge and already the swift intellect of his mind had risen to that challenge. It was the chance to prove himself, to be a bonus to his grandfather. It was a task that no one else could do. He looked again at Shiva. 'Dadaji?'

'It is a great honour, Ramesh, you do not need me to tell you that,' Shiva said.

'No.' Then he looked across at Viki and realised that this responsibility was only a small portion of what the maharajah had to bear. And for the first time in his life he clearly saw Vikram Singh, Maharajah of Baijur, behind the charming, easy-going Viki. He was an Indian, he knew what he had to do.

'I will be happy to serve you always,' he said quietly.

Viki leant forward and touched his arm. 'Thank you, Ramesh.' He smiled briefly for the first time since they had sat at the table. 'I knew that I could trust you.'

Chapter Fifteen

Jane came out of the bungalow and waved to the *khansama*, holding her small packet up in a gesture of thanks. The cook waved back, smiling and nodding, and as Jane placed the waxed paper bag in her basket, he opened the kitchen window and called, '*Namaste*, memsahib!' standing with two house boys to wave her off. Jane grinned, climbed on to her bicycle and adjusted her hat, making sure it was quite secure on her head. She had this procedure every morning, with one or another of the servants waving her off, but it never ceased to delight her. Turning her bike round and setting her feet on the pedals, she glanced back, waved a final time and cycled off, down the drive, out on to the main driveway to the palace and then towards the city.

Ramesh was early in the city. He stood outside the bookshop waiting for the man to open it, and watched the business of the street going on around him. He was in the poorer section of Baijur, it was the only place a poetry bookshop could afford to have premises and he stared at the day-to-day living of the people as they started another day of life on the pavements – their cooking over small charcoal fires, their washing at the taps on the street corner, the rolling up of their bedding and the repairs to the plastic sheeting, the strips of canvas that covered them at night as they started another day of life on the pavements. It wasn't unusual, it was a sight to be seen all over Baijur, all over India, with so many people living on the streets but he had been away for too long, it shocked him every time he saw it, and it filled him with helplessness.

Turning away towards the bookshop, Rami looked at the posters pasted across the window to take his mind off the scene behind him but it was impossible, the noise level was a constant reminder. He listened to the din, the loud incessant chatter, the shouts and laughter of the children, the motor rickshaws, cars and cattle, and in the end gave up trying to distract himself. He turned, leant back against the wall and watched.

The next thing he saw made him stand bolt upright.

'My God!' He stepped forward and waved his arms in the air. 'Jane? Jane! Over here!' He hurried to the edge of the road and called her again. Finally she looked up.

'Rami! Hello!' She straightened and put her hand up to her eyes to shield them from the sun. 'Wait there! I'll come across.' She said something to the woman squatting on the pavement, who smiled and reached out to touch her hand, then she wheeled her bicycle to the edge of the road, waited for a break in the traffic and crossed.

'Good morning, Rami!' Jane propped her bicycle up on the kerb. 'What are you doing here?'

Rami glanced behind him at the poetry bookshop. 'I came to buy a couple of books.' He looked at her face and smiled. Every time he left her he expected that she would be different the next time he saw her but she wasn't, not ever, she was always exactly the same, the honesty of her smile, the clear, open look of her face charmed him. 'What about you? What are you doing here?'

Jane took off her hat and dropped it in the basket. She flicked her hair back in an attempt to make herself look a little more appealing. 'I come here to draw, quite often.' She had forgotten how attractive Rami was, or maybe not forgotten, she thought, avoiding his gaze, deliberately ignored. 'I've made a few friends,' she said, glancing back at the woman she had been talking to. 'People pose for me, I give them a few rupees.' She blushed as she said this, waiting for Rami's disapproval.

'That's very kind,' he said.

Jane looked at him. 'Phillip says it's stupid. He says it's not my problem.' She dug her hands in her pockets and glanced away again. 'I bring a bit of food most days, for the children, a few sweets, some fruit, *khansama* packs me a little bag.' Her cheeks were burning but she felt she'd been caught out so she might as well confess the whole thing. 'I don't tell Phillip, I don't think he would understand.'

Rami was silent for a few moments, then he said, 'You would make him feel ashamed, Jane, as you do me.'

Jane looked up and Ramesh smiled at her. 'I think—'

'Mrs Mills, Mrs Mills!'

They both swung round.

'Mrs Mills, Mrs Mills!' A small gang of children chanted at Jane from across the road, breaking off into fits of giggles. Jane laughed. 'Wait there!' she called across. 'I have something in my basket for you!' She turned to Rami. 'If you'll excuse me?'

He grinned. 'Of course!'

Jane reached into her basket and took out the bag, glancing across the road as she did so. 'No!' she shouted at a little girl who had jumped off the pavement. 'Wait there! I am coming across to you!' She hurriedly looked right and left but couldn't see a break in the traffic.

'Usha! Wait there!' The little girl had darted into the middle of the road and was waiting to run across to Jane. Jane stepped off the pavement but the traffic was relentless. She saw a break, a van some way off and hurried forward. She didn't look left and nor did the little girl who had seen the same break. She was two paces away when she heard Rami's voice. Glancing back, she saw his face, the look of horror, then turning her head sideways she caught sight of the truck. It was the last thing she saw. Diving forward, she caught the child off balance and pushed her back with such force that the little girl's body cracked as it hit the ground. The child screamed. The screech of brakes, the scream and Rami's voice were all she remembered. Then she felt a thud, then nothing. The sky went black.

'Oh my God! Jane!' Rami had run out into the road but it was too late. He heard the wailing of the child, saw her mother scoop her up, but Jane lay motionless, inches away from the truck. He knelt, his hands shaking and gently brushed the hair from her face. He put his fingers on her neck, felt her pulse and, moments later, bent his head. 'Thank God for that,' he murmured. He looked up at the crowd that had started to form. 'She's alive! You, run into the bookshop and get the owner! It's over there.' He pointed behind him and took his *kurta* off, rolling it up and gently placing it under Jane's head. 'Hurry!' he shouted after the man.

Seconds later the owner ran across the road to Rami. 'Rameshji! Who is it? A friend, eh?' He knelt by Rami's side.

'Yes. Ashok, call the palace, they will take care of it, tell them I am here and it is Mrs Mills. They will send an ambulance right away.' The bookshop owner scrambled to his feet and set off. The traffic had stopped and people began to press round to see what was happening. The crowd had doubled. 'Ashok?' Rami shouted. 'Tell them there is a child as well, they will need transport for her! I will take care of it, tell them that I will pay!' The man held his hand up in answer as he ran. 'And hurry,' Rami murmured under his breath. 'Please, please hurry.'

It was dark when Jane came round. The day had disappeared as it always did, quickly and without twilight, and Rami stood at the window, staring out into the grounds of the clinic, looking at the dark shapes of the trees against an ink-black sky. He turned as he heard Jane sigh and was looking at her as she opened her eyes.

'Ramesh?' She moved her head towards him and lifted her hand. 'Ouch, that hurts!'

'Jane!' He hurried to the bed. 'Thank goodness!' The relief in his voice made her want to smile but her face was too sore. 'How do you feel?'

Jane frowned and rolled her eyes upwards. 'Do I have a bandage on my head?'

He smiled. 'Yes, you have a cut on your forehead and a broken nose.'

'Oh God!' She groaned. 'I must look wretched!'

'You also have a bruised shoulder and a sprained wrist, on the left hand, thank God!' She was right-handed. 'You were very, very lucky!'

'What happened? I got hit, yes?'

He nodded.

'By a car?'

'No, a truck. You managed to get the child out of the way but—'

'Usha?' Jane's face creased with worry. 'Is she all right? What happened to her? She's not—'

Rami lay his hand over Jane's 'She's here, in the clinic. She's fine.' He squeezed her hand. 'You saved her life,' he said. 'She would have been killed by that truck.'

'I did?'

He laughed quietly. 'Yes, you did.'

'So where am I? And what time is it?'

'You're in a private clinic, one that the maharajah uses.' He glanced at his watch. 'And it's seven p.m.'

'God! Seven o'clock!' Suddenly Jane tried to lift her head off the pillow. 'Phillip! What about Phillip? He'll be worried sick!'

Rami gently pushed her back down. 'Phillip knows where you are, and what has happened. Relax, you must not get excited.'

'He does?'

'Yes, he . . .' Rami broke off as Jane looked away. He

saw her eyes fill with tears. 'He rang to see if you were all right.'

Jane nodded, bitterly disappointed, and her tears ran down to stain the crisp white cotton pillowcase. 'I'm sorry, it's the shock of the accident,' she said, but it was more. It was the terrible, sick feeling that Phillip didn't care, that he should have, could have been there but he chose not to be. She turned her face right away so that Rami couldn't see the extent of her distress.

'He is in a very important meeting, Jane, he really couldn't get away,' Rami lied, cursing himself for being so tactless. Phillip had rung but once he knew it wasn't serious he told the nurse he would see Jane in the morning, when she felt better. 'He thought you should rest,' he finished lamely and turned away. Taking his bag off the chair, he said, 'So, you'll have to make do with me, I'm afraid, if you are not too tired, that is.'

Jane brightened slightly. He really was so very kind. 'No, I'm not tired at all, just a little sore.'

'Well, I have just the thing to take your mind off your aches and pains,' Rami announced, taking a box from his bag. He sat down and pulled the table up to Jane's bed. 'There were two things that I learnt in England that proved invaluable whilst I was there.'

Jane smiled. 'Really?'

'Yes, really. The first,' he said, standing to pour her some water, 'was to always carry an umbrella, whatever time of the year, whatever the weather.' He held the glass for her and Jane took a couple of sips.

'The second?' she asked, lying back.

Rami produced the box and laid it on the table. 'Scrabble,' he said. 'Part of the English way of life.'

Surprised, Jane started to laugh, but it hurt too much. 'Please, don't make me laugh! My face feels as if it's done ten rounds with Cassius Clay!'

'Oh dear, oh dear me, Mrs Mills, I am so sorry to be making you laugh!' Rami pressed his palms together and nodded his head as he spoke in his Delhi accent. He smiled as Jane moaned through her giggles. 'Now, the game!' He took the board and felt bag of letters out of the box and began to set the Scrabble up. Jane watched him and thought how considerate and gentle he was, how different from Phillip. Suddenly, she didn't mind about Phillip, well, not as much as she had.

'Jane?' Rami glanced up, his face suddenly serious. 'Remember to remind me that I have to ask you something when you are feeling a little bit better. For some help with a task I have to do. Please?'

She nodded. 'What task?'

He smiled. 'When you are feeling better.'

'Is this to make me recover quicker? Or else be consumed with curiosity?'

'Perhaps.' He finished organising the game. Sitting by her side that afternoon, he had decided to ask her to help him with Viki's work, to illustrate what he would write. He had decided, without knowing why, that he would trust Jane Mills with his life. 'Shall we start, Mrs Mills?' he asked.

'Yes, if you like, Mr Rai.'

He held out the bag. 'There is something I had better tell you, before we play.'

Jane's face fell. 'Oh?'

He smiled. 'Yes. That I am excellent at Scrabble and you will never beat me.'

'Oh really?' Jane took her letters.

'Yes, really.' Rami took his. 'Oh.' He had three Us, a Z and a Q, and two Ts. 'Except on a Tuesday,' he said, 'I never play well on a Tuesday.'

Phillip knocked lightly on Jane's bedroom door and glanced quickly at his watch as she called out for him to enter. It was nine-fifteen and he was due in a meeting with Viki at half-past. He had ten minutes to spare. Shouldn't take longer than ten minutes, he thought, fiddling with the rose on her breakfast tray, he was, after all, her husband and his word would be final.

'Hello, darling.' He crossed to the bed, carefully placing the tray on the bedside table and leaning in to kiss Jane's cheek. She turned the better one towards him and he kissed the only patch of skin that wasn't discoloured with bruising. 'How are you this morning?'

'Fine, thank you, Phillip.' Jane sat up and tensely pulled her robe in a little closer, covering her chest. Ever since the accident, since his obvious lack of concern, she had really begun to find his company irritating, insincere more than anything else and this made her uneasy. She had also begun to lose patience with him, she didn't bother to cover her feelings up quite as carefully as she might have done.

'What can I do for you this morning?' she asked curtly.

Phillip poured her tea, then handed her the tray. 'Janey, I wanted to talk to you, about this dinner tonight,' he said. 'Sugar?'

Jane shook her head. 'Just lemon. And the answer is still no, I don't feel ready to face anyone yet.'

Phillip plopped a slice of lemon into the cup. 'You look perfectly all right,' he said tersely. 'There's nothing wrong with you that a little bit of make-up won't cover.'

Jane clenched her jaw. 'Phillip!' She turned her face full on to him. 'Look at me, for goodness sake! I have the remains of two black eyes and most of my face is bruised! Not to mention the scar on my forehead!'

Phillip averted his eyes from her face. She was right, he thought grudgingly, she did look a bit of a mess. 'No one will be in the slightest bit bothered about what you look like, Janey,' he said, more kindly. 'It's just an evening with old friends, Johnny and his wife are desperate to meet you and you've only been to the club once in the whole time we've been here.' He handed her the tea. 'Please, Jane, it would mean a lot to me.'

Jane looked away. 'I'm sorry, Phillip, but no, I'm really not up to it.'

'Well, you've been quite up to gallivanting about with that bloody Indian fellow! Every day for over a week now you've been out with him and you say you can't face a dinner with friends! What's he got that I haven't, Jane?'

'That is totally uncalled for!' Jane shoved the breakfast tray to the side and stood up. 'I think you'd better leave!'

Phillip turned angrily away. He put his hands up to his temples and took a breath. 'Look, I'm sorry, Jane, you're right, it was totally uncalled for.' This was his last chance to have dinner with Johnny and Hannah Wakeman and he was sick of making excuses, sick of missing out on what was going on at the club because Jane refused to go. 'It is odd, though,' he said, 'that you are fit enough to go out and about with Mister Rai but not to go out in the evenings with me.'

Jane sighed. 'Phillip, we've been through all this! I told you, I go out for a couple of hours and draw, I'm helping him with a book he's writing, that's all. I don't have to make polite conversation or be witty or social, I don't have to face anyone except Rami. It's completely different to being seen at the club!'

'Is it?'

Jane suddenly slumped down on the bed; she was tired of all this, this was the third time it had come up and she had lost the energy to fight any more. She simply couldn't be bothered. 'Look, if it really means that much to you, Phillip, I'll come.'

He saw her face, miserable and exhausted, ashen behind the angry purple, blue and yellow bruises but he was unmoved by the sight. 'You promise?'

Jane looked up at him and suddenly it hit her. It was more than irritation, more than lack of patience. When had it happened? When had they lost touch, stopped liking each other almost? She supposed it must have been the accident, she couldn't think of any other explanation for it. Miserably, she nodded. 'Yes, of course, if you insist,' she said. As if she would go back on her word!

Phillip turned towards the door. It was only a dinner, an evening at the club, for Christ's sake, why did Jane have to make such heavy weather of it? It wasn't as if she were any beauty, devastated at losing her looks.

'Right then,' he said coolly, glancing back, his hand on the door. 'I'll see you tonight. We're expected at eight.'

Jane sat and stared blankly at him. She heard the chill in his voice, the slight hint of disdain and she looked down at her hands. Can people change so quickly, she thought, or were we like it all along, I just never stopped to think?

'It's evening dress,' he remarked, 'I'll be home to change at seven-thirty.' Then, leaving the room, he closed the door behind him as Jane sat motionless on the bed and without any emotion at all, watched him go.

'My God! That's the most fascinating story!' Hannah Wakeman, in a low-cut halterneck dress, leant forward and her bosom trembled as she laughed. She took another gulp of her gin and leant drunkenly against Phillip. 'It's soooo spooky!'

Jane moved further away, outside the circle. No one noticed.

'So what happened next?' Johnny asked.

'Yes,' someone else butted in, 'that's surely not the end of it?'

'Well, the bird Colonel Mills had found was apparently one of a pair and . . .' Phillip broke off, turning towards the bar to stub out his cigarette, then he drank down the last of his whisky and turned back to finish his story. 'And this Indian fellow had the other one. When he fled . . .'

Jane edged silently out of the open French doors and stepped on to the terrace. No longer within hearing distance of a story she could repeat off by heart if she'd had to, she took a deep breath and relaxed for the first time all evening.

Glancing up, she stared at the moon, full and bright in the sky, a globe of eerie light against a backdrop of ink black. She wondered where Rami was under the eyes of the moon, what he was doing, then she stopped herself.

She wondered it so often now it had almost become second nature but she knew it was something she had to stop, it wasn't right and she shouldn't do it. She smelt the warm scent of jasmine in the air and again she thought of him, he loved jasmine. She walked down on to the grass, so different from English grass, it was thick and springy, the blades cut like a razor.

She gazed up, walking all the time and watching the moon, mesmerised by it, listening to the sounds of the night, the gentle rustle of the flame trees, the birds and the constant clicking of the *tiddi*. She stood and looked back, some distance from the club, and could see the figures in the bar, lit up in the night sky, like actors on a stage. Unreal, unconnected to her. She walked on.

She knew there were the ruins of a water garden at the end of the club's land, she had heard Rami talk about it and she found herself heading towards it, not for any reason, just aimlessly, the warm air caressing her face and bare arms, the moonlight guiding her way. She stepped through a stone arch, overgrown with creepers and walked along a low stone wall, holding the hem of her evening dress up so she wouldn't trip. Then she jumped down. She found herself in an open space and looking ahead saw the moon on the ground, reflected in the still black waters of the pools. She saw Rami.

'Hello, Jane.'

She stood perfectly still. He said her name as if he had expected her and a shiver ran the length of her spine. He held out his hand and she walked across to him, taking it. They sat by the edge of a pool, their faces staring back at them from the water, their hands locked together.

'Did you know I would come here?'

Rami shrugged. 'I felt it but I didn't know. I do not think we really know anything, Jane.' He looked down at her face in the water and, leaning forward, he placed his finger on the water, on the reflection of her lips.

'Don't!' Jane flicked her hand across the image, dispersing it. 'Don't stare at my face! It's horrible! Ugly!' She covered her eyes.

Rami sat for a few minutes, then gently he reached out and took her hands away. 'You are beautiful, Jane,' he said. He held both of her hands and pressed them against her chest. 'Here, this is where true beauty is, in the heart.' Jane closed her eyes. 'You will always be beautiful to me, because I know your heart.' He took her hands away from her body and bent his head to kiss them. Then he eased her towards him, lifted her face and with infinite tenderness kissed her eyes, the black and bloody eyes, her cheeks and finally her mouth. His lips brushed hers and her whole body sparked.

'No!' She backed away. 'Please don't! I . . .' She stood quickly, frightened by her response and tugged her hands away from him. 'We mustn't! Please, Rami!'

'But, Jane!' He reached out and caught her, pulling her to him.

'No!' She jerked away. 'Please, no!' For a moment they stood like that, suspended in time, confused, frightened. Then Jane ran. She held her dress and ran blindly towards the lights in the distance. She stumbled several times and nearly lost her footing, she heard the cry of his voice behind her but she didn't turn, she couldn't turn.

On to the grass she ran, the electric light sweeping over the lawns, her figure cut out against the dark shapes of the trees, she ran on, up the steps of the terrace and into the safety of the noise and laughter spilling out from the club into the night air. She heard Phillip call her and gripped the wall for support.

'I'm out here!' she shouted. 'I'm just coming in!' Her voice wavered but she held on to it, summoning all her strength. She stood straight and smoothed her dress, taking a deep breath to compose herself.

'Is dinner served?' she asked from the doorway, smiling and blinking rapidly to adjust her eyes to the glare. Phillip walked over to her, taking her arm. He was drunk, had hardly noticed she was gone. 'Yes, my darling,' he said. 'Dinner is served!'

'Oh good!' Jane somehow managed to say. 'I'm absolutely starving!' And together, they joined the rest of the gang and went in to eat.

London was cold. The summer had died a death in mid-July and the country shivered in an unusually chilly spell for the time of year. It was seven-thirty p.m., the night of Mitchell Harvey's gala dinner, and Suzanna Harvey lay in bed with the blinds drawn, the covers pulled up over her head. Her evening dress was still in its box, it hadn't even been pressed and the clock by the side of her bed bleeped incessantly as the alarm went off. She came to for a few moments, heard the rain on the windows and then rolled over and blanked out again.

Downstairs, Mitchell poured himself another whisky and paced the floor. He swung round with the knock on the door.

'Enter!'

Suzy's maid came in and hovered by the door, nervously fiddling with her fingers. 'Mrs Harvey is still asleep, sir,' she said, losing her voice halfway through and having to clear her throat. 'I've tried to wake her but I can't seem to . . .'

'For God's sake what is wrong with you people? Can't you do anything? Christ!' Mitchell looked at his watch. 'I'll have to go and fucking get the slag up myself!'

The maid winced at his language and hurriedly backed out of the door as he came towards her. She pressed herself against the wall and felt the force of his anger as Mitchell banged past her and into the hallway.

'Suzanna!' he hollered up the stairs. 'Get up, Suzanna! Now!'

He stormed up and the maid ran along the corridor to the kitchen where she locked the door. She had seen one of Mr Harvey's rages before and they scared the living daylights out of her.

Upstairs, Mitchell banged the door open and walked into Suzanna's bedroom. 'Jesus Christ!' He strode to the window, drew the blinds and then walked across to the bed. He yanked back the covers. 'Get up, Suzy!' he shouted.

She rolled over and opened her eyes, staring blankly up at him, then she covered her head with her arms.

'Did you hear me!' Suddenly turning, he grabbed the alarm clock and smashed it against the wall; it stopped bleeping.

'What . . . ?' Suzy eased herself up into a sitting position. She shook her head to try and clear it.

'Oh Christ!' Mitchell saw the state of her. 'You fucking bitch!' He lashed out and swiped her across the face. The blow knocked her sideways but she hardly noticed, she lay on the bed and looked up at him with her glassy, unseeing eyes. Mitchell had to turn away to stop himself from punching her. Picking up an empty bottle of vodka, he closed his eyes for a moment, the muscle in the side of his face twitching as he tried to control himself. 'What else have you taken?' he shouted, turning back and taking her shoulders. He shook her. 'Suzanna? What else have you taken?'

She looked at him, confused and he let her go. She slumped down. 'Fuck you then!' he spat. 'Go ahead and die, you stupid bitch!' He walked away from the bed but stopped at her dressing-table. He picked up the phone. He didn't want her to cop it, he couldn't afford the scandal. He dialled his physician and spoke quickly, giving instructions. He wanted her taken care of, out of the way for the moment. He didn't want any more embarrassment, she was too much of a liability.

'No, not tonight, in the morning. I'm pretty sure it's just booze. Yes, at the clinic.' He hesitated before answering the next question. His doctor was right, he could ring his solicitor, get her certified in the next week. He glanced across at her. No, he might need her, later, she was well connected and could be useful again. 'No,' he said. 'Not yet. Just dry her out, get her straight.' He took one of the small cigars he smoked out of his top pocket and lit it up. 'For as long as it takes,' he said. 'Yes, months if that's necessary.' He flicked his ash into a small Meissen tray on the dressing-table. 'Right, I'll tell the staff to expect you then.' He hung up. That taken care of he felt mildly vindicated. He hated the bitch, always had, after the initial triumph of marrying into society had worn off.

'Goodbye, Suzanna,' he said, crossing to the door. 'Sleep well.' And looking back at her pathetic body, slumped in a heap, he walked away from her, smoking his cigar and dropping the ash on the carpet.

Suzanna came round several hours later. She opened her eyes, a blinding pain shot through her head and a surge of panic rose in her chest. God! What the hell had happened? Sitting upright, the sharp pain went down to the back of the head and she put her hands up, clutching the base of her neck. Nausea rose in her throat and leaning over the side of the bed, she retched violently. Nothing but bile came up; she was completely empty. She rested back, breathless and dizzy. Then she remembered, remembered it all and the panic started again. She dropped her legs over the side of the bed, groped for her dressing-gown and stood, gripping the bedside table for support.

Mitchell's gala dinner. She looked at her watch, her heart pounding in her chest. It was eleven-thirty, the blinds were open and the night stared in at her, black and intrusive. It was too late to do anything, he must have had to go without her. She took a step forward, her legs weak, and glanced down. She saw the alarm clock. 'Oh God,' she murmured. Her head was throbbing.

Making it over to the dressing-table, she looked in the mirror. The side of her face was swollen, the skin distended with fluid and a bruise had begun, under her eye and spreading down over her cheek bone. He must have given her a hell of a smack. She put her finger up and touched the swelling. It was so sore she winced. Dropping her hand down on to the dressing-table, she knocked the small dish by the phone, saw the ash, Mitchell's cigar ash and her body froze. He always smoked when he talked on the telephone. Who had he called? From up here in her bedroom? She dropped her head down, suddenly sick and dizzy. Then she looked up and faced herself in the mirror. He is going to get rid of me, she thought, quite coldly and rationally. She knew Mitchell's ways, she knew how he operated.

She took a breath to steady herself. Her reflection stared back at her, sad and haggard, a disappointed face. She closed her eyes. 'Oh, Christ, Phillip!' she whispered. 'I need you, I need you so much.' A warm tear fell on to her hand and she put it to her mouth and licked it. She looked at herself again. I have to get away, she thought, I have to escape him. She straightened and held her head up. I must leave, I have to. She took another big breath, filling her lungs and holding it for a few moments, she let it out slowly, watching her face in the mirror. It made her feel better, marginally and she did it again and again. A minute or so later, she let go of the dressing-table and stood alone, her back straight, her head up. She knew where she was going, she only wished she had done it years ago.

Crossing to the bed, she took off her robe and night-dress and went into the bathroom. Her hands shaking, she ran a hot bath, cleansed her face, packing her things quickly and neatly into a bag, then immersed herself in the bath. Clean, she came out of the bathroom, packed an overnight bag, dressed and made up her face. She had stopped trembling, the fear and panic had hardened into anger, into her fight for self preservation and the adrenalin pumping round her body gave her incredible strength. Ten minutes on she was dressed and ready to go; there was one last thing to do.

Downstairs in Mitchell's study, Suzanna went to his

desk and took out the small silver box she knew he kept there. She turned it over and read the number of the safe engraved on the back. Mitchell thought she was stupid, he never knew how much she observed, took in. She went to the drinks cabinet, clicked open the false door at the back of it and unlocked the safe, her ear close to it, listening for the clicks. She counted, gently turning the dial, holding her breath. The safe opened.

Placing her gloved hand inside, she took out the contents and laid them carefully in the vanity bag she had open on the floor beside her, counting as she did so. The last thing she removed was the velvet bag with her jewellery in and she smiled as she placed it on top of the money; Mitchell loved her jewellery with a peculiar lust. She closed the safe, relocked it and replaced the door. Finally she stood.

She walked out into the hall and, certain of her solitude, she opened the front door and stepped out, walking down the steps of the Regent's Park house on to the street. Thank God they were in London for the dinner, she thought, turning up the collar of her jacket and heading off on to the main road to find a taxi. She shivered and clutched her bags a little tighter. If they'd been in Wiltshire, Christ knows if she would ever have got away alive.

Chapter Sixteen

Phillip rolled over in bed and ignored the knocking at his door. It was five a.m. and it wasn't time to get up.

'Go away!' he called, pulling the covers up over his head. 'Bugger off!'

But the knocking increased.

'What the bloody hell . . . ?' He sat up and threw the covers back, reaching for his dressing-gown and striding across to the door. He yanked it open.

'What the devil is all this about?' he demanded. 'It's five a.m.!'

'Please, sahib, there is a call for you.'

'Well, why the hell didn't you tell me through the door?' Phillip put his hands up to his face and wearily rubbed his eyes. 'You people are so bloody incompetent!' he sighed. 'Who is it, bearer?'

'A lady, sahib, calling from abroad.' The bearer lowered his voice. 'I didn't want to say, sahib, in case memsahib was woken.' Phillip coughed. It had to be Suzanna. He flushed and said, 'You were right, well done.'

The bearer folded his palms and bowed his head. 'Please, sahib, she is waiting for you to go to the telephone.'

'Right, erm . . .' Phillip glanced back at the bearer from the doorway of the sitting-room. 'Best not to mention this to the memsahib.'

'No, sahib, thank you, sahib.'

Phillip turned, silently clicked the door shut behind him and walked on to the phone.

'Hello?'

'Phillip?'

His stomach flipped. 'Suzanna! Where are you? What's happened, why are you ringing?' He had told her where he would be but had never given her his number.

'I'm in Switzerland.'

'With Mitchell?'

'No, alone.'

He swallowed, his throat suddenly dry. He heard her silence down the line and knew she was weeping.

'I've left Mitchell,' she sobbed, 'I had to. I got on the first plane out of London!'

'Oh Jesus!' Phillip slumped down into a chair. He didn't know what to say, how to react. This was his worst nightmare, it could ruin everything. Gripping the receiver, he said, 'What are you going to do?'

Suzanna took a breath. She had stopped crying but her emotions were like a rollercoaster and she would stop and start weeping without reason or dignity. 'I'm coming to India,' she said weakly, 'I'm leaving for Delhi tonight.'

Phillip held his breath. He held down the panic that

seized him and threatened to overwhelm him, making him say things he would regret. He clenched his jaw.

'Phillip?' Suzanna cried. 'Are you still there?' Her voice was unstable, the tears threatened again.

'Yes, of course I'm still here.' He knew that he loved her more than the world and yet at this precise moment he hated her. He would have to go to Delhi, to sort her out, organise things for her. He couldn't leave her in this state, God knows what she'd do. The burden weighed heavily, the thought of it wore him down. 'I'll come to Delhi,' he said, 'I'll leave this afternoon.'

Suzanna on the other end began to weep again and the fleeting moment of hatred passed. Phillip's heart ached at the sound of her. 'Don't cry, baby, please, don't cry,' he whispered. 'I'll take care of you, I promise.' He glanced out of the window at the beginning of the day. He would tell Jane he had a meeting, get the next flight and be gone for a couple of days. He could afford a couple of days out of his schedule but not much longer, though. He hoped to God she was sorted in a couple of days.

'Suzy, I'll be there by tonight,' he said, 'I'll be at the airport tomorrow to meet your plane.' And without another word, he hung up.

Phillip tipped the boy who had carried the luggage up as Suzanna walked across to the window in the sitting-room of their suite and flung it open. She stepped out on to the balcony and wrapped her arms around her body. Despite the heat she hadn't been able to get warm since she had left England; the fear of Mitchell chilled her to the very core. She looked out at the gardens of the hotel, the sight of Delhi in the heat-hazed distance and shivered. She waited for Phillip.

Phillip stood inside the room and watched her. He could hardly believe it had only been six weeks since they'd been together that last night, he could hardly believe that this was the same woman he had loved for as long as he could remember. She was so thin, her shoulder bones dug into him as she'd leant against him in the taxi from the airport and her face had narrowed, highlighting the perfection of her features, the enormous size of her slanted, sad, grey eyes. She looked so vulnerable, almost the same as she had when he first saw her, so fragile and needing that his heart had wrenched at the sight of her and his body had ached with a desperate want to touch her, to comfort her. She needed him, in a way he had never been needed or wanted or desired in his life before, he was her lifeblood and that thought filled him with such power and such longing that it took his breath away.

Suzanna turned. 'Phillip?'

He went to the glass door and stood there, just looking at her. She put her hand out to him and he leant forward, taking it and pulling her towards him. He felt the tremble in her body and his own body responded, an involuntary emotion.

He put his hands to her shirt and slowly unbuttoned it, his fingers stiff, shaky. She wore nothing underneath, she never did with him. He eased it off her shoulders and gazed at her body. He could see the outline of her ribs just beneath the pale brown skin, skin so soft and smooth it tasted like cream. He bent his head and gently kissed her torso, his mouth travelling up to the sharp hollow of her neck. Suzanna wrapped her fingers in his hair and held his head close to her body. She let out a breath, a breath it seemed she had been holding since she left England and finally she relaxed. Closing her eyes, she moaned quietly as he lifted her skirt and pressed his mouth to her thigh and she smiled, with love and deep, deep relief, while the tears streamed silently down her cheeks.

In bed that night, Phillip lay awake while Suzanna slept quietly beside him. He knew he had to tell her, he knew that she had to go back to Mitchell, that neither of them could afford the scandal but he had no idea how to say it. She was so unstable, so abandoned in her passion, giving herself entirely up to him that he really was afraid if he left her she would just break down. It would be like taking the ground from under her feet. He rolled on to his side and stared at the shafts of moonlight that had slipped into the room. He had to tell her, though, he didn't know what else he could do.

'Phillip?' He felt a moment of guilt, as if he'd been caught out. 'Can't you sleep?'

He rolled over and looked at her. 'No. I thought you were asleep.'

Suzanna was lying on her back and she stared blankly up at the ceiling. 'I was,' she said quietly, 'but I often wake up after half an hour or so.' She smiled, wearily. 'I don't seem to be able to make it through the whole night any more.' Phillip reached out for her and she moved towards him, curling into his body. 'Why can't *you* sleep?'

'I don't know,' he lied.

'It's because of me, isn't it?' He stayed silent and gently

stroked her hair. 'Phillip?' She moved so that she could look up at his face. 'Tell me, please.'

He pressed his finger to her mouth. 'Sssh, it's nothing, the heat perhaps, that's all.'

He closed his eyes and it was then that Suzanna knew. She felt the most extraordinary pain in her chest, as if her heart had cracked. 'You want me to go back to Mitchell,' she said blankly. 'You don't want me here.' She moved away from him and sat up, holding the sheet over her breasts. 'You don't want any scandal.' She dropped her head forward and closed her eyes. The pain came again, so intense it made her wince. She held her breath to stop it.

'Suzy?' Phillip knelt up and moved to her. 'Suzy? Are you all right?' He put his hand on her shoulder but she didn't react. 'Suzy?' He began to panic, she wasn't breathing properly, her face was ashen. 'Suzanna?' Phillip shook her gently. She stared at him wide-eyed, she couldn't breathe, the breath was stuck in her chest, she couldn't let it out, the pain was too great. 'Suzy!' he shouted. 'For Christ's sake, Suzy! What the hell . . . ?' He shook her harder and she started to gasp, unable to swallow any air. 'Oh Jesus!' Phillip suddenly struck her across the face, a slap, loud and sharp, but not painful and she screamed, a wrenching, terrible noise. Then she drew breath. Finally she began to sob.

Phillip held her. 'You have to go back,' he whispered. 'You can't stay in India, you must have known that, Suzy, you must have known . . .' He kissed her hair, his arms wrapped around her frail, thin back. 'Suzy, please, it's for the best, you have to trust me, it's for our future.'

'But Mitchell . . .' She drew back and looked at him.

'Mitchell is going to kill me,' she cried, 'I know it, I'm sure of . . .'

Phillip soothed her. She wasn't seeing things properly, she was overwrought. 'Suzanna, I promise nothing will happen to you, you have to stop all this . . .'

'This what?' She wiped her face, instantly angry. 'Fantasising? Is that what you were going to say?' She jerked away from him and hugged her knees into her body, digging her fingers into the flesh. Suddenly she felt completely hopeless. She laid her head on her knees and closed her eyes. What was the point? None of it made sense to her any more, she was tired, exhausted and empty. Phillip was all she had and no matter how hard she tried to believe, she didn't know if that amounted to very much any more. She tried to think of something to say, anything, but she couldn't; her mind was totally blank, her body numb.

'Suzy?' Phillip touched her shoulder, trying to bring her back to him. 'Suzy, you will listen to me, won't you?' She shrugged. She didn't know what she would do. 'You'll go home?' He had to have her word, he would only be here another day, he needed to know she would be safe, that he would be safe. 'Suzy?'

'I'll do whatever you want me to,' she answered listlessly but she didn't know if it was the truth. She wondered if she knew anything at all.

'Only until this is over, until I'm back in London, you do understand that, don't you?' He leant in close to her and took a strand of her hair, winding it round his finger. Even in anger, in desperation she aroused him. 'You trust me, don't you, darling?'

'Phillip, I . . .' She broke off and took his kiss. What

was the point in explaining? What was the point in anything?

'There has only ever been you,' he whispered, pulling her towards him with the strand of hair. 'There will only ever be you.'

Suzy looked away. 'Jane?' she murmured. It was hardly a sound but it hung in the air between them for a moment, like a steel divide.

'Jane means nothing,' Phillip said. He looked at Suzanna. 'That's the truth.' But Suzy couldn't tell any more, truth or lies. He had asked her to believe so much that she wasn't sure she believed any of it. Phillip let go of the strand of hair and cupped the back of her neck with his hand. He kissed her hard, holding her head, digging his fingers into her hair. 'I love you, Suzy,' he whispered. 'Jane is only there for us.' He kissed her again and she opened up to him, pulling him back on to the pillows with her, wrapping her legs over his. Phillip moved, his hands either side of her head he held himself above her and looked down at her face. She filled him with strength. 'Jane is ours,' he murmured, 'I promise you.' But Suzanna didn't hear him. All she heard was an empty, hopeless silence.

Rami looked across at Jane, her eyes closed, her head leant back against the cushions on the cane sofa. He smiled at the peace between them, the contented silence that he so enjoyed and glanced at his watch. It was late and he had to get going.

'I know,' Jane said, hearing the slight movement. 'It's late and you ought to get going.' She opened her eyes and sat upright. 'Do you really?'

Rami got to his feet and walked over to her. He

bent his head and lightly kissed her forehead. 'Yes,' he said, 'I do.'

She smiled at the kiss. They touched only briefly now, now that they knew what lay beneath the surface but they couldn't stop touching altogether. They simply couldn't do it.

'OK,' Jane said. She sighed, stretched and then stood. 'Thank you for your company tonight. I would have been perfectly all right on my own but I'm glad I wasn't.'

'Thank you for dinner.' Rami pressed his palms together and bowed his head. Jane smiled; she loved his perfect courtesy. 'Shall I walk you to your bicycle?'

'If you like.'

He went to hold out his hand but stopped himself at the last moment. Jane noticed it but said nothing. She would have loved to hold his hand but she couldn't, she was married. It wasn't much of a marriage but it was a vow, in the eyes of God, and that was important to Jane. They walked down the steps of the verandah and around the outside of the house to the front. They walked close together, only inches apart but they didn't make contact.

'Are you all set for tomorrow?' Rami asked as they reached his bicycle. He had planned a big journey for them, to one of the distant temples of Baijur.

'I think so,' Jane answered. She never knew where they were going, Rami was peculiarly pedantic about that.

'Good.' He got on to his bicycle and bent to put the clips on. 'I'll see you tomorrow then,' he said, his feet ready on the pedals.

'Yes, tomorrow.' Jane stood back as he moved off.

'Goodbye, dear Jane,' he called, waving over his shoulder.

'Cheerio!' Jane stood and watched until he had disappeared down the drive and out of sight. 'Dear, dear Rami,' she finished, and hugging her arms around her, she walked back into the house, alone.

It took Rami about half an hour to cycle back home and the house was in semi-darkness when he arrived; he presumed everyone was asleep. He left his bicycle by the front steps for the boy to put away and walked into the house, nodding to the bearer who was squatting on the verandah waiting for him. As quietly as he could, he walked along to his room and, dismissing the boy, he switched off the lamps and went out on to his balcony. He gazed up at the stars and said his prayers, new prayers, different from the ones he had said for most of his life. Then he walked back inside, undressed and, thinking as he always did, of Jane, he lay down and went to sleep.

Shiva sat at the desk in his study and smiled. He had heard Rami come in, later than usual and he knew that Major Mills was away. The gods are moving the paths of fate for me, he thought, they are showing me the face of kindness. He stood and walked across to the small statue of Kali he had taken to keeping on his wall and took it in his hands. The black goddess, who wears a garland of skulls, the symbol of destruction and recreation. He ran his fingers over her body, the multiple arms and legs, the grinning, violent face. 'I worship you, Kali,' he said aloud, 'for you shall give me what I want.' Then he replaced it and made his way through the silent bungalow to bed.

Chapter Seventeen

Suzanna sat in the suite with the blinds drawn and a drink in her hand. She had been weeping. Her eyes were swollen, her face streaked with tears. She sipped a vodka tonic and stared blankly at the wall. She didn't know what to do.

An hour earlier she had been lying here with Phillip and now he was gone. She had had to say goodbye, she had clung to him in the hotel reception, begged him not to leave her, but he had. He had calmed her down, dried her tears and gone. Left her, here in Delhi, completely alone.

Suzanna took another sip of the drink. It wasn't strong enough so she added a splash more of vodka and reached for her cigarettes. She hadn't told Phillip about the money, about stealing from Mitchell, she didn't know why not. She had planned to, to convince him that she should stay but after that first night there wasn't any point. He didn't want her here, there wasn't much point in anything now. Suzanna added a half-smoked cigarette stub to the collection in the ashtray and leant her head back against the cushions. He thought she could go back, she had even convinced him that she would book her plane, that she'd leave this evening. Suzy smiled bitterly. If she ever set foot in the UK again, if Mitchell ever found out where she was, she would be dead. Mitchell would not forgive.

She lit the last cigarette in the packet and crushed the box in her hand. Standing, she walked to the telephone to dial room service for another packet and a couple more tonics. She picked the receiver up, scrabbled round for the list of numbers and unable to find it in the semi-darkness, she crossed to the window and pulled open the blinds. The brilliant afternoon sun hit her and she covered her eyes, her vision blurred. Moments later she removed her hand and looked out.

There was a scattering of people around the pool, golden brown bodies on blue and white striped towels. The water was clear, shimmering in the sunlight and the pool boys stood around in immaculate white jackets and black trousers, hurrying across to sunbeds at the click of a finger. Suzanna stared down, mesmerised by the gently moving water, by the sudden glorious image after the dismal darkness of the room. It looked so inviting, so incredible. She opened the French doors and stood on the balcony. She loved the sun, adored lying in it, adored being brown. It boosted her, she always felt, recharged her energy, filled her with life. She lifted her face up to the light and closed her eyes. The warmth was delicious, it soothed her. She took a deep breath, filling her lungs and letting go of it slowly, her whole body relaxing as the breath filtered away.

Then she opened her eyes again and went into the suite. She felt dizzy for a few moments, off balance and she held on to the wall. Recovering, she walked through to the bedroom and sat on the edge of the bed. She thought for a few seconds, her hand pressed against her temple, then she pulled her shirt over her head. Why not go out into the sun for an hour or so, she decided, why not relax in the warmth? What else did she have to do, except sit up here in the dark, miserable and alone? She unfastened her skirt, letting it drop to the floor and left it there. Naked, she bent and rummaged in a bag for a dress and her sunglasses, found what she wanted and slipped the dress over her head. She still felt wobbly, a little unstable on her feet but she did feel better, uplifted slightly, focused. She would buy a bikini at the hotel boutique, some suncream. She checked she had cash in her handbag and dropped the bottle of vodka in there, along with her room key. She definitely felt better now, she felt she had a purpose. For once, she knew what to do next.

Mick Capper sat on a sunbed in the shade of an umbrella and watched the poolside. He was a deep, nutty brown, his hair bleached pale streaky blond and he wore black nylon trunks that fitted him perfectly, a gold bracelet and a pair of Ray-Ban aviators. He was looking out for Suzanna Harvey.

Mick knew a stroke of luck when he saw one and he knew what to do about it as well. That was Mick's strength, sniffing out an opportunity, had a nose like a boxer his mates back in London used to say, and Suzanna Harvey was an opportunity, she was one hell of an opportunity, ripe and just ready for the picking. Mick smiled and clicked his fingers for the boy to bring him a beer.

Mick had been checking out that morning, he'd decided to move on, when he saw her, decided the hotel was a dead loss, nothing doing and he couldn't afford to waste time. But at the reception desk he'd spied Ms Harvey, the lady with married boyfriend departing, floods of tears, sobbing, the works. He'd stood at the desk and eyed them across reception, the cut of the bloke's suit, the Chanel skirt and top, the massive diamond the lady wore and he'd made a split-second decision. He cancelled his check-out and rebooked his room. Yes, he thought, spotting her instantly now and watching her settle herself on to a sunbed, Mick Capper certainly knew a stroke of luck when he saw one. He lifted the magazine, high enough to cover his face but low enough to secure his view, and rested back. No hurry, don't want to rush her, he thought, seeing the slug of vodka she added to the tonic she'd just ordered, give her plenty of time to relax in the sun. Babes were a hell of a lot easier relaxed in the sun.

Suzanna drifted off. She dropped her hand over the side of the sunbed, her arm completely relaxed and let her head loll to one side. Her eyes were shut and the sounds of the pool slowly faded, she saw a wonderful blank space in her mind and sighed. Seconds later she woke up.

'Oh! Christ what . . . !' She sat up and shielded her eyes from the sun, looking up at the figure by the side of her sunbed. Her heart was pounding and her head ached. She felt confused, disorientated.

'Gosh, I'm so sorry, I didn't mean to startle you.' The American accent stepped into the shade and came into view. He was smiling. 'I thought I should move the umbrella,' he said. 'You were going a little red on your legs and I was afraid you might burn.' He shook his head. 'I really do apologise, I honestly didn't mean to startle you but this sun is so fierce.'

Suzanna relaxed back. She *was* going red on her legs and the man was rather good-looking in a slick sort of way. She reached for her drink but the glass was empty.

'May I get you another?'

She hesitated. 'No, thank you but I, erm . . .'

He reached up and tilted the shade for her unasked. 'That's better,' he said. 'Are you sure you wouldn't like another?'

He really was very attentive. Suzanna looked at his face. He was nicely spoken too, a soft American drawl. 'Well, all right, thank you.' She reached for her dress and slipped it over her head. 'Would you like to join me?'

'Yes, thanks.' The man sat on the edge of the facing sunbed and Suzanna noticed how tight his trunks were. She glanced away.

'Charles Swan,' he said, holding out his hand, his American-in-town act was probably his best.

Suzanna looked up. 'Suzanna Harvey,' she answered and they shook.

'Very nice to meet you, Suzanna. Are you in India long?'

'I don't know, I . . .' Suzy's voice trailed off and she was relieved at the appearance of the boy.

'What are you drinking?' He knew exactly what she was drinking.

'A tonic water,' she said. 'Er, with vodka,' she added. Mick smiled. He ordered the drinks and rested back on his hands, looking at her.

'Business or pleasure?'

'Sorry?' Suzanna found his gaze disconcerting. It was a very long time since anyone had looked at her like that.

'What are you here for?'

She thought for a moment, then said, 'Holiday. What about you?'

'Business,' he answered. 'Only I'm taking a couple of days hard-earned rest.'

'I see.' Suzanna took her drink off the tray the boy held out and waited for Charles to do the same. 'Cheers,' she said, 'and thank you.'

'My pleasure.' Mick sipped his beer. 'So, Suzanna, do you like India?' He watched her face. He always used this question, it opened them up, led to all sorts of things.

'I don't know, I've not seen much of it.'

Mick nodded. 'Just Delhi, right?'

Suzanna finished her drink. She was thirsty, she clicked for the boy. 'Not even Delhi,' she said. 'The Taj Mahal Hotel.' She laughed hollowly.

'Would you like to see Delhi?' Mick kept his eyes on her face. 'I have some free time, I could always show you—'

'No.' Suzanna cut him short. 'Thank you very much, it's terribly kind of you but no. I don't think so.'

He shrugged casually to cover his irritation. He'd moved too fast, he should have been more careful. 'If you change your mind at all, if you need any company,

230

for dinner maybe, just let me know.' He smiled and pressed his palms together, imitating the Indian way. Suzanna smiled back.

'That's better,' he said. 'You don't smile often enough, it changes your whole face.'

Suzy looked up at him. It was the nicest thing she'd heard in months. He was right though, she didn't smile often enough, she was far too sad nowadays. 'We could meet up for dinner,' she said suddenly, without thinking, 'in the hotel restaurant.'

Mick grinned. 'Hey, that would be really nice! To tell you the truth I could use the company.'

Suzy laughed; she was glad she'd suggested it. He was genuinely pleased, he wanted to be with her.

'Shall we meet in the bar for a drink first?' he asked.

'Yes, all right. What time?'

'Say I book a table for eight and we meet around seven-thirty?'

'That sounds lovely.'

Mick held out his hand and Suzanna took it. 'I shall look forward to it, Suzanna.'

'Suzy, everyone calls me Suzy,' she said.

He nodded and grinned a second time. It had worked like a charm, always did. 'See ya later then, Suzy.'

'Yes, thanks.' The boy arrived with her drink and she held up her hand to wave before she took it and swallowed down a hefty gulp. She felt good, the sun, the vodka, here on her own, independent for once in her life and she knew what was going to happen next, she didn't have to think about it. She watched Charles walk into the hotel and waved a second time as he turned and glanced back from the doors. Thank

God she didn't have to think about what would happen next.

Jane and Phillip sat in silence. Dinner was over, they sat on the terrace in the flickering lantern light and looked in opposite directions. Phillip thought about Suzanna, he missed her, he longed for her and he felt guilty about her. He also felt guilty about Jane. He felt alone and for the first time since he had imagined all this he felt the terrible pang of doubt. He wondered what the hell he was doing.

Jane thought about nothing in particular, she wouldn't let herself think about Rami and she had no feelings about Phillip, so she simply stared at the floodlit gardens in the distance and wondered how the maharani's roses were doing. She started when she heard Phillip's voice.

'Janey?' She looked round. 'Janey, I think we should talk.'

She sipped her water and watched him over the rim of the glass but she remained silent. It was he who had disappeared off to Delhi without warning or explanation and it was he who had returned difficult and morose. Jane had nothing to say.

'Jane, when did things get so silent between us?' He leant forward and touched her hand on the table. It lay lifeless under his own. 'You're not unhappy, are you?'

'No, Phillip, I am not unhappy,' she answered. She could have said so much more, made accusations, voiced her opinions but she couldn't be bothered. She wasn't sure she really cared that much any more.

'Jane, I need you, you know, I really do.' He picked her hand up and squeezed it. He wanted some sort of physical contact, he was down, he wanted some comfort from his wife. 'I don't want things to go on the way they are.'

Jane sighed. She placed her glass on the table and sat forward. 'Nor do I, Phillip,' she answered honestly. It was no life, this silent hostility.

'Jane, can we sleep together tonight? Try to sort this out?'

But Jane immediately recoiled. She sat back and looked away. 'No,' she answered quietly, 'I don't think so, not tonight.'

Phillip kept his eyes on her face. 'Please,' he said, 'just in the same bed, just close to each other, that's all.' He had no more desire to make love than Jane did but he needed the solace of her, he needed physical reassurance.

Jane faced him. How could she refuse? She was his wife for pity's sake. She stared down at her lap and nodded her head.

'Thank you, Jane.' Phillip reached out and took her hand a second time. 'Thank you.'

Suzy stepped into the lift with Charles and he pressed the fifth-floor button. They smiled at each other as they travelled up in silence, each of them watching the floors light up on the elevator panel. The lift stopped, the door opened and Suzy stepped out. 'I'm just up here on the right,' she said as she dug in her bag for her key. 'Thank you for seeing me to my room.'

Mick shrugged. 'It was a pleasure Suzy, thank you for a wonderful evening.'

She turned to him and smiled. 'It was nice, wasn't it?'

'It was delightful.' Mick dug his hands in his pockets. 'Look, erm, Suzy . . .' he broke off.

'What?'

'Nothing, you'll think I'm interfering.'

She smiled. 'No I won't, come on, tell me, what is it?'

'Well.' He hesitated a second time for effect, then said, 'I know it's none of my business but over dinner you said you've been pretty uptight recently and can't sleep, I just kind of thought that maybe I might be able to help.'

Suzanna stiffened but Mick noticed it. He played the next bit very, very carefully.

'I get the same you see, when the work gets on top of me.'

She nodded and relaxed again. Charles had talked a great deal about his work, he was creative, a writer, and he'd said he thought Suzy was creative too. He could tell these things, sense them. 'Well look, I, er, have a couple of pills here,' he said quietly, 'little things I take every now and then, when I get a bit kind of stressed.' He brought his hand out of his pocket and held it out, palm up. Suzanna stared down at two pink capsules.

'Here, take them.'

Suzy shook her head. 'Thanks, I appreciate it, but no thanks.' She smiled to cover her shock. He could be anyone, offering her drugs, she turned away towards the door. 'I must get into bed,' she said quickly. 'It's late.'

Mick caught her hand as she turned. 'God, Suzy, I'm sorry, I didn't mean to offend you.'

'No, no you haven't offended me!' She laughed nervously.

'Look, I'm only trying to help, that's all. Please, don't be shocked.'

Suzanna looked at him. He popped one of the pills into his mouth and swallowed. 'They really help me unwind,' he said, 'help me sleep.'

Suzy still wasn't sure but Mick pressed the little pill into her hand. 'Take it,' he said. 'Flush it down the toilet if you don't want it.' He smiled. 'I'll never know.'

Finally Suzanna smiled back. She had no intention of taking it but there was no point in being rude. 'I must go,' she said. 'Thank you again for your company.'

'And yours,' Mick replied.

'Right then.' She put the key in the lock and Mick turned towards the lift. He pressed for it and it opened immediately. 'Goodnight, Suzanna,' he said before stepping into it. 'Sleep tight.'

'Goodnight, Charles.' She waited for the lift doors to close again, then she let herself into the suite, dropped the little pill into the ashtray on the table and went through to the bedroom to get ready for bed.

It was two a.m. and Suzanna woke with a start. Her heart was racing and she felt sick. Rolling on to her side, she opened her eyes and saw the light from the bathroom, it reassured her and she sat up.

It happened a lot now, a few hours of heavy, vodka-induced sleep, then she woke, suddenly, with a fright and a stale, dull taste in her mouth. She knew the drink didn't help, only made it worse really but if she didn't drink she wouldn't have slept at all.

Dropping her legs over the side of the bed, Suzy stood, and groped her way in semi-darkness to the bathroom. There she poured some water from the jug, drank it down and sat on the edge of the bath, looking at herself in the mirror and thinking about Phillip. She missed him so much it hurt. She wrapped her arms around her body, hugged herself and let her head fall on to her chest. What if I rang him, she thought, just to say a few words, just to know he wasn't so far away. She glanced up and saw the dark shadows under her eyes. If I spoke to him I might be able to sleep, if I could just reassure myself. She stood up and walked out of the bathroom, switching on the lights in the bedroom and sitting on the edge of the bed.

Opening the bedside drawer, she took out her diary and turned to the back page. She had written down his number, from his business card while he was in the shower. She hadn't meant to, but she'd seen it, there in his wallet and she couldn't help herself. Phillip didn't want her to have his number, he said he'd call her daily in the UK but she took it all the same. If I can just hear his voice, she thought, picking up the receiver, I'll feel all right, I'll know that he's there for me. She dialled the operator and read out the number in her book, then she replaced the receiver, sat back and waited for the call to come through.

Jane wasn't asleep. She lay next to Phillip, listening to him breathe quietly and evenly and looked out at the night sky. The moon was a slither, a tiny slice of iridescent light covered every now and then by a passing cloud. It was hot, hot and still and silent, only the small sound of Phillip's sleeping, steady and slow, broke the unending, suffocating quiet.

Suddenly the phone rang.

The sharp, shrill bell shattered the night and Jane

started with fright. She had had a telephone extension fitted into her bedroom while Phillip was away and cursed that fact now. She took a breath to calm herself and reached for the receiver. It could only be bad news, she thought, switching on the light, who else would telephone at this time of the night? Phillip rolled over and opened his eyes as Jane answered the call.

'Hello?' Her voice was unsteady. 'Hello? Jane Mills speaking. Who is it?' She looked at Phillip. 'It's silent,' she said, 'there's no one there!'

'Hold on for a while,' he answered her, sitting up. 'It sometimes takes a minute or so to connect.'

Jane did as he said, they waited in silence.

'Here, give me the phone.' Phillip was unnerved. He took the receiver. 'Hello? Who's there?' He held it close to his ear. 'Hello?' Then he heard her. A soft, heavy breath, a sob, so quiet he almost missed it and he knew. His heart plummeted, he held on for a moment longer, then he reached across Jane and replaced the receiver. 'God knows who it was,' he said, 'but if it's urgent they'll ring back.' He swung his legs over the side of the bed and stood. 'You go back to sleep, darling.' He pulled on his bath robe. 'I'll stay up for half an hour in the sitting-room, see if anyone calls back.' He walked around the bed, kissed her lightly on the cheek. 'I'll finish the night in my room,' he said.

Jane nodded. She waited for him to leave the room and relieved, she plumped up her pillow, switched off the light and settled down for the rest of the night.

But Suzanna didn't ring back. She dropped the receiver into its cradle after hearing Phillip's voice and stood, walking through to the sitting-room of the suite. She found the small pink pill that Charles had given her and popped it into her mouth, swallowing it down. Then she returned to the bedroom, lay down on the bed and curled herself into a ball, hugging her knees in tight, squeezing her eyes shut. Jane means nothing to him, she kept saying over and over again, Jane means nothing to him. But the image of Jane and Phillip in bed was locked in her mind, it plagued her, sickened her and tortured her. And it did so until the pill took effect, her body finally relaxed and she at last fell into a deep, black and heavily drugged sleep.

Twelve hours later when Suzanna woke, the sun was high in the sky, directly overhead and as she drew back the curtains, shielding her eyes from the bright white light, she realised that the morning had gone and that for the first time in months she hadn't woken with a terrible feeling of fatigue. She sat down on the edge of the bed and stared out at the sky, a perfect clear blue and sighed heavily. She felt tired but a different tired from what she knew, a relaxed feeling that made her limbs heavier, her whole body looser. She felt better too, she was hungry, had an appetite without any vodka inside her.

Standing, she went to the telephone and dialled room service to order some lunch but, glancing down, she saw her diary open and remembered the call last night. She hung up, her appetite suddenly gone. She dropped her head into her hands and wished she could sleep some more, blank it all out, sleep away the pain and give her body, give her mind a chance to recover. She slumped on to the bed and lay there for a while, her eyes closed, trying to shut her mind off. Then suddenly she sat up, picked up the phone and called reception.

'Room 114 please,' she said and waited for the ring-ing tone.

Mick sat on his balcony and watched the poolside down below; he wasn't moving from his room until he saw Mrs Harvey. He reckoned that she'd probably call him but if she didn't then he wanted to be on hand when she appeared. Either way, he'd got it covered.

Relaxing back on his sunlounger, he moved on to his side to tan under his arms and made sure the pool was still in view. Closing his eyes for a couple of moments, he imagined what lay ahead and unable to help himself, he felt the stirring of a magnificent erection.

The phone by his bed rang.

Jumping up from his sunlounger, he hurried in from the balcony and took a breath before he answered; he didn't want to sound rushed. He held the receiver and said, 'Yup. Charles Swan speaking.' Then he clenched his fist in a gesture of triumph. 'Hi there,' he said, smiling. 'Hey, glad to hear it. I told you, didn't I? Those pills are magic!' He laughed. 'Yeah, I'm sure I can, just one of the little babies? Yup, no problem at all, Suzy. What d'ya wanna do, come up here and get it, or will I bring it down for you?' He reached across the bed for his shirt. 'Right! No probs, Suzy. I'll be right there!' And he hung up, threw his shirt over his head, pulled on his shorts and took the pill he had already prepared from a small dish in the bathroom. He winked at himself in the mirror and walked out of the room, along the corridor and down to the lifts. Within minutes he was knocking at the door of

Suzanna Harvey's suite with a ready smile and a measured drop of the highest quality LSD in the small pink capsule he held in his hand.

Suzanna stood. She went to pour Charles another cup of coffee but the pot moved on the table. She screwed her eyes up and saw the table move, the rug under it lifting it up into the air like a magic carpet.

'Jesus!' She sat down and put her hands up to her head. 'What's happening? I . . .' She shook her head from side to side, trying to clear her vision but the room started to move, the walls buckled, bulging in the middle, great chunks of plaster coming off and falling heavily to the floor. She coughed on the dust. 'My God!' she cried. 'There's an earthquake! Quick! The whole place is . . .' She jumped up but her legs gave out and she stumbled, hitting herself hard on the table. She fell forward and slumped down against the sofa. She couldn't see Charles. Was it Charles? Who was it? She wasn't sure if anyone had been there, she didn't know what she was doing there. She began to panic. 'Where am I?' she called out from the floor. Nothing looked right, the room was a mess, it was moving, the floor rolled and she felt sick, she thought she was going to vomit and turned her head to the side. Suddenly it stopped. It changed colour, the whole room changed colour and beautiful shapes of red and gold, orange and turquoise floated up from the rugs, drifting across the walls.

'Phillip?' She tried to look for Phillip, he'd been there only a few moments ago, they'd been having coffee, she had taken a pill to help her sleep. Was it Phillip? Had she taken a pill? She lay back and stared up at the ceiling.

The colours had moved on to the ceiling and they looked so amazing she could hardly breathe. 'Phillip?' she called out again. 'Phillip?' Then she closed her eyes and let the shapes dance in the air and the room twirl her round and round.

Mick stood up as Suzanna closed her eyes and walked through into the bedroom. He always used LSD, it was a mind bender and by the end of the day she wouldn't know what the hell had happened, let alone who Charles Swan was and what he looked like. He opened the bedside drawer and took out the velvet bag Suzy had placed there. He dropped it into a plastic bag he carried in his pocket and started on the rest of the room. He was systematic, a professional and there wasn't much that escaped his attention. He went through the entire suite in a matter of minutes and when he was sure he had everything, he walked across to the door, glanced back at Suzanna Harvey, smiled, and stepped out into the corridor. He went back to his own room, finished his packing, adding the money and the bag of jewellery to his case, then he showered, dressed and went down to reception to check out. Exactly half an hour later he had gone.

Suzanna saw the last colour drift out through the window and opened her eyes, standing to follow it on to the balcony. Outside the sun had moved lower in the sky and it suffused the world with a warm, golden light. Suzy smiled; it was so beautiful she wanted to cry. As she made her way out towards the gold, she glanced sideways at the mirror above the sideboard, expecting to see her face, tanned, drenched in that same wonderful light. She smiled at her reflection, gazing for a moment at her own beauty. Then suddenly, she screamed.

Her face changed, it changed right in front of her eyes. The light died and her cheeks sagged, great hollows in her face appeared, the skin around them wrinkled and bagged. She put her hands up and clawed at the flesh, her eyes sank down into the black shadows below them and her face started to bleed. She screamed again. Her mouth twisted and her teeth were black. She clawed harder, frantically trying to drag the skin away from her face, her fingers covered in blood.

'No!' she screamed, yanking the mirror from the wall and smashing it down on to the ground, shattering the glass into a thousand tiny pieces. She sank to her knees and began to sob. 'No, please God, no,' she cried, biting the inside of her mouth to stop it twisting, not feeling the pain. 'Oh God, no . . .' She covered her head with her hands and curled herself up. 'Oh God . . .' she moaned, over and over again. 'Oh God, no . . .'

When she came round all she could feel was pain. It was dark and she was lying on the floor, her knees curled up tight, her body cold and stiff. She opened her eyes and moved, the metallic taste of blood in her mouth making her feel sick, the pain of her face knocking her dizzy. Disorientated and frightened, she staggered across to the wall and felt for the light switch. Clicking it on, she gasped. The room flooded with light and she saw where she had been lying, the carpet littered with glass and stained with blood. She held on to the wall and made it into the bathroom. She had no idea what had happened, her mind was blank.

Turning on the light over the sink, Suzy had to grip the edge of the unit as she saw her face. It was horrific. Gently, she touched her eyes, swollen and bruised, then she leant forward and ran the cold tap. She fumbled in her wash bag for some cotton wool, and dipping it in the cold water, she held her breath and put her trembling hand up to swab the cuts on her cheeks. She felt sick, she couldn't stop shaking and the pain was making her wince. Moments later, she realised what had happened.

Dropping the cotton wool, she ran into the bedroom and pulled open the drawer. It was empty, the velvet bag had gone. At the wardrobe, she ripped the door open and frantically rummaged through the piles of clothes, flinging them on to the floor. The money wasn't there. Fifty thousand pounds in cash had gone. She held on to the wall and started to cry, pathetic, wailing sobs. She had been robbed, the jewels and the money had gone. She had been robbed and Suzanna had nothing left.

Several hours later, she sat in the concierge's office in silence and waited for his phone to ring. He sat opposite her, avoided her eye and drummed his fingers on the desk. He had no idea what to make of the incident.

'Mrs Harvey, I must be asking you a final time if you will consider giving a statement to the police,' he said. 'It is most essential that they know what was stolen from you.'

Suzanna looked up. 'I have no idea what was stolen,' she said blankly, 'and I have no wish to make a statement.'

The concierge sighed heavily. 'But there must be someone who you would like me to contact for assistance, Mrs Harvey?'

Suzanna shook her head. 'All I would like, please, Mr Kapoor, is a good price for my ring and my earrings.'

'Yes, that is taken care of, Mrs Harvey, but I am just thinking that . . .'

Suzanna held her hand up to silence him. She wanted nothing except the money for the earrings and ring she had found in her wash bag, the only things the thief had missed. 'Please, Mr Kapoor, no more questions.' She couldn't take the risk of being on police files, of Mitchell finding her. 'I am tired, I would just like to get this settled and check out.'

The concierge nodded, just as his phone rang. He picked it up, spoke quickly and smiled across at his guest. His conversation took a couple of minutes, then he replaced the receiver and said, 'I have a good price from my brother-in-law, Mrs Harvey, he will be here with the money in half an hour.'

Suzanna nodded. She almost broke at this point, she felt relief swamp her and tears sprang to her eyes. She looked away. 'Thank you,' she said quietly and she rose, nodded at the concierge and went up to the suite to pack.

Chapter Eighteen

Jane finished her dinner and rang the small bell on the table for the bearer to come and clear. She was tired tonight, Phillip was out and all she wanted to do now was have a bath and go to bed. She patted her mouth with her napkin and rang the bell again, calling, 'DhaniRam? I have finished.' Then she scraped her chair back and stood, taking her cardigan off the back of it and draping it over her shoulders. She could hear voices inside the house and, ringing her bell a third time, she walked in from the terrace and followed the noise through to the hall. There she stopped short.

'Oh!' She walked towards a woman slumped on the chair in the hall. 'It's all right, DhaniRam,' she said to the bearer, 'I'll take care of this.' He dropped his fingers away from the woman's arm and stepped back, muttering in Hindi.

'Hello, may I help you?' Jane couldn't see the woman's

face, her head was covered with a shawl and she looked away, towards the darkness outside. She was wearing European clothes though, expensive ones by the look of it and Jane could tell by the skin on her arms that she wasn't Indian. Jane moved closer and touched the woman's arm.

'Are you all right? Is there something I can do for you?' The woman turned.

'Oh my dear! Your face! What on earth . . . ?' Jane glanced over her shoulder. 'DhaniRam? Can you send for the doctor? Now please!' She knelt down to the woman's level. 'Are you all right?' The woman stared blankly at her. 'Will you come inside for a while, let my doctor have a look at your face?' Jane stood and gently helped the woman to her feet. 'Come on,' she said kindly, 'it's all right, you're amongst friends now.' And leading the way inside, Jane held the woman's hand while she quietly began to sob.

Twenty minutes later, her face bathed properly and dressed by the doctor, Suzanna Harvey sat on the white sofa in Jane and Phillip's sitting-room and stared blankly across at Jane. She picked at her fingernails absent-mindedly, her hands trembled. She took in the order of the room, the framed wedding photograph, the immaculate pale Jane, and a huge swell of anger washed over her. It should be me, she thought, a bitter taste rising in the back of her throat, sitting here, helping someone, it should be me. She clenched her hands together in her lap, locking her fingers, digging her nails into the flesh. Then she looked up and unable to stop herself, said, 'You're not at all like I expected.'

Jane turned away from the window and looked at the woman. She had the oddest sensation, down in the pit of her stomach, a nervousness, a small, tight knot of tension. She saw an expression of distaste on the woman's face and a gentle quizzical look crossed her own. 'I'm sorry?' she said, 'I don't understand.'

The anger erupted, a terrible, intense need to hurt, to strike out. 'No,' Suzanna answered coldly, 'I don't expect you do.' She bit a fingernail and tore the skin, making it bleed and, placing her hand on the sofa beside her, she left a small smear of dark red blood on the cream silk.

Jane winced. She had begun to feel panicky, trapped almost and she took a deep breath to calm herself. She went to stand, to call DhaniRam for some drinks, anything to relieve the tension but as she did so Suzy said, 'You think you're so smug, don't you? You think you've got it all here, servants, position, Phillip.' Her face twisted suddenly as she said his name and Jane's stomach lurched. She held on to the arm of the sofa and froze.

'Well you haven't!' Suzanna cried suddenly. 'Phillip is mine! He's mine! He always has been and always will be!' A sob caught in the back of her throat and she gasped for air. 'I love him ... he ... he loves me!' She stood and lashed out, knocking the photograph frame from the table and smashing it on the cold marble floor. Jane watched with horror. She tried to call DhaniRam but her voice dried up in her throat.

'He doesn't want you!' Suzanna cried. 'He married you to get his job, to keep me! He told me that you were there for us, to screen us to make sure ... to make sure ...' Suddenly she lost track of what she was saying and her voice trailed away. 'To make sure ...' She put her hands up to her face, her eyes were blank and confused. 'Oh God . . .' She began to weep. 'Look at me, look at my face,' she murmured. 'Oh God . . .'

Jane took her hand off the sofa. She had been gripping it so hard that she'd left an imprint of her fingers on the silk. She moved back, away from the woman, frightened, her body sweating, her legs weak. She had never seen such emotion, such violent anger. She edged towards the door, her back to the wall, her eyes continually on the woman. She held her hands in front of her body, protectively, ready to defend herself. She was shaking.

'He said it'd be all right,' Suzy whispered. 'He said to trust him . . .' She looked up as Jane made it to the door. 'He's my life, you know.'

Jane nodded, not daring to move. She heard a commotion behind her in the hall and prayed it was the bearer. She pressed herself back, holding her breath.

'He said to trust him, he said he knew . . .' Suddenly Suzy's head jerked up. Phillip had appeared in the doorway behind Jane.

'Jesus! Suzy!' He ran forward and pulled her in to his body, surrounding her with his arms. 'Oh my God . . . my darling! What's happened?' Suzanna started to cry again and he stroked her hair with infinite tenderness. 'Please, baby, don't cry, don't . . .' He broke off and glanced behind him. He saw Jane, saw her frightened, confused face and shut his eyes, trying to blank it out. 'Suzy, please, please don't cry,' he whispered. Gently he released her and helped her down on to the sofa. He dug in his pocket for his silk handkerchief and tenderly wiped her eyes, careful of the dressings. He turned.

'Jane?'

Jane heard her name but she didn't react. She stood motionless, pressed back against the wall, shocked and confused by what she had just witnessed. She shook her head.

'Jane? I . . .' Phillip moved towards her but she backed away, out of the door. 'Jane, please . . .'

She stood outside the room and stared at him inside it. She had seen his face, seen the love, seen the terrible fear there but she had to hear it, she had to know from him.

'Is it true?' she asked. Her voice was hoarse, hardly a whisper. Phillip closed his eyes for a moment, then he nodded.

'How long?'

He walked towards her. 'Jane, please, it doesn't matter how . . .'

'How long?' she shouted.

He dropped his head and his shoulders slumped. 'Three years,' he murmured, unable to look up. 'Three years.'

Jane stared at him for a moment longer, then she turned and ran. She ran down the steps of the bungalow, down the drive and across the palace grounds. She saw nothing and heard nothing. She ran as fast as she could, she didn't know where she was going or what she was doing but she knew she had to get away, she knew she had to escape this horrible ugly mess.

Jane didn't know how far she had run or for how long when she stopped. She slowed to a walk, her whole body pounding, the blood roaring in her ears. It was dark, the clouds covered the moon and it was hot and still, the air trapped close to the earth, wrapped close around her body.

She didn't for a while know where she was, she wandered across a lawn, the grass dry and rough under foot, she saw bushes ahead, a creeper-covered wall and then she recognised the arch, the opening to the water garden. She carried on, through the opening and down on to the low stone wall, walking along it until she jumped down into the open space and walked across to the still, black waters of the pools. She sat on the edge of one as she had done that night with Rami and curled her knees up under her. She laid her cheek down on her knees and closed her eyes. She didn't think about Phillip, she didn't think about anything, she felt empty and numb.

Rami came to the water garden from the road. He left his bicycle on the ground and climbed over the lowest part of the ruined wall, dropping down the other side, silently and easily, with the grace of a cat. He stood and looked at Jane, here alone just as Shiva had told him she was, her head bowed in sadness, her body curled up in a gesture of defence. He moved forward, his footsteps silent on the ancient mosaic tiled floor and reaching her, he knelt down before her and gently lifted her face up.

'Jane?'

She felt no alarm at the sight of him, no fright. She had sensed his presence, it was almost as if she had been waiting for him. 'My grandfather told me you had run away, I came after you.'

'How did he . . . ?'

Rami put his fingers up to her lips to silence her. He did not know and he did not care. Moving his hand to her hair, to the back of her neck, he gently eased her face towards his. He loved her, of that much he was certain, he loved her gentle strength, her kindness and her humility. He loved everything about Jane Mills in a way he had never loved before and knew he would never love again. He had found the keeper of his soul and, as he kissed her, moving his hands across her back and pulling her body down to his, he knew that this would change his life and that he wanted it to be changed.

Jane closed her eyes. For one peculiar moment she remembered her father and what he had said about love. She smiled fleetingly and realised that he had been right, that she had found someone she would die for just as he'd said she would. Then she opened them again and looked at Ramesh as he broke their kiss and dragged his mouth down over her throat to her neck, slipping the buttons of her shirt through their holes, easing the material back, exposing her, caressing her. She wrapped her fingers in his hair, the black of it stark against the white of her breast and she moaned as his lips found her nipple. His tongue darted across it and she felt such a sharp desire run through her that it was almost painful. She wrapped her bare legs over his, and he pulled at her skirt, bunching it up over her hips, fumbling with his own *churidar*. He moved over her and looked down at her face, her eyes half-closed, her mouth parted. Then he knelt back and slowly he finished unbuttoning her shirt, his fingers trembling now, struggling slightly with the zip of her skirt. Gently he eased her clothes down over her narrow hips and the lean, long thighs and stared at her naked body, her pale gold skin as smooth and warm to touch as sun-drenched marble. He undressed himself, letting her help him, flinching, not with pain but with intense pleasure at her touch. Finally, he rolled his silk *kurta* and placed it as a pillow under her head. He covered her with his body and she moved her legs apart, high up over his hips, she looked up at the sky and for that one second the clouds parted and she caught sight of the moon. She cried out and her face was lit with its extraordinary, pale white light.

Phillip stood in the sitting-room and looked anxiously out at the driveway to the bungalow for sight of Jane. He was worried sick, he had sent a servant to that Indian Ramesh Rai's place and another over to the club. He hoped to God nothing had happened to her, he would be in for a hell of a scandal if it had.

Turning away from the window for a few minutes, he walked out of the sitting-room and along the passage to the guest bedroom where Suzanna was asleep. He glanced in, watched her for a few moments filled with longing and despair, then silently he closed the door again. As he went back to the sitting-room, he saw Jane come up the steps of the bungalow and stopped in the hall, facing her.

'Where've you been?' he asked.

Jane looked away. 'Walking,' she answered coldly. 'Why?'

'I was worried.' Phillip walked out towards her but stopped as she backed down the step. 'Janey, I'm sorry,' he said, 'I really am.'

Jane turned to look at him. She didn't know what to say in reply. She knew the love he felt, she understood him and she pitied him but she didn't forgive him. He had dishonoured his word, married her knowing at the time that he was shaming the vows he made. She couldn't forgive that. She knew and she understood because she too loved, with a force and passion that astounded her but she had fought it and struggled with it until tonight, until there was nothing left to fight or struggle for.

She put her hand on the balustrade and leant wearily against it, pulling herself up the steps. She walked past Phillip and into the bungalow. He caught her arm.

'Will you stay, Jane?' His voice was desperate, pitiful.

She carefully removed his hand. 'Yes,' she answered, 'I'll stay.' She had no choice, she could not leave Rami, not now, not after tonight, even though an affair was impossible. But she could not live alone here, she knew that, the scandal would be too great, it would destroy Rami. She looked up at Phillip's face. 'But I'm not staying for you, I'm staying because I want to.'

He nodded and hung his head, relief swamping him.

'I never, never want to hear of this woman again or catch a hint of scandal. You do understand that, don't you?'

Again he nodded and Jane carried on into the house. She stopped in the hallway and glanced back. 'I can understand your love, Phillip,' she said sadly, 'but I cannot understand the deceit, the dishonour.' And without another word, she turned and went inside to bed.

Chapter Nineteen

It was mid-October and Mitchell Harvey sat in his office on the Embankment, at the top of a huge stone Victorian building overlooking the Thames and buzzed his secretary. He had a file open on the desk in front of him.

'Send in my next appointment, Miss Warner,' he said over the intercom. He released the button and sat back to wait.

'Morning, Mr Harvey.'

A young man came in, half Indian, half English. He wore an expensive suit and tie, his shirt was handmade. Mitchell knew; he'd paid for it. Mitchell nodded at him.

'Sit.' He pointed to the chair in front of his desk and the young man did as he was told. Mitchell looked at him for a few moments, enjoying the sight of him, then he said, 'You saw her yourself?'

The young man nodded. He was pleased with himself, he almost smiled.

'And you have the address?'

He patted the soft leather case he held on his lap. 'Here, with the rest of the details.'

Mitchell stood and turned his back on the young man, looking out of the window at his spectacular view. He was angry, just the mention of her incensed him, and the muscle in his jaw twitched. It had taken too long to find her after that incident in Delhi, ten weeks they'd been watching out, three months Imran had been away. He knew she'd slip in the end though, Suzanna wasn't bright, she had to make a mistake sometime, he'd always been certain of that. Mitchell smiled and the muscle was still.

'You have the money, my things?'

'Yes, they're back in the safe.'

Mitchell came back to the desk. He flipped the file open and looked down at the photograph of Suzanna with a blond man. He turned it over and fingered the next shot. Poor Suzy, couldn't spot a con man inches from her nose. He closed the file on the picture of Mick Capper face down in a ditch; he had a bullet through the back of his head.

'Where is she?'

Imran had been waiting for this question. He opened the briefcase and squared his shoulders, passing a number of files across the desk. He was pleased with himself, he had reason to be. 'In Baijur, like you said she'd be.' He leant forward. 'Mills moved her, though, three times, practically every three weeks, which is why I couldn't suss it at first.' He ran his tongue provocatively over his lips. 'They must have met up at different places every time, he hardly ever went to hers and when she went out she always wore Indian dress.'

Mitchell's mouth curled into a sneer; Suzanna was a racist, it must have pained her terribly to give up her Chanel for a sari.

'Anything else?'

Imran took his cue: he always knew when to stop. 'It's all in the files,' he finished. 'I'll let you go over the details in private.'

Mitchell nodded. He opened the first brown folder and glanced down. A few moments later he looked up again.

'Well done,' he said.

Imran nodded. He waited for Mitchell to make another comment but when he didn't, Imran asked impatiently, 'What do you want me to do next?' But the moment he said it he knew he'd made an error.

Mitchell stopped reading but didn't look up. 'I will tell you when I am ready,' he snapped. 'Don't push me.'

Imran looked away. You never knew with Harvey which way he'd swing. He was an evil bastard, you had to watch every step. Several minutes later, Mitchell closed the file.

'Have you made any arrangements for lunch?' he asked. Imran shook his head. 'Good. We'll go to my club then.'

He stood, unlocked a drawer in his desk and slipped the files inside. He didn't want anything done for now, he needed to think it through carefully. She had to go but he didn't want any whiff of scandal. Locking the drawer, he walked around the desk and stood in front of the young man. He touched the thick, jet black hair. 'I've missed you,' he said. Imran flinched; this was a part of the job he didn't like.

'Come on.' Mitchell moved towards the door and glanced back as Imran stood. Success always gave him a hell of an appetite. 'I booked a table for two at midday,' he said. 'We don't want to waste the afternoon eating, do we?'

It was late, past midnight, and Shiva Rai sat at his desk in the slumbering silence of his house waiting for his call. The end was near and he was finally ready. He had waited patiently for this, he had lived for it, a wish passed on his father's deathbed, a debt of honour that should have been paid many years ago. Events, circumstances, too many things had conspired against him, thwarted him, made him wait. But now, now he had won. He had manipulated the maharajah, persuaded him of his need to be advised, given him the idea. And then, after a long search he had found Major Mills, in the English royal house and he knew his luck had finally turned, he knew he was going to get what he wanted. He had advised the maharajah and Mills had been brought back to India, brought back to finally answer for his family's crimes.

But Shiva was tired, he had been planning for too long, his whole life it seemed and now, now that it was almost finished, he was suddenly weary of it all. He wanted for it just to be over.

The phone rang. He was ready; the time had come. Picking up the receiver, he spoke quickly and quietly. He wrote down an address along with a sum of money on the note pad in front of him and smiling briefly, he hung up. He made one last call, read out what he had written down, confirmed the instructions, the timings of Phillip's visit and saying nothing else, replaced the receiver. His spies had served him well. He was finished; it was done.

Standing, he crossed to the window and looked out at the sky, that great expanse of black that saw all the sins of the world. What did his little one matter? It was a small immorality in the sea of human evil. It was deserved and it was just.

Hearing an owl cry, Shiva Rai shuddered. A superstitious old man, it was a bad omen and it unnerved his sense of calm, of righteousness. He backed away from the window, not wanting to hear it again and hurried across the room to the door. He turned off the lamps from the main switch and took the key to his study from a silk cord that hung from his cummerbund. Then he closed the door behind him as he stepped out into the passage and locked it. The next time he entered that room it would be over. A hundred years of dishonour would be wiped from the name of Rai.

Chapter Twenty

The weather had cooled. It was autumn and the harsh heat of high summer had softened to an easy warmth, bright sunny mornings with fresh easterly winds and temperate afternoons that faded slowly into cool evenings.

Rami sat on the steps of the Rai bungalow in the mellow midday sun and watched the mechanic at work on Shiva's Land Rover. He was expected at Viki's hunting lodge up in Meejat for lunch with his grandfather and the maharajah and he was already late; he should have been on his way two hours ago.

He kept his eyes on the legs that stuck out from under the jeep and waited, impatiently tapping his fingers on the stone step where he sat. His grandfather rarely asked him for lunch, it had to be something important and he was worried that he would offend. Shiva was up in the hills hunting with Viki and a party of politicians, Rami had been honoured to be invited.

'Any luck?' he called, standing and heading down to the mechanic. The man slid out from under the Land Rover.

'I'm sorry, Ramesh Sahib, but I think you have a problem with the oil.'

Rami sighed irritably. 'Can you fix it?'

'Oh most certainly, but not right away, sahib.' The man sat up and wiped his hands on a rag. 'I can do it maybe in an hour.'

Rami nodded. There was no other way up to the lodge, a taxi would never make it. 'OK,' he said, turning back to the steps. 'Do the best you can.' And he sat down again and tried to take his mind off the waiting.

Phillip locked his office door and walked across the terrace and along the passage to the front of the palace. He exchanged greetings with the two uniformed guards on duty and walked through the doors that were held open for him. A taxi was waiting at the entrance.

He gave the address he wanted and climbed into the car. It wasn't the right address but it was close and he'd go the rest of the way on foot. He was looking forward to this afternoon, with the maharajah away, he was taking a well-earned rest. Glancing behind him as the car pulled out on to the main road and watching the distance for a few minutes, he satisfied himself that no one had seen him and, winding the window down, he sat back with a cool breeze on his face and relaxed.

Suzanna was waiting for him in the hallway of her rented bungalow at exactly one o'clock; she knew he would be on time. He knocked at the door twice and she opened it, standing to the side out of view, letting him inside the house. They stood facing each other for a few moments, both aware of the luxury of spending the afternoon together in private and then Phillip lifted her up and carried her through to the bedroom.

'God, I want you,' he said as he placed her on her feet in the darkened room. He glanced across at the window just to check the blinds were fully drawn, then he kissed her, pulling her dress up and pressing her urgently back towards the bed. Suzy waited a few moments then she tore her mouth away.

'No,' she said quietly. 'Wait.' She walked away from him and along the passage. A minute or so later, she came back with her hands full of long silk scarves and saw the briefest flicker of a smile pass across his lips. She dropped them on the bed and turned. 'Take your clothes off,' she instructed. 'All of them.'

Phillip swallowed. He unbuttoned his shirt, pulling his tie down and letting them both drop to the floor. Bending, he pulled off his socks, undid his flies and tugged his trousers down over his hips. He was fully erect.

Suzanna placed her fingers on him and stroked, twice, her hand moving the whole length of him. 'Lie down,' she commanded. He shivered with anticipation and did as she asked.

Taking the scarves, she lifted his arms above his head and tied his wrists with the first one, not tight, but tight enough, then she parted his thighs, tying each of his ankles to the post at the corner of the bed. She watched his face and lifted her dress above her head, standing in just her stilettoes and a gold chain around her slim, curved waist. She moved forward and bent her head, darting her tongue over the tip of him, her heavy breasts falling forward and touching his thighs. He groaned and struggled to move his arms.

'You can't touch, remember?' she said, lifting her head away. She climbed up on to the bed and knelt over him, raising her body up, the sharp heel of her shoes digging into his flesh. She cupped her breasts and fingered the nipples, wetting the end of one finger so that the pink tip glistened with saliva. Then she moved forward so that her hips were above his face and smiled. 'Only with your tongue,' she murmured, 'and your cock.' And parting her thighs further, she lowered herself down, moaned at the exquisite pleasure and closed her eyes, just as the shadow of a figure passed across the wall in front of her.

Jane sat up in bed with a sheet over her and drank the camomile tea that the ayah had brought her. She had been writing her diary. It was a while since she had done so, she had been too unwell but she felt better today, less tired and less sick and she reckoned that she might at last be coming to the end of her illness. She finished her tea, optimistic at the prospect of her afternoon with Rami, and stood, placing the cup neatly back on the tray for the servant.

Jane had taken to resting over lunch, it was the worst time of the day for her, when the sun was at its highest and food smells seemed to drift all over the city. But at least she had been luckier than most who suffered from Indian tummy, even though she was sick at lunch, she usually felt better most evenings.

Walking through to the bathroom, Jane ran the taps in the sink and splashed her face with cool water. She tied her hair back and dabbed a little rouge on her cheeks.

She had no idea where they were going that afternoon and she had no idea what to wear. Rami had sent a message last night telling her to meet him at an address in the city, probably a temple, she thought, deciding on long trousers to be safe, but you could never tell with Rami and this book he was writing, he was constantly full of surprises.

Jane went back into the bedroom, laid her clothes out and began to dress. She slipped her feet into her sandals and collected up her diary, sketch book and her satchel. Then she walked along the corridor, had a quick word with the bearer about what time she would return and hurried down the steps to her bicycle. She didn't want to be late; the message said one-thirty and it was probably a twenty-minute cycle ride.

Phillip lay breathless on the bed, his face covered with Suzanna's rich dark hair, his sweat-dampened body smothered with her own. He had the most glorious feeling in his whole body, it was more than sexual satisfaction, it was a strange euphoric power that coursed through his veins like adrenalin. He had everything, he knew that now, he had total control of the situation, he had the power to do anything. It had worked, marrying Jane, having Suzanna and soon having the social position he'd always dreamt of. It had all worked, he had everything and nothing could take it away from him. He closed his eyes and stroked Suzanna's back. He had it all.

The blow came out of nowhere.

Before he knew what was happening, Phillip felt Suzy's body wrenched from his own, heard her scream and felt the spasm of fear shoot up his spine. He yanked his legs up, tearing the silk and rolled on to his side but it was too late. Another blow hit him across the back of the head and he lost consciousness. He never heard Suzanna begging for her life or the terrified howling as she saw the knife that came up from the assassin's side and cut her throat.

Jane drew to a stop outside the bungalow and stayed on her bicycle looking up at the house before checking her piece of paper a second time. This was the right place, according to the message, it just didn't look anything like she had expected. She climbed off her bike and leant it up against the wall, walking towards the front door of the bungalow. It was open; Rami was obviously expecting her.

Walking through to the sitting-room, Jane called out and felt the smallest shiver of unease as her voice echoed in the empty silence. She wandered back into the hall and along to the bedroom, calling out again and nervously pushing the door open. She peered inside.

'Oh my God!' Her hand flew up to her mouth as the nausea hit the back of her throat. She gagged, gulping down air to try and stop herself retching. She staggered forward and saw Suzanna's hand move. Dropping to the floor, she heaved Suzanna's naked body on to her lap, pressing her hands on to the gash, trying to stop the flow of blood. 'Oh Jesus, oh Jesus,' she cried, 'don't die!' She started to sob as the blood seeped out uncontrollably, soaking her hands, her clothes. 'Oh Jesus, no! Please . . .' She bent her head to try and resuscitate Suzanna. 'No, please don't die, don't . . . !' She saw the eyelids flutter and the arm twitch as the muscle went into spasm. She let the body go. Suzanna was dead, she was already dead. Crawling back, Jane put her hands up to her face. She couldn't stop sobbing. Clambering to her feet, she held on to the wall and groped her way out of the room, her bloody hands staining the white plaster. She backed down the hall, still crying, terrified noisy sobs, and at the open door she turned, ran down the steps and out on to the street, knocking a small child out of the way, oblivious to the mother's wail of protest. She ran to the main road, out amongst the cars and flagged down a taxi, screaming Rami's address at the driver and crawling inside, curling herself up into a ball and clawing frantically at the bloody clothes wet on her skin.

Rami stood by the open door of the Land Rover as the mechanic started up the engine and thrust his foot down hard on to the accelerator. He gave a small cheer as it roared to life and glanced quickly at his watch. If he left now then he'd just make it there for the last of the lunch. The mechanic got out and Rami climbed up into the cab, placing his *kurta* on the seat beside him.

'You think it'll be all right now?' he called. The mechanic nodded. 'Great, thank you!' Rami shifted gear and reached for the handbrake. Slowly he released the clutch and the jeep moved forward. He put his right hand up in a salute and swung the Land Rover round. He accelerated off down the drive, stopped at the main road and glanced to his right before pulling out. It was then that he saw Jane.

Jane ran towards him, along the main road, covered in blood. Her face was streaked with it, her hair matted with it. She was crying as she ran.

'My God . . . Jane . . .' His voice died on his lips.

Jumping down from the cab, he ran towards her, his heart pounding with fear. He caught her in his arms and held her sobbing figure close to him, shielding her from the road, from the stares of the passing traffic. As soon as she calmed, he pulled back.

'Are you hurt? Jane? Are you injured?'

She managed to shake her head. She was shivering with the shock, her whole body trembling uncontrollably. Rami hurried her to the jeep and helped her up. He jumped in beside her and slamming the car into reverse, he spun round and tore up the drive to the house.

Inside, he carried her to the bathroom and ran the taps in the bath. He ripped the wet, bloody clothes from her body and helped her down into the water, looking away, painfully remembering that one time they had made love. He fetched some towels, thankful that his mother and sisters were out and found a *shalwar kameez* and some pyjamas for her to wear. Back in the bathroom, he held the towel for her and wrapped her in it as she stood helpless, shaking so violently she could hardly move. He cradled her body into his and whispered to her, lying next to her on the floor, trying to soothe her and trying to warm her cold shocked body.

Some time later, she was still. She laid her head against his shoulder and he stroked her hair. Her breathing evened.

'Jane?' His voice was no more than a faint whisper. 'What happened?'

Jane opened her eyes and lifted her head. She looked at him. 'Phillip's dead,' she said blankly.

Rami started. He jerked back. 'Dead!' He couldn't

believe it. 'How? My God, Jane! How?' He gripped her shoulder and sat up.

'Murdered,' she said dully, it was as if she still didn't quite understand it. 'Suzanna's dead too,' she said, shaking her head. 'I held her.' It was a murmur. 'I tried to help her . . . I . . .' She broke off and Rami pulled her up to him, holding her so tightly she could hardly breathe. He released her and stood, pulling her to her feet.

'Jane,' he faced her and held her shoulders. 'Jane, listen to me. This is bad, very bad, all right?' He spoke to her as he would a child. 'You have to get dressed now and we have to talk to the police. You found them dead, is that right?' She nodded. 'Where?' He looked at her face, her blank eyes. 'Can you tell me where?'

Jane shook her head. 'You know,' she murmured, 'you know where . . .'

Rami turned away. She was in shock, incoherent. He quickly unfolded the small pile of clothes and helped her to dress, all the time his brain reeling, the panic tight in his chest. He didn't know what the hell had happened and all he could think was please God, don't let Jane be involved.

Leaving her alone for a few moments, Rami hurried along the passage and called to the head bearer to dismiss the servants for the rest of the day; he didn't want anyone else implicated in this. Then he went back to Jane, took her hand and led her down to Shiva's study, taking the key from his grandfather's suite and letting them both into the private hallowed room. He sat her on the divan and crossed to the window, standing in a shaft of sunlight, suspended in agonising indecision. Until he had found out exactly what had happened, he didn't know what to do. He turned as Jane got up and walked across to Shiva's desk.

'Jane?'

She stood in front of a neat pile of papers and held the paperweight in her hand. It was a small, heavy jewelled bird, exquisitely set with diamonds, emeralds and rubies, the work of Rami's great, great grandfather. It was Shiva's, the bird of fate, he had often called it and Rami looked at her as she turned it over and over in her palm, the way that his grandfather did.

'Jane? Are you all right?' For one terrible moment he thought that the shock had deranged her mind, that perhaps she had done something that had sent her over the edge. Then she looked at him.

'There was a man, Colonel Reginald Mills,' she said, 'the commanding officer of the Fourth Battalion of the Dragoon Guards up at Moraphur in 1857, the year of the Mutiny.'

Rami stood still. He knew the name Moraphur, it was where his family came from and he knew the story of the Mutiny, of Jagat Rai. He looked at Jane's face. The confusion had cleared, the blankness had gone from her eyes. She held the bird out to him and it caught the light, the stones glittered. He felt his chest constrict.

'In revenge for the murder of the Europeans, among whom was his wife, Colonel Mills executed many Indians, threw many more into jail. The story goes, so Phillip has told me, that he blamed one family in particular, I don't know who, but two men, a father and a son. He ruined them, confiscated their lands, businesses, wealth.' Jane stopped and glanced down at the bird. 'He stole a small keepsake from this family for himself, they were jewellers and he took a piece of their work. It is in the British Museum, I've seen it myself, donated by Phillip's father . . .' Her voice faltered and she broke off for a moment. 'It is a small jewelled bird,' she said, 'one of a pair.' She looked up at Rami. 'It is the partner of this one here, I would stake my life on it.' Her hand closed over the bird and she held it tightly in her fist. 'The father died in prison—'

'And the son swore to honour his father's death,' Rami finished for her, 'and to pass this oath on down through the generations.' He repeated the words he had heard so often from Shiva. 'It is a matter of great family honour, the man who revenges Indrajit Rai's death will be a god among gods.'

Jane began to tremble. She squeezed her fist tighter and the skin on her hand stretched taut and white over her knuckles. 'Major Phillip Reginald Mills,' she whispered, 'great, great grandson of Colonel Reginald Mills . . .' A sob caught in her throat.

'No, Jane, no!' Rami moved towards her but she backed away. 'It's impossible! Why now? Why not years ago? Why let this vengeance wait for so long?'

'Because there has never been a Mills in India, not until now! There has never been the chance before.'

'No, Jane!' Rami cried. 'It cannot be . . .' He shook his head, he didn't believe it, he couldn't believe it. This sort of thing died with the birth of the New India, it was crazy, superstitious, ridiculous! 'No,' he said, turning away from her, 'no, Jane, I simply do not believe it.'

'But, Rami, you must! Don't you see? How could it have happened without a Mills in India? How could it have been done until now? My God! Your grandfather may even have influenced Phillip's job here . . . you said he was instrumental in many of the maharajah's decisions, you said . . .'

'No! Jane, stop this! This is folly, this talk of vengeance! Stop please!' Jane stared at him across the room, then she glanced down at her hand and opened the fist. A thought so terrible struck her that for a moment it took her breath away.

'Perhaps you knew this already,' she said, 'you sent me there, you arranged to meet me . . .'

Rami spun round. 'I what?' He moved so fast across the room and grabbed her shoulders with such force that Jane cried out.

'I did what, Jane?' He shook her, not realising what he was doing. 'What address?'

Jane's teeth rattled inside her head and her vision blurred. She dropped the bird. 'Stop it!' she shrieked. 'Stop it!' Rami abruptly let her go and she slumped down, holding her head. He stared down at her. 'I got a message,' she cried. 'You told me to go to that address! I got a message last night, to meet you there!'

She started to sob and Rami sunk to his knees, pulling her in close to him. 'Oh God, Jane, please don't cry. I'm so sorry, darling Jane, please . . .' He kissed her hair, pressed her face close to his chest. 'Shiva,' he murmured. The name went round and round in his head. Shiva. Shiva invited him to the lunch yesterday, Shiva knew Jane trusted him, Shiva knew she would go where he asked her to. I should be there now, he thought, I should be out of Baijur, up at Viki's lodge and Jane would have no one, Phillip is dead, his mistress is dead and Jane was seen covered with their blood. He swallowed down the intense fear that rose suddenly in his throat and squeezed his eyes shut tight. When he opened them again he saw the bird, lying on the floor, the stones glinting in the light, like tiny darts of evil. He pulled back from Jane and said, 'Who saw you, Jane? Who and where?'

Jane shook her head. 'I don't know, I . . .' She closed her eyes, trying to think back. 'Lots of people saw me!' she cried. 'I took a taxi, jumped out near your house, I ran from the bungalow, into the street!' She caught her breath. 'Oh God, Rami! They'll think I . . .' She leapt up, darting across to the window. 'Can anyone see me here? Does anyone know I'm with you?' She began to panic again, her whole body pounding with fear. 'The servants? Where are they?' She ran over to the desk and grabbed the phone. 'I've got to get away! I'll phone the airport, I have to leave now!' She dropped her hands down on to the desk and hung her head, momentarily paralysed by anxiety. Then, frantically, she started to rifle through the papers on the desk. 'There must be a number for the airport here! There must be—'

Hurrying across to her, Rami put his hand over hers and stopped it. 'Jane, don't!' He picked it up and held it tight. 'Don't panic, please! I'm here, we'll think this through.' He replaced the receiver and glanced down at the pad by the phone as he did so. He saw the address Shiva had written the night before.

'Do you remember the place you went to?' he asked quietly, hanging his head.

'No! I . . .' Jane took a deep breath to calm herself. 'All I remember is that it was near the Bazaar, on the other side of the Chawlor district.' Rami ripped the corner off the paper and screwed it up into a tight little ball.

'Rami, what? What are you doing?'

He turned away for a moment, then he faced her. 'Nothing, Jane,' he answered. He kissed the hand he held and Jane looked up at him. His eyes were filled with infinite sadness.

'You are right,' he said. 'You must get away to safety. We have to make plans.' He released her hand and picked up the telephone. 'I will call Bodi.' He registered the fear in Jane's eyes. 'It is all right,' he reassured her, 'we can trust him, I promise.' He looked at her, at the clear honest face he loved so much and said, 'I am sorry, Jane, for all this.' He knew now that Shiva had used him, used them both. 'If I had not loved you, if you had not loved me . . .'

Jane put her finger up to his mouth and silenced him. 'I would never have lived a true life,' she said and she moved away from him while he rang Dr Yadav and spoke quickly and quietly in order to save her life.

It was almost dusk by the time the arrangements had been made and Jane stood by the window in Shiva's study, watching the sun go down over Baijur for the last time. She had her back to the room and heard the murmur of conversation behind her as Bodi explained the final details of her flight to Rami. She didn't turn around though, she didn't want to know what would happen when she had gone, or hear the lies that would be told. It was too eerie, it was as if she had already disappeared.

She shivered as she heard an eagle cry and felt a movement behind her. Rami placed his arms gently around her and laid his cheek close to hers. 'You must leave,' he whispered. 'It is the signal.' She closed her eyes to remember his soft, warm breath on her cheek and they stayed like that for as long as they could. 'We must go,' Bodi said behind them.

Jane opened her eyes again. 'I am ready,' she answered. She turned into the room and took the shawl and cloak Bodi held out for her. Rami helped her on with them and tucked the shawl over her face, securing it. All he could see were her eyes, the clear, pale grey eyes. Bodi opened the door of the study.

'When we have gone,' he said to Rami, 'you are to wait thirty minutes then raise the alarm as I said.' Rami nodded. Jane followed Bodi along the passage, out of the back door of the bungalow and down the steps into the garden. It was quiet and dark, only the sound of the *tiddi* could be heard. Turning towards the clump of trees at the far end of Shiva Rai's land, Bodi saw the flash of a torchlight and said, 'Come, they are waiting for us.' He quickly embraced Rami. 'He will not trust you, my son,' he said hurriedly. 'You must be strong, tell him again and again that you know nothing, that she fled from the house when you went to get help.' Bodi released him. 'You do understand that, do you not?'

'Yes, I understand.' Rami moved to embrace Jane but she put her hands out to stop him. She couldn't bear it to have to tear herself away from his body, from his arms. She stood and looked at him for a few moments, then quickly she reached up and brushed his lips with her own. She said nothing.

'I will come for you,' Rami whispered urgently. 'I promise you . . .' But she had turned away, waiting for Bodi's signal to run.

The eagle cried a second time and Jane felt a hand on her back.

'Now! Run!' She took Bodi's cue and together they darted out of the cover of the house and across the open space towards the trees, two dark figures running under the shadow of the clouds.

'Go on, go!' Rami cried silently after them. 'Go like the wind!' And he stood and watched them until the darkness of the trees engulfed them and all he was left with was their fleeting image and the echo of the eagle's cry.

Chapter Twenty-One

Mitchell Harvey stepped off the plane at Delhi Airport and on to Indian soil for the first time. The warmth hit him, a rush of humid air that made him sweat on contact, the smell of it peculiar to India. He walked down the steps and on to the tarmac, carrying a briefcase loaded with US dollars, and boarded the bus. He spoke to no one, made no eye contact. He was in a filthy temper and had been since he'd left Dubai. He would negotiate the final price, deliver the cash then fuck off out of this God-forsaken place. Two days he'd give it, two miserable stinking days, that was all.

Imran was waiting with a car outside. He met Mitchell as he came through arrivals and deduced his mood immediately. He wasted no time on peripherals.

'I've agreed a price, subject to your approval,' he said. 'There's no need to go to Baijur.'

Mitchell kept hold of the briefcase. 'How much?'

'Ten thousand US dollars.'

Mitchell stayed silent as he followed Imran out of the airport to the waiting Mercedes. Inside, away from the smell and heat, he sat back and loosened his tie.

'It's too much,' he said. 'Our friend in Baijur's got greedy.'

Imran had pre-empted Mitchell's response. 'He pretty much controls the police force down there,' he replied. 'He will guarantee what goes into the report.'

Mitchell took a cigar out of the top pocket of his suit and lit it up. 'So he removes Suzanna's name from the file and the inquest, for ten thou?'

'And he organises a road traffic accident report.'

'Very neat. Who is this man?'

'An Indian official, of sorts. There's always someone to help if the price is right.'

Mitchell said nothing and Imran shut up. Mitchell didn't have any choice but he wasn't going to point that out.

'What about the charity story?'

'That's extra.'

'Christ! He is a greedy bastard!' Mitchell flicked his ash on the floor of the car. 'How much extra?' he said after a pause.

'Three.'

'Shit!'

Imran waited for a minute or so then said, 'So far there's been nothing released, we're in a good position. If you move quickly, deliver within the next twenty-four hours, this man can release a news story with witnesses to the CNS. It'll be something like – wealthy British woman on charity mission is tragically killed in road accident.' He paused. 'You stay till the end of the week, release a press statement from Delhi, where you flew immediately from Dubai on hearing the news, distraught, shocked etc. etc.'

Mitchell smoked on in silence. He finished the cigar and ground it out under the heel of his shoe. 'What about Mills?'

'I didn't ask. I didn't think he was important.'

Mitchell glanced out of the window. 'He isn't.' He turned back to Imran. The boy had done well, he was proving to be a valuable asset.

'OK. Do it,' he said. 'Then come back to Delhi for a few days.' He dropped his hand heavily on to Imran's thigh. 'I'll wait for you there.'

Imran kept his face averted, he didn't want Mitchell to see the revulsion in his eyes.

'And Mills' wife, the one they think did it. Where is she?'

'I don't know, no one knows.'

Mitchell removed his hand, instantly angry. 'Then find her,' he snapped. 'And damn fucking quick!' He took out another cigar, his relaxed friendly mood over. 'I don't want to be embarrassed by some maniac wife turning up with the full monty!' He lit up a second time. 'So get that fucking woman out of the way! D'you understand?'

'Yes, sir.'

Mitchell said nothing else and they drove on to the hotel in silence.

It was freezing in the garden, the sort of glorious clear, cold English December morning, where the ground was covered with white frost and the pale blue sky touched the tips of the bare trees. John Bennet sat alone in the greenhouse, the panes of glass frosted over, his breath making clouds of steam in the icy air. He perched on the edge of the bench, a handful of compost in his hand and a half-potted bowl of pansies and ivy at his side. He was motionless. He hung his head and stared at the floor, littered with clumps of soil, gravel, sawdust and he waited for the sound of the car to disappear up the drive.

'John?'

He glanced up. Caroline Bennet stood in the doorway. 'He's gone,' she said. 'You can come back into the house now.'

John winced at the tone of voice she used. She was tired, as stressed as he was but the difference was she had hardened to it. She had let a moment of doubt intrude on her thoughts and Jane had ceased to be the daughter she remembered, she became the woman in the Mills case and all her mother wanted was for it all to be over, over and forgotten.

'What did he want?'

'The same as all the others, a different angle, a photograph, one of the wedding.' She snorted derisively. 'As if we would let these people into the privacy of our lives! It's insulting!'

John held out his hand and she came across and took it. They stayed like that for some time, not looking at each other, both sad, both grieving, but separately.

'I just wish we knew where she was!' John said suddenly. 'I wish I knew she was all right!'

Caroline snatched her hand away. 'Give it up, John!' she snapped. 'For God's sake!'

He looked up at her. They went round and round in circles like this, every day, every night. He couldn't rest, he knew Jane hadn't been involved, he knew his daughter and he worried, he worried himself sick, night after night. But Caroline, she tried to blot it out, to forget it in any way she could.

He stood and dropped the soil on to the ground, brushing the palm of his hand on his gardening trousers. He didn't understand his wife, he never had. It had been months now but he couldn't give up hope, he wouldn't ever give up hope, but the prospect of that, the loneliness of it dismayed him. He followed Caroline out into the garden, abandoning his potting, unable to finish anything these days.

'D'you want coffee?' she asked.

John shrugged. 'I thought I might have a look at the roses,' he answered. Caroline's nostrils flared but she said nothing. The roses were his and Jane's, they reminded him so acutely of his daughter and she didn't understand why he had to keep punishing himself like this. She walked away from him towards the house.

'Don't be long,' she called back. 'It's cold, you'll get a chill.'

He nodded and watched her disappear inside. Then he turned towards the rose garden, the pruned and clipped bushes stiff with ice and smiled sadly at the memory of Jane's love of her roses.

Chapter Twenty-Two

March, 1966

Jane sat on the verandah of her small house in the hills above the mountain town of Ghanerao, in the south-eastern part of the state of Balisthan and looked across the valley as the sun crept over the landscape. It was early morning, the coolest part of the day and the mist was just beginning to lift. She let a long thin shaft of warm sunlight gently caress her face as she leant her head back and folded her hands in her lap. She let her mind drift, her daily thoughts of Rami mixed with a calm happiness and peace that she had lately begun to feel. She was tired, she hadn't slept well and as the shaft of sunlight lengthened and widened, sliding across the verandah to warm her whole figure, she closed her eyes and sighed contentedly.

'Memsahib? Memsahib?'

Jane opened her eyes and realised that she must have dozed off. She saw her ayah and smiled. 'Hello, Usha,' she said. 'Gosh. I must have fallen asleep.' She sat up, with difficulty and the ayah stepped forward to help her. Giving a little laugh, she took the hand she was offered.

'Is that my tea?' she asked, settling herself.

'Yes, memsahib, and there is something for you to eat, something that will be giving you strength.' The ayah smiled and came forward, laying the tray on a small cane table by the side of Jane's chair. She gently placed a hand on Jane's stomach. 'Something that will be giving you both strength.'

Jane smiled. She had got to know this Indian woman well over the past few months, she trusted her. It was a small household, all of the servants chosen by Bodi, but the ayah was the only other woman Jane came into contact with. She would have been very lonely without Usha's company. Jane took the tea and sipped, looking over the rim of the cup at the valley as it came to life.

'Is your brother coming to Ghanerao this month?' she asked, as the ayah cut the fruit for her.

'Yes, memsahib, he is coming a week on Saturday.'

Jane sat still and continued to sip but she couldn't quiet the sudden racing of her heart. Usha's brother worked for Dr Yadav and he would bring Jane's letter from Rami. She finished her tea and exchanged the cup for the small plate of peeled fruit. 'Thank you,' she murmured distractedly; she was already thinking about the letter. Rami would know now, she had kept it a secret for as long as she could but she had had to tell him, in her last correspondence. It was getting close, she needed help, she needed a midwife, maybe even a doctor. She wondered what he would say, whether he would be pleased, or anxious, angry even. She longed for his writing, for Usha's brother to visit his family in Ghanerao and bring Rami's words. She longed for his answer to her letter, telling him that she was pregnant with his child.

Shiva looked at Rami across the table in the restaurant of the gymkhana club in Baijur and watched him sip his water. Rami, the chiselled beauty of his face calm and composed, averted his eyes. He knew Shiva was watching him, he felt the force of the gaze and he continued to look away. He had planned this meticulously, he had been working on it since he received Jane's letter and he wasn't about to make any mistakes at this stage.

'You leave at what time?' Shiva asked, clicking his fingers for the waiter.

Rami turned back to his grandfather and shrugged. 'Later, some time this evening,' he answered. 'Viki wishes me to keep it secret.'

Shiva nodded. He was handed the wine list and surveyed it with the waiter standing at his elbow. Rami knew he wasn't really looking, he was playing for time, for effect. 'Chablis,' he ordered, his habitual choice, 'the '63.' He glanced up and closed the list. 'You are being escorted?'

'Yes, by three of Viki's men. They will be escorting me to the city limits to ensure I am not followed.'

Shiva nodded. He looked away and smiled, raising his right hand in greeting to one of the English contingent from ICI. He didn't trust Rami, hadn't trusted him from that first moment that Jane Mills disappeared but whatever way he followed him, whatever way he watched him, it always came to nothing. He was very, very careful. The wine arrived and Shiva tasted, then nodded. It was poured and he took a mouthful.

'How long will you be gone?'

Rami shrugged. 'As long as it takes,' he answered.

Shiva momentarily lost his patience. 'For goodness sake, Ramesh!' he hissed. 'I am your grandfather! You might at least have the courtesy to tell me what is going on!'

Rami sat silent. He had been waiting for this moment in his task for Viki, the very last part, the removal and hiding of the family wealth. He had prolonged it for as long as he dared, waiting until he needed the cover, knowing that Shiva wouldn't dare try to follow him on royal instructions. He was going to see Jane, for the first time in four months and he was using the final chapter of Viki's book as a cover.

'I am unable to tell anyone anything,' he said, 'I am sorry.'

Shiva's nostrils flared but it was the only outward sign of the intense anger he felt. His grandson was insolent! He was deceiving him and Shiva knew it, he sensed it, felt it. He had never had the justice that was deserved. Without a culprit, the Mills murder had faded from view, become just another unsolved crime. Without Jane Mills to elevate it to a scandal of the highest proportion it had been forgotten and this pained Shiva, he didn't like his jobs only half done.

'But you will be back for the wedding?' Shiva raised an eyebrow. 'It would be a great insult not to return for the wedding.'

'Of course, I will be back in time for the first ceremony.' Rami knew he had three days before the celebrations began. He could just make it in three days.

Shiva smiled. So Ramesh was heading south-east. He clicked for more wine and sat back to enjoy his second glass. He wouldn't attempt the desert terrain to the west in just three days, he was obviously heading for the hills above Ghanerao, that was a three-day trek. He sipped the wine and looked across at his grandson. You have slipped, Ramesh, he thought, his lip curling slightly in a sneer, you are not as clever as you think you are. And he dragged his eyes away from the face that had disappointed and deceived him and began to plot the course that his men would have to take.

Imran Devi stood on the corner of the bazaar and peeled an orange, dropping the peel on to the ground and kicking it idly into the gutter. He had been in Baijur for over four months now, his Hindustani was perfect and his olive skin had burnt a dark Asian brown. He wore native dress, a fine muslin *kurta* and *churidar*, his slippers were soft kid, embellished with gold leaf. He was a high caste Indian, he lived in a suite of rented rooms in a bungalow on the Eastern drive and filled his days doing very little, keeping out of sight, watching, listening. He rang London once a week and he waited.

He was waiting now. He had arranged to meet someone, he was early but that didn't matter and he was tense. The meeting was important, if his information was right then there wasn't much time. He glanced up as an Indian joined him on the street corner and stopped to light a cheroot.

'You wanted to see me,' the man said, flicking the lighted match to the ground. 'You have some work?'

Imran dropped the remains of his orange into the

gutter. 'Yes,' he answered, 'I have.' He turned towards the crowded streets of the market. 'Come,' he said. 'This way.' And he led the way through the bazaar to a small coffee shop and a tiny, dark back room he had hired for his purpose.

Dr Bodi Yadav had left Baijur two days earlier. He had said goodbye to his wife and family for his extended visit to Europe and a medical convention at which he was presenting a paper in London and Paris. They didn't ask any questions, it was something he had done before and his wife was used to his business trips away from home.

But Dr Yadav didn't leave for Delhi, he didn't board the British Airways flight for London, he had no intention of doing so. He waited for two days in a small town on the western side of Balisthan, a dried-out, fly-infested place that no one ever visited and few had ever heard of. He made the last of his arrangements and took delivery of some things he had ordered in Delhi. When the time came, he would be with her. He was ready.

He loaded the jeep and collected the food that had been prepared for him. He was anxious and he was frightened. He had taken every possible precaution, he was certain that they could not be followed but he didn't for one instant doubt Shiva Rai's determination, his shrewd cunning and an evil streak he had had the misfortune to have seen on too many occasions.

Just before darkness fell, Bodi Yadav left the town, taking the desert road east towards Baijur, cutting across country and stopping forty miles south of the city, off the road, under cover of the trees and in the place he had marked for Rami on the map. He hid the vehicle from view, climbed out and, having made sure that the place was deserted, sat by the side of the road to wait.

He didn't have to wait for long. Rami too had left before darkness fell. He had driven out of Baijur in a Land Rover, Viki's men watching the roads and following him twenty miles east of the city. Satisfied that he had departed unseen, they turned back and Ramesh continued on forty miles along the main Balisthan route south. At a junction that split east or west, he cut cross country. Bodi had prepared him for the next stage. The terrain was rough, difficult, the road turned to track and often petered out into open county. He followed the map, pinned to the dashboard and drove with a compass in his hand. It was gruelling, the sky was dark and the land in deep tracks of black shadow. He peered hard through the windscreen, his eyes trained on the foreground, watching the distance every now and then, watching the mirror for any sign of light behind him. It took him three hours.

Bodi looked up at the faint roar of an engine in the distance. He had been dozing, the small fire had almost gone out. He stood, turned his head to the right, then the left and, looking to the west, he listened hard. The night was breathless, the air still and the noise carried. It was Rami, it came from the west. He kicked the coals of the fire and scuffed the ground, covering the ashes with sand. He walked back to the jeep, uncovered it and climbed inside. Starting the engine, he drove into view and, able just to make out a glimmer of a headlight on the horizon, he waited for sight of Rami.

An hour later, they parked the two vehicles at the back

of a small deserted garage in a village several miles across country from the main road and Bodi climbed out. He quickly embraced Ramesh, then, opening the back of his jeep, he began to transfer his things across to the Land Rover, piling them on top of the rows of metal boxes. They were taking only one vehicle, it was safer, the other one Bodi had arranged to be collected the following day. The small task took a matter of minutes. When he was finished, he glanced at his watch.

'It shouldn't be long,' he said. 'We're early.' Rami nodded. The road up to Ghanerao was rarely used, the Land Rover would be obvious and the lights seen for miles around. Bodi didn't want to risk it. He had arranged for a guide to help them up through the rough ground, away from the road, circumventing the village and driving straight up to the small house that Jane rented. It was a hell of a journey but it was by far the safest. Villagers talked, they could arouse suspicion further afield.

Bodi walked back to his jeep and locked it. He leant against the bonnet. 'Where the devil is this chap?' He didn't like the hold-up; it made him nervous. He glanced behind him as a figure materialised out of the darkness.

'Jhoti Sahib?' he hissed.

'Yes.' The figure came into view. 'You are ready?'

Bodi nodded and looked towards Rami. The man was younger than he'd been led to expect but there wasn't time to worry. 'We are ready,' he said. The man walked over to the Land Rover.

Rami opened the door for him and he climbed up, placing a canvas bag on the seat beside him and taking out a spotlight. He looked at Rami's map, then ripped it off the dashboard and folded it away. He replaced it with his own.

Bodi climbed in behind him and waited for Rami. He had a sixth sense, something was making him edgy and he was anxious to get away. Rami took the driver's seat and started the engine. He switched on the headlights.

'Which way?' he asked.

Jhoti nodded to the east. 'Take the road for about two miles and then we cut off.'

Rami shifted into gear. He glanced in the mirror and moved the Land Rover forward. Bodi checked the road behind them, watching until the deserted garage disappeared from view, then he settled back and rested for a few moments. He would be needed when they moved off road, another pair of eyes would be vital even with the beam from the spotlight. He untied the cotton scarf he wore over his mouth and loosened it, winding down the window, relieved at the cool breeze on his face. They were in for a long night, but, if the gods continued to smile, a safe one. He sighed and closed his eyes for a moment. Please the gods a safe one.

Imran Devi picked up the phone immediately it rang. He listened, wrote a number of things down, then replaced the receiver. He dialled another number, spoke quickly, issuing instructions and hung up. He walked through to his bedroom, lay down on the bed and stared out of the window at the black, starless sky. The time had come but he still couldn't stomach the thought of it.

Somewhere, at the back of a small garage off the Pindi Road heading south-east, someone had just made themselves fifty rupees. Life was very cheap in India.

Chapter Twenty-Three

Jane woke with a start. She hadn't slept well for weeks now, the baby kicked at night, its feet lodged just below her breasts, and she woke fitfully, every couple of hours, to shift position, to try and get comfortable. Now, lying in the dark, she listened to the night sounds, staring at the sky through the window, a little afraid, a little lonely. She rolled on to her side and tried to close her eyes. It was silent, eerily calm and she could count the beats of her heart. Suddenly, she heard a noise, a sharp crack outside.

Struggling, she sat up and switched on the lamp, flooding the room with light. She put her hand up to her chest and pressed her palm hard against her racing pulse. She took a couple of deep breaths, gently easing her legs over the side of the bed and dropping her feet on to the floor. She stood up slowly, silently and crept to the long, half-open window. It was cold and she shivered, wrapping her arms around her, covering her swollen belly. She peered out into the dark, very frightened now, ready to call the bearer. Then suddenly the door opened behind her and she swung round.

For a moment she didn't believe it. She stood, ashen-faced, frozen to the spot, then she stumbled forward, relief and joy making her weak and Rami caught her, taking her weight and holding her close to his body.

'Jane, my darling Jane,' he murmured into her hair. 'Dear, dear Jane.'

She jerked back. 'Is it you?' she cried. 'Is it really you?'

He kissed her face, her lips, her eyes. 'Yes, it is really me,' he whispered fiercely. He placed a hand on her stomach. 'And this? This is really you?'

Jane nodded and covered his hand with her own. 'It is you and me, both of us.' She looked down at her belly, at their baby, growing inside her. 'Do you mind?' she asked quietly.

Suddenly Rami laughed, loudly, joyfully. 'Mind?' He shook his head and stroked her through the thin muslin of her nightdress. 'It is the most wonderful thing,' he answered. He knelt and lifting the muslin, he kissed the skin stretched tightly across her belly, he kissed their baby. Jane held his head, her fingers wrapped in his hair. 'One pure moment of love,' he said, looking up at her, 'one union, blessed by the gods.' Jane closed her eyes as he gently kissed her again and the baby moved under his touch. Then silently, she began to cry.

Later, lying curled up with his body wrapped around her, his hand across her womb, Jane felt the movement inside and, staring out at the sky, she said, 'What is going to happen to me?' She pressed her hand against Rami's, against her stomach, 'To us?'

Rami kissed her hair. 'Sssh, Jane, it is all right, you will be with me, you will be safe.' He stroked her skin.

But Jane moved so that she could look at his face. 'Safe?'

He didn't answer her.

'Safe?' she said again. 'What do you mean?' Her voice rose in panic. 'They haven't found who murdered Phillip?' She shifted and with difficulty, sat up 'Tell me, Rami,' she said. 'Tell me the truth. Everything.'

Rami rolled on to his back and looked up at the ceiling. He was silent for some time, not sure what to do, what to say. He didn't want to lie to her but he did want to protect her. At least for the moment, to protect her and the baby.

Jane reached over and switched on the lamp. Rami covered his eyes, the sudden light making him wince.

'Please,' she said, 'I have a right to know.'

Rami sat up as well. He faced her, crossing his legs, taking her hand in his. He looked down at it, at the strong capable fingers, the pale freckled skin.

'They have not found who murdered Phillip,' he said. 'You are the suspect, they are not looking for anyone else.'

Jane caught her breath. She had been fuelling a blind hope, believing in the truth. She had honestly thought they would find the murderer, she had prayed so hard that the misery of this isolation wouldn't last. Pulling her hand away from Rami, she covered her face. 'Oh God,' she breathed, 'my poor baby . . .'

Rami leant forward and cradled her body in to his. 'Janey, it's all right,' he said. 'We will overcome this, I give you my promise, we—'

'How?' Jane suddenly cried, pushing him away. 'How for pity's sake?' Her face creased with anxiety. 'How . . . ?' She stopped and stared down at her belly as a spasm of pain shot through her womb. She gasped and clutched the bed.

'Jane?' Rami sprang forward. 'Jane, what is it?'

Clenching her jaw, Jane shook her head. 'Nothing,' she hissed. 'A pain, that's all . . .' She started to breathe deeply, seconds later her grip relaxed. 'The ayah said it's normal . . .' Her breathing regulated. 'She said it's normal a few weeks before.'

Rami let out a sigh. He took both of Jane's hands and kissed them, pressing the palms to his mouth. 'God, I love you, Jane,' he said. She smiled sadly. 'I will look after you, both of you, I promise you that.'

Jane glanced away.

'Bodi has applied for a job for me, in America,' he said suddenly, 'a teaching job.' He hadn't wanted to tell her until he was sure but she needed to know now, he had to reassure her. 'He is able to get me a passport . . .' Rami smiled. 'Not legally of course, but I will put you on it, you and the baby.' He touched her stomach as he said this, 'We can leave India, cross over to Pakistan and go from there . . .' He broke off. 'Jane? What is the matter? What?'

She shook her head and wiped her tears on the back of her hand. She would never see her family again, she would always have to be someone else, the idea of it, the very thought of it mortified her. 'Nothing, I . . .' She sniffed and attempted to smile. 'I'm sorry . . .'

Rami tilted her chin up so that he could see her eyes. She looked at him, at the man she loved and for a moment she remembered something Phillip had said to her once, something about losing the only thing that mattered and she remembered what she had told him. 'I would do anything to keep it,' she had said. How odd, that it had turned out to be a prophecy for both of them.

Rami kissed her, gently, on the mouth. 'Are you sure it is nothing?'

'Yes, I am.'

He stared at her for a moment longer then leant forward and placed a pillow behind her so that she could lie back comfortably. He reached across her and switched off the lamp.

'Try to sleep a little,' he whispered, wrapping his arms around her. 'Get some rest.' And, closing her eyes, Jane lay in the warmth and comfort of his embrace and felt her body slowly begin to relax and the kick of tiny limbs inside her.

Outside, Bodi sat on the verandah in the dark and looked out at the valley. He was too tense to sleep, he needed time to wind down. *Khansama* was making him something to eat and he held a bowl of fragrant hot tea in his hands, warming them, watching the steam rise up into the cold night air. He listened to the silence, a peculiar silence that belonged to the mountains, a clear, still hush and he drank the scalding liquid, thankful of the warmth in his belly.

He heard a sound.

At first he leant forward, not sure if it was a sound or just his imagination. The night was so intense it could easily have been in his mind. Then he heard it again. He stood up.

Jane's house was built on a ledge of rock on the hillside and the verandah looked right out across the valley. Walking to the edge of it, Bodi stretched forward, turning his head to the right, standing perfectly still, holding his breath. It came again. He had heard right! It was miles off, some distance along the valley but it was without doubt the roar of an engine. It was faint, hardly a noise really but it was definitely a car. Hurrying inside, Bodi called to the bearer.

'Is anyone expected down in Ghanerao tonight?'

The bearer shook his head. He knew the comings and goings of the town, he knew everything about the small community, that was one of the chief reasons he had been recommended to Bodi. 'There is nothing at this time of the night, sahib,' he said. 'The first delivery comes along the pass road at seven o'clock.'

Bodi thought for a moment. 'How long is it from the town up here on the road?'

The bearer shrugged. 'I don't know, sahib, two hours maybe, maybe three.'

'On foot? Cross country?'

The servant smiled, 'My boy can run down in thirty minutes, sahib. He is very fast.'

Bodi crossed to the window and looked out for a few minutes, then he turned. 'Wake the boy,' he instructed, 'then wake the other servants. We must start to pack. I will wake memsahib.'

He moved off towards Jane's bedroom. 'And tell *khansama* to pack some food for us, and some hot drinks.' The bearer nodded, disappearing along to the servants' quarters. 'God knows we're going to need it,' Bodi murmured under his breath and went to wake Jane and Rami.

Jane sat, wrapped in a blanket on the verandah. She was dressed and wide awake with Rami by her side while Bodi stood apart from them, his eyes trained on the horizon, waiting for the signal. He didn't know what to expect, he didn't know how they could possibly have been followed but he wasn't taking any risks. From the hillside across the valley the boy could see along the pass road for miles, he could see the lights of a car at a distance of thirty to forty kilometres and he had instructions to flash his torch three times if the signal was danger. Bodi gripped the painted wooden rail that ran around the verandah and waited. Behind him Jane and Ramesh were ready, they were prepared for the worst.

Minutes later, he turned. He looked at Jane's face, pale in the dim lantern light, her body stiff with fright, and nodded. 'We must go,' he said. 'We have been followed.' And he led the way through the house, still in darkness, to the waiting Land Rover, helped Jane up into the small space left in the back and settled her with blankets and pillows. They were travelling cross country, it would be rough and she would be uncomfortable at best, in pain at the worst. He took the passenger seat, opening out his map and waiting for Rami to climb up. He glanced behind him.

'Try not to worry, Jane dear,' he said. She nodded blankly but he couldn't offer her any other words of reassurance, he didn't have any to give.

They had been driving for two hours before they heard

her. The steep, rugged landscape was impossible to navigate, Rami was driving at speed and the Land Rover had hit countless crevices and ridges, taking it in the suspension but knocking a hell of an impact into the vehicle. Jane gripped the roll cage, her teeth gritted against the pain, her breath coming in short, sharp gasps. She had stifled her cries, biting on the inside of her mouth, the desperate pain starting in the round of her stomach and searing deep down into her pubis, but it was coming now in huge waves, washing over her, drowning her. She let out a scream and bent double, clenching her fists.

Bodi swung round. 'Oh my God!' He leant towards Jane and grabbed her hand, unclenching the fist. 'Jane, Jane hold on, try to breathe deeply! Take my hand, that's it.' He leant the upper half of his body right over the seat. 'That's it, good! Now squeeze it when you feel the contraction . . . Good! . . . Harder, breathe! Good girl . . . well done . . . breathe, try to relax as it eases off.' He glanced sidelong at Rami. 'We have to stop,' he hissed, 'I have to examine her, it might be close.'

Rami nodded, and heading for a clump of trees on a flatter piece of land, he slowed the Land Rover and stopped. He switched off the engine and headlights and reached under the seat for the torch to hand across, but Bodi was already out and opening the back door.

'Jane, are you able to lie back against the bags?'

Jane nodded. She shifted position as another pain washed over her and cried out. Bodi calmed her, holding her hand, talking her through it. A minute later, when it had passed, he bent to lift her legs on to the seat and felt the hem of her dress, the whole back of it saturated with blood. He didn't bother to examine her. She was crying now, whimpering with pain, frightened out of her wits, and Rami knelt on the front seat, leaning over, stroking her forehead, his own face ashen with the shock. Bodi reached for another blanket from the back and tucked it over her. There was nothing he could do at the moment. He hurried round the front of the jeep as Jane screamed with another contraction.

'For God's sake, Bodi,' Rami shouted suddenly, 'do something!' He tried to quieten Jane, looking up at Bodi as he held her hand, murmuring to her. Bodi placed his hand on the boy's shoulder, knowing his fear, his panic. 'I will do everything that I can,' he said. 'We must stay calm and we must find a place where it is possible to deliver the baby.' Jane was bleeding heavily, they didn't have much time.

Bodi took out his map and scanned it for no more than a few seconds, then he said, 'Get in the back with her, Rami, I want you to put a pillow under her hips to raise her up slightly and I want you to comfort her.'

Rami nodded. Gently he eased Jane's legs and slid a pillow beneath her bottom. 'Where are we going?' he asked, looking up at Bodi. Bodi shrugged. 'We are going to a hospital marked on the map,' he answered. He knew it, knew the English doctor who worked there. The relief flooded Rami's face and he said no more. There was no reason to frighten the boy, he would worry if he knew the truth, he might even panic and they were already in too much danger to take that risk.

The colony was hidden away, halfway up the hillside, a small camp of typical hill-people's bamboo huts, thatched roofs and mud floors. It was pitch black and silent, a sleeping community, but as the Land Rover made it up the half-finished road and the noise of the engine shattered the still night silence, people woke, torches were lit and they straggled out into the open to see what the commotion was. Bodi turned off the full beam and dipped the headlights but it was still obvious. Rami sat and stared out in shocked silence.

Bodi drew to a halt and opened the door. He climbed out and called to a figure holding a torchlight.

'Dr Hayes? Is he here?'

The figure limped forward, his cut-away shoes showing the sores on his deformed feet. 'He is in bed, at his bungalow.'

Bodi moved towards the man. 'Can you take us there?'

The man nodded. His right arm was badly disfigured and his hand hung limply by his side. He called over to someone to take his torch for him so he could get in the jeep. Rami jumped out.

'Bodi! Are you mad?' He lunged forward and knocked Bodi's hand away as he went to touch the leper. 'For God's sake, Bodi! What are you doing?'

Bodi swung round. 'I am doing what I have to!' he snapped. 'We need a doctor, we need help!'

'But the infection?' Rami's voice was tight with panic.

'I am a doctor, Ramesh!' Bodi hissed. 'I would not put you at risk!' Rami hung his head. 'Go to Jane,' Bodi instructed. 'You must get her out, the hospital is not far, as I remember it, you must help her there while I get Dr Hayes.'

Rami hesitated for a moment. 'Is it safe here?'

'It is the safest place we will find, Rami,' Bodi answered. 'Not many venture to this colony.'

Rami nodded and, flinching as he heard Jane cry out, he ran back to the jeep and began to help her down on to the ground.

The small village was buzzing as Jane climbed down from the Land Rover. A crowd had formed in the centre of the huts, faces mutilated by leprosy stared at the pregnant woman as she leant heavily on the man with her and moaned with the pain. A woman stepped forward.

'It is this way,' she called, 'I will light the ground for you.'

Rami winced at the sores on her hand as she held up the torch for him. He nodded. 'Thank you,' he called back, 'thank you.'

A short time later, Jane lay on the bed, her face wet with sweat. Her vision was blurred, she could see Rami but he kept fading, his face losing clarity as the pain washed over her. She gritted her teeth, and gasped for air. She had hardly the energy to breathe.

'All right, Jane, here it comes . . . now push, Jane! Push!'

She bore down on the pain in her womb, clenching her jaw, gripping Rami's hand so tight that her nails left tiny bruises on his skin. She screamed. Nothing happened.

Dr Hayes leant over her, his face close to hers. 'One more time, Jane, I want you to do it one more time. We're nearly there, I want you to push really hard when I count three. All right?'

Jane's eyes closed, she was so tired, her eyelids were so heavy. She fought to keep them open, to see Rami's face. There was a tiny break in the pain and she was so tired.

'Jane? Can you hear me?'

She forced them open. 'Yes,' she murmured.

'Good!' Dr Hayes glanced over his shoulder at Bodi. She was bleeding so heavily now that Bodi couldn't swab quick enough. He'd have to do a section if she couldn't get the baby out in the next few minutes. He broke out into a fresh sweat. She wouldn't last it, not with this blood loss and no transfusion. Bodi caught his eye. He took a fresh swab and moved forward, wiping the perspiration out of Hayes' eyes.

'All right, Jane, here we go . . .' He could see another contraction building up, her face creased with pain. 'Ready, Jane . . . One, two three . . .' Rami gripped Jane's hand. 'Push, Jane . . . Come on . . . Push. Hard . . . That's it . . . Come on, bear down, come on . . . Push!' He glanced briefly back at Bodi. 'I've got the head!' he cried. 'I've got it!'

Jane began to weep, she was so weak, the life draining out of her as she haemorrhaged.

'I've got the baby, Jane! Come on, not long now! I want you to push again! Ready, Jane!' Dr Hayes was shouting at her, aware that she was losing consciousness. 'Come on, Jane, one last push! Come on . . . Push!' He shouted over his shoulder. 'Forceps!' Bodi stepped forward but he had his hands on the shoulders. 'Here it comes . . .' He pulled the slippery body out, his hands covered in thick white vernix, his gown soaked with blood. 'I've got her!' He slapped the baby hard on the back and a piercing howl hit the room. 'Your daughter! A little girl, Jane!'

Cutting and clamping the cord, he then reached for a sheet and wrapped the baby up, handing her quickly across to Rami. He glanced at his watch. 'Five-fifteen a.m.,' he said, then he looked at Bodi. Bodi shook his head. Jane had lost too much blood, she continued to bleed.

Rami took the baby and held her close to Jane. 'Look, Jane,' he whispered, 'a little girl, Jane, our baby.' He reached forward and stroked her brow. It was cool, the skin felt dry, papery. Jane didn't open her eyes. 'Janey?' He leant in to her, cradling the baby to his chest. 'Look, Jane, please look . . .' He lifted her eyelid but the eye was blank. 'Jane?' He glanced up at Bodi, then back at Jane. 'Janey?' he cried. He shook her. 'Jane . . . !' Suddenly he pulled back. 'Bodi! Bodi, do something! Oh God!' He stared at her, all the time holding the baby close to his breast. He looked round. 'Bodi!' he shouted. 'Bodi? Please?'

Bodi stepped forward and went to take the baby, to try and offer comfort but Rami jerked away. He stood motionless staring at the doctor, staring at Bodi, staring at the blood. Then he turned away. 'Leave us alone,' he said. 'Please.'

Bodi touched his arm. 'Rami, don't do this, you can't do anything, you . . .'

Rami shook his head. 'Please, Bodi,' he whispered. 'Please . . .'

Bodi stepped back. He glanced briefly at Dr Hayes and together they left the room.

Moving back to the bed, Rami bent and gently kissed Jane's cheek. He could see the pulse in her neck and placed his finger on the vein, feeling the last of her life. Then carefully holding his daughter, he climbed on to the bed and lay down next to Jane, the baby between them. He put his arms around her and laid her head on his shoulder. As the last of the night gave way to the dawn, he held Jane as their baby lay sleeping on her breast, stroked her hair and comforted her. By daybreak she was dead.

Bodi sat by the fire outside, warming himself. The dawn had broken but the light was still dim, the air was cold, the ground hard with frost. He looked round at a movement behind him and saw Rami, the baby wrapped in a blanket in his arms. He waited.

'Bodi?' Rami came across to the fire. He squatted down in front of the man he trusted like a father. 'Bodi, I want you to take the baby out of India,' he said. 'I want you to take her to safety.'

Bodi placed both his arms on Rami's shoulders. 'You are her father, Rami,' he answered. 'You must—'

'No!' Rami held the baby out. 'She will not survive Shiva, you know that, Bodi!'

Bodi nodded. It was true, if they were found now, they would all be killed. Rami continued to hold the baby out to him and he took it, looking down at the tiny half-covered face.

'But you? What will you . . .'

'Here . . .' Rami held a package out. It was wrapped in cloth and bound tightly with a leather thong. 'This is for her.' He leant forward and gently placed his finger on her cheek. 'This is her inheritance.' He tucked the package in Bodi's arms, then he stood.

'Go now, Bodi,' he said fiercely. 'There may not be much time left.' Bodi looked up at Rami's face in the firelight. It seemed that his eyes burnt with a strange kind of energy and that frightened Bodi. He got wearily to his feet. Rami was right, there wasn't much time. 'Rami?'

Rami looked back. He had already moved into the

shadows and Bodi could hardly see him. 'Rami, what have you named your daughter?' he called.

Rami stepped into the light and Bodi saw such pain on his face that his heart wrenched. 'I have named her Indu,' Rami answered. 'She is called after the dawn.' Then he turned and walked away. He walked into the shadows and Bodi stood watching him and straining his eyes until he disappeared from view, a lone dark figure, one that Bodi loved and one that he knew he would never see again.

It was late afternoon when Doctor Hayes stood on the hillside and put his hand up to his eyes to shield them from the sun. He watched the river in the valley down below and the figure of the young man carrying the body of his English wife on to the light raft. It was Indian custom to commit the dead to water, who was he to interfere.

Rami laid Jane's body wrapped in cloth carefully in the boat. He tied the leather straps to her ankles and climbed in beside her. Pushing himself off from the bank, he paddled the light raft downstream, into the centre of the river, the widest, deepest part and then left the boat to drift. He uncovered Jane's face and knelt down next to her.

Tying his own ankles, he attached the straps to the rocks he had carried on board and picked up the axe. He leant forward and smashed a hole in the bottom of the boat, watching the water slowly come up around his legs. He lay down, his face close to Jane's, his lips almost touching hers, then he put his right arm up and with a razor he slashed his wrist. He flinched at the pain, and looking at the blood already flowing from his veins, he cut the other arm.

He embraced his love, encircling her with his arms, with his blood and finally he closed his eyes. The water swirled up around their bodies, it slowly turned red and Rami was united with Jane for all eternity.

Dr Hayes watched the small boat in the centre of the river as it gently floated downstream. The sun sank low in the sky and it became difficult to see properly, the whole scene perfused with a glorious golden light. He turned away for a moment as a shout drifted across the air from the colony and when he turned back the boat had disappeared. He ran down the steep, rocky slope towards the river, staring at the watery horizon but after several hundred yards he gave up and slumped down on a rock. It was pointless. He shook his head, put his hand up and gazed out once more. The boat had gone. He watched the moving river for some time, thinking about Bodi Yadav, thinking about India, then he stood and turned back towards the colony. He was sad but he was also elated by the power of the love he had witnessed. He would keep his promise to Bodi. No one would ever know what had happened there, the life and the death would go unregistered and the secret would be kept.

It would be kept until it was ready to be revealed.

Chapter Twenty-Four

Delhi, 1967

Shiva Rai walked down the steps of the British consulate offices at the high commission and towards his waiting car. He nodded to the driver who held the door open for him and climbed inside. He was tired, weary of the whole business and he laid his head back against the leather seat, closing his eyes. He had found what he wanted, found Brigadier John Bennet, found where the baby would be, if, and only if, it had survived.

'Where to, Shivaji?' The driver looked back at him.

'To my solicitor,' he answered, without opening his eyes. 'In the old quarter.' He felt in his top pocket for the papers. They were all there and he sighed with relief. He had left everything to his cousin, what remained anyway, along with the debts. Now he had to lodge the papers, put them away, not to be opened until his death. He patted the pocket again, superstitiously.

He was too old to do it, he didn't have the energy

now but his cousin, a greedy, malicious man, he would do it, he would complete the cycle, finish the job. Shiva was certain of it, that was why he had chosen him. He would do it. Finally.

He opened his eyes and looked out at the wide streets of New Delhi, the monuments, the state buildings and he smiled. It was the thought that he could die peacefully and respectfully that cheered him. That he could die knowing he had laid the course.

And oh, what a course!

He saw the streets narrow, the buildings increase and the people on the pavements suddenly start to appear as they entered the old quarter of Delhi. This was his India, old India, the India of honour and dishonour, of justice and revenge. The India he knew hadn't died, he had simply laid it to rest until the right time. He had taken care of the future, and he had made sure, quite, quite sure, that he had buried it in the past.

PART 3

Chapter Twenty-Five

Bombay, June 1989

Jimmy Stone walked into the executive lounge in the Sea Rock Hotel and gave his name to the waiter on the door. He was directed to a table and asked to wait — his contact had not arrived yet. Sitting, he ordered a large gin and tonic, crossed his legs and glanced down at his new shoes, hand-made and paid for by the advance on this deal, crocodile skin loafers with a gold buckle. He bent and wiped his handkerchief over them, removing a faint smear on the glossy black surface, then he sat back, smug and content, and looked around the room.

His contact saw Jimmy from the door. He smiled. Jimmy Stone had taken a while to find but seeing him now, the Indian realised that he was perfect. Good-looking, charming, an expert liar and dispensable. He walked forward and joined him at the table.

'Jimmy.'

'Yes, that's right!' Jimmy stood up, grinned and offered

his hand. The Indian shook it briefly, distastefully, then dropped it, taking a seat. He clicked for the waiter, ordered himself a drink, then placed his briefcase on his lap and took out an envelope.

'Everything that we discussed is in here,' he said, handing it over. Jimmy took it and went to open it. 'Please,' he placed a restraining hand on Jimmy's arm. 'Open it in private.' Jimmy nodded and, folding it in half, he slipped the envelope inside the top pocket of his jacket, tailormade in light grey wool, also paid for by the deal.

'So, all I have to do is sign and you get all the bills, is that right?' He smiled and popped a peanut confidently into his mouth. 'Whatever I spend?'

'That is correct.' The Indian glanced away. Stone was an arrogant fool, the worst kind. He looked back. 'You must do what it takes,' he said. 'We have complete confidence in you.'

Jimmy continued to smile. 'And the final payment?'

'When you return to India, as we agreed.' The Indian stirred the drink that had just been placed in front of him. He held it up.

'To a successful trip,' he said.

Jimmy clinked his glass against the other man's. 'Yeah,' he answered. 'And all that lovely money.'

Sussex, June 1989

John Bennet poured boiling water into two mugs of instant coffee, added milk, then sugar and reached for the biscuit tin in the cupboard. He laid the biscuits out on a plate and placed all the coffee things on to a tray, leaving it on the side while he went outside. He walked out of the back door into the garden, down along through the roses, just coming into bloom, and across to the new potting shed he'd had built next to his old one. He knocked on the door.

'Indi! Coffee's ready!' He waited. It was drizzling, a damp, chilly summer day and he wanted to get back inside. He knocked again, this time loudly and impatiently. 'Indi!'

The door flew open.

'Hi, Gramps!' Indu Bennet stood blocking the door, smudges of dirt on her face, her hands thick with soil. She wiped them on her jeans and John tutted; he did the laundry.

'What are you doing in there?' he grouched, digging his hands in his pockets. She had become very secretive of late and it was beginning to annoy him.

Indi smiled. 'Nothing.' Then she laughed. 'Don't be such a grump, you'll know soon enough!' She came out into the drizzle and hooked her arm through his. 'Did I hear the word coffee?'

'Hmmmm.' John peered round her into the shed.

'Grandpa! Don't!' Indi slammed the door shut. 'It's a surprise! Don't spoil it for me.' She narrowed her eyes and smiled. 'You're a wily old bugger sometimes.'

John burst out laughing. 'Less of the old, Indu Bennet.' She was outrageous but her energy, her wit and intelligence never failed to inspire him. 'Coffee's ready inside,' he said. 'Come on.' He turned back towards the house and patted Indi's hand. 'I'm stuck on the crossword,' he remarked as they walked on in. 'Perhaps you'd like to have a look at it?'

'Yup, no problem!' Indi was a crossword fiend. 'It's the

quick one, is it, Gramps?' And she laughed at the look of horror that crossed John's face.

The sitting-room had faded over the years, the colours of the chintz roses were muted, the velvet had paled and worn but the wood was still highly polished, the rugs in perfect condition, the grate swept and the fire relaid every morning. Caroline Bennet had been dead ten years and John ran the house with military precision.

As she plumped down into the sofa and put her feet up on the stool, Indi watched John carefully place the tray on the side table and reach for the biscuit plate, offering it across. He was a good-looking man, her grandfather, he didn't look his seventy-two years, he was fit and capable, strong still, with an active life. Indi adored him.

She took a biscuit and crunched, still looking at him, still thinking and absent-mindedly dropped crumbs on the floor. 'Sorry.' She bent to scoop them up.

John shook his head, then smiled. Silently, he handed her a plate.

'Thanks.'

He sat opposite her, crossing his long legs, relaxing back with his coffee. He looked at Indi. 'So,' he said, 'what are you going to do with your summer vacation?' He drank, then placed the mug on a mat, on the table at his side. 'You have to do something, Indi, you can't just sit around in Sussex and waste this opportunity. Once you start your internship you might never see the light of day again, maybe not for months . . .' He smiled. 'Years perhaps.'

Indi smiled back. She pulled her legs up under her, long and slim, like John's, like her mother's and nursed the mug of coffee, silent for a few minutes. 'To be perfectly honest,' she replied, 'I don't know what to do.' She swirled the brown liquid round and round in the cup. 'I'm quite happy here,' she said, glancing up, 'I've got the choir, the garden.' She grinned. 'I've got you, Gramps. What more do I need?'

John said nothing. Indi Bennet was twenty-three years old, she had just passed her medical exams and started at St Thomas's Hospital in September. For as long as he could remember, she had done nothing but study: science, maths, medicine. She sang with the Bach Choir in London and she had a passion for roses but that was as far as it went. No boy-friends, no rebellions, no fashion, a pair of precious faded Levi's and a collection of John's old shirts, no make-up, no hairstyles, just her crop of dark brown curls and her clear, honey-coloured skin. She had a small circle of close friends, all girls, and she read the *New Statesman*, *Private Eye* and the *British Medical Journal*.

John took up his coffee and finished it before he spoke. He didn't want to push Indi into anything, he loved her company, loved having her around, but he worried that she hadn't seen enough of life, that she was too naïve. He wanted her to go away, to Florence maybe or Venice, he wanted her to travel Europe, to do something, anything, before she ended up working sixteen hours a day in an NHS Hospital.

'Had you thought about staying with the Frasers in Tuscany at all, Indi?' A couple from John's regiment had retired to Italy. 'You know they'd love to have you and you'd be free to do what you wanted, they have a nice studio apartment in their farmhouse which you could have.' He smiled reassuringly but saw that Indi wasn't looking at him, she was fingering the petals on a rose in the bowl behind her.

'Is this the Binton Silver Medal rose?' she asked, turning back.

John sighed heavily. 'Yes, Indi,' he said, 'you know damn well it is.'

'Lovely perfume.' She rubbed the petal she pulled off between her fingers and then sniffed. 'Almost peppery.' She smiled across at her grandfather. 'That's one of your best I think, Gramps, don't you?'

John shook his head but he couldn't help grinning. She was headstrong and fiercely determined but she was never unpleasant, never rude, she never had been.

'All right, Indi, conversation closed,' he said. 'Aunt Clare is coming on Sunday for lunch, perhaps she'll persuade you.'

Indi pulled a face. The only thing Aunt Clare had ever convinced her of was that shopping was a jungle. She shopped like an animal stalking its prey. Indi stood and drained her mug.

'Don't bank on it.' She stepped round the table and leant down to kiss John's cheek. 'Please don't worry about me, Grandpa, I like it here, I always have.'

'I know, that's why I worry.'

'You'd worry more if I ran around London with a ring through my nose, unemployed and changing boyfriends more often than I change my knickers.'

'Indu!'

'Well, it's true!' She smiled. 'Count your blessings, Gramps.'

John reached for her hand. 'I do,' he said, squeezing it, 'I do.'

Chapter Twenty-Six

Indi stretched her hands behind her back, twisted to the right, dipped her shoulder and finally caught hold of the zip. She yanked hard, it gave way and the back of her dress opened up.

'Jeeze! Thank God for that!' She wriggled out of the sleeves and let it drop to the floor, stepping out of it and bending to pick it up.

'If you insist on wearing the same dress you've worn since you left school, Indi,' her friend Mary said, 'it's hardly surprising it feels tight.'

'Tight! I can only just reach top C in it!'

Mary smiled and shook her head. 'Here.' She took the long black dress and zipped it back up, slipping a hanger inside while Indi pulled on her jeans and a striped shirt. She threw a big wool jumper over her head and slipped her loafers on, then turned to Mary and took the dress, stuffing it into a carrier bag.

'You going straight home, Mary?' she asked.

Mary, her dress neatly wrapped in cellophane and hung over her arm, stood watching Indi with exasperation. 'Yes, I am,' she answered. She tutted, then turned towards the coat-rack. How Indu Bennet managed to turn up at concerts with a crumpled dress, no make-up and hair that had a mind of its own, and get away with it, she had no idea. Mary hung her dress on the rack while she put on her raincoat, fastened all the buttons and belted it tightly around her waist. She took her dress and again hung it over her arm, smoothing it as she did so.

'See you at practice on Wednesday, then?'

Indi nodded. She was struggling to get a comb through her hair and glanced up briefly. 'Yup, see you then!' she called, her eyes watering. 'Have a good weekend, Mary.'

Mary smiled. 'Thanks, Indi, and you.' And leaving Indi alone in the dressing-room, the last as always to get changed, she made her way along to the stage door and went out into the clear night air.

Indi called goodnight to Fred the doorman and opened the stage door, putting up her umbrella before she stepped out into the drizzle. She pulled the sleeves of her sweater down over her hands and shivered in the chill, damp night. Turning towards the main road, she jumped over a puddle and started to hum what she had been singing that night, quietly, imitating the conductor and dodging the puddles as she went.

'Hello? Erm? Hello?'

The shout came from behind her. Indi turned.

'Hello! Yes, you! Hello, wait!'

She was at the corner of the street, where it met the

main road and looking back she saw a figure hurrying towards her from the other end of it. She narrowed her eyes and wondered whether to ignore it. Too late. The figure was a fit agile young man and had reached her before she had the chance to make up her mind.

'Hello! Gosh, I thought I'd missed you. I've been waiting at the wrong door, you see, and when you didn't come out I asked and they told me this one was here so I legged it all the way and well . . .' The young man stopped and quickly drew breath. 'I caught you, just in time!' He smiled. 'Lucky eh?' He stood, breathless in front of her, his face wet from the rain, his curly blond hair covered in drops that glistened under the street lights. He dug his hands inside his raincoat and pulled out a dried rose, bound with silk thread, the petals smelling of faded summers. He held it out.

'For you,' he said. 'From a fan.'

Indi took the flower. She blushed terribly and looked away. She didn't know what to say.

'I've seen you sing three times now,' the young man went on, 'I think you sing beautifully, I can tell your voice, I can tell it apart from all the others. You have a perfect contralto voice, don't you?'

Indi smiled. 'Not perfect, no.'

'I knew it, I told you I could pick it out!' He smiled back. 'I think it's perfect.'

Indi laughed, she couldn't help it. 'It's very kind of you to say so, but obviously you're not a music buff.'

The young man smiled. 'I've only just started going to concerts,' he said earnestly, 'I'm doing a course, correspondence, teach yourself classical music . . .' He stopped. 'You're laughing at me,' he said.

Indi put her hand out and touched his arm. 'No, not at all!' She looked at him. 'Everyone has to start somewhere, I think it's admirable that you're interested enough to find out about it.'

'I suppose you know everything there is to know about classical music.'

Again Indi laughed. 'I know what I sing, but that's about it, I'm afraid.' She smelt the rose, gently fragrant still. 'Now roses, there's a subject I do know everything about.'

This time the young man laughed. 'Roses?'

'Yes! Roses! I grow roses, with my grandfather, at home in Sussex. We enter competitions, we've won quite a few actually. We often . . .' Indi broke off. The young man was staring at her and it made her uneasy. 'Anyway,' she said quickly, 'I must be off, it's late and I have to get the last train back.'

The young man shook his head, as if breaking a trance. 'I'm sorry,' he said, 'I was staring, wasn't I?'

'Yes.' Indi looked towards the main road, avoiding his eye.

'I don't mean to, it's just that you're so pretty, that's all.'

Indi turned back to him. She knew lots of men from medical college, she knew all the lines and how to ignore them but there was something strangely honest about this young man, something rather naïve and appealing. She smiled and he grinned back, the skin around his eyes crinkling and a small dimple appearing on both cheeks. It was a boyish smile, uncomplicated, attractive.

'Are you singing next weekend, at this festival thing in Westminster Abbey?' Indi nodded. 'Would you like to have a coffee with me, before the performance?'

She hesitated. She never, ever went on dates, never. 'I don't know, I . . .'

'It'd be brilliant if you could, you could maybe tell me something about the piece you're singing.' He looked at her questioningly. 'It would do wonders for my street cred.'

Finally Indi smiled. 'Yes, all right then,' she said. 'Thanks.'

He grinned. 'Shall I meet you outside?'

'Yes, early though, I have to get ready in plenty of time for the performance.'

'What time then?'

'Six?'

'Brilliant! Six it is.' The young man dug his hands in the pockets of his raincoat. 'Thanks, Indu, I'll really look forward to that.'

Indi looked at him, puzzled. 'How did you know my name?'

He shrugged. 'I told you, I'm a fan.' Then he glanced up the street and seeing a free taxi, jumped off the kerb and waved it down. 'You'll miss your train otherwise,' he said, walking towards it. 'What station?'

'Victoria.'

'Victoria station, mate,' he said to the cabbie and handed over a tenner. 'Keep the change.'

'Please don't!' Indi protested. 'I can get the tube, honestly!'

'It's late,' he said, shrugging, 'and I don't want you to miss your train.' He opened the door of the cab and waited for Indi to climb in.

'You really didn't have to,' she said, settling herself inside and yanking the window down.

'No, but I wanted to.' He slammed the door shut. 'See you next Saturday, then?'

She smiled. 'Yes, see you Saturday.' The young man stepped back and held up his hand in a wave. 'Wait!' Indi cried, suddenly leaning out of the window. 'I don't even know your name!'

The young man laughed. 'Jimmy Stone,' he called, as the cab moved off. 'Jimmy Alexander Stone!' And he dug his hands in his pockets again, turned and walked away.

John heard the front door and picked up a magazine, flicking idly through it. He heard Indi drop her things in the hall, then cross to the sitting-room, cracking the door open and poking her head round.

'Hi, Gramps!' She shook her head, smiling. 'You didn't have to wait up, you know.'

'I know, I didn't!' He dropped the magazine on to the sofa. 'How'd it go?'

'Well, as usual.' Indi came in and perched on the edge of the armchair opposite him. 'I met a fan,' she said, 'after the concert. He came to the stage door and gave me a rose.'

John smiled. 'Very smooth.'

'He wasn't, not at all, he was . . .' She broke off, not quite sure what Jimmy Stone was. 'He was nice,' she finished. 'Unpretentious, pleasant.'

'Urgh! Avoid pleasant, Indi, it's a cover-up for either plain evil or downright boring!'

Indi laughed. 'When did you become such an expert on men, Gramps?'

'No expert, just a cynic.'

'Well, I'll let you know,' she said, 'if it's evil or boring.

I'm having a coffee with him next Saturday before the concert.'

'Oh really?' John raised an eyebrow.

'Yes really.' She stood. 'And don't pretend you're not pleased, Grandpa, I can see the smug satisfaction all over your face!'

John laughed. 'I'm pleased, all right! Now go to bed.' It was true, he was pleased, he wanted Indi to meet more young men, get out a bit.

Indi turned at the door. 'Night, Gramps,' she said.

'Goodnight, Indu.' He stood himself, reaching to switch off the lamp.

'Thanks for waiting up.'

'I told you—'

'I know,' she interrupted, 'you didn't!' And she blew him a kiss, then disappeared off to bed.

'. . . Yup, the last train, Gramps, it's twelve forty-five. No, I'll get a cab to Victoria and one the other end. No, don't bother, honestly, it'll be really late. Yes, OK ' She smiled. 'Yup, I will, thanks . . . OK. Bye!'

Indi hung up and waited for the extra twenty pence piece she'd put into the payphone to drop down into the change tray. It clinked its way through, she picked it up and stuffed it into the pocket of her jeans, wishing she'd worn something smarter now. Heading off towards the changing area to collect her dress, Indi glanced at her watch and wondered if she might still catch Mary. She hoped so because she didn't even have a comb with her tonight.

'Hi, Mary! You look nice.'

'What d'you want, Indi?' Mary turned away from the

small cracked mirror and put her hairbrush back in her handbag. She reached for her lipstick.

'Can I borrow your brush and a bit of make-up?' Indi asked sidling into the room.

Mary looked up. 'You never wear make-up!' She handed her brush over.

'No, but I thought I might try a bit of lipstick, something on my eyes?' Indi started to brush her curls and Mary thought how thick and glossy her hair was.

'What's the occasion?'

'Dinner, with a friend.'

Mary smiled. 'A male friend would that be? The young man you were having a coffee with earlier perhaps?'

Indi blushed. 'Yes.'

'Come here.' Mary took her little make-up purse out of her handbag and scraped a chair back. 'Sit. I'll do it.'

'Oh great! Thanks, Mary.' Indi plonked herself down and crossed her legs.

'What about your clothes?'

'What's wrong with my clothes?'

'Nothing, I just . . .'

Indi swivelled round on the chair. 'I don't look that awful, do I?' She bit her lip.

Mary placed her hands on Indi's shoulders and turned her back round. 'You don't look awful at all,' she answered honestly. 'I don't know how you do it but even those tatty old jeans don't look as bad as they should do.' She tilted Indi's face back and quickly applied a coat of mascara, a sweep of blusher and a dab of natural lip gloss. 'There!'

Indi stood and peered in the mirror. 'Thanks, Mary,' she said, 'I really appreciate it.' There was very little difference, just a heightening of the shape of her eyes, cheeks and lips. Indi finished brushing her hair.

'Where're you going to eat?'

'I don't know, it's very last minute, we only really met for the first time properly tonight.'

'And he's nice, is he? He's certainly very good-looking.' Mary applied her own lipstick and glanced at Indi in the mirror.

'Oh yes! He's charming, he . . .' Indi broke off and smiled sheepishly. 'He's very nice thank you, Mary.' She took her jacket off a hanger and pulled it on, picking up the carrier bag with her dress in. 'Wednesday practice?'

'I'll be there!' Mary took her own raincoat off a hanger and carefully folded it over her arm.

'See you Wednesday then, Mary!' Indi hurried across to the door. 'Bye!'

Mary turned to wish her good luck but she'd gone. 'Yes, see you Wednesday, Indu,' she said to herself. 'Have a nice evening, thank you, Mary, I will.'

Indi met Jimmy at the entrance to the cathedral; he was waiting for her on the steps. He stood as she approached him and grinned, his hands in his pockets as they always seemed to be, his raincoat open, the collar turned up. He jumped down the steps, two at a time and held out his arm. 'Ready?'

'Yup, ready.' Indi slipped her hand through his arm.

'If you see a cab, scream!'

Indi laughed, then suddenly saw a free taxi. 'Ahhhhhhh!' It was a piercing howl.

Jimmy did a double take, then dived into the road and

flagged the car down. 'I didn't mean literally,' he said, bundling her inside. 'My God, what a voice!'

Indi giggled. She sat back as Jimmy gave the name of the restaurant and stared out of the window. London looked entirely different from the inside of a black taxi cab she thought, it looked like another city. They drove on and she continued to stare, the luxury of a taxi one that she could seldom afford. At Piccadilly, the car stopped and Jimmy jumped out, holding the door for her. 'Greens,' he said as she climbed out, 'I hope you like oysters.'

He paid the driver and took her hand, leading her inside. 'I've booked a table for two,' he told the head waiter, 'Stone, ten-thirty.'

'Yes, Mr Stone, this way please.'

Indi held her breath. She spotted a well-known actor dining with a young member of the royal family and blushed as she went past their table.

'Jimmy!' she hissed as they sat down. 'How on earth can you afford a place like this!'

Jimmy grinned. 'Ask me no questions and I'll tell you no lies!'

She narrowed her eyes. 'Seriously,' she said.

'Seriously,' he answered, 'I take photographs, travel photographs, for glossy books on Africa, Venetian palaces, that sort of thing. It pays well and it gives me lots of free time.'

'To teach yourself classical music?' Her voice was heavy with sarcasm. He'd been leading her on, that much was obvious.

He touched her arm, only briefly. 'Yes, to teach myself classical music. I left school at seventeen with three O-levels, one of them photography. I've done bloody well for myself in the last ten years but I don't know much about anything. Not about music or literature, the classics, that sort of thing.'

Indi glanced away. 'I'm sorry,' she said, 'I didn't mean to be rude.'

'Rude?' Jimmy smiled. 'You should hear some of those bitch art directors I have to deal with! Now that's rude.'

Indi smiled back.

'So, now you, Indu Bennet. What have you done in the last ten years?'

Indi shrugged. She felt embarrassed talking about herself, she rarely did it. 'Studied, taken exams, passed them, sung in the choir . . .'

Jimmy put his hands up. 'Whoa, wait! What sort of exams? Let's not rush through it.'

'O-levels, A-levels, my medical exams. I've been at St Thomas's studying medicine, I start my stint as a young doctor in September.' Jimmy whistled through his teeth. 'I know, I'm not looking forward to it either! Eighty-hour weeks, stress, pressure, living off doughnuts.'

'Doughnuts!'

'Yes, it's the only take-away food I like.'

They both laughed.

'And you're half Asian, Indian perhaps, am I right? Where do your parents come from?'

Indi glanced down. She fiddled with the napkin on her lap for a few moments. 'Yes, you are right, I am half Indian,' she said. 'My father was from Balisthan.'

Jimmy reached across the table and lifted her hand up, placing it on the table to stop her fiddling. He looked at her face. 'It's a very beautiful part of India,' he said, 'I've got a commission coming up there quite soon, a shoot for a book on Indian architecture. You say your father *was* from there?'

'Yes, he, erm, they, my parents were killed in a car crash just after I was born.' Indi hated recounting this fact, it always produced a reaction, pity mainly. 'I've lived with my grandfather all my life, until I went away to medical school, that is.'

'I see.' The waiter came up with the menus and Jimmy said nothing until he'd gone again. 'What about your Indian family? Your father's family?'

'I don't know, I never asked really.' She shrugged. 'They were never talked about so I never gave them much thought.' Saying it now she thought she sounded quite pathetic, but it wasn't like that, it was an untouched subject, something never referred to. It would have been difficult, impossible really as John was strangely closed about it, she knew it upset him.

'Have you ever been to India? To where you were born?'

'No, I, erm . . .' She smiled. 'Sorry, I sound rather dull, don't I?'

'Not at all!' Jimmy nodded across to the waiter. 'Shall we order?'

'Yes, yes please.' Indi looked down at the menu then glanced sidelong at Jimmy. She was relieved that bit was over and she was pleased he hadn't said *sorry*, or *how terrible for you*, the way most people did. She liked Jimmy Stone, she decided, choosing moules marinière and Dover sole from the menu, he was different, unlike anyone she knew, honest, unpretentious . . .

'Indi?'

She looked up and saw the waiter by the table.

'Oh, sorry.' She gave her order and closed the menu, handing it over.

'Wine?'

'No, thanks, I'd prefer fizzy water.'

He ordered a large bottle of Abbey Well and then looked across at her. 'You should, you know,' he said.

'Should what?'

'Go to India,' he went on, 'see where you were born. You'd like it, you'd probably feel quite at home there.'

She shrugged. 'Maybe.' It wasn't that it hadn't ever occurred to her, it was more a question of time, of priorities, of hurting and offending her grandfather. She smiled. 'I'll think about it.'

'Do that. I should be getting my brief through any minute now, I can't wait to go back.'

'D'you know India quite well, then?'

'Pretty well. I travel a bit, in between assignments, drift really, I suppose.'

'What about your family?'

Jimmy shrugged. 'What about them? There's very little to say, I'm afraid.'

Indi looked down, embarrassed. Jimmy reached for her hand and held it in his own, turning it over and inspecting the palm.

'Very interesting,' he said, narrowing his eyes. 'It looks to me like you're going to meet a charming young man with a J in his name . . .' He glanced up at her and grinned. 'And that you're going to have a great deal of fun with this young man. Something, I think, you haven't had much of before!'

Indi pulled her hand away but she did laugh. 'Singing's fun!' she protested. 'I love medicine, my gardening!'

Jimmy rolled his eyes, then flopped back in the chair, letting his body go limp.

'Jimmy!' He stayed like that, only he let his tongue loll out. 'Jimmy!' Indi whispered fiercely. 'Jimmy, please!' Several diners glanced over. 'Jimmy?' Indi began to feel uneasy. She leant across the table and gently poked him. Suddenly he leapt forward and caught her hand. She screamed.

Jimmy burst out laughing and Indi, after the initial shock, started to laugh as well. 'God, you're horrid!' she cried. 'Really mean!'

He kept hold of her hand and gently put it to his mouth. The kiss was quick, soft and warm and Indi felt the tremor of it through her whole body.

'I'm sorry,' he said. He dropped her hand and she took it back, holding the patch of skin under the table where he'd kissed it.

'Are you always this mad?' she asked.

He nodded. 'Always,' he answered. 'Life's too short to take seriously.'

'Is it?'

'Absolutely!' The waiter arrived with the drinks and Jimmy sat back while he poured the water. 'Why?' he asked, taking a sip. 'Don't you like it?'

Indi held her own glass to her lips. 'I don't know,' she answered honestly, 'I'm really not quite sure.'

The following morning, Indi lay in bed and listened to the sounds of the coffee grinder down in the kitchen below. It was a Sunday morning ritual, fresh coffee, croissants, church and the *Sunday Times*, not a word spoken for several hours. She could smell the aroma of the croissants in the oven but she didn't want to get up. She wanted to lie in bed and think about last night, she wanted to go over every detail and try to make up her mind about Jimmy Stone before she talked to her grandfather about him. But Indi could hear John's movements below, she could hear him filling the jug for the percolator, opening the oven door, getting out the plates, and she sighed, sitting up and dropping her legs over the side of the bed. She had never missed a Sunday breakfast with John and she wasn't about to start now. Pulling on her dressing-gown, she stood and made her way along to the bathroom.

'Hello, darling.' John had a pair of oven gloves on as Indi walked into the kitchen and glancing over his shoulder at her, he smiled, then bent and took a tray of hot croissants out of the oven.

'Hmmmm, they smell delicious!' she said.

'Home-made.'

'Don't lie, Gramps!' Indi crossed and kissed him on the cheek, picking the Waitrose wrapper off the side and dropping it in the bin. She saw John smiling.

'So, how was last night?'

'It was good, a nice evening.'

'Nice?'

'Yes, fun! Different.'

John placed the plate of croissants on the table along with the coffee jug and pulled out a chair. 'Sit, and tell me what different means, Indi?' He sat himself and shook out his napkin, leaning across the table for a croissant.

'I'm not sure really,' Indi said. 'To be honest I couldn't really make up my mind about him. He's terribly good-looking, funny, bright. He's a photographer, he takes pictures for design books, art history books but he's not at all arrogant or snotty about it.' She stopped and looked across at John. 'We talked a lot about India, Gramps, he's going there on a job this summer.'

John continued to eat his croissant, his face impassive but he felt a knot of tension in the pit of his stomach. India, it was a word he could hardly bear to hear, not since Jane disappeared there, not since that terrible business with Phillip all those years ago. 'So why can't you make your mind up about him, then,' John asked, 'if he's so good-looking and modest?'

Indi shrugged. 'I don't know. I just get a feeling, that's all, a sort of sixth sense. It's probably all imagination but I somehow can't quite believe he's for real.'

John finished eating and poured them both some coffee. 'Forget him then,' he said. 'There are plenty of young men out there, Indi, there's possibly even one for someone as difficult as you!' He smiled as he handed her the milk jug. 'Your time is precious, Indi, don't waste it on someone who doesn't deserve it.'

She sipped her coffee and toyed with the croissant on her plate. Jimmy had asked to see her on Monday night and she'd left it open, said she would ring him. Perhaps Gramps was right, perhaps she shouldn't bother, perhaps she should just ring and say no thanks, she wasn't interested, she had double-booked, and couldn't make Monday night. Looking up, she saw that John was watching her and said, 'You all right, Gramps?'

He nodded and patted her hand. 'Just fine,' he said. Standing, he walked across to the fridge and refilled the milk jug even though it was still half full. He didn't want Indi to see this young man again, he didn't want her head filled with ideas of India, of her heritage, her ethnic background. He didn't want Indi hurt, not now, not at the beginning of her life, her career. She didn't need to know about Jane, about Phillip, she didn't need to know any of it, not yet, not until she was settled, until she had someone who loved her, someone who would help to soften the blow. He turned and looked at the back of her head. He loved his granddaughter, he loved her so much it hurt at times. He had lied to protect her, he knew that, Caroline had known it too and he only hoped to God that one day she would understand that.

He walked across to her and ruffled her hair. 'What's the verdict then? Going to see him again?' He sat down and placed the milk jug between them.

'What d'you think?' Indi answered, smiling.

'Oh, I wouldn't bother.' He was sure the young man was perfectly nice but he didn't want his granddaughter involved in anything Indian.

'No, maybe not.' Indi poured herself another coffee and offered the pot across. 'I think I might just go and ring now,' she said, 'let him know.'

'Now?' John looked up at her as she stood.

'I'll be back in a minute,' she said. 'Have my croissant, Gramps, I can't eat it.' And she disappeared out of the door.

Jimmy lay in bed and smoked a cigarette. It had gone well, he was pleased. He should be able to get it done within the month, if he was smart. Not that it mattered of course, there was no time limit, just a nice fat cheque on delivery. He smiled as the phone rang and leant over the edge of the bed, fumbling round on the floor for it. He picked the receiver up and yanked the wire so it could reach his ear.

'Hello?' He sat up. 'Good morning, Indu, how are you? Good, glad to hear it!' Scratching his armpit, he flicked his cigarette ash into the remains of last night's coffee. 'What, Monday?' he said, noticing a hesitancy in her voice. 'Yes, I did actually!' he lied. 'But I'm not telling you, it's a surprise.'

He dropped the cigarette stub into the mug and it made a hiss as it went out. He leant forward, reaching for the paper, thinking quick. 'It's pretty hard to cancel but I guess I could give the tickets away if I had to.' He scanned the entertainments page. 'Why, don't you want to come?' He hit on the right ad. 'Oh, Indi, really? No, I guess not, but it is a shame, I tried really hard to get tickets for the Royal Opera House, it's a complete sell out.' He waited as the other end went silent. He needed Monday night, it would be impossible to start up again if she dipped out at this stage. 'Indi, are you still there?' He let out a sigh of relief. 'It isn't a problem if you really can't make it, honestly, I can give the tickets away.' He was sweating. 'I know it would be a terrible shame, I was so looking forward to it.'

He bit his thumb-nail. 'Can you? The other person won't mind you cancelling at this late stage?' A shot of adrenalin surged through him. 'Oh great! I'm really pleased.'

He reached for his cigarettes and lit another one up. 'Shall we meet in Covent Garden? At the Crusting Pipe?' He heard Indi hesitate again. This was going to be more difficult than he had first thought. 'How about the Opera House itself, then, outside at seven? Good, we'll do that.' He dropped his feet over the side of the bed and stood. 'I'm really glad you can make it, Indi, really glad.' He bent and picked the phone up, holding the receiver in the crook of his neck and walking naked to the window. He lifted a slat in the blind and looked out. 'OK, Indi, I'll see you tomorrow then,' he said. 'Yes, take care. Bye!' He hung up. 'Shit!' he said aloud. 'Fucking shit!' He left the phone on the window-sill and walked through to the sitting-room. He had rented the flat unfurnished and had a phone, a TV and a bed. In the empty kitchen he opened all the cupboards, hunting for a Yellow Pages; under the sink he found one. He took it back to the bedroom, looked up booking agents and dialled the first one on the page.

'Yes, hello,' he said, 'I hope you can. I need two tickets for *Madame Butterfly* at the Royal Opera House tomorrow night.' He chewed his thumb-nail again. 'No, I'm not concerned with price,' he snapped irritably, 'I'll pay whatever it takes!'

Chapter Twenty-Seven

For the second two weeks of June, a massive high rested over England and the summer weather lived up to all expectations. The sky was a pale azure blue, streaked with feathery clouds, the sun shone and a faint south-easterly breeze blew in off the coast of Sussex.

Indu Bennet lay in a field on her back under the shade of an old oak tree and stared up at the pattern the leaves made against the blue of the sky. Her head rested on a cushion and she wriggled her toes against the soft wool of the rug underneath her. Reaching to the side, she felt for her wine glass and, finding it, carefully tipped it up to her lips and sipped the champagne. She closed her eyes and sighed.

'You're not going to sleep are you, Indi?'

She smiled but kept her eyes closed. 'No, I'm just resting from the view.'

Jimmy rolled on to his side and looked at her. She was

beautiful, half Indian jasmine, half English rose, a heady combination of the exotic and the delicate. He traced the line of her face, from her brow down to her chin with his fingertip and she opened one eye. 'Oi!' She grinned. 'I'm trying to relax here, Mr Stone, it was you who told me to chill out in the first place, remember?'

Jimmy smiled and dropped his hand away. He sat up, taking the bottle of champagne out of the cooler and pouring himself another glass. Beside them lay the remains of their picnic, ordered and packed by Claridges, the hamper open, their plates, cutlery and dishevelled napkins strewn over the grass. Jimmy took an apple from the fruit basket and bit into it. 'Have you given my idea any more thought, Indi?' he asked, pulling his legs into the lotus position.

Indi opened both eyes and glanced sidelong at him. 'No, not really,' she answered. 'Why?'

'The brief's come through,' he said, 'Balisthan, the Mogul Palaces of Balisthan.'

Indi sat up. 'Really?' She cuffed him on the leg. 'Jimmy! Why didn't you say so earlier?'

'I wanted today to be perfect,' he said. 'Relaxed, easy, no decisions to be made.'

Indi leant forward and kissed him lightly on the mouth. 'You are sweet,' she said. He caught the back of her head and held her face close to his but she looked away, lowering her eyes and pulling back. He released her. 'OK, have it your way.' Smiling, he took another bite of the apple.

'You don't mind, do you?'

He shrugged, still grinning. 'Why should I? It's the way you are, it doesn't bother me.' He looked at his apple, deciding which bit to try next. 'It frustrates me, yes, but it doesn't upset me.' He bit. It didn't upset him in the slightest, he was in it for the money, nothing else. Sleeping with her would have been nice, a perk of the job but he wasn't going to push it. He couldn't afford to take that sort of risk.

'So when are you off?' she asked.

'At the end of the month.' He glanced up quickly to check she wasn't too shocked. She was thinking, her forehead creased in the odd frown she had when concentrating, the corner of her lip bitten. He flicked her arm. 'A penny for them?'

'They're worth more than a penny, Jimmy!' She knelt forward, poured herself some more champagne, then stood and walked away from him, some way down the hillside. She sat on the grass and looked at the view. She had no idea what to do.

In the past two weeks Indi had seen a great deal of Jimmy Stone. She'd had nothing else to do and he was persistent, constantly arranging things for her, fun things, extravagant things, jaunts and trips that men her own age would never have thought of. She liked him, he was good fun, easy going. He was completely different to anyone she had ever known before. And now he had asked her to go to India with him, all expenses paid, no ties, just for the company, just for the crack. He was leaving in a couple of weeks and she hadn't told John, she hadn't said yes and she hadn't said no. She couldn't make up her mind and she didn't want to make a mistake either way.

Sipping her champagne, she heard Jimmy come up behind her. He sat down and reached for her hand.

'I see a major trip abroad coming up,' he said, looking

down at her palm, 'with a very good-looking, charming young man.'

Indi smiled and continued to stare at the view. 'It is an offer you can't refuse,' he went on. 'The chance of a lifetime!'

Indi gently pulled her hand away. 'Don't, Jimmy!' she said. 'I'm trying to think.'

He shrugged and sat in silence next to her for a few moments. Then he said, 'I don't see what the problem is, Indi, I honestly don't.' She turned towards him. 'All I'm asking is for you to come to India with me for a while, for as long as you like. I'll book an open ticket, you can come home when you want to, stay as long as you want to. It'll be fun, Indi, really good fun! I really like you, I adore being around you, it would make working there so much more enjoyable if you were with me!' He took her hand again. 'What's the problem with that, eh? I couldn't make it any easier now, could I?'

Indi smiled. 'No, no you couldn't,' she said. 'I do realise that, it's just . . .' She sighed heavily. 'Oh I don't know.' She shrugged and pulled a face. She did know, she knew exactly what was holding her back but she didn't want to discuss it. Her grandfather was a subject she found impossible to talk about.

'So you'll come then?'

'Maybe . . .' she looked back at the view, 'maybe not.'

John hated India, he had always made it quite clear that he never wanted Indi to go there, or have anything to do with the country. She presumed it was losing Jane there that had turned him or maybe there was something else? Whatever it was, she knew he would take a proposed trip to India very badly. Very badly indeed.

344

Jimmy stood up and held out his hands. He knew not to push things, he had to work slowly, thoroughly, he didn't want to bully her into making the wrong decision. Indi took them and he pulled her upright.

'Race you down the hill?' he said.

'Yes, all right . . . Hey!' He sprinted off and she set after him, her bare feet skimming over the grass and the fine cotton of her skirt billowing out behind her as she ran.

The picnic was followed by a long walk across the Downs, then collecting up the rubbish and driving in Jimmy's car to a pub on the edge of the River Arun. They sat out by the water as the day finally faded and watched the twilight, cool and especially long, as it gracefully eased the day into night and brought the shadows to life.

Jimmy drove Indi home. She asked him in but he refused, he had a meeting in London early in the morning and had to be getting back. She climbed out of the car and quietly closed the door, holding up her hand to wave and stepping out of the glare of the headlights. She watched him disappear off down the drive, then she put her key in the door and went into the house. The lights were on in the sitting-room.

'Hello, Gramps.'

'Hello.' John put the paper down. 'Did you have a nice day, Indi?'

'Yes, a picnic up on the Downs, then a drink at the Mucky Duck at Roundal, by the river.'

'Lovely.' He looked at her face, flushed from the sun, the honey colour turning a darker brown, the colour of sandalwood, and she smiled at him, a warm, familiar smile, honest and clear, like Jane's had always been. 'You see rather a lot of this Jimmy Stone, don't you?' he said as Indi came into the room. 'He's obviously very nice.'

'Hmmm.' Indi glanced down at the headlines of the paper John had just put down.

'It's not serious, is it?'

Indi suddenly looked up. 'No! Of course not!' She blushed and John laughed, reaching out for her hand.

'You'll have to learn to stop blushing like that, Indi,' he said. 'None of your patients will take you seriously if you go crimson every time you're embarrassed.'

Indi smiled and sat down on a footstool, hugging her knees. She waited for John to pick up the paper again, then she said, 'Jimmy wants me to go to India with him, Gramps, in a couple of weeks' time.'

John held the paper steady but his body flinched. 'Does he now?' He kept his face hidden for a few moments longer, making sure he was composed when he looked at her. He lowered the paper. 'And what did you tell him?'

'I haven't told him anything yet, I thought I'd talk to you first.'

'I see.' Keep calm, his inner voice was saying, for God's sake keep calm. 'And who exactly is this Jimmy Stone chap? What do you know about him, Indi?'

'He's a photographer, I told you, he works freelance for various publishers, he's twenty-seven and he lives in London.'

'Is that all?'

'No! That's not all, Gramps! We've talked about loads of things, what he likes, what he's done with his life, where he's travelled.'

John nodded, trying to keep his face impassive. 'What

about his parents, Indi? His background, what school he went to?'

'I can't believe you just asked that, Gramps! What does any of that matter?'

'Not a lot, but at least you should know where he comes from!'

Indi bit back an angry retort. 'He doesn't talk about his parents,' she said tightly. 'Not everyone does. And he hasn't talked about his school so presumably it's not Eton!'

'There's no need to be sarcastic, Indu!' John snapped. 'I am asking this for your own good!'

'Oh really?'

'Yes really! Think about it. India isn't Blackpool, a train ride away, it's a complex, difficult country with a man you hardly know. Please, Indi, be sensible!'

'I am being sensible! I want to go.'

'Obviously!'

They both glared at each other for a moment, then Indi looked away. She never rowed with Gramps, never! She could hardly remember a cross word between them. She turned back to him and said, 'Look, I'm sorry, Gramps, it's just that I think I'd really like to go, to see where I was born, to be a bit independent. I don't want to upset you, honestly I don't.'

John heard the plea in her voice but he wasn't able to see sense; he panicked at her words, lashed out stupidly. 'You will upset me, Indi,' he said harshly, 'if you go to India.'

'But why?' Indi threw her hands up in the air. 'You've never told me anything about India, about my parents, just that they were killed in a car crash in 1966! That's it, that's all you ever said! I don't understand why you don't want me to go, why you have this dislike of a country you've never been to!'

John sat still and looked away. How could he explain now? And yet how could he risk letting her go to India to find it out on her own? What could he tell her? About her mother, about Phillip Mills and his awful bloody murder. That Jane ran away? That she was pregnant by an Indian lover and accused of murdering her husband, ran away to have the baby. That she and the Indian were killed and the baby was smuggled out of the country to England, to him and Caroline, her grandparents. That was all he knew, yet how could he tell her all this now? Without warning, without proof? He turned back to her. 'Indi, I forbid you to go to India,' he said, knowing he had no other way open to him. 'I absolutely forbid you!'

Indi looked incredulously at him. 'How can you? How can you forbid me, Grandpa? I'm twenty-three years old, I can do whatever I please!' She stood up and stormed over to the door. 'You know, you were the one who said get out, do something with your summer vacation and now, now I want to go to India for a few weeks, a month at the most, you've suddenly changed your mind!' She shook her head, exasperated. 'I don't understand, Grandpa, I just don't understand you!'

'I wouldn't expect you to!' John suddenly shouted. 'But I have my reasons!' He stood up and flinging the paper down, he crossed to the window. He stood with his back to her and stared out at the garden in darkness. In hindsight he knew that he should have told her then but he just couldn't do it. Perhaps it was too difficult to even admit to himself without the pain of having to tell Indu. He stayed silent, closed up.

'I don't want to go without your approval,' Indi said quietly, 'but I do want to go, Grandpa, I want to see where I was born, I want to go . . .'

'Go then!' John cried suddenly, swinging round to face her. 'But you go without my approval, you go in the knowledge that you make me very unhappy indeed!'

Indi shook her head. 'Please don't make me feel guilty, don't burden me with that,' she murmured. 'Tell me what it is, explain, please, Gramps.'

But John was old, he had suffered the terrible loss of his beloved daughter, the shame of her accusal and he was tired, he couldn't face any more emotion. 'I'm sorry, Indi,' he said, 'but I won't explain and I won't be here for you if you go to India, you can no longer rely on me.' He turned away, unable to look at her face. 'That's it, go to India and you go entirely alone. If you get into trouble then it's your problem.'

Indi put her hand up to her mouth and a sob caught in the back of her throat. This was awful, she didn't understand any of it. How could she go under these circumstances? And yet . . . Jimmy's words went round and round in her head. She was twenty-three, an independent person, she had to start living, she had to break free! She had to see life while she still had the chance. Opening the door, she turned to leave. 'Gramps, I . . . ?' Her voice failed her but he didn't look round. Silently she went upstairs to her room and in the darkness lay down on the bed, curled herself up into a ball and cried confused and angry tears.

*   *   *

John made his early-morning cup of tea and placing the mug and a couple of biscuits on a tray, he went through into the hall and picked *The Times* up off the floor, placing it on top of the tray. He carried it all back upstairs to bed. There wasn't much point in getting up yet, there was nothing to get up for, so he laid the tray on the bedside table, kicked off his slippers and climbed back into bed. He looked at the date on the front page of the paper and sighed heavily. It was only Tuesday, Indi had been gone for nearly two weeks now and it felt like a month. He glanced out of the window, knowing that today was the date she had planned to leave for Delhi and, despite the sunshine, he felt as miserable as sin.

John got up. Leaving the tea, he wandered through into Indi's old bedroom and stood in the tidy, immaculately clean room, longing for the mess of papers, books and clothes, all strewn about the floor. Mrs Jones had done a good job, too good a job, he thought, and, crossing to the window, he opened it to let some air into the room, to give it some life. He heard the postman.

'It's amazing,' he said aloud, 'how important the post becomes when you've nothing else to occupy your mind.' And leaving Indi's room, closing the door firmly behind him, he went eagerly downstairs for his letters.

The first one John opened was from The Rose Growers' Association. It was marked I. Bennet but he was the only member in the house so it was obviously a typo and should have been J. He ripped the back of the envelope and unfolded the page, scanning down the paragraphs and hurriedly reading the contents. Halfway down he stopped and peered closely at it, going back to the first line and rereading it more closely. Then he sat down on the bottom stair and closed his eyes. It was Indu's letter, he had opened it by mistake. It was Indi's registration of her first hybrid rose, the John Bennet Rose. He swallowed hard and standing, held on to the bannister while he fumbled in his pocket for his handkerchief. He blew his nose then walked through to the kitchen and out of the back door into the garden. He went into Indi's potting shed and stood, just inside the door. There it was, her weeks of secrecy, a deep red bloom, the John Bennet Rose.

Minutes later, he was back in the house, the shower was running and he was hunting though an old suitcase he stored under the bed for something he had hidden many years ago. By nine-thirty, he was shaved, showered and dressed. He took his car out of the garage, started it up, then left the engine running while he dashed back to the potting shed for a moment. Finally ready, he climbed back into the car, shifted into gear and headed off up the drive, out on to the main road, to the A29 and then on up to London.

Indi stuffed the last of her shirts into her bag and hollered down the stairs for Jimmy to come and help her close it up. He was sitting drinking coffee with Aunt Clare. He ran up the three flights of their Chelsea town house and swept Indi up into his arms.

'Jimmy! Stop it!' she squealed. He dropped her, slapped his own wrist then knelt on the floor beside her bag. His mood was jubilant. It had taken every last ounce of effort, every last breath of persuasion to get her to come but he'd done it. They were on their way, nothing could stop them now.

'Right! Is that everything?'

'I think so.'

'I bloody well hope so because I'm not unzipping this once I've got it closed. It's stuffed full!'

Indi knelt beside him. 'Sorry,' she said sheepishly. He was right, it was her only bag but she'd made up for that by the sheer size of it. She pressed the sides together while Jimmy yanked on the zip, stretching the fabric of the bag to its full tilt. They struggled, heaved, swore a couple of times and finally got it done. Indi was ready. She checked her small rucksack for her essentials and valuables, then looked at Jimmy.

'I'm ready,' she said. 'Let's go!'

He picked up the bag, moaned at the weight and, grinning, he followed her down the stairs to Aunt Clare.

'Indi?' Aunt Clare stood in the doorway of the kitchen and watched Indi swallow down her travel sickness pill with a glass of water. She hesitated a moment before saying, 'Indi, I just wondered if you might want to, erm, er, phone Gramps?'

Indi glanced up. She saw the look on Aunt Clare's face and sighed. 'I've tried,' she said quietly. 'Three times this week. No reply.'

'Try one last time?'

Indi hesitated. She understood nothing and it hurt as much now as it had two weeks ago. 'I don't know.' She shrugged. 'I don't understand him, Clare, I don't know what I've done, except want a bit of independence.'

Clare touched her shoulder. 'He has his reasons.'

'Yes, that's what he said.' Indi was silent for a few moments. 'May I use the phone, then?'

Clare smiled. 'Go on, we don't have to go for five minutes or so.'

Indi walked into the hall and dialled West Sommerton. She stood, her back slumped against the wall and listened to the empty ringing tone, then she dropped the receiver back in its cradle. 'No answer,' she said sadly.

Clare shrugged. 'Right!' She covered her disappointment. 'Let's get off then, give you plenty of time to check in.'

Indi smiled. 'Thanks, Clare, thanks for putting me up and taking me to the airport with Jimmy. I really—'

Clare came across and kissed Indi's cheek. 'I'll miss you,' she said, 'and so will Dad.' Then she hugged her niece and together they walked back into the hall where Jimmy was waiting with the bags.

John parked the car in the short-term car-park and hurried towards terminal three, praying that they hadn't already gone through to departures. He spotted the British Airways desk across the concourse, put his spectacles on and saw Indi's figure checking in. He shouted, waved his arms in the air and seeing her turn and catch sight of him, he made a dash towards her. They met somewhere in the middle.

'Indi!' John hugged her tightly and closed his eyes for a moment. Then he pulled back and looked at her. 'I thought I might miss you!'

Indi took a hanky from her sleeve and blew her nose loudly. 'Well you didn't,' she said. Then she smiled and hugged him again. 'Thank goodness!'

She took his hand. 'D'you want to come and meet Jimmy? He's over by the check-in.'

'Yes, yes of course!' John held her back for a moment as he dug in his top pocket. 'Indi, I have something for you,' he said, 'something important.' He brought out a package, it was wrapped in cloth and tied with a leather thong.

'What is it?' Indi peered at it. 'I'm not going to get stopped at customs for it, am I, Gramps?' She grinned.

John held it out. 'Indi, be serious for a moment, it's important.' She glanced up at him. 'I was given this when you arrived in England. I've never opened it, I have no idea what it is but I can only assume it is something to do with your parents. It belongs to you, I was keeping it until . . .' He broke off, then he shrugged. 'Until I thought you were ready for it, I suppose. Here.' He handed it to her. 'Take it, put it away safely and look at it when you want to.'

Indi turned the package over in her hands, then she unzipped the hidden pocket in her rucksack and slipped it inside. 'Thank you,' she said. John leant forward and kissed her.

'Always remember who you are, Indi.' He gently tucked a loose curl of hair behind her ear and she smiled. 'And that you are very special, to me. I know what I said, but,' he shrugged, 'I am always here for you, remember that too.' He stood back a pace. 'Now, I suppose I had better meet this young man of yours.'

'He's not my young man, Gramps, he's just a friend, that's all!'

'Right! Then I'd better meet this young man of yours who's not your young man, so to speak, but just a friend!'

Indi laughed. 'He's over here, with Clare.'

John hesitated a moment. 'Ah, Indi, I forgot something.'

He again dug in his pocket and this time gently lifted out a deep red rose. He took the lapel of her jacket in his hands and slipped the bloom into the buttonhole. 'The John Bennet Rose,' he said. 'Wear it with pride, Indi, it's very beautiful.'

She lifted the rose and smelt it, then she smiled. 'You like it?'

'I love it!' And placing his arm around her shoulder, John hugged his granddaughter, swallowed back his sadness and walked with her over to the British Airways desk to check in for her flight to Delhi.

Chapter Twenty-Eight

Indi gripped the seat and gritted her teeth. She squeezed her eyes shut tight, held her breath and, stomach churning, she waited for the wheels to hit the ground. The Air India plane dipped, seemed to lift off into the air again then suddenly drop, like a stone, on to the runway. There was an almighty bump, the fuselage went up once more, Indi's stomach lurched, then it landed a second time with a series of thuds. The wheels were down. Suddenly a round of applause broke out and Indi opened her eyes. The engines thrust into reverse, the brakes came on and the plane screeched along the tarmac, the interior rattling and shaking so much that several of the overhead lockers flew open and the man next to Indi had his bag fall out and hit him hard on the knee. It slowed, Indi's teeth stopped aching and minutes later it ground to a halt. She let go of the seat and glanced across at Jimmy. He had slept through the whole experience.

'Jimmy!' She shook him gently. 'Jimmy, we're in Baijur.' Indi took out her handkerchief and wiped her palms on it; she was sweating badly.

Jimmy opened his eyes and rubbed them, stretching and yawning. 'We're down, are we?'

'Yes, thank God!'

He glanced across at her. 'You have a problem with the flight?' His tone was patronising.

'No, no problem.' She smiled tightly, more out of relief than anything else. Then she unfastened her seatbelt and waited for the man next to her to stand up before sliding out of her seat and squeezing into a space in the aisle to reach for her bag. She was pushed and jostled, waited for several minutes while people shoved past her, then she lost patience and elbowed a large man hard in the ribs as he pushed to get past her and blocked his way. She finally got her bag, called across to Jimmy and kept the crowd behind her waiting while he clambered out of his seat, took his hold-all from the overhead locker and led the way to the exit.

Outside, on the steps of the plane, Indi felt a rush of warm air on her face, saw the pure blue sky above and smelt the breeze, the Indian breeze. She put her hand up to shield her eyes from the sun and glanced across at Jimmy, smiling broadly at him.

'I can hardly believe I'm here!' she called, against the noise of the airport. He nodded and taking her arm, hurried her down to the waiting bus.

Once they were through arrivals, Jimmy found them a taxi, paid the porter and climbed inside, anxious to be away.

'Come on, Indi,' he called out the window, 'don't

dawdle!' She was straining to look at the view, up on tiptoes, gawping like a tourist and it was beginning to get on his nerves. 'Hurry up!'

Indi climbed into the taxi beside him. 'What about the cameras, Jimmy?'

'I asked already,' he answered sharply. 'They've been sent on to the hotel.'

Indi looked at him quizzically for a moment, then shrugged and settled back. He had been in an odd mood since they landed at Delhi, impatient with her, lacking his usual sense of fun. She thought it might be the camera thing, he had apparently sent all his camera equipment on ahead but it hadn't turned up in Delhi and there was no sign of it now. She looked out of the window and tried to ignore his mood. The taxi started, she glanced down to check she had her rucksack, and then went back to the scene out of the window. They drove on in silence, Indi's excitement took over and she forgot Jimmy's tension. Jimmy sat and picked at his fingernails, all his energy focused on one thing. He was almost there now, only a few more hours and he'd have finally made it.

The taxi deposited them on the road above the boat jetty and the lake lay below, the water shimmering in the sunlight, the palace, a white carved building floating serenely in the middle. Indi got out of the car while Jimmy paid, and walked across to the wall, looking down on the view.

'My God! It's incredible!' she called over her shoulder. Jimmy came up behind her and followed her gaze. 'Yes, it is.' He started down the slope towards the jetty and Indi hurried after him. 'Jimmy! Where are you going?'

'To catch the boat,' he called back, 'come on!'

Indi caught him up. 'What d'you mean, come on?' She fell into step with him. 'Where are we going?'

Jimmy stopped and faced her. 'That's where we're staying,' he said, 'in the Lake Palace Hotel.'

'It's a hotel?'

'Yes,' he snapped, suddenly tired, eager to have the whole thing over and done with. 'It's a hotel!' He started walking again and Indi looked behind her at the taxi driver struggling with their bags. She followed Jimmy to the jetty and saw the boat waiting, two uniformed boat men standing ready to help them aboard. She grinned and shook her head. 'I can't believe it,' she said. 'Jimmy, this is amazing!'

Jimmy was already on the boat. 'Yes, I suppose it is!' He looked across the water at the hotel and for the first time all morning, he smiled.

The porter left Indi's bag just inside her room and she tipped him with a few of the rupees Jimmy had given her. She had travellers' cheques but she hadn't had time to cash them yet, so she'd borrowed twenty pounds in Indian currency from him and was using that. She walked over to the French window and opened it, stepping out on to the balcony, high above the water, to look at the view.

'What d'you think?' She swung round. Jimmy stood in the doorway to her room, watching her.

'I think it is just beautiful,' she answered.

'Good, the lady's satisfied, then.' He came in and

dropped down on to her bed, bouncing up and down to test the springs.

'Did your cameras arrive?' Indi leant back against the balustrade and looked at him inside.

'Cameras?' He went blank for a moment then suddenly he smiled. 'Ah, yes, they were in my room waiting for me.'

'Good, then the gentleman's satisfied too.' Indi came in from the balcony. 'So, what are we going to do today?'

Jimmy's face fell. 'Oh God, Indi! Didn't I tell you?' He smacked his palm against his forehead. 'I've got a meeting in the city with the art director. She left a message for me at reception.'

Indi shrugged off her disappointment. 'It doesn't matter,' she said.

'Yes, yes it does!' Jimmy thought for a few moments. 'Look, why don't I arrange a guide for you at reception and you could go off for a few hours on your own, see a few things in Baijur?'

Indi pulled a face. 'Oh, I don't know, Jimmy.'

He jumped up. 'Go on, Indi, you'd have a great time, I promise. These guides are brilliant and I'll ask for the best one they know.'

She smiled; his enthusiasm was hard to resist. 'OK. Thanks, I'd like that.'

'Excellent!' He headed towards the door. 'I'll go and fix it up now.' He turned back in the doorway. 'Indi, I have to be off in ten minutes or so and I've got to change first so look, why don't you freshen up, maybe grab some room service and I'll get reception to call you when the guide arrives.' He came back into the room and kissed her cheek. 'I, my darling girl, will catch up with you later.'

Indi smiled. As he went to leave a second time she called him back. 'Jimmy?' He popped his head round the door. 'What time will you be back tonight?'

He shrugged and rolled his eyes. 'To be honest, Indi, I don't really know. These things can take one hour or twenty, with the art director driving you to every location to sum it all up!' He came into view. 'If I'm not back by dinner, then go ahead and eat without me and I'll see you in the morning. OK?'

She nodded.

'Oh, and give me your passport while I'm at it, and any valuables, I'll bung them in the hotel safe before we both go out.'

Indi took her rucksack off the bed and dug in it for her travel pack. It had her airline ticket, her passport, her vaccination certificate and her travellers' cheques in it. She handed the whole thing over to him and he gently flicked her chin. She smiled.

'That's better. You're here on hols remember and, unfortunately, I'm here to work!'

'I know, I know!' She gave him a little shove. 'Go on then, go to work. I don't want you to be late for your meeting!'

Jimmy smiled. 'Bye for now.' He tapped her leather travel folder on his leg and blew her a kiss.

'Bye!'

Moments later he had disappeared.

Indi's guide, a young Indian boy, helped her into the motor rickshaw and then stood on the roadside and bargained for several minutes with the driver while she sat inside, holding her handkerchief over her face. The traffic of Baijur's busiest road roared past, the dust swirled up and the exhaust fumes blackened the air. As she sat there, the life of the city swarmed all around her, the noise, smell, colour and sheer pace of it all taking her breath away, literally. She waved at a group of dirty, scruffy children who ran shouting along the road and threw them a handful of sweets she'd bought off a road-side stall. Then she looked across at the guide and saw that a price had been agreed; she was on her way back to the Lake Palace.

'Thank you, Ashok,' she said, holding out her hand. 'You have been very kind, I've enjoyed my tour very much.'

He shook her hand, graciously took the tip she handed to him and then folded his palms together and bowed his head. 'If you would like to see some more of the city, Miss Bennet, then I would be happy to be showing it to you.' He pulled a business card from the inside of his *kurta* and handed it across.

'Dr Yadav?' Indi looked up from the card. 'What are you a doctor in?'

'Medicine, Miss Bennet, I am just qualified. I am helping to pay back my fees for the college by guiding for a short time.'

Indi smiled. 'I have just qualified too, in medicine.'

'Oh, goodness me! That is a very big coincidence, Miss Bennet! Very big indeed.' He beamed and Indi smiled back.

'Yes. Well, I wish you good luck, Ashok, with your guiding and your medicine,' she said.

The guide bowed his head again, a little lower this time, smiling and nodding. 'Thank you, Miss Bennet, I am wishing you the same thing.' He spoke a few words of Hindi and the driver of the motor rickshaw nodded, starting the small, noisy engine.

'Goodbye, Ashok!' Indi called. 'And thank—' She was interrupted by a loud bang from the exhaust and jumped out of her skin.

Ashok put his hands over his ears as the bangs sounded twice more – knowing they were due – then he shouted, 'Goodbye, Miss Bennet!' over the racket of the engine. 'Perhaps we meet another time?'

The small vehicle moved off and Indi over-balanced, gripping the seat and slipping to one side. She straightened and held her hand up in a wave. 'I hope so!' she shouted. 'Goodbye!' She watched Ashok as he stood and waved to her from the edge of the road, the only motionless figure in the constantly moving street. The rickshaw veered dangerously round the corner and moments later he disappeared from view. Indi faced the front, held on to the bars of the patched-up roof and clenched her jaw against the thump and swerve of the wheels around the pot-holes in the road.

Back at the boat jetty, she climbed down, thanked the driver and tipped him; the guide having paid for the rickshaw already, it being included in his price for the day. It was late, the air had cooled and the sun was beginning to sink in the sky. As she boarded the boat with the scattering of other hotel guests, she took off her sunglasses, slipped them into her bag and looked at the water bathed in the strange red and gold light of sunset.

She was tired, it had been a long day and she hadn't yet fully recovered from the ten-hour flight to Delhi but nothing could take away the sensation of the warm breeze, the sight of the palace floating out across the water and the sky, a dark purple and blue streaked with fiery orange. Indi settled on to her cushion, nodded at the other passengers and smiled as the boat set off. It was odd, but since arriving in Baijur she had felt strangely at home.

An hour later, Indi rang Jimmy's room once more while the boy placed her tray on the bedside table and uncovered it. She hung on for as long as she could, letting it ring, then she replaced the receiver and rummaged in her bag for a tip for him. He thanked her and departed, leaving her alone to eat. She was disappointed but she was also sleepy after a long hot bath, so she curled herself up on the bed, flicked the remote control on the telly and reached for the tray. She uncovered her meal, picked at it for a few minutes and deciding she was too tired to eat, laid it on the floor. Indi switched channels to an Indian action movie without the volume and making herself comfortable, settled down to watch it and to wait for Jimmy's return. Twenty minutes later, she was sound asleep.

'What?' Indi rolled over and pushed the covers down, away from her face. She heard the knocking again and blinked several times to try and get her eyes into focus. She sighed, opened them fully and saw it was daylight outside, full-blown morning.

The knocking continued, loudly.

'Yes . . .' she croaked, 'I'm coming!' She lifted the blankets and saw that she was fully dressed, the clean clothes she had put on after her bath now crumpled and slept in. She must have gone straight out last night while watching TV and at some point crawled under the blankets. She looked across at the television; it was still on. 'Oh God,' she moaned, spying the mess on the tray by the bed. She stepped over it and went to the door.

'Yes?'

'Please, madam, room cleaning.'

Indi sighed. 'Look, can you come back later? I'm not dressed or up yet.'

'No, madam, room cleaning now.'

Indi held on to the door. She had slept so heavily, so deeply that it felt as if someone had coshed her on the head. She gripped the handle and said, 'I'm sorry but I do not want you to clean the room yet. Please come back later.' She went to close the door.

'Please, madam, new guest arriving! Must clean room now!'

Indi opened it again. 'What d'you mean new guest arriving? I'm booked in for two weeks!' She saw the cleaner's blank face and realised he had only the one sentence in English. 'Wait,' she said, 'I will ring the manager now.' She held up her hands. 'Wait there, all right? I am going to ring the boss.' She made all the arm actions and finally the man nodded. She shut the door.

Hurriedly she rang reception and asked for room 117. She listened to the empty ringing tone in Jimmy's room until the switchboard cut her off and she experienced a momentary flash of panic. 'Calm down,' she told herself. 'This is a silly misunderstanding.' But she had begun to sweat, tiny beads of perspiration on her brow. She rang reception again. 'Hello, this is Miss Bennet in room one three four, may I speak with the manager of the hotel, please?' She waited to be put through. 'Ah, good morning!' she said, as brightly as she could manage, 'I hope so Mr Banerjee, I have a slight problem with my room, number one three four, and I was wondering if you might be able to clear things up for me . . . ?'

Ten minutes later, Indi sat small and helpless in a large leather armchair in the manager's office and watched him on the phone to the police. Her heart was pounding, her hands sweating and she felt sick, dreadfully sick. She listened to the Hindi, not understanding a word of it and thought, *you stupid, stupid girl! What did you know about Jimmy Stone? What did John try to tell you? You stupid, stupid girl!*

The manager hung up. 'Please, Miss Bennet, the police are on the way over to the hotel now. Please be telling me again your story so that I am clear when they arrive.'

Indi swallowed and fiddled nervously with her hands in her lap. 'I, erm . . .' She stopped and cleared her throat; her voice had failed her. 'I, erm . . . came to India with Mr Stone, we arrived at the hotel yesterday morning. He told me he was working here, that he had a meeting and he, erm, er, took my travel documents to put them in the hotel safe before we both went out for the day.' She stopped and took a breath. It was becoming increasingly hard to speak without losing control, the tears lay just beneath the surface and she was holding on to her dignity by a hangnail. She clenched her hands together. 'When I arrived back last night, I tried to call his room but could get no reply, it was the same this morning . . .'

'So you did not know that Mr Stone had checked out yesterday lunchtime?'

'No! I . . .' Indi put her hand up to her face and bit on her knuckles. *How could she know that? What on earth had happened?* 'No,' she continued, her voice strained, 'I had no idea he was checking out. He told me that we would be here for two weeks, that he'd booked me in for two weeks. He was paying for my stay, he was . . .' Indi broke off, appalled by the hotel manager's expression. 'It wasn't like that!' she cried. 'He was a friend from London, he wanted the company while he was working here! He . . . Oh God!' She put her hands up and covered her face, unable any longer to stop the flood of tears. 'Something must have happened to him,' she sobbed. 'There must be some kind of mistake, I can't believe . . .' She bit her lip and forced herself to stop crying. Blowing her nose, she said, 'I don't understand it all, Mr Banerjee, something must have gone wrong.'

'Then you did not know that you had reservations for only one night?'

'No! Perhaps he changed his mind, perhaps . . .' She gave up.

'But the booking was made several weeks ago, Miss Bennet.' The manager looked down his computer sheet. 'It was a telephone booking, from Bombay.'

Indi's head jerked up. 'Bombay? What the . . . ?'

'Yes, that is quite correct, from Bombay. When Mr Stone left, Miss Bennet, he paid only the one bill.'

Indi closed her eyes for a moment, her head had begun to spin. She had no idea what was going on, Jimmy had disappeared, he'd taken her passport, her money and her tickets and now the manager was going on about Bombay and reservations. She rubbed her hands wearily over her face and said, 'Look, Mr Banerjee, could I have another room for a day or so? I am sure this is all a misunderstanding, I . . .' She broke off at the sight of his face.

'We have no rooms available, Miss Bennet, we are fully booked for the next month. I am very sorry but this is our peak season for tourists.'

'But where will I . . . ?' Indi sat and looked down at her hands in her lap. She sat like that for several minutes, paralysed by the sheer desperation of her predicament. Then she glanced up. 'May I make a telephone call please?'

The manager stared at her across the desk. India was full of hopeless cases, European drifters. Penniless, they booked into hotels, left in the middle of the night without paying. He'd seen too many of them in his short career with the hotel chain, this one was no different, they all spun ridiculous lies, told him stories. He tapped his pen on the desk.

'I will have to ask you for cash, Miss Bennet, for the telephone call.'

Indi swallowed. She picked up her rucksack and took out her purse, she had just two pounds in Indian money. 'I think I have enough to call the British consulate,' she said in a small voice, 'at the high commission in Delhi.'

The manager sat stony-faced while Indi laid the notes on the desk, then he nodded. He passed her the telephone. 'Go ahead, Miss Bennet,' he said, 'the operator will dial the number for you.'

Oliver Hicks was taking a year's sabbatical from his regiment before he had to decide whether to become a career soldier or leave the army for good. He had secured an easy, boring job through his father, for the experience of India rather than the actual work itself and he sat in a small poky office at the back of the high commission in Delhi, his feet on the desk, his head back and his mouth slightly open as he slept. His boss was out of the office, he finished at lunchtime, for a few days off, and he had completed everything he'd been asked to do well in advance of his holiday. It was hot, even at that time of day, the fans whirred but the warm air was just wafted around the room, rustling papers and making it more uncomfortable. Oliver, in the warmth, had been unable to keep his eyes open. He had dozed off.

At eleven-ten, the telephone rang.

Oliver started and sat bolt upright. He felt momentarily disorientated then he lunged across the desk for the phone. 'Hello! Passport office, Oliver Hicks, passport clerk speaking.' He shook his head and blinked several times, stifling a yawn with his hand. 'Hello?'

'Erm, hello? I've been put through to you and I'm not sure if I've got the right person but I've had my passport stolen and my money and I . . .' The voice was female, she sounded young.

Oliver reached for a pad. 'If you'd like to give me the details, miss?'

'Yes, I . . .'

The line crackled and Oliver shook the receiver. It sounded like the girl was crying. 'Are you all right?' he asked. 'Look, why don't you tell me what happened and I can get some forms filled in for you.'

'I came out with a friend,' the girl said, 'Jimmy Stone, to Baijur and now he's disappeared, he's gone with my passport and my money and everything!'

Oliver rolled his eyes, another victim of love. 'Do you have any money at all?'

'No! I haven't even got somewhere to stay! I . . .'

'It's all right, calm down now. Look, I can telephone your next of kin for you in the UK and have some funds wired out to you if you give me a number and your address in Baijur. All right?'

'Yes . . .' The line went silent and it sounded as if the girl was weeping again.

'Are you all right?'

'Yes . . .' There was a loud blowing noise and Oliver smiled, he couldn't help it. 'My grandfather in the UK should be able to wire some money out, he's Brigadier John Bennet, the number is West Sommerton . . .' Oliver started for a moment at the name. 'Have you got that?'

'Oh, yes, erm . . .' He scribbled frantically. 'Yes, got it! Where are you?'

'I'm at the Lake Palace Hotel in Baijur, the number here is . . . Look, can you hold on for a moment?'

Oliver said yes but his brain was somewhere else. He knew Brigadier Bennet, or rather knew of him! Jesus! Brigadier John Bennet, DSO, OBE, had been in command of Oliver's regiment from '63 to '68! He apparently survived some sort of awful personal scandal to become one of the government's chief defence advisors. He must have been a hell of a soldier! God, Brigadier Bennet's granddaughter! Lord, what a coincidence!

'Hello?'

'Yes, hello!' Oliver jumped back to the present.

'I've got the number here . . .' She read it out. 'I haven't got a room here but the manager has said I can wait at the hotel for your call.'

'Right, fine. Can I just ask you, miss, is that Brigadier Bennet of the Queen's Regiment?

'Yes.'

'Right!' Oliver could hardly believe it! 'Erm, can you give me your full name, miss?'

'Yes, Indu Bennet. Do you want my home address?'

'No, only your grandfather's address.'

'It's the same. It's Turnpike House, West Sommerton, West Sussex.'

'OK, got that. Look, d'you want me to have a word with the manager, to tell him that we are helping you?' It wasn't his jurisdiction but Oliver suddenly felt personally responsible for this girl. Brigadier Bennet's granddaughter! Imagine!

'No, it's all right, I'm in his office now, he can hear what's going on. If you could just ring my grand-father please.'

'Right, I'll do that straight away and I'll call you right back.' Again it wasn't his job but that wasn't important now. 'Hang on there and don't worry, things will be fine.'

The girl had started to cry again and Oliver's heart went out to her. 'It's OK,' he said. 'Please don't worry, we'll get this sorted out.' He heard her blow her nose again.

'Thanks,' she said.

'I'll ring you back, OK?' Oliver replied. 'Bye for now.' Without waiting for her answer, he hung up. Scrabbling in his desk drawer for the UK telephone list, he yanked it out, scattering the mess that was in there with it and ran his finger down the codes. He found the code for West Sommerton and wrote it next to Brigadier Bennet's number. Then he picked up the receiver again and dialled the switchboard operator.

'Can I have an outside line, please?' He waited, heard the dialling tone then dialled Great Britain. Seconds later, he was through to Sussex and waiting for his call to be answered.

John woke with a start at the sound of the phone ringing down in the hall. He hurried out of bed, thinking, it must be Indi, pulled on his dressing-gown and unable to find his slippers in the faint dawn light, went downstairs in his bare feet. He picked up the receiver and bent to switch on the lamp as he did so. It was six forty-five.

'Hello?' The line was bad, he heard a crackle then nothing for several seconds. 'Hello?'

'Hello, Brigadier Bennet?'

'Yes, speaking.' He felt the sudden thumping of his heart in panic.

'Good morning, my name's Captain Oliver Hicks, I work for the British consulate at the high commission in Delhi and I'm calling about your granddaughter, sir, Indu Bennet.'

'Yes?' John gripped the receiver. 'What's happened? What is it?'

'She's quite all right, sir, but I'm ringing because she's had her passport and money stolen in Baijur. Would it be possible to wire some money to a bank in Baijur today to tide her over while we get on with processing some travel documents for her?'

'Yes, yes of course! I'll go down to my bank as soon as it opens. She is all right, is she? She's not harmed in any way?' John slumped down on to the bottom stair, the sudden shock made him momentarily weak.

'No, not as far as I know.' There was a pause then the young man suddenly said, 'I am going down to Baijur this afternoon, sir, to see that she's all right.'

'You are?' John was surprised.

'Yes.' Hesitation again. 'Yes I am!'

'That's terribly good of you! I didn't catch your name.'

'Captain Oliver Hicks, sir, of the Ninth Cavalry Division.'

'I see.' John felt enormous relief, his regiment. He felt as if he knew this young man. 'Thank you, captain,' he said, 'I greatly appreciate your help.'

'That's quite all right, sir, I had some leave coming up. Can I give you some bank details?'

'Yes, yes please. Could you hold on for a moment while I fetch a pen?' John stood and reached to the hall table. He took the note-pad and pen off it and sat down again. 'Right, captain, fire away!' he said. And scribbling in his slightly arthritic scrawl, he wrote down the name of the bank and all its details.

Oliver hung up and thumped the desk with his fist.

'Oh shit!' he cursed. 'Damn, damn and shit!' Then he smacked his palm against his forehead. Why? Why did he do it? Why did he have to go and open his big mouth? He had to interfere, he had to impress, didn't he? It had just popped out, he'd been so zealous in trying to help that he'd gone and offered his three days' hard-earned holiday to go to Baijur and sort this silly girl out! Why couldn't he keep his big mouth shut? He always did it, always!

He stood up and paced the room. He'd have to cancel his night out with Rob Jones, he'd have to book a flight, or a train if the planes were busy. Oh God! He slumped down into his chair. He was so bloody impulsive, that was his trouble, university and five years in the army should have taught him to think before he acted. Instead he was still the same old Oli, jump in, head first and think about it afterwards, think about it when you've either cracked your head on the bottom or caught a nasty bout of flu because the water's too cold!

He sighed heavily and reached for the telephone. He'd better dial the ticket agency, then ring the Lake Palace Hotel. He'd committed himself now and whether it was a good idea or not, he had to bloody well go through with it.

Indi sat on the terrace in the shade of a striped awning and read an old copy of *The Times*. She was thirsty but she had no money for a drink and she was tired; the trauma and the weeping had exhausted her. She kept one eye on the hotel lobby as she read, for sight of the man from the high commission, and tried to ignore the intrusive glances from several of the hotel's male guests. She was agitated, she felt vulnerable and glancing briefly up at the lobby, she saw a tall young man staring at her, his light brown hair cut short, the slight curl in it cropped and his tanned face set in a determined expression. She thought he might be about to approach her and lifted her paper up to hide her face. If she hadn't been so anxious, if she hadn't been so depressed, she might have considered his look appealing. As it was, his stare thoroughly annoyed her. She rustled *The Times* and sighed irritably, crossed her legs and clenched her jaw. When she heard footsteps, she got ready to pounce.

'Erm, excuse me?' Oliver stood in front of *The Times* and glanced briefly down at the long slim legs that came out from under it, the shape of the thighs clearly visible through the thin cotton of the long Indian skirt. They were nice but he wasn't here for pleasure. He ignored them and glanced up at the paper again. Damn! England were a hundred and twenty-six for seven against Australia. Damn, damn damn! He shook himself. 'Hello?' he tried again. 'I'm looking for—'

'Whatever it is,' Indi snapped, dropping her paper, 'I'm sure that I can't help you!' She glared at him and noticed that his eyes were green, a vivid intense green. 'Sorry,' she said sarcastically. 'Now, if you don't mind.' She lifted the paper again and tutted behind it.

Oliver moved away. He was in a rotten mood, the flight had been terrible, he was hot, tired and the last place on earth he wanted to be was Baijur. Rude young woman! He had a good mind to say something pertinent back, only he didn't want the aggro of an argument. The sooner he found Indu Bennet, sorted her out and left on the next flight out the better! He walked back into the hotel and across to reception. He would ask the manager where she was, better that than risk upsetting some other stroppy holiday-maker.

Five minutes later, he stood in front of the same young woman. He coughed politely and waited for her to lower her paper. He had seen her hurriedly lift it to hide behind as he approached and it annoyed him. As if he'd be interested in someone as arrogant as that! He liked his women soft, and attractive as she may be, he couldn't stand aggression.

'Excuse me,' he said coolly, 'but I was looking for a

young woman called Indu Bennet. I'm from the high commission in Delhi. You wouldn't know where I could find her, would you?' He stared at the paper and saw the hand holding it tremble slightly. He coughed again. Moments later the paper was lowered.

'You've found her,' Indi said in a small voice. 'I'm Indu Bennet.' She glanced briefly at him, then she avoided his eye and flushed deep red.

'Ah, I see.' Oliver was enjoying the moment. 'Captain Oliver Hicks,' he said. 'We spoke on the telephone.'

'Yes, yes of course.' Indi still hadn't looked up. She tangled her fingers in her lap and her face continued to burn. Oliver pulled out a chair and sat down. At least she has the grace to be embarrassed, he thought. He reached for his briefcase and placed it on his knees. 'I have some forms here, Miss Bennet, for your travel documents,' he announced, unbuckling the satchel. 'We need to go through them and then I can take them back to be processed in Delhi. All right?'

Indi looked up. 'Yes, fine.' She met Oliver's eye and he saw for the first time the shape of her face, her dark honey-coloured skin and her eyes, brown with specks of green that caught the light and looked strangely unreal. She bit her lip and the dark red colour drained from it where her tooth held the flesh. His stomach flipped and he had to shift on the hard wrought-iron seat to cover his erection. He looked away, down at the forms and completely forgot for an instant what he was doing here. He swallowed, then glanced up again. 'Would you like a drink?' he asked. 'While we do these?'

Indi smiled. She put her hand up to her hair and tucked a stray curl back behind her ear. 'Yes please, I'd love one.

I've been dying of thirst here but I spent my last rupee on the telephone call to the commission. I literally don't have a penny!'

Oliver laughed, rather stupidly he thought, and for no particular reason. He clicked for the waiter. 'What d'you want?'

'An orange juice, please.'

He gave their order to the boy, then took a pen out of his pocket to fill in the forms. 'Talking of last rupees, did the draft arrive at the bank by the way?'

Indi glanced down. 'I, erm, I don't know, I'm afraid. I didn't have the money to get into the city from here.' She looked back up at him. 'I hope you don't mind but I was waiting for you to arrive. I hoped we might go together.'

Oliver dragged his eyes away from her face. 'No, not at all.' He fiddled with the papers for a few minutes. He was cross with himself, he didn't want to be here, he had promised Rob Jones that he'd be back just as soon as he'd filled in the forms and that they would have their boys' night out. There was a flight leaving that evening and he had booked a seat on it. Now he was saying yes to gallivanting all over Baijur because he'd fallen for the face and the legs. He looked up and saw her watching him. God, she really was beautiful!

'It is all right, is it?' she asked nervously.

'Yes, yes fine!' he blurted. Damn, he'd missed his chance now! Stacking the forms, he slipped them back in his case and fastened it. 'Shall we head off now, then?'

Indi nodded. She bent for her rucksack, her shirt gaped and Oli glimpsed the curve of her breast just visible above black lace. He stood quickly and looked out across the terrace to the lake beyond. The last thing he needed was a pash on Brigadier Bennet's granddaughter! Jeeze! 'Ready?' he asked, abruptly turning round.

'Yup! Ready.' Indi answered.

And together they walked towards the lobby of the hotel, both thinking about something else and neither of them seeing the figure who stood and, some way behind, followed them out.

The bank clerk shook his head. He had been shaking it for the past five minutes despite Oliver's protestations. The draft had to be processed, like anything else, at the bank in Delhi, forms had to filled out, signatures obtained, it had to be cleared at the bank here in Baijur, more forms filled out and then, only then, could it be cashed. No, he didn't know when it would be ready for collection, it might be tomorrow, it might be three days. These things took time, even urgent things took time, in India.

Oliver smacked his fist down on the counter in frustration and the bank clerk looked blankly at him. He shook his head and shrugged. He was about to utter the same excuses when Oliver interrupted him. 'Don't bother!' he snapped. 'I understand the problem!' He walked over to Indi who was sitting miserably on the complimentary seat and looking on in silent agony.

'No money,' he said. 'Sorry.'

She jumped up angrily. Yanking open the door of the bank, she stormed out into the street, close to tears and stood, her hands over her face, counting to a hundred.

'Hey!' Oliver came out after her. He touched her shoulder from behind. 'Hey, it's not that bad!'

'Not that bad!' Indi swung round. 'How can you say

that?' She threw her hands up in the air. 'I've got no money, I'm stuck here until my banker's draft manages to get through the bloody Indian bureaucracy and I've got nowhere to stay!' A sob caught in the back of her throat. 'And you say it's not that bad!'

'Whoa! Hang on a minute.' Oliver's patience was also frayed. He'd spent two fruitless hours in the bank, he had undoubtedly missed his flight, he now had a responsibility thrust on him that he didn't need and, to cap it all, here she was shouting at him in the middle of the street! As if any of it was his fault! He took a deep breath and said, 'Look, I'm sorry and all that but it's really not that bad . . .'

'How would you know?' Indi cried. 'What do you know about it anyway?'

'Nothing!' Oliver suddenly shouted back. 'But I am here to help and the least you can do is be a little more grateful!'

'Grateful? Ha! I didn't ask you to come, did I?' Indi had lost all sense of perspective. The stress and frustration of the day suddenly erupted and poured out, like burning molten lava. 'Let's get one thing straight,' she shouted. 'You came here off your own bat, I didn't ask you, OK?'

'No! But where the hell would you be if I hadn't, eh?' Oliver yelled back. He had had enough as well. He'd made one hell of a mistake coming here, him and his bloody impulsive decisions. He wished he'd never set eyes on her, arrogant little cow! 'If it hadn't been for your grandfather then I would never have bothered.' He glared at her. 'And, frankly, I wish I hadn't!'

Indi's face was burning with indignation, her chest

heaved but she'd calmed down a bit. 'No,' she snapped, 'I wish you hadn't either!'

'Good! We're agreed then.'

'Yes, we're agreed!'

They each stood their ground for a minute or so, then Oliver said angrily, 'I suggest that we go back to the hotel, pick up your bags, then find somewhere for you to stay. Is that all right?'

Indi resented his sarcasm. 'Yes,' she said icily, 'that's quite all right.'

'Good!' Oliver growled. He turned down the street. 'Come on.'

'Right!' Indi growled back. 'I'm coming!' And two paces behind, she followed him down the street until they found an empty motor rickshaw and took it back to the hotel.

They were both in a foul mood as they stood at the reception desk in the Lake Palace and watched the clerk telephone the eighth hotel on his list for a reservation. It was summer, Baijur had had an enormous tourism drive across Europe and was now twenty per cent overbooked. There was nothing to be had, either in the top range or the middle range of hotels and Oliver point-blank refused the bottom range; he didn't want to go back to Delhi with flea bites.

'I am most sorry, sir, but I am not getting any luck with a room for you.'

Oliver sighed. This was all he needed, a perfect end to a perfect day! 'Nothing?'

'No, sir, there is nothing available.'

He glanced across at Indi who stood with her back to him, staring out at the water in the fading light. 'And you have nothing here?'

The clerk looked at his computer sheet again. He ran his pen down it, shaking his head as he did so. 'No rooms at all, sir, I am most sorry.'

Oliver leant in to the desk and glanced at the list. 'Is there anything at all? We'll take anything.'

The clerk went to another list. He looked for several minutes, then suddenly he glanced up. 'Ah! I am finding one thing at least, sir!' He smiled. 'I have the royal suite that is empty for a few days, sir.'

Oliver swallowed. 'The royal suite?' His voice came out a little higher than usual.

'Oh yes, it is very, very good, sir, a very good room. I can highly recommend it. Oh yes!'

Indi turned. 'They have a room?' The relief on her face was apparent.

'Yes, the, erm, royal suite,' Oliver answered.

She looked at the clerk. 'We'll take it,' she said.

'But it's hugely expensive,' Oliver hissed.

'Then I'll pay for it!' Indi hissed back. 'For God's sake! It's all there is!'

Oliver looked up at the clerk. 'Thank you, we will take it,' he said. 'If someone could show us to the room now?'

'Oh yes, sir, yes indeed!' The desk clerk clicked for the boy and beamed at them. They had gone up in his estimation, they were people to be considered now. 'Please, the boy will show you up now.'

Oliver and Indi both moved off at the same time and collided, knocking into each other and springing apart immediately. But they didn't apologise to one another, they simply separated, ignored it and went after the boy in relieved and angry silence.

*   *   *

It was midnight when Oliver woke up. He glanced at the luminous dial on his watch, saw the time and rolled on to his side to get back to sleep again. He pulled the sheet in and glanced across at Indi on the other side of the huge king-size bed, a bolster between them, her side of the bed rumpled and chaotic, the sheets all over the place and one long brown leg kicked out, naked up to the very top of her thigh. He squeezed his eyes shut and sighed, wondering what the hell he was doing here.

'Are you awake, Captain Hicks?'

He opened them again. 'Yes.' He had cooled off, he didn't want to go on with the tense silence. 'It's Oliver,' he said, 'not Captain Hicks.'

'Right, Oliver.' Indi rolled over to face him. 'What did you mean about my grandfather, Oliver? Earlier? You said if it wasn't for—'

'I know what I said,' Oliver interrupted. 'I'm in the Ninth Cavalry Division, Brigadier Bennet is . . .' He broke off. 'He's a kind of regimental hero, everyone knows about him, he's highly respected. And, when you said his name, I kind of . . .' He stopped again, then he smiled at himself. 'This sounds stupid,' he said, 'but I kind of wanted to do something to help, to impress him, I guess.'

Indi smiled back. 'No, it's not stupid.' She reached out and touched him on the arm. 'Thank you,' she said.

Oliver looked down at her hand. She had long elegant fingers and oval nails, cut short, unvarnished. 'That's all right, Miss Bennet,' he replied. He rolled over, away from her.

'It's Indi,' she said quietly, 'not Miss Bennet.'

'Goodnight then, Indi,' Oliver whispered.

'Goodnight,' she answered. 'Sleep well.'

*   *   *

But Oliver didn't sleep. He lay in the dark and listened to the sound of Indi's breathing, light, so quiet he almost couldn't hear it and he wondered again and again what he was doing here. Indi Bennet was like no one he had ever met before and she scared the living daylights out of him. She had riled him, infuriated him, aroused him and now charmed him, all in ten hours. She was wonderful, exotic, strong, sensuous, but she was dangerous. And Oliver Hicks didn't need dangerous, he didn't need dangerous in any shape or form.

Chapter Twenty-Nine

The following morning, while Oliver finished breakfast and Indi showered, the call came through to their suite. He had left a message with the bank, as soon as it opened, that if the banker's draft cleared they were to call the hotel right away. It was ten-fifteen and he took the message with a mixture of relief and disappointment. The money had arrived, Indi could stay on for as long as she liked and he was no longer needed. He rang the airport and the station. There were no flights but he could get a train out at midday, so he began to pack his small rucksack and check he had all the details on the forms. Indi came out of the bathroom.

'Oliver? What's happened?' She was wearing a white towelling bath robe, belted in tight around her small waist and her hair was wet. Oliver thought she was the most beautiful sight he had ever seen and he flushed, then looked away.

'The bank rang,' he answered, stuffing his sweater into his bag. 'The money's through, and I called the station. There's a train back to Delhi at midday which I will be on.'

'I see.' Indi rubbed her hair with a towel, then sat on the bed. 'How long d'you think it'll be before my documents come through?'

'Not long, a few days, possibly a week.' Oliver clipped the top of his rucksack down and slung it on the bed. 'I might as well head off now,' he said. 'Get on with it!'

Indi shrugged; she wasn't sure if she wanted him to go. She watched him put the files into his briefcase then suddenly said, 'If you don't mind waiting for five minutes, I could come into the city with you and see you off.' She knelt and pulled a shirt out of her bag. 'I have to pick my money up anyway.'

'OK.' Oliver didn't quite know how to react. 'I'd, erm, like that. Thanks.'

Indi stood with her clean clothes in her hand. 'I won't be a minute.' She headed back towards the bathroom. 'Don't go away!'

Oliver laughed, a little too readily and sat down on the edge of the bed. He looked at his hands, out at the view, then back at his hands again. He wanted to get going, to be off out of Baijur and away from Indi Bennet before he had a chance to think about it. He didn't want to be any more involved than he already was – Indi was too attractive and far too complicated to hang around with. Minutes later she appeared in the doorway.

'OK, I'm ready!' She had literally pulled a shirt and skirt on, tied her sandals and flicked her fingers through her wet hair. She looked fresh and natural and deadly sexy.

Oliver cleared his throat and stood, heaving his rucksack on to his shoulder. 'Right,' he said gruffly, 'let's go!' He walked towards the door and waited while Indi collected up her things and slung them into her own rucksack. She joined him and they walked out of the suite, along the passage and down to reception.

'Excuse me. Miss Bennet? Madam, please, excuse me.'

Indi glanced behind her. 'Oh, yes?'

The boy stood with a slip of paper in his hand. 'Please, for Miss Bennet, a message.' He handed it to her. 'Please.'

Indi dug in her bag and gave the boy a tip, then she opened the message, read it and glanced across at Oliver. 'I've got a call coming through,' she said. 'Probably from Gramps.' She shrugged. 'I'd better go back and wait for it.'

Oliver nodded. 'I should get going,' he said, 'I don't want to miss my train.'

'No.' Indi looked away for a few moments, then said, 'What about the money you lent me?'

'You can post it on, or drop it in to the high commission on your way back through Delhi.'

'OK.'

They stood awkwardly for a few moments.

'Right,' Oliver said.

'Yes, erm, right.' Indi held out her hand and they shook. 'Thank you, Captain Hicks.' She smiled. 'I'd, erm, better get back for my . . .' she glanced behind her. 'For my call.'

'Yes, yes you had.' Oliver smiled as well. 'Goodbye, Indi. It was nice to meet you.'

'Yes, and it was nice to meet you.'

They continued to stand there, looking at each other.

'Bye then.' Indi took a step back.

'Yes, bye.' Oliver stayed where he was. If it had been any other woman he might have kissed her, but with Indi he didn't want to even attempt it. God knows where it would end up. He watched her as she held up her hand to wave.

'Bye!' she called again.

'Goodbye!'

Finally, she disappeared down the passage and Oliver turned towards the hotel entrance and the boat waiting on the jetty. He walked out into the brilliant sunlight and nodded to the boat man.

'Five minutes to wait please, sir,' the boatman said. 'Other passengers are coming.'

'OK. Fine.' Oliver dropped his rucksack on to the ground and sat down on it. He looked out across the water and saw the city of Baijur up ahead, hazy in the distant heat. Well, at least he'd seen Baijur, he thought, the last state in India to have had a maharajah, and he'd sorted Brigadier Bennet's granddaughter out. He felt a bit miserable though, despite the success of the trip. Truth was, he didn't really want to leave.

Indi walked back towards the suite and saw the door ajar. The cleaners must be in, she thought, dropping her rucksack off her shoulder and holding on to it. She swung the door wide open and walked across to the telephone, dropping her bag down on the sofa and calling out. She turned towards the bedroom and that was when the blow hit her. It came from behind.

She went down. Her legs buckled and she fell forward,

clutching for the sofa and clasping it with both hands. She gasped for breath and managed to heave herself up, lunging for her bag at the same time as the man did. They struggled with it and swinging round, half crouched, Indi smacked her head hard into the man's pelvis. She heard a cry and brought her fist up again into his crotch, punching it as hard as she could. He fell back and she screamed, scrambling to her feet, gripping her bag. She ran breathless, her legs weak, she sprinted out of the suite, down the passage and through the hotel reception.

'Oliver!' she screamed, darting past a small crowd on to the boat jetty. 'Oliver!' Her legs gave way and she collapsed on to her knees. 'Oliver!'

The boat was fifty feet from the jetty when he heard her. He spun round, shouted to the boatman and stood, muttering apologies to the two other passengers. 'Indi, hang on!' he yelled across the noise of the engine. 'Hang on there, I'm coming!' He saw her drop forward and his stomach lurched. 'Hurry up!' he called across to the boatman. 'Can't this bloody thing go any faster?'

Minutes later they were back at the jetty. He jumped off the boat as it pulled alongside and ran across to her, dropping down beside her and pulling her into his arms. 'God, what happened? Indi, what happened?'

She wasn't crying but she was shocked, her face was ashen and she was shaking. 'A man, in the suite, he hit me . . .' She put her hand up to the back of her neck and Oliver gently lifted her hair. 'Christ! Let's get you back inside, we'll need to get that seen.' He helped her to her feet and with his arm around her, walked her inside and across to one of the chairs in reception.

'Here, sit here and I'll get the desk to call a doctor.'

'No.' She looked up at him. 'It's all right, I've felt it, it doesn't need stitches. It's all right.'

'How would you know? I'll get a doctor, Indi, don't argue.'

She reached for his arm. 'I am a doctor,' she said. 'Well, half a one at least.'

'You are?' He realised that he didn't know the first thing about her.

'Yes.' She smiled at the look on his face. 'You had me down as a silly young thing, didn't you?'

'No! Of course not, I . . .' He sat down next to her. 'I didn't know what to make of you to be honest. I still don't.'

They both smiled.

'Look, can I get you anything? A drink maybe?'

'No, but I could do with some ice.' She touched the back of her neck. 'For this.'

Oliver held his hand up to attract the boy's attention. 'D'you want to tell me what happened?' He ordered tea for them both and a bucket of ice. As the boy disappeared, he said, 'You should report this to the manager, you know, Indi. It could have been very nasty, you were lucky. I wonder if he's tried it on anyone else?' Indi looked down at her hands. 'It's not unusual for tourists to get ripped off when they're abroad,' he went on, 'particularly not in India but you don't expect it in your hotel room! We'll definitely have to say something to the management and the police need to be informed. Did you get a look at him, Indi? I suppose it was a bit quick but you . . .' He stopped. 'Indi? Are you all right?' The boy arrived with the drinks and ice and interrupted him. Oliver organised the tea, wrapped the ice in a napkin and handed it to Indi for her neck. He signed, waited for the boy to leave, then said, 'Is there something you're not telling me? Why do I get the feeling that there's something wrong here?'

Indi said nothing. She held the ice on her neck and stayed silent; she didn't know what to say.

'Indi? It's not connected to this Jimmy Stone thing in any way, is it? You don't think he might have . . .'

'No, I mean it might be . . . Oh! I really don't know what's going on!' She dropped the ice bag on to the coffee table. 'I went into the room to take my call, Oliver, and someone hit me from behind. They tried to grab my bag but I managed to hold on to it and smack them hard in the goolies!' Indi stopped. 'What's so funny?' she demanded.

'Nothing!' Oliver tried hard to cover his smirk but it just didn't work. 'I'm sorry,' he said, breaking into a grin. 'It's the way you "smacked them hard in the goolies"!' Suddenly he started to laugh. 'It just sounds quite funny, that's all!'

Indi smiled. 'I bet it didn't feel funny!' she said. Then she too started to laugh. 'I really gave it all I had. Wallop!' She punched the air and laughed even harder, 'God . . . it must . . . have . . . really hurt!' She gasped for air, crying with laughter. Then all of a sudden she burst into tears.

Oliver instantly sobered and fumbled in his bag for a hanky. 'It's all right,' he said. 'It often happens, it's the shock.'

Indi blew her nose loudly and Oliver remembered the noise from the telephone call. 'That's a charming noise,' he said, smiling.

Indi smiled back and wiped her face. 'One of my most endearing qualities.' She sniffed and took a sip of her tea. 'Sorry,' she mumbled, 'I didn't mean to make a fool of myself. I feel very confused, with everything that's happened.'

'You haven't made a fool of yourself.' Oliver watched her as she composed herself. 'Look,' he said, 'I'll go over to reception, check on your call and then why don't you start at the beginning, tell me the whole thing, how you met Jimmy Stone, when, the trip here, everything. Let's try and sort it out. Hmmm?'

She nodded. It was all beginning to feel a little bit odd, a little bit scary. 'All right,' she said. She waited for Oliver to return from the reception desk and then took a big breath. 'I met him a month ago . . .' And she started on the whole tale, from the giving of the red rose to the last words she spoke to Jimmy Stone.

An hour later, Oliver sat back and clicked for more tea. He didn't know what to make of the whole story but he did know that something wasn't right. The phone call was bona fide, from Brigadier Bennet, but that seemed to be the only thing that was.

'So, Jimmy Stone flies you out to India,' he said, 'gets you to Baijur, then disappears, with all your documents and money, leaving you stranded. Yes?' Indi nodded. 'Then you go back to the room, accidentally catch some-one there and he tries to steal your bag?'

'I think he was after my bag but I'm not exactly sure. He may have been searching the room, he may have been after me, waiting for me.' She shivered.

Oliver thought for a moment. 'Your parents? Your father was Indian, right? Might it have something to do with him, d'you think?'

'No, I mean I doubt it. I know practically nothing about him. I've never even seen a photo. What could it have to do with him?'

Oliver shrugged. 'I don't know. I'm just trying to make some sense of all this.' He was silent for a few minutes, then he said, 'Look, what would you think if I said that maybe your father's family, or someone connected to him wanted to get you out to India? What if they set up Jimmy Stone to lure you out here?'

'That's bizarre! How could they possibly know about me? I know nothing about them.'

'OK, then look, what if Jimmy Stone was involved in something sinister, something dangerous. What if he hid something in your bag and now he's sent someone to collect it?'

'No, he can't have done! I unpacked it all myself, there was nothing in it that shouldn't have been there. I checked the whole bag.'

'Are you sure?'

'Yes!'

'But it makes sense, to keep you here till the goods have been collected.'

'Goods?' Indi shook her head. 'You mean drugs, don't you?'

'Yes, they're a possibility.' Oliver sighed and rubbed his hands over his face. 'Could he have hidden something anywhere else?'

Suddenly both Indi and Oliver looked down at her rucksack. 'In there?' She picked it up. 'Surely not, I . . .' She began to unpack it but Oliver caught her arm. 'We should do that in private,' he said. She nodded.

'Can you face going back to the suite?'

'Yes.' They stood and, glancing over his shoulder, Oliver led the way out of the lobby and back down the passage to the royal suite. Indi handed him the card key and he went in first.

'Shit!' He stood just inside the door and glanced back at her. 'Someone is looking for something, Indi, that's for sure.'

She came up behind him. 'Oh God!'

The room had been trashed. Drawers were open, furniture ransacked, everything turned over. Indi walked into the bedroom where her clothes were strewn everywhere, her wash things scattered over the floor. She dropped the rucksack down on the bed and slumped down putting her head into her hands. She felt thoroughly miserable and bloody scared. She stayed like that for a while and Oliver gave her the chance to recover. After a couple of minutes, she sat straight and reached for the bag, tipping it up, emptying the entire contents out. She rifled through them.

'Anything there?'

She shook her head. Oliver came across and sifted through the small pile. 'Any secret compartments in the bag?'

'No, only a zipped pocket that's hidden under this flap.' Indi unzipped it and pulled out the package John had given her.

'Christ! What's that?'

She shook her head. 'Don't get excited, Oliver, Gramps gave it to me.' She began to untie the leather thong that bound the cloth. 'It belonged to my father, he wanted me to have it.' She uncovered the book. 'It's some kind of diary.' She opened the first page on a water-colour illustration of an Indian elephant and held it out for Oliver to see.

'It's beautiful,' he said. 'What does it say?'

Indi shrugged. 'It's in Hindi, I've no idea.' She flicked through the pages. 'There's some verse in here, some English verse.' She continued to flick. 'And loads of paintings.' She peered closer at one. 'My God! They're my mother's paintings. Look! Here! It says JM, that was her name, Jane Mills.' Indi smiled. 'Wow! Perhaps that's why Gramps wanted me to have it. I've seen a couple of her water-colours at home but they're nothing like these.' She looked up at Oliver. 'It's beautiful, the whole thing. I wonder what it is?'

He took it from her and looked at it. 'You're right, it is lovely.' He turned a couple of the pages. 'Everything is dated, the verses and pictures run on from each other.'

'Let's see.' Indi stood next to him. 'Oh yes!' She followed the dates as he turned the pages. 'I wonder if it means anything? You know, like some kind of story?'

Oliver gave it back to her and sat on the edge of the bed. 'I don't suppose it's valuable in any way?'

'I doubt it.' Indi sat next to him. 'Why?'

'I just wondered if it might be the thing your man was looking for.'

Indi looked down and turned the book over in her hands. 'I shouldn't think so.' Then she glanced up at him. 'But how would we find out if it were?'

He thought for a moment. 'Maybe if we knew more about your parents, about what happened, that might give us a few clues.' He stood and started to put Indi's things back in her bag. 'One thing is for certain, Indi, and that is that things are beginning to look very peculiar, to say the least. Unless of course it's all a massive coincidence.' He finished and turned to her. 'But I doubt that very much.'

'So, what next then?'

'Well, first, let's find out if Jimmy Stone was real and did actually disappear by accident. Can you ring your grandfather and ask him to get in touch with Stone's publishers?'

'Yes, all right.'

'And can you get any more information on your parents from him?'

'No, I don't think so.' Indi looked down at the book. 'He's never said very much at all and I don't want to ask him. He hates India, it upsets him to talk about it.'

Oliver touched her shoulder. 'OK, I've got a friend at the high commission who might be able to help. Rob Jones, he works for the foreign office, he might be able to look up some files.' He smiled. 'Then again he might not.' Looking down at her, he offered her his hands. 'Come on,' he said, 'you make your call and I'll get moving on this mess.'

Indi slipped the book back into the hidden pocket in the rucksack and then took Oliver's hands, letting him pull her up.

'Oliver?'

He turned.

'What about your train?'

Oliver shrugged and smiled. 'What about it?' he answered and he bent to begin on the clearing up.

John put down the telephone thus ending his call to Beckman and Steen, the last publisher on his list. He sighed heavily and slumped down on to the chair in the hall. No one, not one single person in any of the companies on his list had ever heard of Jimmy Stone and no one had a book commissioned on the Mogul architecture of Baijur. Whatever it was that young man had been up to it certainly wasn't art photography. Damn! John put his head in his hands. Damn and blast! He should have enquired a week ago, before Indi even left the country, he should have made sure it was all bona fide before letting her go off with some head-case who didn't know the difference between truth and lies!

He looked up and sighed again. Well, he had to ring, at least let them know what he'd found, even though it wasn't much. He stood again and picked up the receiver, looking on his pad for the international code and the number in Baijur. Once he'd done that then maybe it was time to do a little investigative work himself. If Stone had lured Indi out to that God-forsaken place then there was a reason for it and, by Christ, John was going to find it out.

Suddenly he dropped the receiver back in its cradle and walked from the hall into his study. He would start now and there was only one place to make that start. He unlocked the side cupboard of his desk and took out a heavy stack of newspapers tied with string, a collection he had made many years ago, every *Times* published for nearly two months. He cut the string with his letter knife and lifted the first issue off the pile. History, he thought, looking down at the newspaper, a history he had never been able to face. And taking the paper off the pile, he sat down at his desk, put his glasses on, and finally began to read.

The Baijur gymkhana club, four o'clock in the afternoon

and Oliver glanced at his watch as he stifled a small yawn behind his hand. He was bored and anxious and the heat of the clubhouse was beginning to get to him.

He glanced across at Indi, deep in conversation with the Indian chap they had met there quite by accident and cursed himself for suggesting the venue in the first place. He'd been recommended it, by Rob Jones on the phone that morning, but all it had achieved was two hours in Dr Yadav's company. It wasn't that Oliver had anything against this Ashok Yadav, it was just that Oliver wasn't a doctor and he didn't understand a lot of what they had been saying all over lunch. Besides, this Ashok was a bit too good-looking and got on a bit too well with Indi for Oliver to really like him. Not that he'd worked out his feelings for Indi, nothing like. He felt an enormous responsibility, now that he was here, and she needed his help, that much was obvious. It wasn't anything more than that though, he thought, trying to convince himself and glancing briefly across at her. He felt his excitement immediately flare and looked away. So, he liked attractive women, that's all it was, and who didn't?

Oliver coughed to attract Indi's attention without wanting to interrupt. She looked across at him and smiled.

'Ashok, I think we have to go in a few minutes. Is that right, Oliver?'

'Yes, I'm sorry but we do.' He was finding it difficult to be polite and Indi's forehead creased in a frown. 'Are you ready?'

'Yes, of course.' She stood and Ashok stood with her.

'It has been most fortunate accident of fate to be meeting you again, Indu,' Ashok said, 'I have very much enjoyed our chat.'

'Thank you, Ashok. So have I.' She glanced across at Oliver, prompting him.

'Oh, so have I!' He held his hand out and shook with Ashok.

Ashok turned towards Indi and folded his palms. 'If there is anything that I might be able to do for you at any time, please, please do not hesitate to ask it of me.'

Indi smiled. 'Thank you.' She bent to pick up her bag. 'Oh, Ashok,' she said suddenly, 'there is something that you could do for me.'

'Of course. What is it?'

Indi unzipped the pocket in her rucksack and took out the book. 'Ashok, could you read me the inscription on the front page, it's in Hindi?'

'Yes, certainly, it would be my pleasure.' He took the book and opened it. 'It is very beautiful script.' He read and was silent for a few moments. 'It says, "O Rose thou art sick. The invisible worm . . ."'

'"That flies in the night",' Oliver went on, '"In the howling storm; Has found out thy bed Of crimson joy: And his dark secret love Does thy life destroy."'

Indi looked across at him.

'Blake,' he said, '*Songs of Innocence and Experience.*'

'I know.' She looked then at Ashok. 'Is that all it says?'

He read the line at the bottom of the page and the date. 'It says at the bottom here, "For Indu, from her father," and it is dated March 1966.'

Indi took the book. She looked at the inscription and then at the first drawing but she didn't say anything. She closed the book and put it away. 'Thanks, Ashok, I appreciate that.' She held out her hand and they shook.

'We may meet again, I shall probably be in Baijur for a few more days.'

'Perhaps, I hope so, Indu.'

Indi and Oliver turned towards the door. 'Goodbye, Ashok.'

'Goodbye, Indu and goodbye, Oliver.' Ashok bowed and watched them leave. He waved as they walked down the steps of the club together and he saw them get into a motor rickshaw. Then he walked across to the telephone. Taking out his diary, he looked up the number of the journalist he knew and dialled. He didn't want to waste time, he needed to know the facts, the history, if he was going to make a move. He needed to be sure they really had what he thought and once he knew that, there wouldn't be any time to waste.

Rob Jones had called when they got back to the hotel and Oliver had to phone him back. Indi went into the bedroom to finish tidying while he made the call from the sitting-room of the suite. He dialled Delhi, went through the switchboard and finally got Rob on the end of the line.

'Hello? Rob? It's Oliver, I'm returning your call, sorry we weren't in, mate.'

'No problem, Oli. I've got some stuff here from the files but I'm afraid it's not great news.'

Oliver reached for a pen and the hotel notepaper. 'OK, fire away.'

'Well, it's not as simple as that, Oli, I'm going to have to send you some press cuttings in order to give you the full story. But, in short, the Jane Mills you wanted to know about wasn't involved in any car accident, as far as I can find out. If it's the same one, and I'm pretty sure it is, then she was accused of murdering her husband, Major Phillip Mills, and his mistress, some Indian woman, in Baijur in October 1966.'

Oliver slumped down on to the chair. 'Jesus,' he murmured.

'She disappeared straight afterwards and has never been found since. It was generally assumed she died at some later date or took her own life. There's never been any sighting or word of her for twenty odd years. Oli? You still there?'

Oliver ran his hands through his hair and took a deep breath. 'Yup, still here. Sorry, Rob, it's a bit of a shock, that's all.'

'Yes, I can imagine. Look, I'll send the cuttings by express parcel delivery, they may help to get things into perspective. It was a hell of a scandal at the time, apparently she found him in bed with the mistress and there's a mountain of newspaper coverage.'

'I bet!'

'I'm sorry, Oliver, sorry I couldn't tell you anything better.'

'Yeah, me too.' Oliver had been doodling absent-mindedly on the notepaper and saw that he'd drawn tear drops.

'What's happening at the office, by the way? You want me to say anything?'

He dropped the pen and screwed the sheet of paper into a ball. 'No, not yet. I'll probably be back tomorrow, if not, then I'll ring the boss myself.' He threw the ball across the room and hit the wastepaper basket first time. 'Listen, thanks, Rob, I appreciate this. I'll see you in a few days, OK?'

'OK. If I come across anything else about Baijur in the next twenty-four hours I'll give you a buzz.'

'Great, thanks. Bye for now.' Oliver hung up. As he turned, he saw Indi in the doorway watching him.

'So?' She leant against the door frame. 'What did he say?'

Oliver walked across to her. He stood in front of her and placed his hand on her arm. 'Oliver! What did he say?' She smiled up at him. 'Come on! Tell me.'

'He said that Jane Mills was accused of murdering her husband Major Phillip Mills and his mistress in Baijur in October 1966. She disappeared straight after the bodies were discovered and has never been found.' He looked down, then a few moments later he glanced up at her. 'I'm sorry, Indi, really I am.' He reached for her hand. 'I . . .'

'Stop it!' She knocked his hand away. 'I don't want your pity!' Shoving past him, she walked out on to the balcony and stood with her back to him staring out at the water. He didn't know what to do so he went after her.

'I know how you must feel, Indi, I . . .'

'Oh, you do, do you?' She spun round. 'Christ, that's very intuitive of you!' He saw that she was crying although she seemed unaware of it herself. 'How can you possibly know how I feel?' she cried. 'My grandfather lied to me! He told me a load of old crap, took the moral high ground and all my life he lied to me! He must have known, he must have . . .' She broke off and wiped her nose on the back of her hand. The tears were streaming down her face now and she could hardly see.

'Perhaps he couldn't tell you.' Oliver stepped closer to her. She was dangerously near the edge of the balcony and it scared him. 'Maybe he was trying to protect you,

Indi.' He reached out to her, 'Doing what he thought was right.'

'Right!' She jerked away from him. 'Right!' Suddenly she lost her footing. She stumbled back and fell off balance. She screamed. Oliver lunged forward and grabbed her. 'Jesus Christ!' He hugged her in tight, his heart pounding. 'Nearly lost you then,' he whispered. She started to sob.

'Hey! It's all right.' He gently stroked her hair, his fingers tracing the curls. 'Come on, please, Indi, don't cry.'

Indi pulled back. 'Sorry,' she mumbled. Oliver handed her his hanky for the second time that day and she blew her nose. 'Thanks.'

She went to hand it back to him and they both smiled.

'I think you'd better keep it now, don't you?' She nodded.

'Come on, I'll phone room service. I think we could both do with a drink.' Oliver took her hand and led her back inside. A while later, after the drinks had arrived, he poured her a whisky and took it across to her.

'You OK now?'

'Yes, I think so.' Indi took a sip then forgot the drink and stood abruptly, walking across to where she'd left her bag. She unzipped the pocket and took out the book, sitting on the edge of the sofa to look at it. Oliver watched her.

'Perhaps this means more than we thought,' she said, going through the pages. She was odd, all fired up, angry and determined. 'Perhaps it is connected to my father and mother in some way.' She flicked to the end. 'It must be, Oliver! It has to be!'

Oliver came over to her. 'Yes, perhaps it is.' He took the book and closed it. 'But just for now, let's leave it.'

He wanted to touch her, to make some kind of physical contact but she shrank from him, almost flinching. He moved away. 'Finish your drink,' he said, 'and then let's go and have a massive, eye-wateringly hot curry.'

Indi at last smiled.

'Whatever this means,' he tapped the book, 'it can wait.'

'OK.' She thought for a moment. 'But we have to come back to it, we have to find out.'

Oliver nodded. 'We will, I promise.' He picked up his whisky and drank it down in one. 'Come on,' he said, suddenly unable to be alone with her any more, 'let's go!'

Oliver felt the cool breeze on his back and rolled over. He had only been half asleep and sat up on seeing the empty space on the other side of the bed.

'Indi?' He dropped his feet down on to the floor and, reaching for a towel, wrapped it round his waist and walked out on to the balcony. 'Indi? Are you all right?'

She turned. She was wearing a long, thin muslin shirt and he could see her body quite clearly through the fine gauze. He looked away.

'The verse,' she said, 'in the book, I keep thinking about it, why he wrote it there, the last entry at the front of the book. It is obviously the end, it's dated after the last drawing, yet does it symbolise the beginning as well?' She looked at the book on the cane table. 'I don't understand it, Oliver, I keep thinking that it has to be there for a reason. I can't sleep for thinking about it. Who was he? What did it all mean?'

Oliver pulled a chair out and sat. He rubbed his hands

wearily over his face to wake himself up. '"O Rose thou art sick,"' he began, '"The invisible worm, That flies in the night, In the howling storm; Has found out thy bed Of crimson joy: And his dark secret love Does thy life destroy."' He took a breath. 'The verse is from the *Songs of Experience*, you know that, the passing of innocence to experience, a stormy passage, experience is darkness, corruption.' He looked down at the book. 'What does it mean? Well, to be honest, Indi, it can mean what you want it to. If we were to maybe put it in the context of your parents it could mean any number of things, it would be how we translate it.' He broke off and thought for a moment, then he glanced up. 'What's the matter?'

Indi was staring at him as if he'd just stepped off another planet. 'How do you know all this, Captain Hicks?'

'BA hons, English, Durham University.' He shrugged. 'Anyway, as I was saying. Let's look at what we know. Your parents, Jane Mills is English, right, your father is Indian, they are in love, deeply in love, it is beautiful, a gift of the gods, like a rose, perfect almost, but it is difficult, stormy, she's married, unhappy, they are forbidden to meet maybe, this is the howling storm, maybe he's even referring to the murder?' Oliver stopped for breath. 'Yes, OK. Let's say it's the murder he's referring to. The rose, the perfect love, is sick, a murder has been committed, there is chaos, a howling storm, and there is danger, Jane is in hiding, perhaps with her lover but there is a sick worm, and this worm has found them out.' He broke off and looked at her. 'How does it all sound?'

'Weird!' Indi smiled. 'But impressive. Go on.'

'Ah,' Oliver pulled a face. 'I can't. That's as far as I can get, I think.'

'So, basically, in plain English for the dunce here, you're saying that maybe the verse refers to what happened to them? That they, my parents, were in danger, their love was in trouble, a sick rose, and that someone had come after them?'

'Yuh, more or less. Perhaps.'

Indi thought for a few moments. 'That sounds credible.' She reached for the book and sat down next to Oliver. He glanced briefly at her thighs and then looked away. 'D'you think this book might tell their story and that's why he wanted me to have it?'

Oliver shrugged. He was desperately trying to think of something else, anything else to take his mind off the rush of blood to his groin.

'Maybe the dates, verses and drawings mean something, perhaps a series of events?' Indi suddenly had an idea. She turned to him. 'What if it's like some sort of puzzle, one thing leading to the next?' She shook his arm. 'Oliver?'

'Hmmm, maybe.' He crossed his legs and shifted on the chair, away from her.

'And if it is, then perhaps I should try and follow it, try to make some sort of sense of it.' She looked at him expectantly. 'Well, what d'you think? Oliver?'

He faced her. 'I think you could be right,' he said, 'and I think it might be worth trying to follow the pages, to see where it all leads.' He let out a sigh of relief, he had it under control now. 'But, I also think that this book may be what someone is looking for and there's no way I am going to let you do it on your own!'

Indi shook her head. 'No, I don't want to involve you, Oli, I don't want you to feel you have to,' she said.

'I don't feel I have to.' He shrugged. 'I want to.' It

was the first time he had put any sense to the turmoil of feelings whirring round and round in his head and he felt immediately better for it, more in control. He did want to be with her, he wanted it more than he could remember wanting anything before. He smiled at her. 'All right?'

She smiled back. 'All right,' she said, then she reached forward and gently kissed his mouth, her hand on his cheek. 'Thank you,' she whispered. Before he knew what he was doing, Oliver caught her wrist. He held her fingers and trailed them over his lips, kissing the tips, watching her face. He couldn't stop himself. Then he eased her forward again and kissed her mouth. She responded, instantly, uncontrollably and her whole body almost fell towards him.

'Jesus, Indi . . .' He tangled his hands in her hair, kissing her mouth, her cheeks, biting her lips. She lifted her face and he tore his mouth down under her chin, to her neck, her chest. She moaned as he released her hair and felt for her breasts, yanking the thin muslin up, desperate to touch her hot, damp skin, cool, hard nipples. She pulled herself up and blindly moved towards him, sinking down on to his hips, wrapping her legs around him, raising her arms over her head so he could take off the shirt and kiss the flushed skin of her body. He held her, away from him for a moment, and stared, just a moment, at her breasts, the narrow shape of her hips, the long curve of her legs, her face, the burning green eyes. Then he reached down and fumbled with his towel, pulling it away. He eased her forward, shifting her hips slightly.

'Oh . . . God, Oli . . .' She pulled back.

'What . . .' He continued to kiss her throat, not looking

at her. Then, he sensed a change. He stopped and stared up at her face.

Indi swallowed hard. She had suddenly tensed, her body had tightened up and she sat straight, her arms across her breasts.

'I'm sorry,' she said, 'I can't . . . not now . . . I just . . .' She moved and stood, untangling her body from his. Bending, she picked up the shirt and threw it over her head. She stood, staring at the ground, her head hung, her eyes full of tears. 'I just can't do it,' she mumbled. 'Oh God . . . how awful . . .'

And suddenly she ran, from the balcony into the suite and through to the bedroom, slamming the door behind her.

'Fuck!' Oliver sat motionless for a while, his body still pulsing, then he stood and kicked the chair opposite. It fell and clattered against the table. 'Fuck, fuck, fuck!' He walked into the suite, looked miserably around him and slumped down on to the sofa. He was furious, not with her, but with himself, for getting so bloody carried away, for messing things up in his usual, plough-in-and-think-later way. 'Fuck!' he said again to the empty room, then he slung his legs up and curled on to his side. 'Fuck,' he murmured one last time.

He was in for one hell of a long night.

In the bedroom, Indi lay in darkness and pulled the sheet up to her chin. She was shivering, unable to get warm and she wanted to cry but the tears wouldn't come. She stared, dry-eyed, at the shadows and tried to stop the terrible pounding of her heart. What has happened to me, she thought, what? One moment I'm an ordinary young woman, just out of medical school, just into my last summer of freedom and the next my life has been turned upside down, complete chaos. I don't know who I am, where I came from, I don't know what I want or where I'm going to. She sniffed and wiped her nose on the edge of the sheet. I don't know anything, except how miserable I feel, how confused. What am I doing jumping into bed with the first man I see?

She sat up. The truth was, she wanted to jump into bed with him, she longed to do it. Fat lot of good that would do me, she thought, letting the tears finally roll down her face. Up to my eyes in some sort of awful, sinister history and I want love.

'Well, you can't have it, Indi Bennet,' she cried out loud, weeping openly now and reaching for the handkerchief under her pillow. 'Men always let you down. Always!' She blew her nose and wiped her face. 'Gramps, Jimmy Stone . . .' She hiccuped and sobbed, covering her face with the hanky and trying to suppress the noise. 'All of them! Oliver too, if you give him half a chance!'

She continued to cry, quietly, until the tears slowly dried up and the tightness in her chest eased. Then she gave up on the hanky and blew her nose on Oliver's part of the sheet. He won't be needing it tonight, she thought, thank God. She lay back and closed her eyes. A lucky escape by all accounts, she told herself. The only problem was, it didn't feel like a lucky escape, it felt more like a miserable disappointment.

Chapter Thirty

The man was medium height, thin with a beard. He had no muscle but he was powerful, he carried his power in a machete fastened to his belt. He was an Indian, living in America, ordinary looking, he blended in to the environment. They didn't see him, not once, he was far too skilled for that.

In his hotel room, late in the day, he stripped his shirt off and dropped the belt and knife down on to the bed. He was in a second-class hotel and it pissed him off. He wanted to do the job and get out of there, he hated the heat, the smell, he deserved better than the shit hole he was in. He walked across to his telephone and dialled the operator to place his call, then he went into the bathroom to wash. He was filthy, crawling on the ground, hiding, it was the part of the job he despised. He liked to kill. Women, that was his thing, he was a professional and the suffering turned him on.

The phone rang.

He came out of the bathroom and picked up the receiver. 'Yeah, Khan here.'

'Mr Khan. What have you got for me?'

'Something has happened,' he said, 'I think they have what you want.'

'You think?' The man on the other end was derisive. 'I don't pay you to think, Khan, I want to know!'

Khan swallowed down his anger. 'Yeah, well they've been to three different places in the city today, I watched them, they're at the gymkhana club now. They're following some sort of trail, a map.'

'Are you sure?'

'Yes.' He was more than fucking sure, he'd been close enough to spit in their path.

'Good. We don't have to move yet, then.'

'You want me to leave the girl?' Khan was openly angry. He had been wasting his time, he had been planning . . .

The man on the other end cut into his thoughts. 'If she has what is rightfully mine, then yes, that is exactly what I want you to do.' The man paused. 'For now.' He let his words sink in. 'There is no need to take her, we do not need a bargaining tool, she has what I want. If she did not then it would be a different matter, Mr Khan. You do understand that?' Khan remained silent. 'I want you to keep on them. I will ring in a few days.'

Khan lit up a foul-smelling cigarette. 'I need more money,' he said.

'When I arrive. Not before.'

'No, now! Get someone to deliver it. This place is a dump. I don't do anything until—'

'You do as I tell you! Mr Stone got greedy, look what happened to him.'

Khan dropped his cigarette on the floor and ground it out under his heel. 'What if they find what you're looking for first?'

The man on the other end was silent. 'Then they lead me to it,' he said after a pause, 'and you kill them.'

'What are you looking for?' Khan asked.

'None of your fucking business!' the man snapped. 'Understand?'

Khan took his knife out of its sheath and flicked it across the room. It landed, its tip embedded in the wood of the window frame. 'I understand all right, Mr Rai,' he said. And without another word, he hung up.

John sat on the floor in his study. He had moved the desk, his chair and the small filing cabinet out into the hall and had spread the four relevant newspapers out over the carpet, along with a historical account of the 1857 mutiny open at the chapter on Moraphur and his Polaroids of the jewellery collection in the British Museum donated by Phillip Mills' family. He sat and stared at all this information; he had been sitting there for three hours and had not come up with anything. Picking up his notepad, he started again, thinking aloud. It was the only way he was able to work anything out, talking to himself. He'd done it for years, ever since Caroline died and there had been no one left to listen.

'Right, there's the account of the inquest and the mention of the British consulate asking for an independent coroner's report,' he said. 'Then there's this report, stating quite clearly that it seemed unlikely that the strength of the blows inflicted on Phillip Mills could have been done by a nine-stone woman, unless she was very strong, which Jane wasn't. Also . . .' He leant forward and picked up the paper with the article in, 'There's this odd thing about the Indian woman found. States time of death as two to three hours after Phillip Mills and a clean, skilled severing of the throat. How could Jane possibly have known how to do that?'

John knelt back. 'Come on, John, think!' He dropped the paper down and rubbed his hands over his face. 'The British consulate asked for an independent report, i.e. they weren't happy with what had been filed. The report raises some questions that were never answered. Jane didn't kill Phillip Mills, I know it, so maybe they knew it as well? And if Jane didn't kill Phillip, who did?'

He knelt forward and looked at the book on the mutiny. 'A man with a history in India . . . Colonel Reginald Mills . . . Ah, here it is.' John read the passage he had already gone over twenty or so times. 'Phillip Mills knew India, did he ever mention anything about it?' John thought back. He could only ever remember meeting Phillip four or five times and each time he'd been charming, affable and entertaining but rather shallow. The women loved him though, Clare thought he was terrific, especially that time he came to dinner.

'Dinner!' John suddenly exclaimed. 'The dinner, here. My God! That story, about his family, it had Clare agog!' He sat back on his heels. 'God, what did he say now, what was it . . . ?' He pinched the bridge of his nose between his forefinger and thumb. 'Damn, what was it all about?'

He stretched across the carpet and grabbed the Polaroids he'd taken at the British Museum. 'That's it! After the mutiny and the murder of his wife, Colonel Mills had thrown some Indian into prison where he'd died and then stripped the family of all their wealth and dishonoured them. The family swore revenge.' He looked down at the photographs. 'The family were jewellers, Mills stole a bird, this one, one of a pair.'

John stood up and stepped over the mess, across to the window. He stared out at the garden. 'Surely not.' He shook his head and dug his hands in his pockets. He was getting too old for all this, he wasn't thinking properly, he was imagining things, rambling. Revenge, it was the stuff of fiction, not real life. He turned back into the room and surveyed the floor. But if Jane didn't kill Phillip, then who did? Someone must have set Jane up as the culprit and that took planning, it required patience, skill. John went over each thing he had accumulated in the room, his eyes flicking over the floor. He was a soldier, he had fought in the second world war, he knew what men were capable of, what evils, what suffering they could inflict. He stepped across the papers to the photographs and looked at them a final time.

So, if he was right that someone wanting revenge had killed Phillip and set Jane up, then what in God's name did all of that have to do with Indi? How did she get involved, taken out to India and stranded there? What was the connection, if there was one at all? He sighed heavily and squatted down.

'Dead end,' he said to the empty space. 'Unless . . .' He got up and turned to the books that lined one wall, running his hand down the shelves, looking for something. 'Unless, unless . . . come on, where is it? Ah!' It's a long shot but you never know, he thought, pulling the file down. He flicked through the pages and found the leaflet – Sotheby's Fine Art. He filed everything, always had, thank God. He carried it out to the hall, picked up the phone and dialled the London number.

'Yes, hello,' he said, 'I hope you can. I wanted to contact someone about Indian jewellery, nineteenth century to the present day. You do? Mister who? Oh, well if that's possible then yes. Super, thank you. Of course,' John took up his pen and reached for the pad, 'of course I'll hold on, no problem at all,' he said.

Indi and Oliver were at a corner table in the dining-room of the gymkhana club. They had taken to eating there, it was one of the cheapest and best places in the city and Oliver felt safe there, it was one of the few places he did. In the gymkhana club he didn't have to constantly look over his shoulder, check what was behind them, what could be in front of them. He could relax, of a fashion, and he could forget for a while that what they were doing was potentially very dangerous indeed.

They sat, late in the evening, their dinner over, with the file of press cuttings that Rob Jones had sent from Delhi and the book open on the page they had got to. They said nothing to each other, they read in silence. Every now and then Oliver would glance across at Indi to check she was all right – he couldn't help himself, it was instinctive. Since the incident the other night they had been together all the time and yet not 'together' at all. They circled round each other, saying nothing personal, making no contact. They simply discussed the book, the clues, the trail. He thought he understood, it was so much for her to face up to, all the horror of the truth, and then

there were moments when he just wanted to shake her
and shout, Whoa! Stop a minute, look at me, talk to me!
There were moments when he didn't even understand his
own feelings, let alone hers.

Oliver looked down at the page in front of him and
tried to take his mind off her. He concentrated on the
book, on the clue they were well and truly stuck on. He
read and reread the verse, Sappho, he thought it was and
thankfully it was written in English. For a reason perhaps?
He wasn't sure, but the picture, the dark water-colour that
went with it he was sure about. That it was different from
the rest of the work, that much he was certain of. It
was strangely different, as if something had fuelled it,
something had happened to raise it above the level of
art. It was emotional, vivid, alive. And there was a line
of Hindi at the bottom of the page, written in a different
hand from the rest of the script. That was odd too. He
read the verse one last time, murmuring the words under
his breath.

'If you will come
I shall put out
new pillows for
you to rest on.'

Indi looked up. 'That's beautiful,' she said.

Oliver closed the book. 'Yes, it is, isn't it?' He reached
out and went to place his hand over hers, then thought
better of it. He drummed the table-top with his fingers.
'You look tired, Indi,' he said.

'I am.'

'Are you all right? I mean, all this, it's not too much
for you is it?'

417

She shook her head, not trusting herself to speak. It was awful, every word she read made her feel sick, it was a terrible journey of self-discovery, finding that she was no longer safe and secure in the knowledge of who she was, she was no longer just Indi Bennet, but was now the daughter of a murderess. She cleared her throat.

'Have you seen this, Oli?' she asked, changing the subject. She passed him a photograph in one of the articles. He looked down at it and saw a group picture, Jane and Phillip Mills, the Maharajah of Baijur and Ramesh Rai, the maharajah's close friend.

'It's odd, isn't it,' he commented, 'looking at old photographs in black and white? They seem so far removed from how we are today.'

'God, I hope so!' Indi blurted. 'I would hate to think that I was capable of doing something like my mother did . . . I . . .' Her voice faltered and she turned abruptly away.

Oliver glanced at her for a moment, then he too turned away. He didn't know what to say.

Suddenly Indi scraped her chair back and ran from the table. Oliver saw her shoulders sag and knew she was crying. He sat motionless for a few seconds, afraid of interfering and yet frightened of her being alone, then he gathered their things up and calling out to the waiter that they'd be back, darted out after her.

Indi ran out of the doors of the dining-room and across the terrace, down on to the lawn. She stopped running, once in darkness, and slowed to a walk. The club had remained practically unchanged for seventy-odd years. Formerly open only to the British, it was now open to everyone, and as she wandered down through the flame trees, Indi glanced behind her and saw it lit up, an old colonial building, the same one her mother would have known. She swallowed and stood for several minutes, looking back at it.

'You don't honestly believe that Jane committed the murder, do you?' She turned and saw Oliver. 'Not after all that you've read, about the independent coroner's report?' Indi shrugged and Oliver stepped closer to her. 'Well, I don't,' he said. 'I cannot imagine it and nor should you.' He kept his arms locked by his side because the temptation to hold her, to surround her with his arms, to press her close in to his body, was so strong it made him ache.

'Indi?'

She turned away. 'No,' she answered at last, 'no I don't.' She began to walk on and Oliver walked after her. They went down through the trees to the end of the lawns, the moon lighting the way, and then through an arch in an old wall, hung densely with creepers. They came into the ruins of a water garden and walked down the steps towards the first pool, still strangely kept filled with water, black and still, reflecting the sky. They stopped and Oliver glanced around him, instinctively wary.

Indi sat down on the edge of the pool and looked at her reflection. She saw Oliver behind her and the trees, the pale orb of the moon. Then suddenly, she swung round. 'The water garden!' she cried. 'It's the water garden!' She reached for the bag, pulling it out of Oliver's hands. 'Here! Wait!' Scrabbling in it, she found the book and flicked it open on to the right page. 'Look, Oliver, here!' The drawing was the reflection of the water, the sky, the moon, the trees.

Oliver dropped down next to her. 'Bloody hell! You're right. It's here, this place!' He took the book and studied the page, then he glanced up. 'So? What does it mean? We're here, what's next?'

'Show me the verse.' Indi read the verse, then burrowed into the bag again. She pulled out her guide book and flicked through it until she found what she wanted. She read, then looked at Oliver. 'In the sixteenth century, the Moghul ruler, Mahmud of Alwar fell in love with a dancing girl. He wanted her in the palace but the Begum wouldn't allow it so he built his mistress a palace in the hills overlooking the city. He built her the most beautiful water garden to keep her cool up there in the heat of summer and it says here that the remains of it can still be visited.' She laughed and dropped the guide book down on to the ground. 'That's it! The next place! That's what the verse refers to, love, the giving of gifts.' She leant in close to Oliver to see the book. 'It's brilliant, isn't it?'

Oliver smiled. 'Yes, it's very clever. What it all leads to, God knows.' He continued to look at the painting.

'What's up?' Indi frowned. 'You're not satisfied, are you?'

'I don't know, I . . .' He faced her. 'I'm probably being silly but I can't help feeling that there's something else to it, that it all means more than just the next clue.'

'Like?'

'Like the drawing is so intense, so beautiful and the verse is so specifically about love. I've just got a feeling, that's all.' He went to close the book. 'Oh, and there's this line here, in Hindi,' he read it out, stumbling over the words. 'I wonder what it means?'

'It means, two bodies, two hearts, one soul.'

Both Indi and Oliver spun round. 'Ashok?'

Oliver jumped up.

'Yes, and you are right, Oliver, it does mean more. It is a line about creation, about conception.'

Indi caught her breath. Suddenly frightened, she stood up next to Oliver and felt for his hand. Oliver had been right, this was far more dangerous than she had ever imagined.

'I am working for the Indian government,' Ashok said, 'I have been following you for the last twenty-four hours. I know what is going on and I must tell you that what you are doing is illegal. From this moment that book is Indian property. We work together.'

Oliver felt Indi grip his fingers.

'So,' Ashok stepped out of the dark shadow of the wall. 'I think you had better give it to me, if you want to do what is best for you.'

Chapter Thirty-One

John tightened the knot on his tie as he sat in the reception of the Sotheby's London offices. He had a copy of *Country Life* open on his lap but he couldn't concentrate on it. He was too anxious. It was Tuesday, he hadn't been able to get through to Indi for days and this morning he'd had a call from Captain Hicks, brief and curt, he'd said they were both fine and that Indi would ring when she could. John didn't know what to do. He was worried, even though he had no reason to doubt Captain Hicks. He felt a sense of danger, a strange intuition and, if he hadn't been over seventy, he might well have got on the next plane out to Delhi.

'Mr Bennet?'

'Oh, yes?' He stood and hurried over to the desk.

'Mr Wraughton is free now. Could you take the lift up to the second floor and his secretary will meet you at the lifts.'

'Certainly. Thank you, erm, this way?'

The girl on the desk smiled and touched her hair. He was damn good-looking Mr Bennet, she thought, she liked older men, particularly the masculine, distinguished ones. 'Yes, through the double doors there and the lift is on your right.' She looked up hopefully. 'Would you like me to show you?'

'No, thank you, it's quite all right.' John turned. Flirting was always wasted on him, he wasn't a ladies' man. 'Thanks,' he called. 'See you later.' He walked through the double doors and took the lift straight up.

'Ah, Mr Bennet!' John thanked the secretary who'd shown him in and walked across to Wraughton. He was a young man, no more than thirty-five, John guessed, academic-looking, with a dark suit and small round spectacles. The two men shook hands.

'Please, Mr Bennet, have a seat.'

'Thank you.' John glanced round the room while Wraughton searched under the piles of paper on his desk for his notes. The office was more like a study, it was lined with books, wall to wall, with papers, notes and photographs littering every available surface.

'Ah, here it is.' Wraughton lifted a brown card folder from under a pile of books. 'I've made my enquiries, Mr Bennet, and I've got quite a lot here for you.' He opened the file and took out some photographs. He sat down.

'The photos you sent me of the pieces in the British Museum looked vaguely familiar to me, only I couldn't place them straight away. So, I had a dig through our records. The work is very unusual, Mr Bennet, it's highly stylised and the quality of the stones is rare. It's excellent workmanship, more French than Indian and it belongs to a man called Indrajit Rai.' Wraughton passed across his snaps. 'We've had a number of pieces go through our house, Mr Bennet, these two here for example, several years ago.' John glanced down at the photos. 'I'll give you a bit of the history, shall I?'

'Please.'

'Indrajit Rai was well known for a number of years in the nineteenth century, he was a royal jeweller, served many of the royal houses of India and indeed several of his pieces ended up with Queen Victoria. We in fact saw quite a bit of his work brought over here during that period. However, his work then disappeared for a number of years, fifty years or so I think . . . Let me see,' Wraughton checked his notes, 'yes, nothing came out of India from him up until the early twentieth century.' He shrugged. 'I've no idea why, he maybe had money problems, retired, that sort of thing, but then in 1905 a number of pieces came on to the market again, some of Indrajit Rai's and some new pieces but very much in the Rai style. It turns out his grandson had been building up the Rai house again and was producing superb jewellery which had found a market in Europe.' Wraughton passed across another photograph. 'These were part of the Duchess of Windsor's collection, sold a few months back. She was quite a fan of Rai's work. To put it in perspective, he enjoyed something of the same reputation as, say, Cartier or Fabergé.'

John handed the photo back. 'So what happened? How come I've never heard of Rai?'

'Well, two things mainly. First, two world wars, Rai wasn't European and it was terribly difficult for them to break into the European monopoly on fashion after the war, plus the company diversified, went into other things, built up other business interests. And secondly, and this is the main reason I think, the company suffered huge financial losses in the sixties. Just as the rest of the world was enjoying a boom economy and houses like Cartier went on to become almost household names, the house of Rai was practically bankrupted. They lost millions!'

'How?'

'Well, to be honest I'm not really sure. It was difficult to get a real account of what happened, it was a private company with very diverse investments and we only dealt with the jewellery side.' Wraughton looked at his notes. 'I did ring the man who previously did my job though, he's retired now, lives in Wittering. I was kind of fascinated by the whole thing,' he smiled, 'and, to be honest, Mr Bennet, I've had a few pieces from the house of Rai come through us over the past year so I wanted to find out what had really happened, get the picture in focus, in case any more pieces came up.' Wraughton took off his glasses and rubbed the bridge of his nose, then he slipped them on again. 'Apparently, according to my colleague, it's run by a cousin of Rai's now. The youngest Rai son was involved in some kind of swindle back in the sixties and that's when the business was handed over. The rumour goes, and it is just rumour as far as I can gather, the house of Rai had been working for the Maharajah of Baijur, one of the last royal houses in independent India, making copies of his family's jewels, extensive copies, during the troubles with Pakistan.' Wraughton stopped. 'Are you all right, Mr Bennet?'

John nodded. He had started at the mention of Baijur, it had thrown him for a moment. He cleared his throat and said, 'Fine, thank you. Please, do go on.'

'Well, Baijur is near the border and the maharajah was concerned about political stability. Anyway, apparently the house of Rai made copies of everything, the family's entire wealth and the son, trusted friend of the maharajah, etc, was supposed to hide the real loot. But, he ran off with it! He disappeared, vamoosh, never to be seen again. Him and all the loot!' Wraughton shook his head. 'The family, the house of Rai had to pay it all back and that's what was supposed to have bankrupted them. It's a hell of a story, isn't it?' He smiled and sat back in his chair. 'If you can believe it of course!'

'You don't?'

Wraughton shrugged. 'It's an Indian tale, a story. I'm not sure I'd take it too seriously.' Again he smiled. 'According to my colleague, the son wrote down where he'd hidden the loot, but needless to say, no one's ever found his notes!'

John swallowed hard. 'No, quite.' His heart was pounding and he'd begun to sweat.

'Though God knows what anyone would do to get their hands on that piece of paper,' Wraughton joked. 'If it did exist!' He stopped smiling. 'Erm, Mr Bennet? Are you sure you're all right?' Wraughton got up and buzzed for his secretary. 'Can I get you some water, Mr Bennet?'

'Yes, yes please.' John wiped his face with his handkerchief, then put his head down between his knees. He had never felt dizzy in his life before. He tried to breathe evenly.

'Mr Bennet?' He felt someone touch him on the arm. 'Mr Bennet, your water.'

'Thank you.' John sat up. He took a deep breath and sipped the water. 'That's better. Sorry.' He placed the glass on the desk and his hands were trembling. 'It must be the heat in here.'

Wraughton went immediately to open the window.

'Thanks.' John looked across at him. 'Would you know when all this happened? The disappearance and all that.'

Wraughton came back to the desk. 'I don't think so.' He flicked through the notes. 'Oh, wait! Here, I've got a note that says some time around the beginning of 1966.' He shrugged. 'How true that is I have no idea.'

John finished the water. He stood. 'Thank you, Mr Wraughton,' he said, 'you have been extremely helpful.'

'I have?'

'Yes, extremely helpful.' John held out his hand. 'I appreciate it.'

'No trouble at all, Mr Bennet. I've enjoyed the research.'

John nodded at the secretary and walked towards the door. He stopped and looked back. 'Did this Indrajit Rai come from Bombay or Delhi by the way?'

'Neither,' Wraughton answered. 'Don't ask me why, but he always lived and worked in a small city north of Delhi. An odd little place, Moraphur; famous for nothing!'

John shivered. 'Except the mutiny,' he answered.

'Yes, of course, except the 1857 mutiny!'

'Goodbye, Mr Wraughton,' John said. 'And thank you again.'

'Goodbye. It was a pleasure.'

John walked down to the lifts and stood watching the lights on the panel while he waited for it to come up. He felt in his top pocket for his credit card holder. Bugger being over seventy, he decided, stepping into the elevator. He would be on the next plane to Delhi and nothing was going to stop him. Indi was in danger and he was damned if he was going to lose another daughter in that God-forsaken country.

Indi stood with her back to the hills and looked inward, across the fort, to Oliver's figure, high up on one of the parapets, the rising sun to his left, the dawn sky streaked with its light, fading purple, burning orange. She watched him for a few minutes, solitary and motionless and felt an ache in the pit of her stomach, a familiar ache, longing. She wanted him, she knew that, she wanted to love him but she couldn't, she couldn't let herself do it, not now, not until . . . She saw him move towards the steps to come down and quickly looked away. Maybe not ever. She just didn't know, she didn't know anything any more. So how could she possibly know about love?

'Indu?' She glanced to her right, her thoughts interrupted.

'Ashok.'

The Indian came to stand beside her and they both turned to look out at the hills. 'We are stuck, are we not?' he asked.

'Yes, I think we are,' she answered. 'I'm sorry.'

'So am I.'

They stood in silence for a while. For five days they had worked together now, Ashok, Indi and Oliver, they had found the pattern, uncovered the clues and ended up at the fort, the Tiberis Fort, thirty miles from Baijur, high up in the hills, the last place, the last clue.

'What are we to do?'

'I don't know,' Indi said, 'I wish I did.'

Ashok turned to face her. 'Indu, I have something that

I must tell you,' he said, 'something that I have not been honest about.'

Indi shrugged. She had been angry and disappointed at Ashok's revelation several days ago but she was unable to dislike him. He had been clever and resourceful in their search, kind even, and in different circumstances he might have become a friend. 'Forget it,' she said. 'You don't have to tell me anything.'

'Yes, I do.' He dug in his pocket and pulled out a photograph. 'Here, please look. It is my wife to be,' he said, smiling and holding it out to her. 'Please.'

Indi took the photo. 'She's very beautiful, you must be very proud.'

'I am.' He took the photograph back and carefully placed it in his pocket again. 'Indu,' he took a deep breath, 'I am not a government official, I have lied to you. This is not an official investigation, it is personal, it is something that has to do with my family.'

Indi watched his face. She knew he wasn't lying and it shocked her. 'What has it to do with your family, Ashok?' She bit her lip. 'I think you'd better tell me, now.'

Ashok flushed. He didn't know where to start. He hesitated for a few moments, then said, 'My father died when I was just born, Indi, my mother went to her husband's uncle, the only man in her family, she was one of five sisters. This man took her in, Dr Bodi Yadav, he cared for her and me for my first two years, I called him uncle. In 1966 he became involved in a great scandal here, in Baijur. It ruined him, my family were dishonoured, they never recovered.'

Indi swallowed. 'He wasn't involved in the murder of . . . ?'

'No, I do not think that he was.' Ashok looked down at his hands then up at Indi. 'There was a theft, from Vikram Singh, the Maharajah of Baijur, and my uncle disappeared just after this. The man that was involved was Ramesh Rai, he was a great friend of the maharajah, his family were jewellers, they had worked for the house of Singh for many, many years. He was also a great friend of Bodi Yadav, like a son to him. He disappeared one night with the entire wealth of the maharajah, no one ever heard of him again.'

Indi held her breath. She had the most peculiar feeling that she knew what was coming next.

'Ramesh Rai was working for the maharajah,' Ashok said. 'He was supposed to have hidden the wealth and made a puzzle of where to be able to find it. It was all for political security, Baijur was a very unstable state then.'

'Did he make this . . . ?' Indi lost her voice. She coughed to clear her throat and took a deep breath. 'Did he make this puzzle into a book?'

'Yes, I think so. I think that is what we have. I thought it from the first moment that you gave it to me in the gymkhana club . . . Indu?'

Indi had slid down the wall and squatted, her head in her hands.

'Indu? Are you all right?' Ashok knelt beside her. He touched her arm and she looked up.

'You think my father is Ramesh Rai?'

'I think it must be so. I think you have the puzzle that he made.'

Indi blinked rapidly to try and stop the tears. She desperately wanted to blow her nose and longed for

Oliver to appear with his handkerchief. 'Why tell me now?' she asked, using the sleeve of her shirt instead.

'Because I wanted you to know the truth. I am doing this for my family, I cannot get married until my family has regained its honour; Mira's family will not have me.'

Indi hung her head. It was stupid and she was trying desperately not to but she couldn't stop herself crying. The tears streamed down her face and the sobs caught in her throat. She covered her face.

'Oh my God, Indu, please do not cry. Please do not upset yourself on my account.'

'It's not on your account,' she cried, half weeping, half laughing at his ridiculous assumption. 'It's . . . Oh, forget it!' She lifted the hem of her shirt and blew her nose loudly on it, but the tears still streamed.

Ashok leant forward and gently embraced her. 'Please, do not be upset, Indu, please.' He stroked her hair. 'Please, be calm now.' He pulled back and very briefly kissed her lips, a kiss of friendship, the seal of her forgiveness. He wiped her face with his fingertips. 'Come now, we will go and find Oliver and see if he has been able to solve this last piece of the mystery.' He stood and pulled Indi to her feet. 'Come, let us go.' And, holding her arm, he led her down the stairs to find Oliver.

Oliver stepped into the shadows out of sight and turned towards the view, gripping the wall, his knuckles white with tension. He hadn't been able to hear what was going on, he hadn't been able to see properly, he was too far away, but he had caught sight of them kissing, he hadn't been too far away to see that! He dropped his head down and closed his eyes. The pain of it tore through him and made the black behind his eyes turn red and burn. He knew now, of course he knew! He'd known all along really, only he just couldn't admit it. He was in love with her, he had been from the first moment he saw her. Only he'd been stupid, stupid to imagine for one moment that she might feel the way that he did, stupid to think that she was different, special. One night, one intense moment of passion and I think that's it. What a prat! He had honestly believed that she . . . He stopped himself and opened his eyes. She had never given him any sign, apart from that instinctive passion. Hell, they hadn't even touched since, how in God's name could he have thought all of that? He turned towards the fort and saw Indi and Ashok below in the courtyard. 'You were wrong, Oliver,' he said aloud, 'you were bloody wrong! You fool!' And he swallowed down the hurt, knowing he had no choice, put his hand up and called out to them.

'Oliver? Are you all right?' Two hours later, Indi walked into the suite after him and dropped her bag down on the sofa. He hadn't said a word for over an hour now, not since Ashok had left for home to go over Bodi Yadav's diaries in search of something that might give them a lead. He had suggested it, then sat in stony silence all the way back to the hotel. 'Oliver?'

'Yes!' he snapped. He took a breath and turned away again. He had nothing to say to her, why couldn't she just leave him alone?

Indi shrugged. She didn't need this, she had enough grief of her own. She walked through to the bedroom and took her washbag off the side. 'I think I'll have a bath,' she called, 'and then maybe get some sleep.' They had been up nearly all night, travelling to the fort, climbing up there and then, trying to figure it all out. She went into the bathroom and ran the taps. She was tired, she needed to unwind, think about things. Closing the door, she stripped off, sprinkled some perfumed oil into the water and testing it first with her toe, she climbed in the bath and sank down into the water. She submerged herself and came up seconds later feeling instantly better. She remembered her hair shampoo, it was in the bedroom.

Oliver stared at the closed bathroom door for several minutes before hoisting his rucksack on to the bed. He unclipped it and went to the drawers for his clothes. She didn't need him there, they were almost at the end now and he was peripheral, an extra. She had Ashok, they could solve it between them, they didn't want him messing up their romance.

He pulled his three shirts from the drawer, all freshly laundered by the hotel and dropped them in his rucksack. He crossed to the bed and pulled open the bedside drawer. Now he'd made up his mind, nothing was going to stop him.

'Oliver?' He looked up. 'What are you doing?' Indi stood in the doorway, dripping wet, a towel wrapped round her body.

'Packing,' he answered sharply. 'What does it look like?' He didn't want a scene, he wanted to be left alone to get on with it.

'It looks like something's upset you,' she said. 'Why don't you tell me what it is?'

'Butt out, Indi!' Her presence annoyed him, it was as if she wanted to rub it in.

Indi came into the room. She was suddenly angry, irrationally so. What the hell was he doing? He couldn't just leave, walk out on her! The anger flared dangerously in her chest, fuelled by panic. 'What's that supposed to mean?'

'What? Butt out?' Oliver took the small pile of personal effects and stuffed them in the pocket of his bag. 'Exactly that!' he said.

Suddenly Indi grabbed his arm and shook it. 'Stop doing that!' she cried. 'If you want a row you can have one.' The thought of him going made her faint with pain.

Oliver brushed her off. 'I don't want a row. I just want to leave. OK?' He shoved past her.

'No! It's not OK!' She went after him. 'You can't leave now. How will we manage without you? How will we get any further?'

'On your own,' he said, collecting up his bits and pieces from the sitting-room. 'Like most grown-ups.'

'Like most . . . !' Indi turned away speechless. Her stomach was churning and she wanted to scream. How could he do this? How could he?

'Excuse me.' Oliver brushed past her to get back into the bedroom.

Suddenly she pushed him. 'No!' she shouted. 'I won't excuse you!' It didn't hurt but it unbalanced him for a moment and he stumbled, knocking himself on the door. He spun round and without thinking, pushed her back. Only his strength doubled hers and she smacked into the door frame with a loud crunch. She caught her breath, shocked for a second, then she yelled. 'You fucking bastard! Don't you dare . . .'

She went for him. One instant she was looking at his face and the next she was punching him in the chest, kicking him, screaming at him. He took it for a moment, too shocked to react, then he grabbed her wrists and held them up while she struggled against him. He yanked her hands down to her sides, shoved her back against the door with his bodyweight and went to release her, to walk away. He looked at her eyes.

'Jesus Christ!' Moments later they were kissing. She pressed her body into his and her arms went up around his neck, pulling him down to her, the force of her passion so intense it took his breath away. They sank down to the floor and he ripped the towel away from her. She wound her legs over him as his hands travelled the length of her body, she fumbled with his belt.

'Wait,' he whispered harshly. 'Wait.' He let her go and knelt up, taking off his shirt, unfastening his trousers. She touched him and he closed his eyes. 'God, Indi, I . . .' he broke off and looked at her, naked and beautiful in the early morning light. He finished undressing, then reached for his shirt, rolled it up and gently placed it under her head. 'You are beautiful,' he said.

She caught his hand and kissed the palm, the wrist, then she laid it on her breast. 'Then love me,' she whispered, 'love me.'

Oliver moved over, covered her with his body and she smiled, reaching up to him. He licked the perfumed skin of her breast and gently sucked her nipple. He found her mouth and she wrapped her legs high up round his hips. They kissed, their mouths and their bodies became one and as he moved, slowly, making her cry out, she caught her fingers in his hair and whispered his name, over and over again.

Later, after they had made love again, slowly, tangled

in the sheets of the bed, Oliver woke from a light sleep to find her gone. He rolled over and snapped his eyes open. She was sitting on the floor with his shirt on, her head resting on her knees and a photograph from one of the news cuttings in her hand.

'Are you all right, Indi?'

She looked up. 'I don't know,' she answered. 'This is my father,' she said quietly, holding the cutting up. 'I think, anyway. Ramesh Rai, friend to the Maharajah of Baijur, seducer of married women, accessory to murder perhaps, thief.' She dropped her head back on her knees and Oliver climbed out of bed, going across to her. He knelt down.

'You don't know any of that,' he said. 'Not for sure.'

'I don't know anything at all, Oliver, I am more uncertain of myself now, of everything I am, than I have ever been in my entire life before.'

He glanced away. He had hoped, thought perhaps, that she would be certain of one thing, of him and what she felt for him.

Indi wiped the tears from her cheeks on the back of her hand.

'I thought I knew who I was, where I was going. Now, now I don't even know what to do next.' She didn't dare talk about them, about what had just happened. She couldn't.

Oliver reached out and brushed her hair off her face. 'You are going to find out what happened to your parents,' he said. 'The truth. That's what you're going to do next.'

'How? We've come to a dead end. The Tiberis Fort led nowhere and the verse meant nothing to me. I've no idea where it came from.'

'Hmmm. Look, don't worry, I'm certain something will come up.'

Indi narrowed her eyes. 'What does hmmm mean? Do you know something I don't?'

'I'm not sure, maybe.'

She looked doubtfully at him. 'Are you always this optimistic?'

He leant forward and kissed her bare knee. 'Only after fantastic sex,' he said. She smiled. 'Will you come back to bed?'

'No, I think I'll finish that bath I started earlier.'

Oliver stood and grabbed a towel off the back of the chair. 'Would you mind if I joined you?'

'No, of course not.'

He held out his hands and she took them, levering herself up. 'I'll run the taps then,' he said.

'Yes, OK.' She watched him head into the bathroom and felt a sudden pain in her chest. She didn't want to be in love, she couldn't afford to be in love, not now, not with all the confusion in her head. She laid the photo of her father in the front of the book and put it away in her bag. No, she decided, I will not let myself do this, not now, not at the moment. She sighed and a sinking feeling hit the pit of her stomach. Perhaps I was right earlier, she thought, maybe not ever. And sadly, she went on into the bathroom.

John put his bag down in the reception of the Lake Palace Hotel and went across to the desk to confirm his reservation. It had been hell to get a room here but he'd done it, by paying extra of course and by taking one of the most expensive rooms in the place, one that had just come free and one that he had paid a hefty premium to have cleaned immediately. He smiled as he signed in. Why save it, he thought, when you need it?

He turned from the desk and went across to pick up his bag. He was in a hurry, he bent, not looking in front of him and collided with an Indian head-on. There was a scuffle and John put his hands out to stop himself from unbalancing. He held on to the Indian and felt something hard around the man's waist. He pulled back and looked up sharply. He knew the shape of a knife, could tell one with his eyes closed.

'Oh, excuse me, old chap!' John took in the man's face, an ordinary face, not unpleasant, but the eyes were different, they were hard, unseeing. The Indian turned abruptly away and muttered an apology. He had gone before John realised it.

Brushing himself down, John picked up his bag and stopped at the desk on the way. 'Erm, excuse me?' The clerk looked up. 'Is that chap a guest here? I think I might know him.'

'Who, sir?'

'The Indian fella who was here a few moments ago.'

The clerk shrugged. 'No, I do not think he is a guest here, sir.'

'I see.' John smiled politely. 'Thank you.' He looked towards the terrace. 'Which way to room one three five, please?'

'Out on to the terrace, sir, and then turn on the right.' John nodded and made his way along to his room.

Ten minutes later, he had washed, changed his clothes and rang the desk to ask about Indu. Noting down the number of the royal suite, he ripped the page off the pad, combed his hair quickly in the mirror and left his luggage where it was. He took only the Browning out, carried on a Special Forces licence and locked it in the room safe. Then he set off to find Indu. He had missed her, he couldn't wait to see her.

Oliver finished combing his hair, then went through to the sitting-room of the suite to wait for the room service. They had ordered a late breakfast and it was due any minute. Hearing a knock on the door, he hurried across to open it. He was hungry, looking forward to eating.

'Captain Hicks?'

'Yes?' Oliver looked at the gentleman in the passage. He was confused for a moment or two then recognised the eyes. They were the same eyes.

'I'm John Bennet, Indu's grandfather.' John held out his hand.

'Of course, of course!' Oliver shook it warmly. 'I knew it when I saw you, the resemblance, it's quite striking!' He jumped back. 'God, sorry, please, please come in.' He showed John into the sitting-room. 'Could you wait for a moment, I'll call Indi.'

'Yes, of course.' John unfastened his linen jacket and glanced around him. He heard whisperings in the bedroom, then the door quickly closed, cutting him off.

Oliver leant against it and scowled. 'For God's sake, Indi!' he hissed. 'Get out there and see him!'

Indi sat on the edge of the bed. 'No.' She stared out of the window at the water. Oliver came over to her and grabbed her arm. He pulled her.

'Stop being childish! He's come all this way to find

you, to see if you're all right, I imagine. Go out and talk to him.'

'I said no!' Indi jerked her arm away. 'And get off me!'

Oliver stomped back to the door and opened it.

'Brigadier, Indi's in here.' He walked out of the bedroom and nodded to John. 'Please go on in.' Crossing to the balcony, he stepped out and left them both to it.

John stood in the doorway and stared at his granddaughter. She looked different, older in a way and yet vulnerable. She didn't glance up at him, she kept her face turned away.

'You're angry,' he said, 'I'm sorry.'

'What did you expect?' Indi twisted her fingers in her lap. 'You told me lies, all my life. I shouldn't have had to find out like this, you must have known!'

John leant against the door frame. 'I did know but I tried very, very hard to forget it. I couldn't face it.' He suddenly felt very tired, very old. The anxiety had kept him going, the fear that she might be in danger. Now he was here he realised that he shouldn't have come, he had acted rashly, out of panic. He should have left her alone. 'I didn't think it would do you any good, knowing,' he said, 'I wanted you to be happy, not bogged down with someone else's mistake.'

Indi finally looked up. 'Would you have ever told me the truth?'

'Yes, when you were ready for it.'

'And when would that have been?' She stood and walked away from him to the sliding doors. She saw Oliver out on the balcony and the sight of him made her feel worse, more alone than ever.

'You should go home, Gramps,' she said, glancing back at him. 'I can work this out on my own.'

He nodded. 'Yes, I can see that.' Turning to go, he said, 'At least you're all right. I was worried.'

'Yes, I'm all right.' She shrugged. 'Relatively.'

John walked away from her and out of the room. 'Oliver?' He stood in the middle of the sitting-room as Oliver hurried in from the balcony.

'I'll see you back to your room, Brigadier,' Oliver said.

'It's John, by the way.'

'John then.' Oliver smiled and opened the door of the suite just as room service arrived. 'Take it in, please,' he instructed, 'I'll be back in a while.' Letting John go first, he followed him out into the passage and together they walked back to John's room.

Indi was pacing the floor when he came back. She was chewing her fingernails and had eaten nothing. She stopped as he opened the door.

'Ashok rang,' she said. 'He's found something, in Bodi Yadav's accounts.'

Oliver perched on the edge of the sofa. He wanted her to ask about John, to at least make some reference to him.

'Apparently he made monthly payments on a house in Ghanerao,' she went on, 'up in the hills north of here. Ashok asked his aunt if they ever holidayed there and she said no, she'd never heard of this place!' Indi's eyes were burning. 'Do you see? It must be connected! Perhaps he escaped there, perhaps he sent Ramesh Rai up there to hide. Whatever it is we have to go there. We have to!' She hurried through to the bedroom to collect her things up. 'Ashok's hired a Land Rover,' she called. 'He's coming over here. We're to meet him at the jetty at half-past!' She looked behind her at Oliver in the doorway. 'Oli, get a move on!'

He continued to stand there. 'What about your grandfather?' he asked at last.

Indi stopped what she was doing. 'That's my business,' she said coldly.

'No, it's our business, after this morning!'

Suddenly Indi snapped. Seeing John, Ashok's phone call, Oliver, that morning, everything together had unhinged her and she lost her temper. 'Our business!' she cried. 'After this morning!' She didn't care what she said, she just wanted to be out of there, on her way! 'Please, it was only sex, Oliver! Don't read anything more into it than there is!'

Oliver shook his head, incredulous. After everything, all that had happened between them the past week, after what they had felt that morning, it was none of his business, it was only sex! He leant his head back and closed his eyes. Forget it, Oliver, he told himself, again and again, willing his self-control. Forget it, cool it! Nothing means anything to her any more. He snapped his eyes open and crossed to the bed to get his things together. Trouble was, he couldn't let her go alone and he knew that, even if he did just want to walk out now and leave her to it. He had a responsibility to the brigadier, to himself, and he had to look after her, though God knows why! He grabbed his bag and followed her out into the sitting-room.

'So you're coming,' she said from the doorway of the suite.

'Yes,' he answered. 'Looks that way, doesn't it!'

She stared at him for a moment. 'Why?' she asked, unable to stop herself.

'Because this whole thing is beginning to look bloody dangerous if you ask me and I don't want your death on my hands!' He scowled across at her. 'OK?'

Indi cursed herself for asking. Despite all she'd said, all she had decided, she wanted him to say something different. She shrugged and bit her lip. 'OK,' she replied. 'Come on. Let's go.'

John had seen them go. He was drinking tea on the terrace and had watched them from a distance. God, he hoped Hicks knew how to take care of her! He finished his tea and held his hand up to attract the waiter's attention. As he did so he caught a glimpse of the Indian he'd run into earlier.

Leaving several rupee notes on the table, John stood and walked into reception. There was a boat leaving from the jetty and he could see the Indian outside waiting to board it. He watched him for a few minutes, then turned back towards the terrace. He was being paranoid, he told himself, the man could be anyone. Only John knew eyes like that, he'd seen men who liked to kill many times before.

'Excuse me? Mr Bennet, sir?' He looked round. 'I have a message for you, sir.'

John walked over to the desk and took the slip of paper handed to him. He opened it and read it quickly. It said, 'Have gone to Ghanerao with Ashok, it could be difficult. We may need help.' It was signed Oliver Hicks. Looking out at the jetty, John saw the boat move off. The Indian was on it and he carried a bag; he was headed on a journey, that was obvious.

'Can you get me a guide?' he asked the clerk. 'Someone who knows the northern country, the hills nearer the border? And a jeep, I'll need to hire a jeep.'

The clerk nodded and suddenly smiled. 'Oh yes, Mr Bennet, sir,' he said, 'I have a brother-in-law who is a mountain guide, sir, he will be most pleased to help, I am sure.'

John nodded and folded the paper away in his pocket. 'Good,' he said. 'I'll leave you to arrange that for, say,' he glanced at his watch, 'an hour's time?'

'Oh yes, sir, it is no problem at all.' The clerk frowned for a moment. John stopped.

'Yes? What is it?'

'It is very short notice, Mr Bennet, sir, it might be costing a bit more money for you.'

John sighed irritably. 'Just get it organised, please, I will pay what is required.' And, glancing quickly at the water, seeing the boat almost at the far side, he hurried back to his room to pack a bag and get himself ready for any eventuality.

Chapter Thirty-Two

Indi leant against the Land Rover and put the water bottle up to her mouth. She took a long drink, then passed it over to Ashok.

'I don't understand it,' she said, wiping her mouth on the back of her hand. 'Do you think perhaps that my father and Bodi Yadav planned all this months in advance?' Ashok shook his head. 'Well, why rent that house for months before the theft occurred? It doesn't make sense.'

He finished drinking and put the bottle back in the bag. 'I am certain that my uncle would not have done that,' he answered. 'If he had planned to steal from the maharajah he would have taken care of his family first, I am sure of this. He would not have left my mother, his own mother without a man in the family.'

Indi sighed heavily and looked towards the telephone exchange. 'What on earth is Oliver doing?' she said crossly. 'He's been in there almost an hour now!'

Ashok touched her arm. 'He will be here soon.' He had guessed several days ago what they felt about each other, he was only sorry that neither of them had the sense to admit it.

Indi opened the door of the jeep and took the map off the front seat. 'Well, when Oliver gets back, if he ever gets back, I vote that we go up to the house, have another look there and then think again.' They were in Ghanerao, they had been up to the house, seen it, then come down to the small town again. It was a summer house, rented to the richer residents of Delhi when the city became too hot to bear and it held little interest for them. Indi studied the map again for a few moments then said, 'For God's sake! Where on earth is Oliver?'

'Ah!' Ashok waved to the figure in the distance. 'Here he is!'

Both he and Indi walked across the dusty town square towards him.

'D'you two want a drink?' Oliver called as he got closer. 'There's a small shop round the corner selling bottled drinks.'

Indi frowned; she didn't want to waste any more time. She glanced across at Ashok and he shrugged. Oliver reached them.

'Well I could do with a break,' he said, 'I'm bloody thirsty and I've got quite a bit to say as well.'

'All right.' Indi looked back at the jeep. 'I'll go and lock the Land Rover,' she said.

'Get your bag, will you?' Oliver called. She held up her hand in acknowledgement and walked off. Minutes later she was back, and they set off for the small shop.

'So? What is it you have to tell us?' Indi asked.

They were sitting on the pavement and Oliver had the book open on his lap, making furious notes on a sheet of paper. He glanced up momentarily. 'Hang on for a moment longer,' he said, going back to what he was doing. 'I'll be with you in a sec.'

Indi tutted and sipped her yoghurt drink. Ashok looked down the street. The place was deserted, it was midday and there was hardly a soul around. He noticed an Indian he thought he'd seen earlier but the man disappeared down a side street and he didn't have a chance to get a good look.

'Right!' Oliver sat up straight and Ashok turned to him, instantly forgetting the man.

'This is what I've got,' Oliver said, holding out his notes. 'But it's different to what we originally thought, I'm guessing quite a lot and I don't think it is at all connected to the Tiberis Fort.' Both Indi and Ashok looked surprised. 'I think it was supposed to be,' he went on, 'but then things changed, Rai decided to alter his puzzle. He added the verse and that's the clue we were supposed to follow. It is a completely separate thing from the fort.'

Indi put down her drink. 'The verse?'

'Gerard Manley Hopkins.' Oliver looked down at the first page of his notes. 'I kept having this odd feeling that it was familiar, I didn't say anything because I wasn't at all sure. Anyway, the verse wasn't familiar, but the style was. It's so unique, that's why.' He smiled briefly. 'So, I rang my friend Rob Jones in Delhi, just now. On the way here, in the jeep, I kept going over and over the words and thought the only person it might possibly be, that I could think of anyway, was Gerard Manley Hopkins.' He was excited and he was speaking so quickly that Ashok was having trouble keeping up with him. 'Anyway, that's why I've been so long! Rob had to go to the library to get a copy of the poetry out, then come back and ring me here at the exchange.'

Oliver shifted and crossed his legs in the lotus position. 'It had to be a first verse, that's what I thought, and so he flicked through the collection that he had, skimming every first verse and bingo! He got it! Here.' Oliver lifted a sheet of notes and began to read.

'As a dare-gale skylark scanted in a dull cage
Man's mourning spirit in his bone-house, mean house,
    dwells—
That bird beyond the remembering his free fells;
This in drudgery, day-labouring-out life's age.'

He stopped and looked up at them. 'It's called "The Caged Skylark"! It was the second line that did it, "Man's mourning spirit in his bone-house, mean house, dwells—" It's so typical of Gerard Manley Hopkins and I kept thinking . . .' He broke off and flushed. Neither Indi nor Ashok were following him. 'Anyway,' he said, 'the poem goes on to say, "Yet both do droop deadly sometimes in their cells/ Or wring their barriers in bursts of fear or rage." Then in the third verse, there's the word prison.' Again he looked up, they were both still blank-faced. 'So I got to thinking, once I'd written this all down that it must have meant something, the cage business, the prison, the words fear and anger, and I started to go through the book again.' He turned to the page he wanted and held the book up. 'This page is about conception, creation, love. It was the first time that Jane Mills and Ramesh Rai made love.' He glanced sidelong at Indi's face and saw her swallow hard and look down. 'We're assuming anyway. It's dated 24th July, 1965. The puzzle goes on, right up until October. Then it stops. The Tiberis Fort was painted on 29th September.' Oliver shook his head, it seemed to make such clear sense now he wondered why he'd never thought of it before. 'The murder of Phillip Mills and mistress was the beginning of October,' he continued. 'The verse is dated October.' He took a breath. 'Now I'm assuming, OK?'

Both Indi and Ashok nodded.

'Jane and Ramesh are in love, they are making this puzzle together. At the end of September they go to the Tiberis Fort, Jane paints, that's the next clue, then, at the beginning of October, Phillip is murdered. Now, Jane didn't do the murder, she was set up, that's what I honestly believe, so, she flees, Ramesh Rai helps her escape, knowing she wouldn't be able to prove her innocence, and he enlists the help of a man he thinks of as a father figure, Bodi Yadav. Bodi rents a house in the hills for Jane. She is already pregnant, she must have been if you were born in March, Indi, right? So, Jane sits it out at the house in the hills until Ramesh can organise a proper escape, maybe to another country and until she's had the baby. The house is the prison in the verse, Jane is the caged skylark.'

'My God!' Indi touched Oliver's arm. 'This is brilliant, Oliver, I can't believe you've thought of all this.'

'So, what you think,' Ashok said, 'is that the wealth is hidden around the house, somewhere up there?'

Oliver shook his head. 'No, that's just it. Again I'm assuming, guessing here almost, but I think that is what Ramesh Rai meant to do, bury or hide the maharajah's wealth up there in Jane's house and then send him the book. He would know by then that Ramesh had gone, almost certainly with Jane, perhaps Bodi Yadav was to come back to Baijur with a message. But something went wrong. I think the fear in the poem means something and I think that whoever killed Phillip maybe came after Jane as well. Maybe they meant to kill Jane but got the mistress instead, maybe Jane witnessed the murder, it said in the reports that her hand prints were all over the wall, she might have struggled perhaps, known more than was safe.' Oliver stopped. He rubbed his hands over his face, suddenly exhausted from talking so much. He took a deep breath and looked at Indi. 'What do you think?'

She was silent for a while, then she said, 'I don't know. I think what you've said makes more sense than anything else but where does it leave us? If it's not at the house, then where is it?'

Oliver folded his pieces of paper up and tucked them inside the book. He saw the cutting, the photograph of Jane and Phillip Mills with the maharajah and Ramesh Rai. 'I don't know where it is,' he said, looking at the picture, 'but one thing I am certain of is that your father was a very clever man, Indi. His poetry, his philosophy in this book are concerned with love, with goodness, with religion. I think that he only did what he did because he had to.'

Ashok stood. 'We must go back to the house,' he said, 'we will find something there to lead us, I am sure of it.'

Oliver glanced at Indi. 'Yes,' she said, 'he is right, we should go back up to Jane's house.'

He nodded. He didn't want to waste time, it made him edgy but if it meant something to both Indi and Ashok then he supposed it wouldn't do any harm, providing they were quick about it. 'Right,' he said, handing the book back to

Indi. He stood. 'Do you know the way, Ashok, or shall I map read?'

'Please to map read again for me, Oliver,' Ashok said. And leading the way, he walked silently back to the jeep.

An hour later, John pulled into the dusty square in Ghanerao and stopped. His guide nodded and jumped out. 'I will not be long, sir,' he said, glancing over to the small shop selling drinks, 'I will buy water and ask the keeper for you.'

'Thank you.' John put the battered old Land Rover into reverse and swung it round. He watched the scene in the rear-view mirror and kept the engine running. He was hot, damp with sweat and exhausted, it had been a hell of a drive and he needed a rest but he didn't want to risk it. Oliver's note had been short and tense, John wasn't going to waste time.

'They have been here,' the guide said a few minutes later, as he climbed back into the jeep. 'Earlier, about an hour before. There have been four strangers in the village today.'

John jerked round. 'Four?'

'That is what man said. Two Indians, two Europeans.'

'Damn!' The eyes of the Indian John had collided with flashed momentarily into his mind. 'Where were they headed?'

'To house in hills, sir.'

'You know the way?'

The guide nodded. He had a map and a compass but John had seen him use only the compass so far. He was bloody skilled for a guide. 'Please, drive on,' he said.

John shifted gears and accelerated off. Two Indians, he

thought, putting his foot down, Ashok and who else? A fresh sweat broke out on his forehead and ran down the side of his face. 'Jesus Christ,' he murmured, his hand gripping the gear lever. It was a hell of a long time since he'd felt fear like this.

Khan lay in the thicket on the hillside, the smell of the ground close to his nostrils, his face on the dry, cracked earth. He listened to the voices above him on the verandah of the house.

He waited.

He had his instructions, he knew what to do but the urge to move now was so strong it made him hard, continually and painfully hard. The thought of the kill was so erotic that his erection pressed into the scorched rock as he lay on his stomach and the blood throbbed. He wanted it over, he wanted relief.

Suddenly, he heard a noise. He glanced up.

The girl had clambered halfway down the slope, out of view and sat in the shade of the house's overhang. She looked out at the hills and took off her shirt. Her underwear was soaked with sweat. Stretching her arms behind her back, she unfastened her bra and peeled it off, taking a cloth from her bag. She wiped her chest, around her throat, her breasts, blotting the tiny droplets of perspiration from her torso.

Khan held his breath.

She sat still for a few moments and he reached down to his waist for his knife. He dug the razor-sharp steel against the palm of his hand and continued to watch her. She lifted her skirt and ran the cloth the length of her bare legs, up to her thighs, then to the flat of her stomach. She put the cloth back in her bag and reached for her bra again.

Khan moved. He closed his eyes for a split second and saw her beautiful body streaked with blood, her legs open, her eyes wild with fear and he flinched. He knocked a stone with his foot and sent it rattling down the hillside. The girl jumped up.

'Oliver?' she shouted. 'Oliver?'

'You all right, Indi?'

'Yes . . .' She looked up and saw the figure of the young man.

Khan watched as she pulled on the rest of her clothes and ran back up the hillside, losing her footing a few times, stumbling twice. He smiled.

Stupid, stupid girl. Didn't think to look where the stone came from, didn't think to say what she'd seen. He let go of the knife and brought his hand back up to his face. He wiped the sweat from his eyes. He was looking forward to finishing the job, he thought with relish, it was beginning to look as if this one could well be worth all the aggro.

Oliver pulled Indi up to level ground. 'Are you OK?' he asked. 'You look a bit spooked.'

She laughed nervously. 'I'm fine, really.' They walked over to the jeep. 'Where to?' She dropped her bag on the back seat.

Oliver shrugged. 'Ashok's just looking at the map for ideas, temples etc, something that might have provided inspiration.' He was getting impatient, it made him nervous, all this waiting. He couldn't help feeling they were pushing their luck.

Indi sat down on the ground and looked up at Ashok

as he came round to her side. She shielded her eyes from the sun. 'Come up with anything?'

He shook his head. 'Would you like to have a look, Oliver?'

Oli took the map. 'Don't know what good it'll do.' He ran his finger across it. 'Hey, Ashok? What's this cross here?'

Ashok peered in. 'It was a hospital and a leper colony I think. I remember my mother talking about it and I am thinking it was quite well-known. It had an English doctor I believe.'

Oliver looked up, his face a mixture of shock and excitement.

'The sick rose!' he cried, '"O Rose thou art sick, the invisible worm . . ."' He put his hands up to his face and shook his head in disbelief. 'The sick rose is the leper! The colony, that's where he went, that's where it is!'

Indi pulled herself up. 'I don't believe it! Are you sure?'

'No! Of course I'm not sure but it's worth a try.' He took the bag off the seat and pulled the book out. He looked at the poem. 'It's here, the sick rose, the last clue.' Holding it in his hand, he opened the driver's door of the jeep. 'Come on,' he called, 'let's get going.' Ashok walked round to the passenger side and climbed in.

'Indi?'

Indi took one last look at the house. It gave her an eerie feeling and she shivered despite the intensity of the heat. 'Right,' she said, climbing into the back. 'Let's go.' And, glancing behind her as a shadow passed behind the house, she put it down to her imagination and looked forward again as the jeep moved off.

John and his guide drove off the main road and took the

track that led to the house. They saw the tyre marks of another vehicle and pulling over, John switched off the engine while the guide jumped down to examine them.

'I think it is Land Rover, sir,' he called, running his fingers along the marks. He stood and walked across to the edge of the track, looking across the hillside. He stood like that for several minutes.

'Are you all right?' John had climbed down and walked over to him.

The guide looked at his compass, then listened again. He turned to John. 'There is another vehicle,' he said, 'perhaps fifteen, twenty miles from here. It was here, at house.'

'What sort of vehicle?'

The guide got down on his hands and knees and leant over the hillside. He found the tyre tracks. 'A motor bike. Two wheels. Something for the country, it is thick tyre, here, look.'

John knelt and followed the guide's hand. 'Some kind of motor-cross bike?' He got to his feet again. 'What now? They've gone, have they? With this bike following?'

The guide stood as well. He took the map from his belt and unfolded it, checking his compass, then the map. He located the paper mill and the hospital, the only other landmarks on the map, then he looked across the hills again with his compass. 'Come,' he said, 'we will go across the land. They are on the road, going to here.' He pointed his finger at the map and John nodded. They got into the jeep.

John glanced sidelong at the man. He was beginning to feel suspicious, this man was good, too good. 'How do you know all this?' John asked, reversing down the track.

'I was with Indian army,' the guide said, 'special forces

but I had injury, here.' He pointed to his knees. 'I was given pension but,' he shrugged, 'it is not enough.'

John stopped and looked at him. 'In the bag,' he said, 'in the back.'

The man reached over and brought the bag on to the front seat as John started off again. He took out a nine-millimetre Browning and John watched him out of the corner of his eye. 'You know how to use it?' he asked.

The man nodded. He fingered the pistol. 'Yes,' he answered, slipping it into his belt. 'I know.'

It took three hours of hard driving to make it to the colony. The land had been carved up by the new road to the paper mill and the hospital with its small colony of lepers had been pushed further back into the hills, away from the factory workers. There was no danger in it now, it was treatable, drugs were available, the Red Cross provided help but old superstitions die hard. It was still a leper colony, avoided, disregarded.

Oliver drove along the dirt track up to the hospital and stopped, switching off the engine, the three of them sitting in the sudden quiet after the noise and rattle of the jeep. Indi looked at the dilapidated building, recently half-repaired, then climbed out. She went up to the doors and pulled one open, walking inside.

Ashok started to get out but Oliver stopped him. 'Leave her on her own a while,' he said. Ashok looked at the hospital, then shrugged. They could both see Indi through the glass doors in the reception talking to a European doctor and they watched on in silence. Minutes later, she dropped her head down on to her chest and covered her face with her hands. The doctor, a man in his fifties, put his arm around her and hugged her. Oliver turned away.

'I think she's found it,' he said quietly.

Ashok started. 'What . . . ?'

'The truth,' Oliver finished. Then he climbed out of the jeep and walked away.

'Oliver?' He looked round. He had been standing on the hillside looking at the river down below and saw Indi in the distance. She waved at him and he started towards her.

'You were right,' she said when he reached her. 'Now come and meet Dr Hayes. He has something he wants to show us.' Oliver waited for her to make some sort of move, to hold his hand or touch him in some way, but she didn't. She walked off, expecting him to follow and he did exactly as she wanted.

'It's over here,' Dr Hayes said to the three of them when they reached the caves that were set into the rocky slope. It had taken about twenty minutes of walking from the colony and he was out of breath, trying to explain. 'At least I think it is. I've never been in here, I didn't want to sully the feeling of sanctity.' He stopped and stood to get his breath. 'I'll let you go in alone,' he said. 'It's your business after all.' He looked at Indi and squeezed her arm. 'Good luck, I hope you find what you're searching for.'

She looked ahead. 'Thank you,' she said, 'I hope so too.' She walked forward into the cave as Hayes started down the slope back towards the colony then she stopped and turned. 'This is yours as well,' she said to Ashok. 'Are you coming?' He glanced quickly at Oliver, then nodded. He followed her into the cave and the two of them left Oliver behind.

Oliver sat down on a rock and dug his hands in his

pockets. 'Oh well,' he quipped glibly to himself, covering the hurt, 'it was nice while it lasted.'

The next thing he knew he was flat on the ground.

Indi stood in the darkness and shone her torch around the cave. It was still and airless, deathly quiet. She saw the stacks of security boxes, three, four, five she counted, six boxes piled on top of each other in each stack. She walked forward to the last stack and flashed the light, catching sight of a small package on the top, wrapped in cloth and some sort of plastic cover. She moved forward, picked it up and unwrapped it. She saw at once it was her mother's diary and closed her eyes for a moment in relief. This was what she had been looking for. She flicked through the pages. This was it, the whole story, the truth.

'Ashok,' she whispered behind her, 'it's all here, it's . . .' Suddenly she heard the thump. It echoed off the walls and she spun round. 'Ashok?' She flashed the light up and down. 'Ashok?' She saw his face. 'Oh my God!'

Dropping the torch, she staggered back, groping behind her. She was breathing fast and hard, the darkness engulfed her and she lost her footing. Clutching at the wet, slimy rock, she managed to right herself, clawing forward.

A hand grabbed her arm. She screamed and it covered her face. An arm went round her neck.

'Not here . . .' a voice said, 'not now, not yet.' She felt the cold tip of a knife on her breast through the thin fabric of her shirt and she jerked with fright. It grazed the skin, drawing blood, making her flinch.

'Stupid!' he hissed. 'Stupid girl!'

He yanked her head back, wrenching her neck and walking her backwards. She started to cry. 'I want to see you before I kill you,' he whispered, his hot breath on her throat. 'In the light.'

She struggled to breathe, to stop the uncontrollable sobbing. She could hardly walk and he had to drag her along the rock, hauling her up every time her legs gave way, twisting her whole body, tearing her skin on the filthy, bat-infested walls. 'I want you to feel the pain,' he hissed, 'the fear.' Then he laughed, a high-pitched manic laughter that rebounded off the rock and sent the bats swooping overhead.

John ran along the edge of the slope and motioned to Mulraj above the cave. He dropped to his knees, felt the sharp pain of arthritis and swore under his breath. He crawled along the ground to the cover of the rocks and saw the figure at the edge of the cave. He watched, then swung his arm up over his head in a split-second movement to give Mulraj the signal. The man staggered out, dragging Indi in a neck lock and Mulraj aimed the pistol. A shot rang out, Indi screamed and fell to the ground. John ran forward.

Before he saw it a machete flew through the air and hit him in the shoulder. He fell, rolling over, digging the blade deep into the flesh. Mulraj was down and over the body of the assassin when he stumbled on them. He clutched his arm, his face ashen, the blood seeping through his fingers.

'Indi? Jesus! Indi?' He knelt down and lifted her head up, cradling it in his lap. She was bleeding where she'd hit her face on the rock but she opened her eyes, dazed, shocked. 'Gramps? What the . . . ?' She lifted her head round, saw his arm and scrambled to her feet. 'My God, Gramps!' She bent forward and inspected the wound. 'You're too bloody old to be playing soldiers!' she suddenly snapped. Then leaning forward and touching his forehead with her own, she said, 'But Christ am I glad that you did.' And she burst into floods of tears.

Two hours later, Oliver stood by the jeep and waited for the guide, Mulraj. He had a nasty lump on the back of his head but he was all right, fit enough to travel, and he was leaving. He had said his goodbyes.

He smiled as Ashok came towards him, nursing a sling over his right arm and a bandaged head.

'You are off, Oliver!'

'Yes, in a few minutes.'

Ashok held out his good hand, the left and they shook warmly.

'What will you do?' He meant about Indi, and Oliver knew that but he didn't know what to say. She didn't need him, not at the moment, not with so much going on in her head. Perhaps not at all. It hurt, the pain was far worse than any crack on the head but what could he do? 'Return to Delhi,' he said, 'hand in my notice and go back to the army.' He glanced in the direction of the hospital. At least one good thing had happened to him, he'd finally made up his mind about the army. John Bennet had convinced him; if he ended up even half the soldier the brigadier was then he'd be happy.

'They will find out the truth now,' Ashok said, following Oliver's gaze.

'Yes, I'm glad.' He turned to the Indian. 'What about you? What will you do, Ashok?'

'Once the truth is known and the wealth is uncovered I

will restore my family's honour and I hope I will be getting married.'

Oliver grinned. 'Congratulations!'

Ashok bowed. He took out his photograph and handed it across. It was an honour only befitting a friend. Oliver looked, then handed it back. 'You must be very proud,' he said. They were the same words Indi had used.

'Well, here's Mulraj!' Oliver turned to the guide. 'Are you ready?' The guide smiled and bowed. He slung his bag on the seat and climbed into the jeep. Oliver looked at Ashok. 'Good luck,' he said. 'With everything.'

Ashok nodded. 'And good luck to you, Captain Hicks.' He stood back as Oliver climbed up into the driver's seat and started the engine. He slammed the door shut.

'Goodbye!' Oliver called out of the window. He reversed, turned the wheel and swung the jeep round.

'Goodbye!' Ashok shouted as they moved off. 'Goodbye, Captain Hicks!' And he stood, watching the cloud of dust all the way up the track until the jeep turned into the main road and disappeared from view.

Chapter Thirty-Three

It was October and as Indi hurried out of the hospital entrance, she pulled the collar of her coat up high around her face. She was tired, hungry, her legs ached and to cap it all it was freezing. She shivered, bought an *Evening Standard* from the news-seller on the corner and walked quickly along to the tube. It was six-fifteen, she had been on duty since four that morning and she had a mood like a thunder cloud.

At the tube station she had to queue for her ticket, she got the heel of her shoe trapped in the slats on the escalator and a month's worth of old receipts fell out of her wallet as she got her ticket out. She stood in a crowd for the train, pushed and shoved her way on, finally found half an inch of space and managed to get the *Standard* out of her bag. She sighed miserably.

Ever since she had returned from India she'd felt

miserable. Dr Bennet, about to sell a major portion of the Maharajah of Baijur's jewellery collection which the legal profession had somehow decided was rightfully hers and to give a huge chunk of money to charity, should be feeling pretty damn chuffed with herself. No, she felt lousy, unhappy, dissatisfied and lonely. Lonely! Ha! She'd never felt lonely in her life before! Well, not since she went to India anyway.

Indi struggled to get the paper up and read the front page. She saw a young man out of the corner of her eye try to look at the headlines and she rustled it irritably. She turned the page.

'Erm, excuse me?'

She sighed and shifted away, holding the paper a bit higher.

'Hello? I'm looking for . . .'

God! Some people were so bloody tiresome! 'Whoever it is,' Indi snapped as she dropped the paper, 'I'm sure . . .' She stopped and let the paper go. It slithered to the floor, shedding its pages. 'Oliver!' she croaked.

He smiled. 'I'm looking for Indu Bennet,' he said, 'I wanted to tell her that I love her.' There was an instant silence in the carriage.

Indi stared at his face as it blurred out of focus and Oliver silently handed her a handkerchief.

'Do you know where I might find her?'

Indi blew her nose. 'Yes,' she whispered. 'Here.' She wiped her eyes. 'I love you too,' she murmured.

Oliver frowned. 'I'm sorry, I didn't hear you.'

Indi cleared her throat. 'I love you too!' she shouted over the noise of the train. He shook his head and put his finger behind his ear. 'I love you too!' she suddenly yelled.

'Good!' He smiled. 'That's settled then.' And as he leant forward to kiss her, the entire carriage broke into a round of applause.

Elle

Maria Barrett

She has nothing but a name and a dream of revenge...

Ruled by a tangled and violent past, Elle shuts her heart to love in a ruthless search to find her mother's murderer.

Glamorous, brilliant and rich, poised at the pinnacle of her career as the young head of a prestigious banking company - she must risk losing the key to her past and the love of her life as she engages her enemy.

Elle introduces an exciting new writer destined to catch your imagination and sweep into the bestseller lists. A story of one woman's lonely fight that grips the reader from beginning to end.

<u>Dangerous Obsession</u>

Maria Barrett

From the day of her mother's death to her husband's
murder, Francesca has known only hatred, violence
and jealousy. Until, fleeing her past to forge a new
life in England, Francesca at last finds kindness - and
with Patrick Devlin, true, passionate love...

But a peasant girl from Italy is no asset to an aspiring
politician, and Patrick ends their affair, leaving Francesca
to rebuild her world a second time. Yet, as she
gradually makes her name as a fashion designer
and he is promoted to the cabinet, neither can
forget what they once shared.

And Francesca's past is never far behind...

Deceived

Maria Barrett

At the age of thirty-one, Livvy Davis seemed to have all the good things life could offer. Wealth, beauty, intelligence - all rewarded with a stimulating media career and a fantastic lover.

But behind James's dazzling good looks and high-flying job lurked a fatal flaw; a weakness which would shatter the foundations of their love and throw Livvy into a turmoil of misery.

Sacked from her job, evicted from her luxury flat and facing criminal charges, Livvy has no choice but to turn to the man whose unrequited love for her proves to be a godsend - not only helping her get back on her feet, but also providing a chance for sweet revenge...

☐ Elle	Maria Barrett	£4.99
☐ Dangerous Obsession	Maria Barrett	£4.99
☐ Deceived	Maria Barrett	£4.99
☐ Deceptions	Judith Michael	£5.99
☐ Inheritance	Judith Michael	£5.99
☐ Forests of the Night	Sarah Harrison	£4.99
☐ The Flowers of the Field	Sarah Harrison	£5.99
☐ The Blackbird's Tale	Emma Blair	£5.99
☐ A Most Determined Woman	Emma Blair	£5.99

Warner Books now offers an exciting range of quality titles by both established and new authors which can be ordered from the following address:

> Little, Brown & Company (UK),
> P.O. Box 11,
> Falmouth,
> Cornwall TR10 9EN.

Alternatively you may fax your order to the above address.
Fax No. 01326 317444.

Payments can be made as follows: cheque, postal order (payable to Little, Brown and Company) or by credit cards, Visa/Access. Do not send cash or currency. UK customers and B.F.P.O. please allow £1.00 for postage and packing for the first book, plus 50p for the second book, plus 30p for each additional book up to a maximum charge of £3.00 (7 books plus). Overseas customers including Ireland, please allow £2.00 for the first book plus £1.00 for the second book, plus 50p for each additional book.

NAME (Block Letters) _____

ADDRESS _____

_____

_____

☐ I enclose my remittance for £ _____
☐ I wish to pay by Access/Visa Card

Number ☐☐☐☐☐☐☐☐☐☐☐☐☐☐☐☐☐☐

Card Expiry Date _____